W9-CZH-214

JUDGMENT DAY

THE SCIENCE OF DISCWORLD IV

Terry Pratchett, Ian Stewart, and Jack Cohen

Terry Pratchett is the acclaimed creator of the global bestselling Discworld® series. He was appointed OBE and a Knight Bachelor in recognition of his services to literature. He died in 2015.

Ian Stewart is a Fellow of the Royal Society, a professor of mathematics at the University of Warwick, and the author of numerous books on math and popular science, as well as science fiction novels coauthored with Jack Cohen.

Jack Cohen is a professor of biology and honorary professor of mathematics at the University of Warwick and has coauthored several books with Ian Stewart.

www.terrypratchettbooks.com

Withdrawn

Withdrawn

JUDGMENT DAY

THE SCIENCE
OF DISCWORLD IV

JUDGMENT DAY

THE SCIENCE
OF DISCWORLD IV

Terry Pratchett,
Ian Stewart, and Jack Cohen

ANCHOR BOOKS
A Division of Penguin Random House LLC
New York

FIRST ANCHOR BOOKS EDITION, DECEMBER 2015

Copyright © 2013 by The Estate of Terry Pratchett, Lyn Pratchett,
Joat Enterprises, and Jack Cohen
Illustrations © 2013 by Paul Kidby and Sandra Kidby

All rights reserved. Published in the United States by Anchor Books,
a division of Penguin Random House LLC, New York. Originally published in
Great Britain by Ebury Press, an imprint of Ebury Publishing, a division of
Penguin Random House Ltd., London, in 2013.

Anchor Books and colophon are registered trademarks of
Penguin Random House LLC.

Terry Pratchett® and Discworld® are registered trademarks.

Grateful acknowledgment is made to Ricky Gervais for permission to reprint an
excerpt from "Why I'm an Atheist" by Ricky Gervais, copyright © 2015 by
Ricky Gervais. Originally appeared on the *Wall Street Journal* blog *Speakeasy* on
December 19, 2010. Reprinted by permission of United Agents on behalf
of Ricky Gervais.

This is a work of fiction. Names, characters, places, and incidents either are the
product of the author's imagination or are used fictitiously. Any resemblance to
actual persons, living or dead, events, or locales is entirely coincidental.

The Library of Congress Cataloging-in-Publication data has been applied for.

Anchor Books Trade Paperback ISBN: 978-0-8041-6900-4
eBook ISBN: 978-0-8041-7225-7

www.anchorbooks.com

Printed in the United States of America
10   9   8   7   6   5   4   3   2   1

And as imagination bodies forth
The forms of things unknown, the poet's pen
Turns them to shapes and gives to airy nothing
A local habitation and a name.
  —William Shakespeare, *A Midsummer Night's Dream*

We don't see things as they are. We see them as we are.
            —Anaïs Nin

Philosophy is questions that may never be answered. Religion is answers that may never be questioned.
    —Anonymous, quoted in Daniel C. Dennett,
    Breaking the Spell: Religion as a Natural Phenomenon

Even scientists believe in God. They've found Him in the Large Hadron Kaleidoscope.
        —door-to-door missionary,
        as reported in *New Scientist*

"I never made the world," said Om. "Why should I make the world? It was here already. And if I *did* make a world, I wouldn't make it a ball. People'd fall off. All the sea'd run off the bottom."   —*Small Gods*

"Come on into the Library. It's got an earthed copper roof, you know. Gods really hate that sort of thing."
        —*Small Gods*

CONTENTS

CONTENTS

JUDGMENT DAY

THE SCIENCE
OF DISCWORLD IV

WORLDS, DISC
AND ROUND

There is a sensible way to make a world.

It should be flat, so that no one falls off accidentally* unless they get too near the edge, in which
case it's their own fault.

It should be circular, so that it can revolve
sedately to create the slow progression of the seasons.

It should have strong supports, so that it doesn't fall down.

The supports should rest on firm foundations.

To avoid an infinite regression, the foundations should do what
foundations are supposed to do, and stay up of their own accord.

It should have a sun, to provide light. This sun should be small and
not too hot, to save energy, and it should revolve around the disc to
separate day from night.

The world should be populated by people, since there is no point
in making it if no one is going to live there.

Everything should happen because people want it to (magic) or
because the power of story (narrativium) demands it.

This sensible world is Discworld – flat, circular, held up by four
world-bearing elephants standing firmly on the back of a giant
space-faring turtle and inhabited by ordinary humans, wizards,

---

* Falling off deliberately is another matter, about which they can be as imaginative as
they wish. See *The Light Fantastic, The Colour of Magic* and *The Last Hero*.

witches, trolls, dwarves, vampires, golems, elves, the tooth fairy and the Hogfather.

But—

There is also a stupid way to make a world. And sometimes, that is necessary.

When an experiment in fundamental thaumaturgy on the squash court of Unseen University ran wild and threatened to destroy the universe, the computer HEX had to use up a huge quantity of magic in an instant. The only option was to activate the Roundworld Project, a magical force field that – paradoxically – keeps magic out. When the Dean of Unseen University poked his finger in to see what would happen, Roundworld switched on.

Roundworld isn't entirely sure which bit of itself its name applies to. Sometimes the name refers to the planet, sometimes to the entire universe. There have been a few mishaps along the way, but the Roundworld universe has now been running fairly successfully for thirteen and a half billion years; all of it started by an old man with a beard.

In the absence of magic, and lacking natural narrativium, the Roundworld universe runs on rules. Not rules made by people, but rules made by Roundworld itself; which is weird, because Roundworld has no idea what its rules ought to be. It seems to make them up as it goes along, but it's hard to be sure.

Certainly, it doesn't know what size it ought to be. From outside, as it gathers dust on a shelf in Rincewind's office, the Roundworld universe – a globe about 20 centimetres in diameter – resembles a cross between a foot-the-ball and a child's snowstorm toy. From inside, it appears to be somewhat larger: a sphere whose radius is about 400 sextillion kilometres. As far as its only known* inhabitants can tell, it may be much larger still; perhaps even infinite.

Such a huge universe seems to be cosmic overkill, because those inhabitants occupy only the tiniest part of its awe-inspiring volume,

---

* This may be misleading since it is the opinion of the inhabitants concerned.

namely the surface of an approximate sphere a mere twelve thousand kilometres across.

The wizards call this sphere Roundworld too. Its inhabitants call it Earth, because that's what the surface is usually made of (except for the wet, rocky, sandy and icy bits): a typically parochial attitude. Until a few centuries ago they thought that Earth was fixed at the centre of the universe; the rest, which revolved around it or wandered crazily across the sky, was of minor importance since it didn't contain *them*.

Roundworld the planet, as the name suggests, is *round*. Not round like a disc, but round like a foot-the-ball. It is younger than Roundworld the universe: about one third of its age. Though cosmically minuscule, the planet is fairly big compared to its inhabitants, so that if you live there, and you're stupid, you can be fooled into imagining that it's flat.

To prevent the planet's inhabitants falling off, the rules state that a mysterious force glues them on. Thankfully, there are no world-bearing elephants. If there were, the inhabitants would be able to walk *round* their world to the point where it meets an elephant. This world-bearing beast of immense power would appear to be *lying on its back*, its feet in the air. (Paint the soles yellow and you wouldn't be able to see it floating in a bowl of custard …)

Roundworld's rules are democratic. Not only does this mysterious force glue people to their world: it glues everything to everything else. But the glue is weak, and everything can – and usually does – move.

This includes Roundworld the planet. It does have a sun, but this sun does not go round the planet. Instead, *the planet goes round the sun*. Worse, that doesn't create day and night; instead, it produces seasons, because the planet is tilted. Also, the orbit isn't circular. It's a bit squashed, which is typical of Roundworld's jerry-built construction. So to get day and night, the planet has to spin as well. It works, in its way: if you're really stupid, you can be fooled into imagining that the sun goes round the planet. But – wouldn't you just know it – the spin also prevented Roundworld from being a sensible sphere, because when it was molten it got sort of squashed, just like its orbit … oh, forget it.

As a consequence of this hopelessly bungled arrangement, the sun has to be enormous, and a very long distance away. So it has to be ridiculously hot: so hot that special new rules have to come into play to allow it to burn. And then almost all of its prodigious energy output is wasted, trying to warm up empty space.

Roundworld has no supports. It appears to think it's a turtle, because it swims through space, tugged along by those mysterious forces. Its human inhabitants are not bothered by a sphere that swims, despite the absence of flippers. But then, people turned up at most four hundred thousand years ago, one hundredth of a per cent of the lifetime of the planet. And they seem to have turned up by accident, starting out as little blobs and then spontaneously becoming more complex – but they argue a lot about that. They're not terribly bright, to be honest, and they only started to work out modern scientific rules of the universe they live in four hundred years ago, so they've got a lot of catching up to do.

The inhabitants refer to themselves optimistically as *Homo sapiens*, meaning 'wise man' in an appropriately dead language. Their activities seldom fit that description, but there are occasional glorious exceptions. They should really be called *Pan narrans*, the storytelling ape, because nothing appeals to them more than a rollicking good yarn. They are narrativium incarnate, and they are currently refashioning their world to resemble Discworld, so that things *do* happen because people want them to. They have invented their own form of magic, with spells like 'make a dugout canoe', 'switch on the light', and 'login to Twitter'. This kind of magic cheats by using the rules behind the scenes, but if you're really, really stupid you can ignore that and pretend it's magic.

The first *The Science of Discworld* explained all that, and much more, including the giant limpet and the ill-fated crab civilisation's great leap sideways. An endless series of natural disasters established something that the wizards intuitively knew from the word go: a round world is not a safe place to be. Fast-forwarding through Roundworld history, they managed to skip from some not very promising apes huddled around a black monolith to the collapse of the space elevators, as some presumably highly intelligent creatures, having finally got the message, fled the planet and headed for the stars to escape yet another ice age.

They couldn't really be descended from those apes, could they? The apes seemed to have only two interests: sex, and bashing each other over the head.

In *The Science of Discworld II*, the wizards were surprised to find that the intelligent star-farers were indeed descended from the apes – a strange new use of the word 'descend', and one that caused serious trouble later. They found that out because Roundworld had taken the wrong leg of the Trousers of Time and had therefore deviated from its original timeline. Its ape-derived humans had become barbarians, their society vicious and riddled with superstition. They would never leave the planet in time to escape their doom. Something had interfered with Roundworld's history.

Feeling somehow responsible for the planet's fate, much as one might worry about a sick gerbil, the wizards entered their bizarre creation, to find that it was infested by elves. Discworld's elves are not the noble creatures of some Roundworld myths. If an elf told you to eat your own head, you'd do it. But going back in time to when the elves had arrived, and kicking them out, just made everything worse. The evil had gone, but it had taken with it any shred of innovation.

Examining Roundworld's history on what ought to have been its correct timeline, the wizards deduced that two key people – prominent among those very few wise ones – had never been born. This omission had to be repaired to get the planet back on track. They were William Shakespeare, whose artistic creations would give birth to a genuine spirit of humanity, and Isaac Newton, who would provide science. With considerable difficulty, and some interesting failures along the way requiring ceilings to be painted black, the wizards nudged humanity back onto the only timeline that would save it from annihilation. Shakespeare's *A Midsummer Night's Dream* tipped the tables decisively by exposing the elves to ridicule. Newton's *Principia Mathematica* completed the job by pointing humanity at the stars. Job done.

It couldn't last.

By the time of *The Science of Discworld III*, Roundworld was in trouble again. Having safely entered its Victorian era, which should have been a hotbed of innovation, it had once more departed from its proper history. New technology was developing, but at a snail's pace. Some vital spur to innovation had been lost, and the gerbil of humanity was sick once more. This time, a key figure had written the wrong book. The Reverend Charles Darwin's *Theology of Species*, explaining the complexity of life through divine intervention, had been so well received that science and religious belief had converged. The creative spark of rational debate* had been lost. By the time the Reverend Richard Dawkins finally wrote *The Origin of Species (by Means of Natural Selection &c &c &c ...)* it was too late to develop space travel before the ice came down.

This time, getting Darwin born was not the problem. Getting him to write the correct book ... that was where everything went pear-shaped, and it proved remarkably hard to nudge history back on track. Contrary to the proverb, supplying a missing nail from a horse's shoe does not save a kingdom. It generally has no effect, aside from making the horse feel a bit more comfortable, because hardly anything important has a single cause. It took a huge squad of wizards, making over two thousand carefully choreographed changes, to get Darwin onto the *Beagle*, stop him jumping ship when he was being as sick as a dog, and perk his interest in geology so that he stayed with the expedition† until it got to the Galápagos Islands.

---

* That is, insults, name-calling and shameless point-scoring.
† Loosely speaking. He remained on land whenever feasible, about 70% of the entire 'voyage'.

6

They wouldn't have succeeded at all, but the wizards eventually realised that something was actively interfering with their efforts to reset history to manufacturer's specifications. The Auditors of Reality are the ultimate Health and Safety officers: they much prefer a universe in which nothing interesting ever happens, and they are willing to go to extreme lengths to ensure that it doesn't. They had been blocking the wizards' every move.

It was a near thing. Even when the wizards successfully arranged for Darwin to visit the Galápagos and notice the finches and mockingbirds and turtles, it took years for him to understand the significance of those creatures – by which time all the turtle shells were long gone, tossed overboard after their contents were eaten, and he'd given away the finches to a bird expert. (He *had* realised that the mockingbirds were interesting.) It took even longer to get him to take the plunge and write *The Origin* instead of *The Ology*; he kept writing scholarly books about barnacles instead. Then, when he had finally managed to write *The Origin*, he still messed up with *Origin II*, calling it *The Descent of Man* – oh dear. *The Ascent of Man* would have been a better marketing ploy.

Anyway, the wizards finally achieved success, even contriving to bring Darwin into Discworld to meet the God of Evolution and admire the wheels on his elephant. The publication of *The Origin* established the corresponding timeline as the only one that had ever happened. (The Trousers of Time are like that.) Roundworld was saved *again*, and could rest undisturbed on its shelf, gathering dust ...

Until—

ONE

GREAT BIG THING

Every university must have, sooner or later, a big or, more preferably, a *Great Big Thing*. According to Ponder Stibbons, head of Inadvisably Applied Magic at Unseen University, it was, he said, practically a law of nature; and it couldn't be too big, and it had to be a thing, and definitely not a small one.

The senior wizards, eyeing the chocolate biscuits on the tray brought in by the tea lady, listened with as much attention as could be expected from wizards momentarily afflicted with chocolate starvation. Ponder's carefully written and argued speech pointed out that studious research throughout Library-space, or L-space as it is colloquially known, revealed that not to have a Great Big Thing would be a pitiful thing; and the lack of such a thing, indeed, in the academic universe, would make the university they were sitting in right now the butt of jokes and sardonic jibes by people who would be ashamed to be called their fellow academics – said jibes being all the more painful because academics know what *sardonic* actually means.

And when Mister Stibbons finished his last well-tuned argument, Mustrum Ridcully, the Archchancellor, put his hand heavily on the last disputed chocolate biscuit and said, 'Well now, Ponder, if I know you, and I most certainly *do* know you, then you never put in front of me a problem without having a proposed solution somewhere up your sleeve.' Ridcully's eyes narrowed a little as he continued, 'Indeed, Mister Stibbons, it would be very unlike you not already to have a Great Big Candidate. Am I not right?'

Ponder didn't bother to blush, but simply said, 'Well, sir, I do know that we in the HEM* do think that there are many puzzles presented to us by the universe that we really need to solve. As they say, sir: what you don't know can kill you! Ha-ha.'

Ponder was pleased with coming up with that remark; he knew his Archchancellor – who had the instincts of a fighter, and a bare-knuckle fighter at that – and so he moved in with, 'I'm thinking of the fact that we simply don't know why there is a third slood derivative, which in theory means that at the birth of the universe, in that very first nanosecond, the universe actually began to travel backwards in time. According to Von Flamer's experiment, that means that we appear to be coming and going at the same time! Ha-ha!'

'Yes, well, I can quite believe that,' said Ridcully glumly, looking at his fellows; and because he was the Archchancellor, after all, he added, 'Wasn't there something about a cat that was alive and dead at the same time?'

Ponder was always ready for this sort of thing and he said, 'Yes, sir, but it was only a hypothetical cat, sir, as it turned out – nothing to get pet-owners all upset about – and may I add that the elastic string theory turned out to be just one more unproven hypothesis, as did the bubble theory of interconnecting horizons.'

'Really.' Ridcully sighed. 'What a shame. I rather liked that one. Oh well, I trust that in its short life it gave some theoretical scientists a living, and so happily its little life wasn't wasted. You know, Mister Stibbons, over the years you have often discoursed with me about the various theories, hypotheses, concepts and conjectures in the world of natural science. You know what? I just wonder, I really do wonder, whether the universe – being of course by its very nature, dynamic, and possibly in some curious sense *sapient* – may now perhaps be trying to escape from your incessant prying, and is possibly driving you into even greater feats of intellect. The little tease!'

---

* High Energy Magic department.

There was a pause from the assembled wizards, and for a moment the face of Ponder Stibbons appeared to be made of polished bronze; then he said, 'What an amazing deduction, Archchancellor. I applaud you! Everybody knows that Unseen University will rise to meet *any* challenge; with your permission, sir, I will set to work on a budget right now. The Roundworld project was only a beginning. Now, with the … Challenger Project, we will explore the fundamental basis of magic in our world!'

He ran to the High Energy Magic building so fast that his progress metamorphosed into a hurtle, which in ballistic terms is exactly the opposite of a turtle and *extremely* more streamlined.

And *that* was six years ago …

Today, Lord Vetinari, tyrant of Ankh-Morpork, glanced up at the Great Big Thing which appeared to be doing nothing but humming to itself. It hovered in the air, appearing and disappearing, and in Vetinari's opinion looking somewhat smug, a feat indeed for something that had no face.

It was, in fact, a rather amorphous blob that seemed to twist magical equations with arcane symbols and squiggles that clearly meant *something* to those who knew about such things. The Patrician was not, on his own admission, a lover of technical things that spun and, indeed, hummed. Nor of unidentifiable squiggles. He saw them as things with which you couldn't negotiate, or argue; you couldn't hang them either, or even creatively torture them. Of course, the dictum *noblesse oblige* came to the rescue as always – although those who knew Havelock Vetinari well knew that he sometimes wasn't all that obliging.

On this occasion Lord Vetinari was being introduced to excitable and occasionally spotty young wizards in white robes – though still of course in pointy hats – who made a great fuss about large conglomerations of mindless and humming machinery behind the blob. Nevertheless, he did his best to look enthusiastic, and managed to drum up some conversation with Mustrum Ridcully, the Arch-chancellor, who it seemed was just as much in the dark as himself; and he congratulated Ridcully because it was clearly the thing to do, whatever the thing *did*.

'I'm sure you must be very proud, Archchancellor. It's extremely good, clearly a triumph, most certainly!'

Ridcully chuckled and said, 'Bravo! Thank you *so* much, Have-lock, and do you know what? *Some* people said that if we turned the experiment on it would bring the world to an end! Can you imagine that? Us! The psychic protectors of the city, and indeed of the world throughout history!'

Lord Vetinari took an almost imperceptible step back and carefully enquired, 'And precisely when was it that you *did* turn it on, may I ask? It seems to be humming along quite adequately at the moment.'

'As a matter of fact, Havelock, the humming is going to end very shortly. The noise you are hearing is coming from a swarm of bees in the garden over there, and the Bursar hasn't had enough time to instruct them to get back to work. In fact, we were hoping that you would do the honours after lunch, if it is all right by you, of course?'

The expression on the face of Lord Havelock Vetinari was, for a moment, a picture: and it was a picture painted by a *very* modern artist, one who had been smoking something generally considered to turn the brain to cheese.

But *noblesse oblige* was a crushing imperative even for a tyrant, especially one who valued his self-esteem, and therefore, two hours later, a well-fed Lord Vetinari stood in front of the huge humming thing, feeling rather concerned. He made a small oration on the need for mankind to further its knowledge of the universe.

'While it is still there,' he added, looking very pointedly at Ridcully.

Then, after posing for the iconographer's lenses, he looked at the big red button on its stand in front of him and thought, I wonder if there *is* any truth in the rumours that this could end the world? Well, it's too late now to protest, and it would be quite remiss for me to draw back at this point. He brightened up and thought, If indeed it's me who blows up the known world, then it might just be good for my image anyway.

He pressed the button to the kind of applause people make when they understand that something important has happened while at the same time having no idea what they are really cheering. After checking, Vetinari turned to the Archchancellor and said, 'It would seem, Mustrum, that I have not destroyed the universe, which is something of a comfort. Is anything else supposed to happen?'

The Archchancellor slapped him on the back and said, 'Don't fret, Havelock: the Challenger Project was started up yesterday evening by Mister Stibbons over a cup of tea, just to make certain that it would start; and seeing that it was warmed up, he left it on. This of course in no way demeans *your* part in the ceremony, I promise you. The formality of the *significant* opening is at the heart of the whole business, which I am proud to say has all gone swimmingly!'

And *that* was six minutes ago ...

TWO

GREAT BIG THINKING

 Great Big Things have a seductive allure, to which Roundworld's scientists are by no means immune. Most science requires relatively modest equipment, some is inherently expensive, and some would finance a small nation. Governments worldwide are addicted to big science, and often find it easier to authorise a ten-billion dollar project than one costing ten thousand – much as a committee will agree to a new building in five minutes, but then spend an hour debating the cost of biscuits. We all know why: it takes an expert to evaluate the design and price of a building, but everyone understands biscuits. The funding of big science is sometimes depressingly similar. Moreover, for administrators and politicians seeking to enhance their careers, big science is more prestigious than small science, because it involves more money.

However, there can also be a more admirable motive for huge scientific projects: big problems sometimes require big answers. Putting together a faster-than-light drive on the kitchen table using old baked bean cans may work in a science fiction story, but it's seldom a realistic way to proceed. Sometimes you get what you pay for.

Big science can be traced back to the Manhattan project in World War II, which developed the atomic bomb. This was an extraordinarily complex task, involving tens of thousands of people with a variety of skills. It stretched the boundaries of science, engineering and, above all, organisation and logistics. We don't want to suggest that finding really effective ways to blow people to smithereens is necessarily a sensible criterion for success, but the Manhattan project convinced a lot of people that big science can have a huge impact on the entire planet. Governments have promoted big science ever since; the Apollo Moon landings and the human genome project are familiar examples.

Some areas of science are unable to function at all without Great Big Things. Perhaps the most prominent is particle physics, which has given the world a series of gigantic machines, called particle accelerators, which probe the small-scale structure of matter. The most powerful of these are colliders, which smash subatomic particles into stationary targets, or into each other in head-on collisions, to see what gets spat out. As particle physics progresses, the new particles that theorists are predicting become more exotic and harder to detect. It takes a more energetic collision to spit them out, and more mathematical detective work and more powerful computers to compile evidence that they were, for an almost infinitesimal moment of time, actually present. So each new accelerator has to be bigger, hence more expensive, than its predecessors.

The latest and greatest is the Large Hadron Collider (LHC). 'Collider' we know about, 'hadron' is the name of a class of subatomic particles, and 'large' is fully justified. The LHC is housed in two circular tunnels, deep underground; they are mostly in Switzerland but wander across the border into France as well. The main tunnel is eight kilometres across, and the other one is about half as big. The tunnels contain two tubes, along which the particles of interest – electrons, protons, positrons and so on – are propelled at speeds close to that of light by 1,624 magnets. The magnets have to be kept at a temperature close to absolute zero, which requires 96 tonnes of liquid helium; they are absolutely enormous, and most weigh over 27 tonnes.

The tubes cross at four locations, where the particles can be smashed into each other. This is the time-honoured way for physicists to probe the structure of matter, because the collisions generate a swarm of other particles, the bits and pieces out of which the original particles are made. Six enormously complex detectors, located at various points along the tunnels, collect data on this swarm, and powerful computers analyse the data to work out what's going on.

The LHC cost €7.5 billion – about £6 billion or $9 billion – to build. Not surprisingly, it is a multinational project, so big politics gets in on the act as well.

Ponder Stibbons has two reasons for wanting a Great Big Thing. One is the spirit of intellectual enquiry, the mental fuel on which the High Energy Magic building runs. The bright young wizards who inhabit that building want to discover the fundamental basis of magic, a quest that has led them to such esoteric theories as quantum thaumodynamics and the third slood derivative, as well as the fateful experiment in splitting the thaum that inadvertently brought Round-world into existence in the first place. The second reason opened the previous chapter: every university that wants to be *considered* a university has to have its very own Great Big Thing.

It is much the same in Roundworld – and not only for universities.

Particle physics began with small equipment and a big idea. The word 'atom' means 'indivisible', a choice of terminology that was a hostage to fortune from the day it was minted. Once physicists had swallowed the proposition that atoms exist, which they did just over a century ago, a few began to wonder if it might be a mistake to take the name literally. In 1897 Joseph John Thomson showed that they had a point when he discovered cathode rays, tiny particles emanating from atoms. These particles were named electrons.

You can hang around waiting for atoms to emit new particles, you can encourage them to do so, or you can make them an offer they can't refuse by bashing them into things to see what breaks off and where it goes. In 1932 John Cockroft and Ernest Walton built a small particle accelerator and memorably 'split the atom'. It soon emerged that atoms are made from three types of particle: electrons, protons and neutrons. These particles are extremely small, and even the most powerful microscopes yet invented cannot make them visible –

though atoms can now be 'seen' using very sensitive microscopes that exploit quantum effects.

All of the elements – hydrogen, helium, carbon, sulphur and so on – are made from these three particles. Their chemical properties differ because their atoms contain different numbers of particles. There are some basic rules. In particular, the particles have electrical charges: negative for the electron, positive for the proton, and zero for the neutron. So the number of protons should be the same as the number of electrons, to make the total charge zero. A hydrogen atom is the simplest possible, with one electron and one proton; helium has two electrons, two protons and two neutrons.

The main chemical properties of an atom depend on the number of electrons, so you can throw in different numbers of neutrons without changing the chemistry dramatically. However, it does change a bit. This explains the existence of isotopes: variants of a given element with subtly different chemistry. An atom of the commonest form of carbon, for instance, has six electrons, six protons and six neutrons. There are other isotopes, which have between two and sixteen neutrons. Carbon-14, used by archaeologists to date ancient organic materials, has eight neutrons. An atom of the commonest form of sulphur has sixteen electrons, sixteen protons and sixteen neutrons; 25 isotopes are known.

Electrons are especially important for the atom's chemical properties because they are on the outside, where they can make contact with other atoms to form molecules. The protons and neutrons are clustered closely together at the centre of the atom, forming its nucleus. In an early theory, electrons were thought to orbit the nucleus like planets going round the Sun. Then this image was replaced by one in which an electron is a fuzzy probability cloud, which tells us not where the particle *is*, but where it is *likely* to be found if you try to observe it. Today, even that image is seen as an oversimplification of some pretty advanced mathematics in which the electron is nowhere and everywhere at the same time.

Those three particles – electrons, protons and neutrons – unified the whole of physics and chemistry. They explained the entire list of chemical elements from hydrogen up to californium, the most complex naturally occurring element, and indeed various short-lived man-made elements of even greater complexity. To get matter in all its glorious variety, all you needed was a short list of particles, which were 'fundamental' in the sense that they couldn't be split into even smaller particles. It was simple and straightforward.

Of course, it didn't *stay* simple. First, quantum mechanics had to be introduced to explain a vast range of experimental observations about matter on its smallest scales. Then several other equally funda-mental particles turned up, such as the photon – a particle of light – and the neutrino – an electrically neutral particle that interacts so rarely with everything else that it would be able to pass though thousands of miles of solid lead without difficulty. Every night, countless neutrinos generated by nuclear reactions in the Sun pass right through the solid Earth, and through you, and hardly any of them have any effect on anything.

Neutrinos and photons were only the beginning. Within a few years there were more fundamental particles than chemical elements, which was a bit worrying because the explanation was becoming more complicated than the things it was trying to explain. But eventually physicists worked out that some particles are more fundamental than others. A proton, for example, is made from three smaller particles called quarks. The same goes for the neutron, but the combination is different. Electrons, neutrinos and photons, however, remain fundamental; as far as we know, they're not made out of anything simpler.*

---

* Ever since the 1970s physicists have speculated that quarks and electrons are actually made from even smaller particles, variously named alphons, haplons, helons, maons, prequarks, primons, quinks, rishons, subquarks, tweedles and Y-particles. The generic name for such particles is currently 'preon'.

One of the main reasons for constructing the LHC was to investigate the final missing ingredient of the standard model, which despite its modest name seems to explain almost everything in particle physics. This model maintains, with strong supporting evidence, that *all* particles are made from sixteen truly fundamental ones. Six are called quarks, and they come in pairs with quirky names: up/down, charmed/strange, and top/bottom. A neutron is one up quark plus two down quarks; a proton is one down quark plus two up quarks.

Next come six so-called leptons, also in pairs: the electron, muon, and tauon (usually just called tau) and their associated neutrinos. The original neutrino is now called the electron neutrino, and it is paired with the electron. These twelve particles – quarks and leptons – are collectively called fermions, after the great Italian-born American physicist Enrico Fermi.

The remaining four particles are associated with forces, so they hold everything else together. Physicists recognise four basic forces of nature: gravity, electromagnetism, the strong nuclear force and the weak nuclear force. Gravity plays no role in the standard model because it hasn't yet been fitted into a quantum-mechanical picture. The other three forces are associated with specific particles known as bosons in honour of the Indian physicist Satyendra Nath Bose. The distinction between fermions and bosons is important: they have different statistical properties.

The four bosons 'mediate' the forces, much as two tennis players are held together by their mutual attention to the ball. The electromagnetic force is mediated by the photon, the weak nuclear force is mediated by the Z-boson and the W-boson, and the strong nuclear force is mediated by the gluon. So that's the standard model: twelve fermions (six quarks, six leptons) held together by four bosons.

Sixteen fundamental particles.

Oh, and the Higgs boson – *seventeen* fundamental particles.

Assuming, of course, that the fabled Higgs (as it is colloquially called) actually existed. Which, until 2012, was moot.

Despite its successes, the standard model fails to explain why most particles have masses (for one particular technical meaning of 'mass'). The Higgs came to prominence in the 1960s, when several physicists realised that a boson with unusual features might solve one important aspect of this riddle. Among them was Peter Higgs, who worked out some of the hypothetical particle's properties and predicted that it should exist. The Higgs boson creates a Higgs field: a sea of Higgs bosons. The main unusual feature is that the strength of the Higgs field is not zero, even in empty space. When a particle moves through this all-pervasive Higgs field it interacts with it, and the effect can be interpreted as mass. One analogy is moving a spoon through treacle, but that misrepresents mass as resistance, and Higgs is critical of that way of describing his theory. Another analogy views the Higgs as a celebrity at a party, who attracts a cluster of admirers.

The existence (or not) of the Higgs boson was the main reason, though by no means the only one, for spending billions of euros on the LHC. And in July 2012 it duly delivered, with the announcement by two independent experimental teams of the discovery of a previously unknown particle. It was a boson with a mass of about 126 GeV (billion electronvolts, a standard unit used in particle physics), and the observations were consistent with the Higgs in the sense that those features that could be measured were what Higgs had predicted.

This discovery of the long-sought Higgs, if it holds up, completes the standard model. It could not have been made without big science, and it represents a major triumph for the LHC. However, the main impact to date has been in theoretical physics. The existence of the Higgs does not greatly affect the rest of science, which already assumes that particles have mass. So it could be argued that the same amount of money, spent on less spectacular projects, would almost certainly have produced results with more practical utility. However, it is in the nature of Great Big Things that if the money isn't spent on *them*, it isn't spent on smaller scientific projects either.

Small projects don't advance bureaucratic or political careers as effectively as big ones.

The discovery of the Higgs exemplifies some basic issues about how scientists view the world, and about the nature of scientific knowledge. The actual evidence for the Higgs is a tiny bump on a statistical graph. In what sense can we be confident that the bump actually represents a new particle? The answer is extremely technical. It is impossible to observe a Higgs boson directly, because it splits spontaneously and very rapidly into a swarm of other particles. These collide with yet other particles, creating a huge mess. It takes very clever mathematics, and very fast computers, to tease out of this mess the characteristic signature of a Higgs boson. In order to be sure that what you've seen isn't just coincidence, you need to observe a large number of these Higgs-like events. Since they are very rare, you need to run the experiments many times and perform some sophisticated statistical analysis. Only when the chance of that bump being coincidence falls below one in a million do physicists allow themselves to express confidence that the Higgs is real.

We say 'the' Higgs, but there are alternative theories with more than one Higgs-like particle – *eighteen* fundamental particles. Or nineteen, or twenty. But now we know there is at least one, when before it might have been none.

Understanding all this requires considerable expertise in esoteric areas of theoretical physics and mathematics. Even understanding the aspect of 'mass' involved, and which particles it applies to, is complicated. Performing the experiment successfully requires a range of engineering skills, in addition to a deep background in experimental physics. Even the word 'particle' has a technical meaning, nothing like the comfortable image of a tiny ball bearing. So in what sense can scientists claim to 'know' how the universe behaves, on such a small scale that no human can perceive it directly? It's not like looking through a telescope and seeing that Jupiter has four smaller bodies going round it, as Galileo did; or like looking down a microscope and realising that living things are made from tiny cells, as Robert Hooke did. The evidence for the Higgs, like that for most basic aspects of science, is not exactly in your face.

To come to grips with these questions, we take a look at the nature of scientific knowledge, using more familiar examples than the Higgs. Then we distinguish two fundamentally different ways to think about the world, which will form a running theme throughout the book.

Science is often thought to be a collection of 'facts', which make unequivocal statements about the world. The Earth goes round the Sun. Prisms separate light into its component colours. If it quacks and waddles, it's a duck. Learn the facts, master the technical jargon (here being: orbit, spectrum, *Anatidae*), tick the boxes, and you understand science. Government administrators in charge of education often take this view, because they can count the ticks (*Ixodidae* – no, scratch that).

Oddly, the people who disagree most strongly are scientists. They know that science is nothing of the kind. There are no hard-and-fast facts. Every scientific statement is provisional. Politicians hate this. How can anyone trust scientists? If new evidence comes along, they change their minds.

Of course, some parts of science are less provisional than others. No scientist expects the accepted description of the shape of the Earth to change overnight from round to flat. But they have already seen it change from a plane to a sphere, from a sphere to a spheroid flattened at the poles, and from a perfect spheroid to a bumpy one. A recent press release announced that the Earth is shaped like a lumpy potato.* On the other hand, no one would be surprised if new measurements revealed that the Earth's seventeenth spherical harmonic – one component of the mathematical description of

---

* Provided all irregularities are exaggerated by a factor of 7000. http://www.new
scientist.com/article/dn20335-earth-is-shaped-like-a-lumpy-potato.html

its shape – needed to be increased by two per cent. Most changes in science are gradual and progressive, and they don't affect the big picture.

Sometimes, however, the scientific worldview changes radically. Four elements became 98 (now 118 as we've learned how to make new ones). Newton's gravity, a force acting mysteriously at a distance, morphed into Einstein's curved spacetime. Fundamental particles such as the electron changed from tiny hard spheres to probability waves, and are now considered to be localised excitations in a quantum field. The field is a sea of particles and the particles are isolated waves in that sea. The Higgs field is an example: here the corresponding particles are Higgs bosons. You can't have one without the other: if you want to be a particle physicist, you have to understand the physics of quantum fields as well. So the word 'particle' necessarily acquires a different meaning.

Scientific revolutions don't change the universe. They change how humans interpret it. Many scientific controversies are mainly about interpretations, not 'the facts'. For example, many creationists don't dispute the *results* of DNA sequencing;* instead, they dispute the interpretation of those results as evidence for evolution.

Humans are hot on interpretation. It lets them wriggle out of awkward positions. In 2012, in a televised debate about sexism in religion and the vexed issue of female bishops in the Church of England, some months before the General Synod voted against the proposal, one participant quoted 1 Timothy 2:12-14: 'But I suffer not a woman to teach, nor to usurp authority over the man, but to be in silence. For Adam was first formed, then Eve. And Adam was not deceived, but the woman being deceived was in the transgression.' It

---

* Recall that DNA stands for 'deoxyribonucleic acid', a type of molecule that famously takes the form of a double helix, like two interwound spiral staircases. The 'steps' of the staircase come in four kinds, called bases, which are like code letters. The sequence of bases differs from one organism to the next, and it represents genetic information about that organism.

seems hard to interpret this as anything other than a statement that women are inferior to men, that they should be subservient and *shut up*, and that moreover, original sin is entirely the fault of women, not men, because Eve fell for the serpent's temptation. Despite this apparently unequivocal reading, another participant stoutly maintained that the verses meant nothing of the kind. It was just a matter of interpretation.

Interpretations matter, because 'the facts' seldom explain how the universe relates to *us*. 'The facts' tell us that the Sun's heat comes from nuclear reactions, mainly hydrogen fusing to helium. But we want more. We want to know *why*. Did the Sun come into existence *in order to* provide us with heat? Or is it the other way round: are we on this planet because the Sun's heat provided an environment in which creatures like us could evolve? The facts are the same either way, but their implications depend on how we interpret them.

Our default interpretation is to view the world in human terms. This is no great surprise. If a cat has a point of view, it surely views the world in feline terms. But humanity's natural mode of operation has had a profound effect on how we think about our world, and on what kinds of explanation we find convincing. It also has a profound effect on *what world we think about*. Our brains perceive the world on a human scale, and interpret those perceptions in terms of what is – or sometimes was – important *to us*.

Our focus on the human scale may seem entirely reasonable. How else would we view our world? But rhetorical questions deserve rhetorical answers, and for us, unlike the rest of the animal kingdom, there are alternatives. The human brain can consciously modify its own thought-patterns. We can teach ourselves to think on other scales, both smaller and larger. We can train ourselves to avoid psychological traps, such as believing what we want to *because* we want to. We can think in even more alien ways: mathematicians routinely contemplate spaces with more than three dimensions, shapes so complicated that they have no meaningful volume, surfaces with only one side, and different sizes of infinity.

Humans *can* think inhuman thoughts.

That kind of thinking is said to be analytic. It may not come naturally, and its outcomes may not always be terribly comforting, but it's *possible*. It has been the main path to today's world, in which analytic thinking has become increasingly necessary for our survival. If you spend your time comfortably telling yourself that the world is what you want it to be, you will get some nasty surprises, and it may be too late to do anything about them. Unfortunately, the need to think analytically places a huge barrier between science and many human desires and beliefs that re-emerge in every generation. Battles scientists fondly imagined were won in the nineteenth century must continually be re-fought; rationality and evidence alone may not be enough to prevail.

There is a reason for our natural thought-patterns. They evolved, along with us, because they had survival value. A million years ago, human ancestors roamed the African savannahs, and their lives depended – day in, day out – on finding enough food to keep them alive, and avoiding becoming food themselves. The most important things in their lives were their fellow human beings, the animals and plants that they ate, and the animals that wanted to eat *them*.

Their world also included many things that were not alive: rocks; rivers, lakes and seas; the weather; fires (perhaps started by lightning); the Sun, Moon and stars. But even these often seemed to share some of the features of life. Many of them moved; some changed without any apparent pattern, as if acting on their own impulses; and many could kill. So it is not surprising that as human culture developed, we came to view our world as the outcome of conscious actions by living entities. The Sun, Moon and stars were gods, visible evidence for the existence of supernatural beings that lived in the heavens. A rumble of thunder, a flash of lightning – these were signs of the gods' displeasure. The evidence was all around us on a daily basis, which put it beyond dispute.

In particular, animals and plants were central to the lives of early humans. You only have to browse through a book of Egyptian hieroglyphs to notice just how many of them are animals, birds, fish, plants ... or bits of animals, birds, fish and plants. Egyptian gods were depicted with the heads of animals; in one extreme case, the god Khepri, the head was an entire dung beetle, neatly placed on top of an otherwise headless human body. Khepri was one aspect of the Sun-god, and the dung beetle (or scarab) got in on the act because dung beetles roll balls of dung around and dig them into the ground. Therefore the Sun, a giant ball, is pushed around by a giant dung beetle; as proof, the Sun also disappears into the ground (the underworld) every evening at sunset.

The physicist and science fiction author Gregory Benford has written many essays with a common theme: broadly speaking, human styles of thought tend to fall into two categories.* One is to see humanity as the context for the universe; the other is to see the universe as the context for humanity. The same person can think both ways of course, but most of us tend to default to one of them. Most ways to separate people into two kinds are nonsense: as the old joke goes, there are two kinds of people: those who think there are two kinds of people, and those who don't. But Benford's distinction is an illuminating one, and it holds more than a grain of truth.

We can paraphrase it like this. Many people see the surrounding world – the universe – as a resource for humans to exploit; they also see it as a reflection of themselves. What matters most, in this view, is always human-centred. 'What can this do *for me*?' (or '*for us*?') is the main, and often the only, question worth asking. From such a viewpoint, to understand something is to express it in terms of human agency. What matters is its *purpose*, and that is whatever *we* use it

* Gregory Benford, a creature of double vision, in *Science Fiction and the Two Cultures: Essays on Bridging the Gap between the Sciences and the Humanities*, edited by Gary Westfahl and George Slusser, McFarland Publishers 2009, pages 228-236.

for. In this worldview, rain exists in order to make crops grow and to provide fresh water for us to drink. The Sun is there because it warms our bodies. The universe was designed with us in mind, constructed so that we could live in it, and it would have no meaning if we were not present.

It is a short and natural step to see human beings as the pinnacle of creation, rulers of the planet, masters of the universe. Moreover, you can do all of that without any conscious recognition of how narrowly human-centred your worldview is, and maintain that you are acting out of humility, not arrogance, because of course we are subservient to the universe's creator. Which is basically a superhuman version of us – a king, an emperor, a pharaoh, a lord – whose powers are expanded to the limits of our imagination.

The alternative view is that human beings are just one tiny feature of a vast cosmos, most of which does not function on a human scale or take any notice of what we want. Crops grow because rain exists, but rain exists for reasons that have virtually nothing to do with crops. Rain has been in existence for billions of years, crops for about ten thousand. In the cosmic scheme of things, human beings are just one tiny incidental detail on an insignificant ball of rock, most of whose history happened before we turned up to wonder what was going on. We may be the most important thing in the universe as far as we are concerned, but nothing that happens outside our tiny planet depends on our existence, with a few obvious exceptions like various small but complicated bits of metal and plastic now littering the surface of the Moon and Mars, in orbit around Mercury, Jupiter and Saturn, or wandering through the outer edges of our solar system. We might say that the universe is indifferent to us, but even that statement is too self-conscious; it endows the universe with the human attribute of indifference. There is no 'it' to be indifferent. The system of the world does not function in human terms.

We'll refer to these ways of thinking as 'human-centred' and 'universe-centred'. Many controversies that grab the headlines stem, to a greater or lesser extent, from the deep differences between them. Instead of assuming that one must be superior to the other, and then arguing vehemently about which one it is, we should first learn to recognise the difference. Both have advantages, in their proper spheres of influence. What causes trouble is when they tread on each other's toes.

Before the early twentieth century, scientists used to think that phenomena like light could either be particles or waves, but not both. They argued – often nastily – about which was correct. When quantum theory was invented, it turned out that matter had both aspects, inseparably intertwined. At about the time that all reputable scientists *knew* that light was a wave, photons turned up, and those were particles of light. Electrons, which were obviously particles when they were discovered, turned out to have wavelike features as well. So quantum physicists got used to the idea that things that seemed to be particles were actually tiny clumps of waves.

Then quantum field theory came along, and the waves stopped being clumped. They could spread out. So now particle physicists have to know about quantum fields, and our best explanation of why 'particles' have mass is the existence of an all-pervading Higgs field. On the other hand, the current evidence only supports the existence of the particle-like aspect of this field: the Higgs boson. The field itself has not been observed. It might not exist, and that would be interesting, because it would overturn the way physicists currently think about particles and fields. It would also be somewhat annoying.

In everyday life, we encounter solid, compact objects, such as rocks, and they make it easy for us to think about tiny particles. We encounter sloshy but well-defined structures that move around on water, and we feel comfortable with waves. In a human-centred view, there are no sloshy rocks, which makes us assume – almost without questioning it – that nothing can be both particle and wave at the same time. But universe-centred thinking has shown that this assumption can be wrong outside the human domain.

The human-centred view is as old as humanity itself. It seems to be the default pattern of thinking for most of us, and that makes sound evolutionary sense. The universe-centred view appeared more recently. In the sense that we're thinking of – science and the scientific method – universe-centred thinking has become widespread only in the last three or four hundred years. It is still a minority view, but a very influential one. To see why, we must understand two things: how science goes about its business, and what constitutes scientific evidence.

For those of us who are willing to pay attention, the universe-centred view has revealed just how big, how ancient, and how awe-inspiring the universe is. Even on a human scale, it's a very impressive place, but our parochial perceptions pale into insignificance when confronted by the mind-numbing reality.

When early humans roamed the plains of Africa, the world must have *seemed* huge, but it was actually extremely small. A big distance was what you could walk in a month. An individual's experience of the world was limited to the immediate region in which he or she lived. For most purposes, a human-centred view works very well for such a small world. The important plants and animals – the ones useful to specific groups of humans – were relatively few in number, and located in their immediate vicinity. One person could encompass them all, learn their names, know how to milk a goat or to make a roof from palm fronds. The deeper message of the Egyptian hieroglyphs is not how diverse that culture's flora and fauna were, but how narrowly its symbolism was tailored to the organisms that were important to everyday Egyptian life.

As we came to understand our world more deeply, and asked new questions, comfortable answers in terms that we could intuitively understand began to make less and less sense. Conceivably the Sun might, metaphorically, be pushed around by an invisible giant dung-beetle, but the Sun is a vast ball of very hot gas and no ordinary beetle could survive the heat. You either fix things up by attributing supernatural powers to your beetle, or you accept that a beetle can't hack it. You then have to accept that the motion of the Sun occurs for reasons that differ significantly from the purposeful shoving of a beetle storing up food for its larvae, raising the interesting question 'why or how *does* it move?'. Similarly, although the setting Sun looks as if it is disappearing underground, you can come to understand that it is being obscured by the rotating bulk of the Earth. Instead of telling a story that offers little real insight, you've learned something new about the world.

It took time for humanity to realise all this, because our planet is far larger than a village. If you walked 40 kilometres every day it would take you three years to travel all the way round the world, ignoring ocean crossings and other obstacles. The Moon is nearly ten times as far away; the Sun is 390 times as far away as the Moon. To get to the nearest star, you must multiply that figure by a further 270,000. The diameter of our home galaxy is 25,000 times as great again. The nearest galaxy of comparable size, the Andromeda galaxy, is 25 times as far away. The distance from Earth to the edge of the observable visible universe is more than 18,000 times as great as that. In round figures, 400,000,000,000,000,000,000,000 kilometres.

Four hundred sextillion. That's some village.

We have no intuitive feel for anything that large. In fact, we have little intuitive feel for distances of more than a few thousand miles, and those only because many of us now travel such distances by air – which shrinks the world to a size we can comprehend. From London, New York is just a meal away.

We know that the universe is that big, and that old, because we have developed a technique that consciously and deliberately sets aside the human-centred view of the world. It does so by searching not just for evidence to confirm our ideas, which human beings have done since the dawn of time, but for evidence that could disprove them, a new and rather disturbing thought. This technique is called science. It replaces blind faith by carefully targeted doubt. It has existed in its current form for no more than a few centuries, although precursors go back a few thousand years. There is a sense in which 'know' is too strong a word, for scientists consider all knowledge to be provisional. But what we 'know' through science rests on much more secure foundations than anything else that we claim to know, because those foundations have survived being tested to destruction.

Through science, we know how big and how old the Earth is. We know how big and how old our solar system is. We know how big and how old the observable part of the universe is. We know that the temperature at the centre of the Sun is about 15 million degrees Celsius. We know that the Earth has a roughly spherical core of molten iron. We know that the Earth is roughly, though not exactly, spherical, and that (with suitable caveats about moving frames of reference) our planet goes round the Sun rather than being fixed in space while the Sun goes round *it*. We know that many features of an animal's form are determined, to a significant degree, by a long, complicated molecule that lives inside the nucleus of its cells. We know that bacteria and viruses cause most of the world's diseases. We know that everything is made from seventeen fundamental particles.

'Know' is one of those simple yet difficult words. How can we know, to take a typical example, what the temperature is at the Sun's centre? Has anyone been there to find out?

Well, hardly. If scientists are right about the temperature at the centre of the Sun, nobody who was suddenly transported there would survive for a nanosecond. In fact, they'd burn up long before they even reached the Sun. We haven't sent measuring instruments to the centre of the Sun, for the same reason. So how can we possibly know how hot it is at the centre, when no person or instrument can be sent there to find out?

We know such things because science is not limited to just *observing* the world. If it were, it would be firmly back in the human-centred realm. Its power derives from the possibility of thinking about the world, as well as experiencing it. The main tool of science is logical inference: *deducing* features of the world from a combination of observation, experiment and theory. Mathematics has long played a key role here, being the best tool we currently have for making quantitative inferences.

Most of us understand in broad terms what an observation is: you take a look at things, you measure some numbers. Theories are trickier. Confusingly, the word 'theory' has two distinct meanings. One is 'an idea about the world that has been proposed, but has not yet been tested sufficiently for us to have much confidence that it is valid'. A lot of science consists of proposing theories in this sense, and then testing them over and over again in as many ways as possible. The other meaning is 'an extensive, interconnected body of ideas that have survived countless independent attempts at disproof'. These are the theories that inform the scientific worldview. Anyone who tries to convince you that evolution is 'only a theory' is confusing the second use with the first, either through intention to mislead, or ignorance.

There is a fancy word for the first meaning: 'hypothesis'. Few people actually use this because it always sounds pedantic, although 'hypothetical' is familiar enough. The closest ordinary word to the second meaning is 'fact', but this has an air of finality that is at odds with how science works. In science, facts are always provisional. However, well-established facts – well-developed and well-supported theories – are not *very* provisional. It takes a lot of evidence to change them, and often a change is only a slight modification.

Occasionally, however, there may be a genuine revolution, such as relativity or quantum theory. Even then, the previous theories often survive in a suitable domain, where they remain accurate and effective. NASA mostly uses Newton's dynamics and his theory of gravity to compute the trajectories of spacecraft, not Einstein's. An exception is the GPS system of navigational satellites, which has to take relativistic dynamics into account to compute accurate positions.

Science is almost unique among human ways of thinking in not only permitting this kind of revisionism, but actively *encouraging* it. Science is consciously and deliberately universe-centred. That is what the 'scientific method' is about. It is like that because the pioneers of science understood the tricks that the human mind uses to convince itself that what it *wants* to be true *is* true – and took steps to combat them, rather than promoting them or exploiting them.

There is a common misconception of the scientific method, in which it is argued that there is no such thing because specific scientists stuck to their guns despite apparent contrary evidence. So science is just another belief system, right?

Not entirely. The mistake is to focus on the conservatism and arrogance of individuals, who often fail to conform to the scientific ideal. When they turn out to have been right all along, we hail them as maverick geniuses; when they don't, we forget their views and move on. And that's how the real scientific method works. All the other scientists keep the individuals in check.

The beauty of this set-up is that it would work even if *no* individual operated according to the ideal model of dispassionate science. Each scientist could have personal biases – indeed, it seems likely that they do – and the scientific process would still follow a universe-centred trajectory. When a scientist proposes a new theory, a new idea, other scientists seldom rush to congratulate him or her for such a wonderful thought. Instead, they try very hard to shoot it down. Usually, the scientist proposing the idea has already done the same thing. It's much better to catch the flaw yourself, before publication, than to risk public humiliation when someone else notices it.

In short, you can be objective about what everyone *else* is doing, even if you are subjective about your own work. So it is not the actions of particular individuals that produce something close to the textbook scientific method. It is the overall activity of the whole community of scientists, where the emphasis is on spotting mistakes and trying to find something better. It takes only one bright scientist to notice a mistaken assumption. A PhD student can prove a Nobel prize-winner wrong.

If at some future date new observations conflict with what we think we know today, scientists will – after considerable soul-searching, some stubborn conservatism, and a lot of heated argument – revise their theories to resolve the difficulties. This does not imply that they are merely making everything up as they go along: each successive refinement has to fit more and more observations. The absence of complete certainty may seem a weakness, but it is why science has been so successful. The truth of a statement about the universe does not depend on how strongly you believe it.

Sometimes an entire area of science can become trapped in a massive conceptual error. A classic instance is 'phlogiston'. The underlying scientific problem was to explain the changes that occur in materials when they burn. Wood, for instance, gives off smoke and flame, and turns into ash. This led to the theory that wood *emits* a substance, phlogiston, when it burns, and that fire is made from phlogiston.

Volume 2 of the first edition of *Encyclopaedia Britannica*, dated 1771, says: 'Inflammable bodies … really contain the element fire as a conftituent principle … To this fubftance … chemifts have affigned the peculiar title of the Phlogifton, which is indeed no other than a Greek word for the inflammable matter … The inflammability of a body is an infallible fign that it contains a phlogifton …' The same edition considers 'element' to mean earth, air, fire or water, and it has a fascinating analysis of the size of Noah's Ark, based on its need to contain only a few hundred species.

As chemists investigated gases, and started weighing substances, they made a discovery that spelt doom for the phlogiston theory. Although ash is lighter than wood, the total weight of all combustion products – ash, gas and especially steam – is greater than that of the original wood. Burning wood *gains* weight. So, if it is emitting

34

phlogiston, then phlogiston must have negative weight. Given enough imagination, this is not impossible, and it would be very useful as an antigravity device if it were true, but it's unlikely. The discovery of the gas oxygen was the clincher: materials burn only in the presence of oxygen, and when they do, they take up oxygen from their surroundings. Phlogiston was a mistaken concept of 'negative oxygen', In fact, for a time oxygen was referred to as 'dephlogisticated air'.

Significant changes in scientific orthodoxy often occur when new kinds of evidence become available. One of the biggest changes to our understanding of stars came when nuclear reactions were discovered. Before that, it seemed that stars ought to burn up their store of matter very rapidly, and go out. Since they visibly didn't, this was a puzzle. An awful lot of argument about the Sun's remarkable ability to *stay alight* disappeared as soon as scientists realised it shone by nuclear reactions, not chemical ones.

This discovery also changed scientists' estimate of the age of the solar system. If the Sun is a very large bonfire, and is still alight, it must have been lit fairly recently. If it runs on nuclear reactions, it can be much older, and by studying those reactions, you can work out *how* much older. The same goes for the Earth. In 1862 the physicist William Thompson (later Lord Kelvin) calculated that on the 'bonfire' theory, the planet's internal heat would have disappeared within 20-400 million years. His approach ignored convection currents in the Earth's mantle, and when these were taken into account by John Perry in 1895 the age of the planet was revised to 2-3 billion years. Following the discovery of radioactivity, George Darwin and John Joly pointed out in 1903 that the Earth had its own internal source of heat, caused by radioactive decay. Understanding the physics of radioactive decay led to a very effective method for dating ancient rocks … and so it went. In 1956 Clair Cameron Patterson used the physics of uranium decaying into lead, and observations of these elements in several meteorites, to deduce the currently accepted age of the Earth: 4.54 billion years. (The material in meteorites formed at the same time as the planets, but has not been subjected to the same complicated processes as the material of the Earth. Meteorites are a 'frozen' record of the early solar system.)

Independent verification has come from Earth's own rocks; in particular, tiny particles of rock called zircons. Chemically, these rocks are zirconium silicate, an extremely hard material that survives destructive geological processes such as erosion, and even metamorphism, where rocks are heated to extreme temperatures by volcanic intrusions. They can be dated using radioactive decay of uranium and thorium. The most ancient zircons yet observed – small crystals found in the Jack Hills of Western Australia – are 4.404 billion years old. Many different lines of evidence all converge on a similar figure for the age of our planet. This is why scientists are adamant that contrary to the claims of Young Earth creationists, a 10,000-year-old planet is completely inconsistent with the evidence and makes absolutely no sense. And they have come to this conclusion not through belief, or by seeking only confirmatory evidence and ignoring anything that conflicts, but by *trying to prove themselves wrong.*

No other system of human thought has the same kind of self-scrutiny. Some come close: philosophy, the law. Faith-based systems do change, usually very slowly, but few of them advocate self-doubt as a desirable instrument of change. In religion, doubt is often anathema: what counts is *how strongly you believe things.* This is rather evidently a human-based view: the world is what we sincerely and deeply believe it to be. Science is a universe-based view, and has shown many times that the world is *not* what we sincerely and deeply believe it to be.

One of Benford's examples illustrates this point: James Clerk Maxwell's discovery of electromagnetic waves travelling at the speed of light, implying that light itself is a wave. Human-centred thinking could not have made this discovery, indeed would have been sceptical that it was possible: 'The poets' and philosophers' inability to see a connection between sloshing currents in waves and luminous sunset beauty revealed a gap in the human imagination, not in reality,' Benford wrote.

Similarly, the Higgs boson, by completing the standard model, tells us that there is far more to our universe than meets the eye. The standard model, and much of the research that led to it, starts from the idea that everything is made from atoms, which is already far removed from everyday experience, and takes it to a new level. *What are atoms made of?* Even to ask such a question, you have to be able to think outside the box of human-level concerns. To answer it, you have to develop that kind of thinking into a powerful way to find out how the universe behaves. And you don't get very far until you understand that this may be very different from how it appears to behave, *and* from how human beings might want it to behave.

That method is science, and it occupies the second of Benford's categories: the universe as a context for humanity. In fact, that is where its power originates. Science is done by people, for people, but it works very hard to circumvent natural human thought-patterns, which are centred on *us*. But the universe does not work the way we want it to; it does its own thing and we mostly go with the flow. Except that, being part of the universe, we have evolved to feel comfortable in our own little corner of it. We can interact with little pieces of it, and sometimes we can bend them to our will. But the universe does not exist in order for us to exist. Instead, we exist because the universe is that kind of universe.

Our social lives, on the other hand, operate almost exclusively in Benford's first category: humans as a context for the universe. We have spent millennia arranging this, re-engineering our world so that things happen *because we want them to*. Too cold? Build a fire. Dangerous predators? Exterminate them. Hunting too difficult? Domesticate useful animals. Get wet in the rain? Build a house with a roof. Too dark? Switch on the light. Looking for the Higgs? Spend €7.5 billion.

As a result, most of the things we now encounter in our daily lives have been made by humans or extensively modified by humans. Even the landscape has been determined by human activity. Britain's hills have been shaped by extensive ancient earthworks, and most of its forests were cut down in the Iron Age so that farms could exploit the land. That wonderful scenery that you find at places like the stately home of Chatsworth – 'nature in all its glory', with a river flowing between sweeping hills, dotted with mature trees? Well, most of it was constructed by Capability Brown. Even the Amazon rainforest now seems to be the result of agricultural and architectural activity by ancient South American civilisations.

The differences between the two Benfordian worldviews are profound, but remain manageable as long as they don't overtly clash. Trouble arises when both worldviews are applied to the same things. Then, they may conflict with each other, and intellectual conflict can turn into political conflict. The uneasy relation between science and religion is a case in point. There are comforting ways to resolve the apparent conflict, and there are plenty of religious scientists, although few of them are Biblical literalists. But the default ways of thinking in science and religion are fundamentally different, and even determined social relativists tend to feel uneasy when they try to claim there's no serious conflict. Benford's distinction explains why.

Most religious explanations of the world are human-centred. They endow the world with purpose, a human attribute; they place humans at the pinnacle of creation; they consider animals and plants to be resources placed on Earth for the benefit of humanity. In order to explain human intelligence and will, they introduce ideas like the soul or the spirit, even though no corresponding organs can be found in the human body, and from there it is a short step to the afterlife, whose existence is based entirely on faith, not evidence. So it should be no surprise that throughout history, science and religion have clashed. Moderates in both camps have always understood that these clashes are in a sense unnecessary. Looking back after enough time has passed, it is often hard to understand what all the fuss was about. But at the time, those two distinct worldviews simply could not accommodate each other.

The biggest battleground, in this context, is life. The astonishing world of living organisms: Life with a capital L. And, even more so, human consciousness. We are surrounded by life, we ourselves are conscious living beings ... and we find it all terribly mysterious. Thirty thousand years ago some humans could carve quite realistic animals and people from bone or ivory, but no one, even today, knows how to breathe life into an inanimate object. Indeed, the idea that life is something you can 'breathe into' an inanimate object is not particularly sensible. Living creatures are not made by starting with a dead version and bringing it to life. Universe-centred thinkers understand this, but human-centred thinkers often see the body – especially the human body – as a dead thing that is animated by a separate, and immaterial, soul or spirit.

The proof of course is that we observe the reverse process on a regular basis. When someone dies, life seems to pass from their body, leaving a corpse. Where did the life *go*?

Agreed, science doesn't fully understand what gives us our personalities and consciousness, but it is pretty clear that personality derives from the structure and operation of a brain inside a body, interacting with the external world, especially other human beings. The person develops as the human develops. It's not a supernatural *thing*, inserted at conception or birth, with a separate existence of its own. It's a process carried out by ordinary matter in a living person, and when that person dies, their process *stops*. It doesn't depart into a new existence outside the ordinary universe.

In a human-centred view, souls make sense. In a universe-centred one, they look like a philosophical category error. In centuries of studying human beings, not a shred of convincing scientific evidence has ever been found for a soul. The same goes for all of the supernatural elements of all of the world's religions. Science and religion can coexist peacefully, and it's probably best that they do. But until religions discard the supernatural, these two very different world-views can never be fully reconciled. And when fundamentalists try to discredit science because it conflicts with their beliefs, they bring their beliefs into disrepute and provoke unnecessary conflict.

However, even though human-centred thinking can be abused, we cannot understand our place in the universe by using *only* universe-centred thinking. It's a human-centred question, and our relationship to the universe involves both points of view. Even though everything in the universe is made from seventeen funda-mental particles, it's how those particles are combined, and how the resulting systems behave, that make us what we are.

THREE

SEEPAGE BETWEEN WORLDS

 The button having been pressed, the Archchancellor had noticed, *not* for the first time, that Lord Vetinari had a most useful talent, which was to be extremely volcanically angry without even slightly losing his composure. *Corpses* would have admired the coldness that he could insert into the most innocent conversation.

But now, in mid-reverie, Mustrum Ridcully heard a scream emanating from the High Energy Magic building. The scream was very closely followed by a number of wizards. They seemed to be fleeing, but he grabbed one and held on tight.

'Here! Has something gone horribly wrong?'

'I should say so, sir! There's a *woman*! And she's *angry*!'

This last wail was larded with the inference that only an Archchancellor could deal with a very angry woman. Fortuitously, Mustrum Ridcully was the very Archchancellor they needed, because for one thing he knew how to soothe, but he also knew when to twinkle and – more importantly perhaps – he also knew when *not* to twinkle. This looked like it could be a vital skill in the case of this particular lady, who was standing in the entrance to the HEM with her arms akimbo and a definite look of annoyance, a look which was tinted with a palpable sense that there had better be an explanation and, moreover, an extremely *good* one.

The Archchancellor took care as he walked towards her, and at exactly the proper moment took off his hat and bowed, not too theatrically, with just the right amount of olde-worlde charm. 'Do excuse me, madam, how may I be of service?' he said courteously. 'I thought I heard a scream?'

She glowered at him. 'Oh, I am sorry, but I punched one of your chaps. Couldn't help it. Found myself where I shouldn't be and thought: When in doubt strike first. I *am* a librarian, you know. And who are you, sir?'

'Madam, my name is Mustrum Ridcully and I am Archchancellor of this college.'

'And what you don't know isn't knowledge, by any chance? No!' The woman watched Ridcully's face and realised that he was as bewildered as her. 'Don't answer that! Just tell me where I am and why. I can't get any coherence with all these men scuttling about like drones around a hive.'

'Madam, I quite understand your feelings myself – it takes ages to get any real coherence out of them. Alas, that is the curse of academia; but with the aforesaid in mind I *will* tell you that you appear to have magically landed in Unseen University, and have been caught up in what I might now call a "science" experiment, although it may seem to you to be like magic, and very hard to explain at the moment. I do have my suspicions as to how you got here, believe me, for my thaumometer nearly went off the scale a few minutes ago, suggesting that what we might call magic is wild.' He paused, before adding reassuringly, 'But don't fret; I'm used to this sort of thing. Running a university does have its ups and downs, and I truly believe I know the cause of this, and we will get it right as soon as possible. May I say that I would be very pleased if you would be our guest until that happy time.'

She looked at him askance, in a slightly dazed fashion, and said, 'Somehow I appear to have turned up mysteriously in something like Balliol College; it certainly reminds me of it, oh my word, yes.

Oh dear, where are my manners?' The woman held out her hand to Ridcully and said, 'How do you do, sir? My name is Marjorie Daw, you know, rather like the nursery rhyme?* And please, I don't know how I got here, I don't know how I can get back to where I belong … and I am feeling rather sick.'

While she was speaking, a white-robed wizard rushed to the side of Mustrum Ridcully and handed him a small piece of paper; then scuttled away quickly.

Mustrum glanced at what was on the paper. 'I believe, madam, that you hail from England, on planet Earth as you call it – a fact which I have just established, since my Librarian can't find any other place in the multiverse where that particular nursery rhyme should be sung.'

She stared at him, the words 'planet' and 'multiverse' rocketing into her brain, back out again and then – because she *was* a librarian – pulling out an index card or two and settling in again for a nice bit of research. Then she crumpled gently downwards towards the lawn, where she was gallantly caught by the Archchancellor.

She came round in a matter-of-fact way, saying, 'Sorry, there must be something about this travelling that doesn't suit me.' Her eyes narrowed and her lip curled as she continued, 'It won't happen again, I *assure* you.'

Ridcully, apparently lost in admiration for this surprisingly amazing woman, led her to the office of Mrs Whitlow, the housekeeper, who very shortly afterwards reported back that the mysterious lady was snoring in the best guest room available. And Mrs Whitlow also gave the Archchancellor a *look* – one of those looks that spoke for themselves – for after all, he had just carried a lady into the university. It concluded that, well, presumably a man could do anything he wanted in his *own* university, but please let there be no hanky or panky or, even worse, *spanky*.

---

* She had rather liked the name until she went to school; the other kids teased her until one day she took umbrage and there was an up-and-downer, after which they showed some respect.

Mustrum Ridcully, on the other hand, did not go to sleep immediately, but instead, once all the guests and visitors had gone, ambled along to the university library, where he spoke to the head Librarian, who promptly carried out the task that Ridcully had presented to him.

Although he had a very pointy hat and, on special occasions, wore very ornate robes, Mustrum Ridcully was also very smart. Smart was a necessary part of life in the university if you wanted to *have* a life in the university. He prided himself on his memory for small things, so within the hour he headed to the study of Ponder Stibbons. He was followed dutifully by the Librarian, whose skill at picking up data fast was legendary.

'Simian* and gentlemen,' Ridcully summarised, 'I am convinced that the Great Big Thing so recently put to work by the wizards of the High Energy Magic building may have struck what I am reliably informed is called a *hitch* ... yes, Mister Stibbons?'

Everyone knows that if you have foolishly done something wrong then your first step must be to determine if the blame can be laid elsewhere, but Archchancellor Ridcully knew where *all* the bucks stopped, and so Ponder's best defence would therefore be to state a clear intention to return the world, as soon as possible, to the *status quo ante*, and by any means necessary.

'On a point of order, Archchancellor,' the wizard replied, 'the word in question is a *glitch* and, as they go, a not particularly bad one, given that as far as we can tell nobody has been injured, I'm pleased to say. According to HEX, Archchancellor, your surmise that we are cross-linked to Roundworld is correct. Well done, sir! Finding a clue in that children's rhyme was an amazing surmise. Unfortunately, it also makes me worry that there may be more ... *seepage* between our worlds ...'

---

* The Librarian of Unseen University, who gets a capital 'L', is an orangutan, because of an accident when a spell escaped from a book of magic. See *The Light Fantastic*.

Ridcully frowned. 'Mister Stibbons. We have meddled in Round-world rather too many times, in my opinion. In fact, as I recall, it was the Dean who caused the place to come into being, don't you remember? He was mucking about with some firmament, so techni-cally speaking he created the place. Mind you,' he went on, 'I think it would be a very good idea if we don't let anybody know about *that*. There would be no end of arguments.'

Ponder nodded vigorously.

Ridcully grinned and continued thoughtfully, with a certain amount of malice aforethought, 'It does seem to me, Mister Stibbons, that we should send an agent in there to see how things are. After all, Miss Daw has stumbled into our world, and therefore we have a duty to see nothing untoward is happening in hers as a result of your ... experiment. Indeed, in the interests of all concerned, I think we should definitely send someone the other way. We *are* responsi-ble for the place.' Mustrum Ridcully stroked his beard, a signal to all who knew him that he was feeling rather nasty and mysterious. 'I think, yes, the Dean himself ought to go and have a look around.' The beard was stroked again, and Ridcully continued, 'For backup, you had better send Rincewind with him; he's been looking a little peaky lately, so a change of air will do him good.'

'Alas, sir,' said Ponder, 'if you recall, and I *know* you recall, the Dean is now Archchancellor of Pseudopolis University, and we haven't inducted a new Dean yet.'

Undeterred, Ridcully said, 'Get him anyway! He was the one who created Roundworld. He can't just shrug it off; he ought to see how the old place is doing. Send him a clacks. We need action today. We want no more seepages!'

FOUR

WORLD TURTLES

 Before the Large Hadron Collider was turned on, there were attempts to get court injunctions to stop it, in case it created a mini black hole and gobbled up the universe. This was not *totally* silly, but it ignored a worse problem: according to the cosmological theory of eternal inflation, any part of the universe could blow up at any moment – see chapter 18.

Thanks to the switching on of the Great Big Thing, Marjorie Daw has seeped into Discworld. Since she is a librarian, we suspect the seepage happened through L-space, the interconnected space of all libraries that ever have existed or ever could exist.

This may not be the first time something has seeped from Roundworld into Discworld either. Long ago, when the Omnian religion was founded, its adherents came to believe that Discworld, belying its name, is actually round. Where did *that* idea come from? For that matter, how did many early Roundworld cultures get the complementary idea that their world is flat?

We can gain some knowledge about early human beliefs from archaeology, the branch of science that examines evidence from our past. The artefacts and records that survive give us clues about how the ancients thought. Those clues can to some extent be clarified by another branch of science, psychology: the study of how people think. The pictures that emerge from the combination of these two sciences are necessarily tentative, because the evidence is indirect. Scholars can, and do, have a field day arguing about the interpretation of a cave painting or a stick with marks on it.

Ancient myths and legends possess a number of common features. They often focus on deep, mysterious questions. And they generally answer those questions from a human-centred viewpoint. The Discworld series takes Roundworld mythology seriously, to humorous effect; nowhere more so than in its basic geography and its magical supports – elephants and turtle. Here we'll take a look at how various ancient cultures imagined the form, and purpose, of our world, looking for common elements and significant differences. Especially flat worlds and world-bearing animals. Here elephants turn out to be particularly problematic, most likely a case of mistaken identity. In chapter 20 we revisit some of these ancient myths, which will illuminate the science of human belief systems.

In a human-centred view, a flat world makes more sense than a round one. Superficially the world looks flat, ignoring mountains and suchlike and concentrating on the big picture. In the absence of a theory of gravity, people assumed that objects fell *down* because that was their natural resting-place. To prove it, just lift a rock off the ground and let go. So a round world seems implausible: things would fall off the bottom half. In contrast, there's no danger of falling off a flat world unless you get too close to the edge.

There is one effective way to counteract this natural tendency to fall downwards: place something underneath as a support. This support may in turn need something underneath to support *it*, but you can iterate the process many times provided ultimately everything rests on something firm. This process, known as building, was effective enough to erect the Great Pyramid of Khufu at Giza, built in 2560 BC and over 145 metres high. It was the tallest building in the world until 1300, when the architect of Lincoln cathedral cheated by using a lot more up and a lot less sideways.

A common feature of human-centred thinking is that it often works well until you start to ask questions that transcend the human scale. Then it has a habit of falling to pieces. The line of thought just described seems fairly foolproof until you go for the big picture. Applying the kind of logical reasoning that drives so many Discworld stories, it is impossible not to ask: *What keeps the world up?* Human-centred thinking provides an obvious and compelling answer: something supports it. In Greek mythology, it was Atlas, bearing the world on his sturdy shoulders. Discworld sensibly plumps for a more plausible support cast: the giant world-bearing elephant. As belt and braces, there is not just one of them, but four – or possibly five, if the legend recounted in *The Fifth Elephant* is to be believed.

All well and good, but both universe-centred science and human-centred myth-making can hardly fail to ask a supplementary question: *What keeps the elephants up?* If the idea of an ordinary elephant hovering in mid-air is ludicrous, how much more so is that of a vast, extraordinarily heavy elephant doing the same? Discworld's answer is A'Tuin, a giant space-faring turtle. The turtle's shell provides a firm place for the elephants to stand. As a cosmology, it all hangs together pretty well … but of course a further question arises: *What keeps the turtle up?*

It might seem that we could go on like this indefinitely, but at this point observations of nature come into play. The natural world provides a long list of exceptions to the belief that the natural place of any object is on the ground: celestial bodies, clouds, birds, insects and all water-borne creatures – fish, crocodiles, hippos, whales and, crucially, turtles.

However, we can prune the list. Birds and insects do not remain aloft indefinitely; wait long enough and they do, in fact, descend to their natural place, typically a tree or a bush. The Sun, Moon and stars do not inhabit the terrestrial realm at all, so there is no reason to expect them to behave in a human-centred way – and they don't. Assigning them to the realm of the supernatural has so many attractions that it becomes virtually unavoidable. The same arguably goes for clouds, which have a habit of producing awe-inspiring phenomena such as thunder and lightning. Scratch clouds. Crocodiles and hippos are out: they spend a lot of time on land. Fish are not renowned for doing that, but no sensible person would try to fit four elephants on top of a fish.

Which leaves turtles.

Small turtles spend a lot of time on rocks, but no one in their right mind would expect a small turtle to hold up four giant world-bearing elephants. Big turtles come out onto land to lay their eggs, but that's a mystical event and it doesn't cast serious doubt on the theory that a turtle's natural place is in water. Where, please notice, *it does not require support*. It can swim. So it stands to reason that any self-respecting giant space-faring turtle will swim through space, which implies that it needs no artificial support to avoid falling. Examining the animal more closely, a world-spanning turtle seems ideal as a support for giant elephants. It is hard to imagine what could perform the task better.

In short, Discworld is, as stated earlier, the sensible way to make a world.

By comparison, Roundworld makes no sense. It's the wrong shape, it's held up by nothing, and it swims through space unaided despite not being the right shape to swim through *anything*. Basically, it's a giant rock, and you all know what rocks do when you throw them in the lake. It is hardly surprising that it took the wizards a long time to come to terms with the way Roundworld organises itself. Accordingly, we should not be surprised to find that pre-scientific humanity had the same problem.

Flat worlds, giant elephants, world-bearing turtles ... how did these enter the human psyche? One of the ironies of human-centred thinking is that it is unavoidably attracted to superhuman questions – the big picture. What are we? Why are we here? Where did it all come from? And one of the ironies of universe-centred thinking is that it is far better equipped to answer human-scale questions than cosmic ones.

If you want to find out how the rainbow gets its colours, you can pass light through a glass prism in a darkened room. This is what Isaac Newton did in about 1670, though he had to overcome some practical problems. The worst was his cat, which kept wandering into the attic to find out what Isaac was doing, pushing open the door and letting light in. So the ingenious scientist cut a hole in the door and nailed up a piece of felt, inventing the cat flap. When puss had kittens, he added a smaller hole next to the big one, which probably seemed logical at the time.* Anyway, once the feline disruption was taken care of, Newton discovered that white light from the Sun splits into colours, and optics was born.

This kind of experiment is a cinch for things like light, which can be confined to a laboratory (if the cat complies). If you want to discover the nature of the universe, however, it's not so easy. You can't put the universe on a laboratory bench, and you can't step outside it to observe its form, or go back in time to see how it began. The wizards can do, and have already done, all of these things; however, neither the scientists nor the theologians of Roundworld are likely to accept that the Dean of Unseen University kicked it all off by poking his finger in.

Instead, human-centred thinkers on Roundworld tend to go for human-level explanations like emperors and elephants, scaled up to superhuman levels to become gods and world-bearers. Most human civilisations have a creation myth – often several, not always compatible. Universe-centred thinkers have to fall back on scientific inference, and test the resulting theories indirectly. Their cosmological scenarios have often fared little better than most creation myths. Some look remarkably similar: compare the Big Bang to Genesis.

---

* Like all really nice stories this tale, told by a 'country parson', may be false. Other versions say that Newton kept losing time from his research by letting the cat out. Selig Brodetsky's *Sir Isaac Newton* and Louis Trenchard More's *Isaac Newton: a Biography* both state that the great mathematician did not allow either a cat or a dog to enter his chamber. But in 1827 J.M.F. Wright, who lived in Newton's former rooms at Trinity College, Cambridge, wrote that the door once had two holes – by then filled in – of the right size for a cat and a kitten.

However, scientific cosmologists do try to prove themselves wrong, and keep looking for weaknesses in their theories even when observations seem to confirm that they're right. Typically, after about twenty years of increasingly good supporting evidence, these theories start to unravel as the observations become more sophisticated: see chapter 18.

Our ancestors needed to rationalise the things they observed in the natural world, and creation myths played a significant role. It can therefore be argued that they helped to bring about today's science and technology, because they long ago drew humanity's attention to the big questions, and held out hope of answering them. So it's worth examining the similarities and differences between the creation stories of different cultures – especially when it comes to world-bearing elephants and space-faring turtles. Along with a third common world-bearing creature, the giant snake.

The world turtle (cosmic turtle, divine turtle, world-bearing turtle) can be found in the myths of the Chinese, Hindus and various tribes of native North Americans, in particular the Lenape (or Delaware Indians) and the Iroquois.

Around 1680 Jasper Danckaerts, a member of a Protestant sect known as Labadists, travelled to America to found a community, and he recorded a Lenape myth of a world turtle in *Journal Of A Voyage To New York In 1679-80*. We paraphrase the story from a 1974 article by Jay Miller.* At first, all was water. Then the Great Turtle emerged, mud on its back became the Earth, and a great tree grew. As it rose skywards, one twig became a man; then it bent to touch the Earth and another twig became a woman. All humans descended from these two. Miller adds: 'my ... conversations with the Delaware indicate that life and the Earth would have been impossible without the turtle supporting the world.'

---

* Jay Miller, Why the world is on the back of a turtle, *Man* 9 (1974) 306–308.

According to the Iroquois creation story, immortal Sky People lived on a floating island before the Earth existed. When one of the women discovered that she was going to have twins, her husband lost his temper and pulled up a tree at the island's centre, the tree being their source of light at a time when the Sun did not exist. The woman looked into the hole thus created, and far below she saw the ocean that covered the Earth. Her husband pushed her into the hole, and she fell. Two birds caught her, and tried to get mud from the ocean floor to make land for her to live on. Finally Little Toad brought up mud, which was spread on the back of Big Turtle. The mud grew until it turned into North America. Then the woman gave birth. One son, Sapling, was kind, and filled the world with all good things; the other, Flint, ruined much of his brother's work and created everything evil. The two fought, and eventually Flint was banished to live as a volcano on Big Turtle's back. His anger can still sometimes be felt when the Earth shakes.

In these myths, there are partial parallels with ancient Egyptian mythology, in which the primal mound or *benben* rose from a sea of chaos. The god Seth wanted to kill his brother Osiris. He constructed a coffin, lured Osiris inside, shut the lid, sealed it with lead and threw it in the Nile. Their sister Isis set out to find Osiris, but Seth got there first and cut him into 14 pieces. Isis located 13 of them, but a fish had eaten Osiris's penis. So she made an artificial one for him from gold, and sang until he came back to life.

The world-bearing turtle never made it into the Egyptian pantheon, but it was common in ancient central America, among cultures such as the Olmecs. To many of these cultures, the world was both square and round, and it was also a caiman or turtle floating on a primordial sea, which represented the Earth and might or might not carry it. The world had four corners, one for each cardinal direction, and a fifth symbolic point at its centre. The cosmos was divided into three horizontal layers: the underworld below, the heavens above, and the everyday world in between.

In another central American culture, the Maya civilisation, thirteen creator gods constructed humanity from maize dough. The world was carried at its four cardinal points by four *bacabs*, elderly deities of the earth's interior and waters, shown carrying a sky-dragon in early depictions but later believed to be drowned ancestors. Their names were Cantzicnal, Hobnil, Hosanek and Saccimi, and each ruled one of the four directions.* They were closely associated with four rain gods and four wind gods. They can appear as a conch, a snail, a spider web, a bee-like suit of armour, or a turtle. In the *Dresden Codex* the turtle is also associated with the rain-god Chaac, which similarly has four aspects, one for each cardinal direction.

At the Puuc Maya site at Uxmal there is a building called the House of the Turtles, whose cornice is decorated with hundreds of the animals. Its function is unknown, but the Maya associated turtles with water and earth. Their shells were used in making drums, and seem to have been associated with thunder. The god Pauahutun, who like Atlas carried the world on his shoulders, is sometimes shown wearing a turtle-shell hat. The Maize God is occasionally shown emerging from a turtle's shell. The Mayan name for the constellation Orion is Ak'Ek' or Turtle Star.

The *Popol Vuh* of the Quiché Maya provides more detail. It tells of three generations of deities, beginning with the creator grandparents of the sea and the lightning gods of the sky. The Mayans were corn farmers, so their human-centred worldview naturally related to the cycle of wet and dry seasons: their creator gods brought rain and the corn cycle into being. Their gods came as a standard package. Each god was associated with an aspect of the Mayan calendar, so one function of the calendar was to specify which god was in the ascendant at any given time. Often gods possessed several different aspects, and some of the major deities had four aspects, one for each cardinal direction, each with slightly different responsibilities.

---

* It's fascinating how priests always know the *names* of the gods.

The *Popol Vuh* tells that before the Earth appeared, the universe was a huge freshwater sea, above which was a blank sky with no stars or Sun. In the sea dwelt the creator grandparents Xpiyacoc and Xmucane. Below was Xibalba, the place of fright, domain of the gods One Death and Seven Death. The gods of sea and sky decided that they would create people to worship them. Since such creatures would need somewhere to live, the gods created the Earth, raising it from the primordial sea and covering it in vegetation.

That was Mayan cosmogony: the origin of the universe. In their cosmology (the shape and structure of the universe) the Earth was a flat disc, but it also had aspects of a square, whose corners were determined by the rising and setting of the solstice Sun, and whose sides were four great mythical mountains. It has been suggested that the notion of a square world reflects the shape of a cornfield. A rope formed a protective perimeter, reminiscent of Discworld's 'circumfence'* but this one was intended to keep out malevolent supernatural beings. Each of the mountains was the home of one aspect of a grandfather deity, Mayan name unknown or uncertain, referred to by anthropologists as God N. The gods' homes could be reached through caves, but these created gaps in the protective perimeter so that evil could enter.

The Earth was next made ready for growing corn. So the children and grandchildren of the creator grandparents, now living on the Earth, set up the Sun and the yearly cycle of the seasons and synchronised them with the movements of the Moon and Venus. There were two children, Hun Hunahpu and Vucub Hunahpu. The first married Bone Woman – the book does not say how she came into being (just as Genesis tells us that Cain's wife 'dwelt in the land of Nod', but is silent about the creation of both Nod and the wife). When Bone Woman died, Hun Hunahpu and Vucub Hunahpu went to the underworld, suffering defeat at the hands of the two lords of

---

* A 10,000-mile long drift net built to catch items falling over the edge.

death. Blood Woman, the daughter of an underworld being, was made pregnant by spittle from Hun Hunahpu's dead head, and gave birth to Hunahpu and Xbalanque, the hero twins. Much of the tale deals with the twins' eventual defeat of the lords of death, which required assistance from their grandparents. Xmucane made a mixture of corn and ground bone into dough, from which the creator grandparents formed the first people. Job done, the hero twins became the Sun and the full Moon.

God N is often shown wearing a net bag on his head. One of his manifestations was as a possum; another was as a turtle. An inscribed stone at Copán bears his name 'yellow turtle', in the form of his image together with phonetic signs for *ak* – meaning turtle. In his turtle aspect, God N represented the Earth, because the creation of the Earth, rising from the primordial sea, was like a turtle coming to the surface of a pool. God N also manifested himself as the four *bacabs*, whom the sixteenth-century Bishop of Yucatán Diego de Landa described as 'four brothers whom [the creator] god placed, when he created the world, at the four points of it, holding up the sky so that it should not fall'.

Benford's distinction is very visible here. The Mayan view, like that of many ancient cultures, was human-centred. They tried to understand the universe in terms of their own everyday experiences. Their stories rationalised nature, by portraying it in human terms – only bigger. But within that framework, they did their best to tackle the big questions of life, the universe, and everything.

To westerners, a turtle/elephant world is most commonly associated with Hinduism. Turtles are often confused with tortoises, as they generally are in American English. Philosopher John Locke's *Essay Concerning Human Understanding* in 1690 mentions an 'Indian who said the world was on an elephant which was on a tortoise'. In his 1927 *Why I Am Not A Christian* Bertrand Russell writes of 'the Hindu's view, that the world rested upon an elephant and the elephant rested upon a tortoise', adding, 'When they said, "How about the tortoise?" the Indian said, "Suppose we change the subject."' The elephant-turtle story remains in common circulation, but it is a misrepresentation of Hindu beliefs, conflating two separate mythical beings: the world-turtle and the world-elephant. In fact, Hindu mythology features three distinct species of world-bearing creature: tortoise, elephant and snake, with the snake being arguably the most important.

These creatures occur in several guises. The commonest name for the world-tortoise is Kurma or Kumaraja. According to the *Shatpatha Brahmana* its upper shell is the heavens, its lower shell the Earth, and its body is the atmosphere. The *Bhagavata Purana* calls it Akupara – unbounded. In 1838 Leveson Vernon-Harcourt published *The Doctrine of the Deluge*, whose purpose is clearly indicated by its subtitle: *vindicating the scriptural account from the doubts which have recently been cast upon it by geological speculations*. In it, he wrote of a tortoise called Chukwa that supported Mount Meru. This mountain is sacred in both Hindu and Buddhist cosmology, the centre of the universe – physical, spiritual and metaphysical – where Brahma and the demigods reside. Vernon-Harcourt attributes the story to an astronomer who described it to Bishop Heber 'in the Vidayala school in Benares'. Since the word 'vidyayala' (note slight difference in spelling) means 'school' in Sanskrit, it is hard to give the report much credit. *Brewer's Dictionary of Phrase and Fable* includes the entry '*Chukwa*. The tortoise at the South Pole on which the Earth is said to rest', but there is little evidence to support this statement. However, Chukwa appears in the Ramayana as the name of a world-elephant, also known as Maha-padma or -pudma. Most likely various mythological entities were being confused and their stories combined.

Some sources say that Chukwa is the first and oldest turtle, who swims in the primordial ocean of milk and supports the Earth. Some also say that the elephant Maha-Pudma is interposed. This story apparently occurs in the *Puranas*, dating from the Gupta period (320-500). Whether the Hindus *believed* this myth, other than in a ritual sense, is debatable. Hindu astronomers of the Gupta period knew the Earth was round, and they may even have known that the Earth goes round the Sun. Perhaps there were 'priests' and 'scientists' – human- and universe-centred thinkers – then too.

The ocean of milk appears in one of the most famous reliefs at one of the great world heritage sites, the Khmer temple complex of Angkor Wat in Cambodia. In one version of Hindu cosmology, the ocean of milk was one of seven seas, surrounding seven worlds in concentric rings. Horace Hayman Wilson's 1840 translation of the *Vishnu Purana* relates that the creator god Hari (*aka* Vishnu and Krishna) instructed all the other gods to throw medicinal herbs into the sea of milk, and to churn the ocean to make *amrit* – the food of the gods. Assorted gods were told to use the mountain Mandara as a churning-stick, winding the serpent Vásuki round it like a rope. Hari himself, in the form of a tortoise, served as a pivot for the mountain as it was whirled around.

Around 1870 Ralph Griffith translated the *Rámáyan of Válmíki* into verse. Canto 45 of Book 1 relates that it didn't go as well as had been hoped. When the gods and demons continued to churn the Ocean of Milk, a fundamental engineering blunder became apparent:

Mandar's mountain, whirling round.
Pierced to the depths below the ground.

They implored Vishnu to help them 'bear up Mandar's threatening weight'. Obligingly, he came up with the perfect solution:

Then Vishnu, as their need was sore,
The semblance of a tortoise wore,
And in the bed of Ocean lay
The mountain on his back to stay.

Despite its neglect in Discworld cosmology, we must now introduce another species of world-bearing animal: the snake.

You'll see why in a moment.

In many Hindu and Buddhist temples, the handrails of stair-cases are long stone snakes, which terminate at the lower end as a many-headed king cobra, each head having an extended hood. This creature is called a *naga*. The *nagas* of Angkor generally have seven heads in a symmetric arrangement: one in the centre, three either side. A Cambodian legend tells of the *naga* as a race of supernatural reptiles whose kingdom was somewhere in the Pacific Ocean; their seven heads correspond to seven distinct races, mythically associated with the seven colours of the rainbow.

The *Mahabharata* takes a fairly negative view of *nagas*, portraying them as treacherous and venomous creatures, the rightful prey of the eagle-king Garuda. But according to the *Puranas* the king of the *nagas*, Shesha (*aka* Sheshanag, Devanagari, Adishesha), was a creator deity. Brahma first saw him in the form of a devoted human ascetic, and was so impressed that he gave him the task of carrying the world on his head. Only then did Shesha take on the aspect of a snake, slith-ering down a hole in the Earth to reach the base of the world, so that instead of placing the planet on his head, he placed his head beneath the planet. As you would.

Why are we talking about world-bearing snakes, not exactly prom-inent in the Discworld canon?

World-bearing elephants are probably snakes that got lost in translation.

The Sanskrit word *naga* has several other meanings. One is 'king cobra'. Another is 'elephant' – probably a reference to the animal's snake-like trunk. Although world-bearing elephants appear in later Sanskrit literature, they are conspicuously absent from the early epics. Wilhelm von Humboldt has suggested that the myths of world elephants may have arisen from confusion between different mean-ings of '*naga*', so that stories about the world-bearing serpent became corrupted into myths about world-bearing elephants. This is, in any case, an attractive idea for a culture that routinely used elephants for heavy lifting.

Classical Sanskrit writings include many references to the role of world elephants in Hindu cosmology. They guard and support the Earth at its four cardinal points, and the Earth shakes when they adjust their positions – an imaginative explanation for earthquakes. They variously occur as a set of four, eight, or sixteen. The *Amarakosha*, a dictionary in verse written by the scholar Amarasinha around AD 380, states that eight male and eight female elephants hold up the world. It names the males as Airavata, Anjana, Kumunda, Pundarika, Pushpa-danta, Sarva-bhauma, Supratika and Vamana. It is silent about the names of the females. The *Ramayana* lists just four male world elephants: Bhadra, Mahápadma, Saumanas and Virúpáksha.

It may or may not be significant that the name Mahápadma is mentioned in *Harivamsa* and *Vishnu Purana* as a supernatural snake. Like dragons in the mythology of other cultures, it guards a hoard of treasure. *Brewer's Dictionary* describes a 'popular rendition of a Hindu myth in which the tortoise Chukwa supports the elephant Maha-pudma, which in turn supports the world'. This variant spelling seems to come from a misprint in a 1921 edition of one of the stories of the *Mahabharata* by the Indian freedom fighter and poet Sri Aurobindo:

> *On the wondrous dais rose a throne,*
> *And he its pedestal whose lotus hood*
> *With ominous beauty crowns his horrible*
> *Sleek folds, great Mahapudma; high displayed*
> *He bears the throne of Death.*

However, this creature is clearly a giant cobra – unless you think the lotus hood is the elephant's ears.

Our main interest in these stories, in the present context, is comparative mythology. The creation myths of many ancient cultures contain very similar elements. It is tempting to explain these similarities in terms of cross-cultural contact. It is becoming increasingly clear that the ancient world, at various times and in various places, was more advanced than we have previously imagined, and there is good archaeological evidence for trade over much longer distances than used to be assumed. However, temptation should probably be resisted, even so, because other explanations are more plausible. One is cultural convergence driven by human psychology and common environments.

Images such as the Earth rising from a primal ocean seem to be the sort of thing that naturally occurs to intelligent but uninformed human beings who try to explain where their world came from using human-centred thinking. Seas rise and fall with the tides, rocks appear and disappear. Floods drown low mounds, and then reveal them again as the waters recede. We take inspiration from nature, make it larger than life, and use our own invention to explain what we can't understand. Creation myths open up windows into the human psyche. Ubiquitous natural phenomena, such as seas, mountains, volcanoes and earthquakes, suggest similar supernatural explanations. All ancient cultures were greatly influenced by the animals and plants that existed in their vicinity. If you live in a land full of possums and jaguars, it is no surprise if you develop possum gods and jaguar gods.

In many ways the *differences* between mythologies in disparate cultures are their most significant features. They suggest that the similarities may often result from some kind of convergent evolution, in which the same general supernatural explanation turns up independently because it has a certain logic – often of the Discworld kind – that appeals to the human mind. Explaining thunder as the gods throwing things, for example.

It is also interesting to see how myths evolve, like Chinese whispers, when they are passed on by oral tradition. Snakes become elephants. When the myths were preserved in written form, they still underwent dramatic changes before the invention of printing made it easy to mass-produce books. Even today, many of us can remember the general outline of a joke, or a story, but not the names of the characters. In mathematical circles, there are some standard stories about famous mathematicians, and the stories never change, but the famous mathematicians often do; the important point is that they should be famous. After that, it doesn't greatly matter who they were – the story is just as funny, whoever you choose. The turtle joke in the next section is an example.

The logic of mythology can also sometimes shed a little light on scientific issues, by reminding us of the principal reason for adopting the scientific method: the human tendency towards self-deception. We all too easily accept some kinds of evidence, or some types of argument, when they confirm what we want to believe; we tend to reject them if they conflict with our beliefs.

In 2012 a Gallup poll found that 46% of American adults agreed that 'God created human beings pretty much in their present form at one time within the last 10,000 years or so'. It was agreed by 32% that 'Human beings developed over millions of years from less advanced forms of life, but God guided this process'. And 15% believed that 'Human beings have developed over millions of years from less advanced forms of life, but God had no part in this process'. The scientific figures, based on a variety of evidence, place the first members of genus *Homo* at about 2.5 million years ago, and *Homo sapiens* – anatomically modern humans – at about 200,000 years ago, with archaic forms dating back perhaps twice as far.

We've mentioned Young Earth creationists in chapter 2. They argue that since Biblical scholarship dates the creation of humans to at most 10,000 years ago, and both the planet and humanity were created a few days apart, the Earth itself must also be less than 10,000 years old. As we saw, the scientific evidence that the planet is far older – homing in on about 4.5 billion years – is extensive, consistent, and comes from a variety of independent lines of thought, all supported by observations. If you insist on denying all of that, however, there is a straightforward way to do so: the scientific view rests on logical inference, not just direct personal experience.

It would seem strange, however, that a creator god should have gone to such extreme lengths, less than 10,000 years ago, to give his creation every appearance of being billions of years old, with humans existing for hundreds of thousands of years. It could be a test of faith, the universal get-out clause, but that's a peculiar reason for deceiving your own creations.*

The turtle-and-elephant universe features early on in Stephen Hawking's rampant bestseller *A Brief History of Time*. He tells us that a famous scientist, possibly Bertrand Russell,† was giving a public lecture, explaining how the Earth goes round the Sun and the Sun shares the rotation of the Galaxy. When he asked for questions, a proverbial little old lady complained that his theories were nonsense: the world was flat and rode on the back of a giant tortoise. 'What does the tortoise stand on?' the lecturer enquired. 'You're very clever, young man,' said the old lady, 'but it's turtles all the way down!'‡

Before the Big Bang theory became the orthodoxy, cosmologists espoused the steady-state theory: the universe has always existed and is essentially static. Although they have now abandoned the steady-state theory, many people still find it more congenial than any theory with an origin. In particular, an origin seems to require a precursor, so it seems natural to ask 'What happened before the Big Bang?'

---

* In 1857 Philip Gosse wrote a book called *Omphalos: An Attempt to Untie the Geological Knot* that argued for this approach – see *The Science of Discworld II: The Globe*.
† In his 1967 *Constraints on Variables in Syntax* the linguist John R. Ross states that it was the psychologist/philosopher William James. In other sources the scientist is variously identified as Arthur Stanley Eddington, Thomas Huxley, Linus Pauling, Carl Sagan, and many others. Insert scientist here.
‡ Notice how 'tortoise' morphs into 'turtle'. Perhaps the lady was American.

Until recently most cosmologists would have answered that since time began with the Big Bang, there *was* no before: it's like asking what lies north of the North Pole. In the last few years, however, many cosmologists have started to wonder if something more interesting might be going on, and whether there is a sensible series of events that led up to the Big Bang – in effect happening 'before' it in a causal sense, even if not a strictly temporal one. In *Figments of Reality*, Ian and Jack wrote:

> Most people seem perfectly happy with 'it's always been like that', finding no difficulty in conceiving of a universe that goes back for ever. Yet nearly everybody finds an infinite pile of turtles highly incongruous … So why are we so happy with an infinite pile of causality: today's universe riding on the back of yesterday's, which rides in turn on the day before's? It's *universes all the way back.*

Mathematical calculations show that an infinite pile of stationary turtles can support itself in a universe in which gravity is a constant force in a fixed direction (call this 'down'). This rather improbable structure works because the force of gravity acting on each turtle is exactly balanced by the reaction force where it stands on the turtle below, so Newton's third law of motion – action equals reaction – is obeyed. Similarly, there is no problem with causality in the infinite temporal pile of universes: each is caused by the previous one, so every universe has a cause. But psychologically, human beings are entirely happy with infinite piles of causality, yet find an infinite pile of turtles ridiculous.

We seem to accept or reject infinite piles of causality in a rather haphazard way, however. The philosopher David Hume rejected one example of what he called 'infinite progression' in his 1779 *Dialogues Concerning Natural Religion.* The context was a discussion of a creator God as an explanation of the material world. The obvious question 'what created God?' leads all too naturally to 'creators all the way back', a line of thinking that Hume wanted to close off. He says:

> Have we not the same reason to trace that ideal world into another ideal world, or new intelligent principle? But if we stop, and go no further; why go so far? Why not stop at the material world? ... after all, what satisfaction is there in that infinite progression? ... If the material world rests upon a similar ideal world, this ideal world must rest upon some other; and so on, without end. It were better, therefore, never to look beyond the present material world. By supposing it to contain the principle of its order within itself, we really assert it to be God; and the sooner we arrive at that Divine Being, so much the better. When you go one step beyond the mundane system, you only excite an inquisitive humour which it is impossible ever to satisfy.

In short, if we identify God with the material universe, we need go no further, and that's great because it stops us asking awkward questions. However, this does seem to imply that the universe created itself. And that seems to leave open exactly the line of thinking that Hume was trying to close (but Spinoza, two hundred years earlier, had already espoused that idea...).

Other scientific issues can be similarly swayed by human psychology. It is difficult to imagine Einstein's curved space (though not impossible for a trained mathematician or physicist), because we foolishly ask 'curved round what?' The answer is that it's not curved *round* anything – it's just curved. Its natural metric – its mathematical measure of distance – is not flat. Space seems to bunch up or spread out compared to a naive model based on Euclid's geometry. On the other hand, we are very happy with an infinite flat Euclidean plane or its three-dimensional analogue, space. It never occurs to us to ask 'flat along what?' But it's an equally sensible (or equally sense-less) question.

These cognitive biases probably stem from the model of space that our brains have evolved to contain, which seems to be Euclidean. This may perhaps be the simplest model that fits our experiences of the nearby world, extrapolated in the simplest way to avoid space having a boundary. Which would be appealing because we don't *see* any boundary. Our minds are very parochial. Our model of causality presumably evolved to match sequences of events that are common in our immediate vicinity, the human-scale world.

When it comes to the crunch, looking at both the theory that time had a specific origin, a finite period into the past, and the theory that it did not, but has always been in existence, then *both* have inherent flaws. This suggests that we are not thinking about the right question. Our view of the universe may be just as parochial and unreasonable as the world-bearing animals of ancient cultures were. Future scientists may view both the Big Bang, and four elephants riding on a turtle, as conceptual errors of a very similar kind.

FIVE

MAGIC ISN'T REAL

 Miss Marjorie Daw, senior librarian, woke up feeling to her surprise rather chipper; full, as it were, of beans. She felt around and everything important still seemed to be there; and most certainly she was sleeping in an extremely good and comfortable bed, leaving only the minor problem that it was not hers – a state of affairs that hadn't pertained for some time. However, anybody who knew the Dewey decimal system by heart was a person not to panic until the situation had been most carefully considered. Clearly she was all in one piece and, she now recognised, *extremely* hungry. Then she noticed that on the little table beside the bed was a prominent handwritten note which said, 'If you require anything, please ring the bell; if you *do not* require anything then don't ring.'

For some reason she was rather taken by the thoughtfulness and careful thinking evidenced by the little missive; it showed a sensible mind of the sort that was in short supply these days. She therefore carefully rang the bell, and it was answered by a brisk young woman who identified herself as Glenda, who began by saying, 'Did you sleep well? Strictly speaking, ladies who are not kitchen staff are not allowed in this university. But quite frankly it doesn't seem to matter all that much, especially if you dig your heels in, and may I say you have some elegantly high ones.'

Still bemused, Marjorie said, 'Yes, Jimmy Choos – not exactly librarian footwear, but it scares the daylights out of the city councillors when it comes to the budget.'

Glenda smiled and said, 'The Archchancellor knows that you are a librarian; I will take you to him shortly. Earlier today I took the liberty of getting together some new clothes for someone of your size and height; they're in the wardrobe of your room if you haven't already noticed, and I will come back to get you in fifteen minutes. Can I answer any questions at this point?'

Marjorie's brain was not exactly spinning – a more definitive description would be that it felt as if it had spent some time in a cocktail shaker. There had been – what? – the sense of motion, gone in an instant; and then, for heaven's sake, some sort of garden party? Then an inconclusive conversation with a bearded man who was probably from Balliol, to judge by his arrogance; although it was also perfectly *charming* arrogance, sufficient to make him appear quite likeable – like a man who has in fact *earned* the right to be arrogant. But beyond that everything else seemed to be a busy mélange of sights, noises and people. She most certainly knew who she was, and also could remember her telephone number, because in fact she had tried it and there was no signal here, wherever this place was. At least, she thought, it is civilised, but I am a long way from home, and … *how the hell do I know the language?*

All she could do was get changed – *remarkable* how the wizards had managed to get clothes exactly in her size – and wait for Glenda to come back, which she did after exactly fifteen minutes, greeting her cheerfully, asking how she was again, then walking with her through the grounds of this strange but hospitable university.

They were shortly joined by the elderly but handsome man who called himself an *Arch* Chancellor, a title Marjorie had never heard of before. She had to admit, though, that he *was* pretty arch, appearing to be more of a showman than an academic; he was indeed flamboyant as, chattering all the time, he carefully took her hand and led her to a table in the garden nearby.

Marjorie was keen on the concept of politeness, so she said, 'Excuse me, sir, but I cannot recall your name.'

'Only to be expected, Miss Marjorie Daw. I am told that your disorientation should shortly go away, which of course is why I am taking tea with you here in an environment that is likely to be more salubrious to you than my study; and besides I like the fresh air and trust that you do too. I have a lot to tell you in a short period but – where are my manners? Do you like meringues?'

He was watching her, still with an innocent expression, and Marjorie drew herself together sufficiently to say cautiously, 'The crackly ones or the soft ones?'

Ridcully said, 'For preference the crackly ones, the ones that crumble and crunch – although the other kind can be brought out if you so wish.' He handed her a plate of shining meringues, and said, 'I thought so; you look like a cruncher if ever I saw one. No namby-pamby, fiddly sticky ones for *you*.'

'And how is it, sir, that I suddenly feel so cheerful?' She paused, suddenly suspicious, remembering the exact-fit clothes. 'Have you been Googling me?'

'No, madam, because I do not know what googling is – although I may be goggling, of course. And now, in this little oasis of quiet in a noisy world, I would like you to sit down and listen to me. An Archchancellor learns how to read people, and you are a most organised person, extremely well read, amazingly so. I can see that, and a colleague of your profession has assured me of all these things, although of course you will not have met him as yet. Various types of coffee and tea will be here very shortly, but before you say anything, please let me explain – and believe me, dear Miss Daw, it's going to be a *long* explanation!'

The outriders of twilight were metaphorically at least putting on their spurs when Ridcully carefully topped up Marjorie's cup for the last time and said, 'And there you are, or more accurately, *here* you are; and to answer your first question: yes, we can get you back to Earth; although if you don't mind I rather prefer the term Roundworld; but that is of no moment at the moment, as it were, because we do have a problem at the moment, which is appearing to make it impossible to send you back the other way. This hiatus should not take very long, and I do apologise; but there's a will, and we are looking for the way; as I said, normally we could do this with almost a wave of a hand, but alas, a mechanical problem has caused something of an obstruction.'

Marjorie drew enough breath for the sentences she was confronting and said, 'Mister Archchancellor ...'

Ridcully quickly held up a hand and said, 'Call me Mustrum, if you don't find that too familiar.'

She hesitated and said, 'Very well ... Mustrum. I do find you quite unfamiliar, but in a very familiar way.' She smiled, and added, 'Of course I am aware of science fiction; and some of it is extremely good. But somehow I don't think it should work with wizards. For truly, after all, magic isn't *real*.' She hesitated again for a moment, and then added, more as a statement than a question, 'Is it?'

REALITY ISN'T MAGIC

 Is magic real?

Most of us no longer think that, not even those who are comfortable with supernatural intervention in everyday life. Magic is superstition, unlike entirely sensible beliefs in virgin births or life after death.

Magic is a human-centred viewpoint. It explains natural events in terms of what people want to happen. Assemble the magical ingredients (which often relate metaphorically to the desired outcome, like a rhino horn to an erection), incant the magic words (words have *power*), and the universe obligingly changes to accommodate your wishes.

On the whole, we much prefer stories about causes, as they hang together better than magical ones. We like to be told that something happens *because* something else did. You have to be quick on your mental feet to avoid the seductiveness of turtle-pile explanations involving causes all the way back, though. Most of us feel more comfortable when the pile is fairly short.

Scientists prefer rational, evidence-based causality. Religious people like to rest their short pile of causes on God, which relieves them of the need to look more deeply, just as Hume advised. Ironically, science lies behind technology, which we use to remodel our world so that it seems to work like magic, as we said in *The Science of Discworld*. When you switch on the light, all sorts of complicated technology goes into action: electricity, conducting wires, plastic insulation, and so on. (If you think a light switch is simple, you're not thinking about what makes it work and how it can be produced.) The electrician and the company that made the switch need to understand the technology in considerable detail, but the user does not. To them, it works 'like magic'. If you could show an iPad to a mediaeval monk, he would probably declare it the work of the Devil. Who else could create moving pictures on a slate? He would certainly find it incomprehensible. So do almost all of its users today. We *want* our gadgets to work like magic, doing what we want because we want it.

In contrast, science is mostly about how things happen 'of their own accord'. Science is universe-centred; magic is human-centred. The two viewpoints come together in technology: here the human-centred view sets our goals, while the universe-centred view helps us to achieve them. So technological magic involves a special kind of causality. Not *natural* causality – the workings of nature's laws – but *human* causality: how we can make nature do what we want.

Our thinking about causality easily gets muddled. We don't really understand what it is. Worry not: neither do scientists. In fact, anyone who claims to understand causality hasn't fully understood the question.

One of the big puzzles about causality is that once you start to trace the causes of even the simplest features of the world, you find an ever-branching backward tree, with many unlikely things coming together at just the right instant to make something else happen. We rest on an infinite pile of coincidences, and the pile gets wider the further back we go. The probability of anything specific happening seems to be zero.

Dawkins starts *Unweaving the Rainbow* with the example of all the people that aren't alive because they've never been born, the sperms that never made it to an egg for fertilisation, all the DNA combinations that were never actualised. These 'potential people', he says, outnumber the sands of Arabia. The ones who *have* been born are the tiniest of minorities.

He quotes Desmond Morris ascribing his love of natural history to Napoleon: if Morris's great-grandfather's arm had not been removed by a cannonball in the Peninsular War, all would have gone differently. If *your* parents, or your grandparents, had never met ... You can see where we're going here: the events that have actually happened are the tiniest fraction of those that *might* have happened.

It's easy to sort this out for Discworld. Narrativium makes sure that things go as they ought, and if there's a problem, there are always the History Monks to set things to rights. But Roundworld isn't like that: when the wizards needed to produce Shakespeare all kinds of things went wrong before they got the right version of him.*

How do you know that *you* are the right version?

Let's examine this problem: all the things that could have happened, versus the tiny fraction that actually did.

Some physicists claim to believe (we find it hard to accept that they actually do, when they get up in the morning) that there's a very simple answer to this conundrum. *All possible things happen.* Each distinct choice starts off a new universe, so that the Trousers of Time are forever bifurcating; everything happens somewhere. This seems absurd, making potential events as real as actual events. It's as if you tossed a coin a hundred times and wrote down the list of what happened: HHTTTHH and so on. Fine. But then you claim that every possible series happened 'somewhere', that HHHHHH, all heads, and TTTTTTT, all tails, happened too, as well as all the other possible combinations. Only ... they didn't happen in this universe, they happened in other ones. You're stuck in the universe where HHTTTHH happened, but somewhere else, the all-tails and all-heads options came up. The newspapers there must have been full of that news, mustn't they? Or are they perhaps in the kind of universe where unlikely things happen all the time?

---

* See *The Science of Discworld II: The Globe.*

This is the world of Schrödinger's cat, alive and dead at the same time until someone takes a look. Ponder Stibbons alluded to it in chapter 1. Well, it's the world of Schrödinger's cat according to quantum physicists, though not according to Schrödinger, who used a cat because cats aren't like that. But electrons are, so quantum physicists view a cat as a sort of super-electron. There is, however, a different view: that HHTTTHH *was* what happened, and that the other possibilities, like the other people whose sperms didn't make it to an egg, or the other histories that didn't result in Morris being a great naturalist, didn't actually happen. Anywhere.

Now, there is a sense in which the classical universe is the superposition of all conceivable quantum states, and that's what the quantum physicists are so keen to explain. But only *one* classical universe arises from of all those quantum alternatives – and that's why a cat is not a super-electron. Feynman explained this in *QED* using light rays as an example. The classical (that is, non-quantum) law of reflection tells us that when a light ray hits a mirror, 'the angle of incidence equals the angle of reflection'. That is, the ray bounces off at the same angle as it hit. In a classical world, there is only one outcome, determined by this simple geometric law. In a quantum world, there is no such thing as a light ray; instead, there is a quantum superposition of wavelike photons, going in all directions.

If you model the incoming ray in such terms, these photons concentrate *around* the classical ray in a particular manner. Each photon follows its own path; even the places where they hit the mirror can be different, and where they go afterwards need not obey the classical equal-angles law. Wonderfully, if you add up all of the waves corresponding to all of the photons – all of the potential quantum states of the system – with the right probabilities, the answer concentrates very tightly around the classical reflected ray. Feynman manages to convince his readers of this technical point (the principle of stationary phase) *without* doing any sums. Brilliant!

Notice how here the entire quantum superposition, of all possible states – including crazy ones where the photon follows wiggly paths, hits the mirror many times, and so on – leads to a *single* classical result: the one we observe. It does not lead to a superposition of many different classical worlds, like the traditional story of a world in which Adolf Hitler won the Second World War coexisting alongside one in which he didn't, together with endless variants in which all possible choices occurred at all possible times.

Yes, but ... Can we somehow pull that quantum superposition apart into many different *classical* scenarios, so that their superposition is the same as the quantum one? Each classical scenario would be a superposition of some of the quantum ones, and we must be careful not to use any of them twice, but is it possible? If so, our objection to the many-Hitlers universe would be irrelevant.

The most reasonable classical variations on the equal-angles scenario involve classical choices about where the incident light ray hits (which determines the angle of incidence) and what angle it comes off at (the angle of reflection). That is, we draw lots of straight lines that start at the light source, hit the mirror and bounce off – possibly with *unequal* angles.

Now, there are indeed photon-paths, submerged in the ocean of all possible quantum states, which mimic all of those classical paths. But if we change the point at which the ray hits the mirror, and try to synthesise that ray as a sum of nearby quantum states, it doesn't work. To make the original set of photon-paths represent the original incident ray correctly, these paths must be assigned probabilities that are concentrated near that ray. The paths near a different ray then have the wrong probabilities to represent that alternative ray. In short, we can't change the point at which the classical ray hits the mirror. But then, paths that reflect at a different angle aren't classical at all; in classical physics they are impossible, because classical paths obey the law of reflection.

This thought-experiment with a mini-universe containing a mirror and a light ray seems to indicate that the quantum super-position concerned determines a unique classical state, *and* that it can't be pulled apart into several different classical states. Perhaps there's a clever way to do that, but not in the world of incident and reflected rays. In short, although this mini-universe has infinitely many different quantum states, there is exactly one superposition that obeys a classical narrative. Since that's true for this simple mini-universe, something like it is presumably true for more complex ones. In particular, although the classical story in which Hitler lost the Second World War can be pulled apart into zillions of quantum alternatives, these states determine a single classical narrative, the one in which Hitler lost World War II. Moreover, this state cannot be pulled apart into different classical narratives by partitioning the quantum states that combine to create it.

If this argument is correct, there's no reason to believe that the constituent quantum states are anything other than useful mathematical fictions.

The main problem underlying Schrödinger's cat is not quantum superposition; it is our inability to model observations in quantum mechanics in a way that corresponds to actual experimental apparatus. Instead of admitting that we can't say what happens when we observe the world, and find just one state out of many potential ones, we insist that the entire universe must keep splitting into pieces that include all possible outcomes. This is just like insisting that the entire universe revolves round a stationary Earth, instead of accepting that maybe the Earth spins instead.

Since many things did *not* happen when you came into being, what about those that did? Were lots of them random rolls of the genetic dice, in which one sperm carrying these genes got there and the other 200 million missed out? Or a specific cannonball took an arm off and missed all the rest … or killed other people? Were other – perhaps all – events strictly determined by what had happened the instant before, which in turn was determined by the instant before that? Do we have to choose between everything that happens being the luck of the draw, or everything being strictly causal and determinate, from the Big Bang onward, through now into the infinite future? So that only one future was ever possible?

The opening chapters of Daniel Dennett's *Freedom Evolves* show conclusively that we can't – ever – decide between these options. They aren't real choices: determinate/indeterminate isn't the way to go, because we can't ever know which applies. The distinction makes sense only in a thought-experiment where we rerun the entire universe again, starting from an identical state, and check whether the same events occur both times. It is a valid distinction for how we *think* about our world, for the kinds of model we propose, but it's not a meaningful statement about the world itself.

We could take examples of events from anywhere and anything, and discuss their provenance: what makes them happen. Here we will look at three. The first example shows how difficult it is to demonstrate a cause in the real physical world, because tiny events can have tremendous outcomes. The second shows how, in our cultural world, small events – or the absence of such events – can take over a social universe and bias it away from the desirable outcome. Finally, we'll show how meddling by humans can completely change biological systems – and we're not thinking of dodos.

In the 1960s Edward Lorenz, a mathematician and meteorologist, discovered that tiny differences in computer input for (a toy model of) weather prediction could lead to large differences in the resulting forecast. From this discovery, together with a variety of other inputs, came the mathematics of deterministic chaos. We have all heard how the flapping of a butterfly's wings in Tokyo can cause a tornado in Texas a month later. This is a fine, dramatic example, but it considerably misrepresents causality. It suggests that only *that* butterfly is needed for the tornado, when actually it's the *difference* made by that butterfly that changes the circumstances just slightly, and flips the balance of causality into another path, a different trajectory on the same attractor. In reality, our world is full of butterflies.

Weather is a dynamic path through the attractor that we call climate. As long as the climate stays the same, the attractor doesn't change, but the path through it can. We then experience the same *kind* of weather, but in a different order. Climate change is more drastic: it alters the attractor. Now the entire range of possible weather-trajectories is different. Nonetheless, much of it still looks like plausible weather from the original attractor, because the attractor may not undergo any radical change – it need not encounter a tipping point. It can get a bit bigger, a bit smaller, or move around a little. We can't observe attractors directly, but we can reconstruct them mathematically from observations, processed in the right way. The simplest way to detect change in the attractor is to observe data such as long-term averages of temperature, size and frequency of hurricanes, likelihood of flooding etc. Many objections to 'climate change' confuse climate with weather.

We wrote a long piece in *The Science of Discworld III* about causality, and don't want to repeat that here. Enough to say that there is not any single cause of any event; it is almost always truer to declare that all of the preceding events contribute, than to point to one cause. However, stories do have a linear structure: A causes B causes C ... The law courts are full of that kind of story, as are most novels, and pretty well all detective stories and science fiction. Even Discworld stories rely on that fictional causality for their coherence. But this is because we are the storytelling ape. A story is a linear sequence of words. It is interesting to speculate whether an advanced alien culture would of necessity concoct such false-to-fact linearly causal stories. Could one always attribute events to three or four, or ten or twenty or a thousand, causes? Or is that the storytelling ape's way of seeing causality?

If we truly live in a deterministic universe, whatever that means, each successive state is the inevitable result of the immediately preceding state, including such minor causes as the gravitational influences of far stars, even the gravitational influences of the beasts on the planets around far stars. This picture is consistent with certain portrayals of the universe, where for some elements (spaceships approaching the speed of light are favourite candidates) what is in the future for some is on the left for others, while to the right are events-past. So every event is already 'there', in some frame of reference. This portrays the whole universe as a vast crystalline structure, with the future just as determinate as the past.

We find this representation as unsatisfactory as the perpetually-dividing Trousers of Time image. Historically, some of it derives from a misreading of Einstein's concept of a world-line in relativity, a fixed curve running across spacetime and describing the entire history of a particle. One curve, calculated using Einstein's equations, so one history, right? It's a valid image in a world with only one particle, whose state can be measured exactly, to infinitely many decimal points. It's not sensible for the vast, complex universe. If you start drawing a curve in spacetime, and allow it to develop as it grows, at any given stage you may have no idea where it will go next, no way to predict its future path. Einstein's equations don't help, because you can't measure the current state of the universe exactly. That's not a deterministic universe in any meaningful sense, but after infinite time you've got just one curve, one world-line – just as before.

Faced with a choice between two extremes, a world that is random or one that is completely predetermined, most of us dislike both. Neither matches our experiences. That doesn't prove either of them is wrong, but it makes a key point: any theoretical model must explain our daily experiences. It may well demonstrate that deep down, things are not as we assume; however, it does have to explain how what we assume emerges from the model, even if it's a misinterpretation of what is 'really' happening in the model. For example, the standard claim that science has proved atoms to be mostly empty space does *not* prove that the apparent solidity of a table is an illusion. You also have to explain why it seems solid to us; then you discover that empty space isn't empty at all, but filled with quantum fields and forces. Which is what 'solid' means at that level of description.

So we would like to find some leeway, some *choosable* indeterminacy in what happens, if only to foster our illusion of having free will. We would like to think that on an appropriate level of description, what we decide to do is not simply what we *have* to do.

Worryingly, the great (though sometimes misguided) philosopher René Descartes would have had sympathy with this approach, but that's because he famously divided the world into two separate aspects, *res cogitans* and *res extensa*, mind and matter. He needed *res cogitans*, the mind, to be freewheeling, so that it could instruct the body, *res extensa*. In contrast, he thought that little of the body's influence, if any, went the other way.

Consider the accidents of history that converged on Descartes, making his world a divided one and resulting in all kinds of anomalies in the present intellectual scene, from Arts and Science departments in universities, barely considering each other to be intellectually proper, to descriptions of minds and souls in popular parlance that are, to say the least, irrational.

In *Essential Readings in Biosemiotics*, Donald Favareau presents a fascinating story that makes a lot of sense. He starts with Aristotle, who wrote some twenty-six essays, only six of which were translated into Latin by Boethius in the sixth century. Two (*Categories* and *On Interpretation*) were about the material world, one (*Prior Analytics*) was about the mind, and the other three (*Posterior Analytics*, *Topics* and *Sophistical Refutations*) were about law and argument. The essay that joined up mind and matter, *De Anima* – Life, or Soul – was not translated until the thirteenth century, so it got left out of the western world's traditional 'works of Aristotle' for a thousand years, based entirely on Boethius. It was, in fact, translated from the Arabic in 1352 by Jean Buridan; all the great libraries then were in Arabia and Spain, and the Muslim religion was in the ascendant. But despite that, it was not then added to the standard 'works of Aristotle'.

In particular, Descartes had access to *Categories* and *On Interpretation*, but not to *De Anima* or *On Sense and the Sensible*, which provided a series of beautiful bridges between mind and body. So, believing himself to be free from preconceptions, but in fact carrying only part of Aristotle's weighty arguments in his memory, he divided mind from matter. That laid a secure foundation for this intellectual separation, right up to Norbert Weiner and *Cybernetics*, when feedback and machinery met.

That accident, that *De Anima* was not available to Descartes, or to Francis Bacon when he published the *Novum Organon* in 1620, which was based on the six essays translated by Boethius, changed the whole European intellectual climate for the next four hundred years. From Newton through to Einstein, physics was delimited with no thought of information. Shakespeare, Samuel Taylor Coleridge, all the way to Kingsley Amis, John Betjeman and Philip Larkin – everyone talked about machinery and industry, but only from outside.

The two worlds, mind and matter, only began to come together with Sigmund Freud and Carl Jung, who were in neither world, nor by any means in both. And then, after the Second World War, during which many scientists had been involved with communication issues, Claude Shannon began to publish papers in which information was treated as a quantitative concept. Soon after that came cybernetics, in which feedback of information interacted with amplification and other physical changes, resulting in changes to output. The safety-valve on a boiler was an early example: when the pressure got too high the valve released some steam. Weiner added room thermostats, which turned the heat off and on. Nearly all amplifiers for sound use 'feedback' to send the output back to the input, improving the sound quality.

Here information is used to control mechanical systems, which introduces a whole new dimension of technological magic. Hidden inside every laptop, iPhone, and for that matter, refrigerator, is a long, complex series of 'spells': the software instructions that make all of the general-purpose electronics carry out the specific tasks needed to make the gadget work. Programmers are today's sorcerers.

However, no one yet thought of linguistics as having anything to do with that kind of information. Only at the turn of the millennium did Steven Pinker, a linguistic psychologist, write *How the Mind Works* from a neurological *and* linguistic viewpoint. The two sides met, productively, after three hundred and fifty years.

Pinker later wrote *The Better Angels of our Nature*, arguing that today's humans are significantly less violent than they used to be. The book presents a wealth of data to support this contention. Nearly all of the reviews disagree; all of these are by people who are statistics-blind. They comment on the very apparent decline of violence in the last few centuries as if it were *only* apparent, unsupported by valid observations. Almost none of the comments are from positions that are modern and balanced; nearly all are from arts *or* science viewpoints, but not both.

Now that the division between mind and matter has been buried, or at least is on its way to the cemetery, how do we think about causality? Well, here is our second example, which splits into three related issues: day and night, the rainbow, and turning a light switch on.

What causes day and night? The answer is easy and obvious.* It is a question of gravitational forces, working according to the law of gravity, and the Earth turning on its axis so that it presents different faces towards the Sun. The Earth turning, about once per twenty-four hours, is what causes day and night. Easy.

---

* Though not obvious to 20% of Americans, who believe that the Sun goes round the Earth, and a further 9% who don't know: see Morris Berman, *Dark Ages America*.

Now let's think about a rainbow. Here things are a little more complicated. Jack sent each of his six children in to school to ask the teacher what made a rainbow. In each case the teacher gave what we've elsewhere called the lie-to-children response:* 'A raindrop is like a little prism, and you've seen how a prism breaks light up into colours.' 'No,' said Jack's children, 'it's the sharp bits on the prism that break up the light, and there aren't any sharp bits on raindrops. Anyway, we understand about raindrops refracting light, we want to know why there's that wonderful great bow in the sky.' And all the teachers said 'I don't know', variously, and two said, 'When you find out, please tell me,' and got great plus points for that.

The children were wrong about the sharp corner of the prism: it still refracts if you round the corner off. But they were right to focus on the shape of the rainbow, rather than its colours. Until you explain the shape, it's not clear why the colours, emitted by millions of different drops of rain, don't smear out.

What actually happens is quite complicated, though known to Descartes. Sunlight striking each drop gets refracted (and broken up into different colours) and then it bounces (total internal reflection) and passes out back towards the Sun, the different colours being further separated. Some fancy geometry shows that there is a focusing effect, because rays that enter the drop behave differently according to where they hit. Most of the light of a given colour comes out in a concentrated 'beam' at an angle of about 67° from the direction it went in. This angle depends on the wavelength, that is, the colour, of the light. So, if you're standing with the Sun behind you,

---

* This phrase is not intended to be derogatory, but it recognises an educational dilemma. In *The Collapse of Chaos*, 'liar-to-children' is a highly respected profession on the planet Zarathustra. The name reflects the occasional need for teachers to simplify explanations, to pave the way for more sophisticated ones later. The Zarathustrans observed that while all such explanations are true for a given value of 'truth', that value is sometimes small.

you see the backward-pointing coloured spray of rays from those raindrops that form a 67° circle in the sky. Someone standing a metre to your right doesn't see *your* raindrops, but those corresponding to a *different* circle a metre to the right of yours.

Many years ago when the world was young, Jack was training to be a rabbi, and he grew up with a reasonably-firm conviction about God, Abraham and the covenant between them (Genesis 9 verse 13). He was delighted by rainbows, and still is. What a nice idea ... but quite a complicated way to achieve it. And didn't light get refracted in exactly that way before the covenant? Now he sees rainbows as grace notes in the physical world, apparently unlikely processes that are delightful, or the evolution of frogs, whose developmental programme has to work in wildly varying temperatures, requiring a longer genome than our own. He doesn't implicate a god in these things, but he is grateful nevertheless. He does genuinely wonder whether humans are the only creatures that enjoy rainbows, or indeed enjoy at all. Still, rainbows were 'there' long before humans came on the scene. Perhaps the crab civilisation (*The Science of Discworld* chapter 31, 'Great Leap Sideways') enjoyed them.

So much for the causality of rainbows: complicated physics, but a delightful outcome.

Now we come to a really difficult bit of causality; turning a light on. You think this is simple too? Not a bit of it. You go into a room from a lighted hallway, and the switch is there. All kinds of clever neuronal things happen, sensory things and motor things, and the result is that the muscles in your arm lift it so that your finger can work the switch. You press (or turn or whatever) the switch, and the connection is made. Now alternating current can participate in a circuit that includes a lamp bulb, possibly with a filament which instantly heats up to about 3000° Celsius, emitting lots of heat and quite a lot of light. It might instead be a fluorescent tube, or an LED that produces light more efficiently, that is, with less heat.

We need to think about you causing your finger to press the switch – but we also need to understand how the electrical system is just sitting there waiting for you to work it.

Jack has a friend who's an electrician, a pleasant, helpful guy that you can phone up and he'll sort your electrical problem out. The electrician has many friends and acquaintances who are academics, and he has, at least *three times*, been in the following situation. Someone has rung up to ask why a socket that they have bought and put into the wall isn't working an appliance that they've plugged into it. When the electrician turns up … well, he discovers that they genuinely didn't know that there have to be wires in the wall connecting the socket to the electricity supply. They thought the socket alone would be enough.

Part of the problem is the old arts/science division, but one of the people concerned was a biologist. What is it about electricity that's so mysterious? We don't think the problem is electricity, or even understanding how it works. It's about cryptic investment. There was a time, quite long ago, when there were gas pipes to many public buildings, to power the lamps so that people could work when it was dark outside, but no electric supply, yet. Jack's mother took over the fifth floor of an old factory in Middlesex Street in the East End of London. There were rotating belts going up through the floors, turning long rods to which her sewing machines were attached, worked by great electric motors in the basement. Jack was amazed, when he went down to see these in the 1960s, that there were also remains of an old hydraulic system: water was piped to the building from a central pumping station, and returned when it had done its work, probably between the 1880s and 1910.

Such investments have been fossilised now, replaced by electric cables; but there had been a succession of power supplies to that building, invisible from outside, just made explicit by a series of bills from The London Hydraulic Power Company. The London Hydraulic Power Company had *181 miles* of cast-iron pipes under London providing power to factories. Who'd have thought that we would have forgotten that? The electric cables to houses are ever so discreet now, but they used to be a pair of wires from a local transformer, draped over the gardens. They still are in many rural districts, but a lot of cables to houses are now underground in British cities and suburbs. (Less so in America and Japan.)

So it's no longer obvious, to anyone who bothers to look, just how much investment there has been in energy distribution. Since the wires are invisible, people aren't always aware that they are present, let alone *necessary*. But that hidden wiring is the reason why we have only to lift an arm to turn the light on.

Our third example, as promised, is biological, and involves the meddling of humans: orchids.

Pick up a flower and look at it. Admire its petals. There were no petals 120 million years ago, just leaves. Some of the leaves may have been coloured, to attract insects, but they weren't petals. Leaves held their own wonders, however: they were flat areas on plants, making photosynthesis more effective. They helped to collect sunlight and to shade other competing plants. Before big leaves evolved, many plants had tiny leaves like scales on their stems; before that, plants were mostly in the seas, with flat 'stems' to collect more sunlight.

Petals are a trick that advanced land plants – angiosperms – use to attract insects (sometimes hummingbirds or even bats) so that they can reproduce sexually when pollen is carried from plant to plant. Originally, petals were leaves, with no reproductive role, sexual or not. But leaves have evolved into colourful arrays – which appeal to the human urge to tinker.

Look at a standard domestic rose; not the ones in hedgerows, which are often 'normal'. The sepals, anthers, perhaps even stigmas, have all been turned into petals. The flower of a cultivated rose is a monstrous concoction that has undone millions of years of evolution by selecting genetic differences over the generations. In any plant nursery there are hundreds of cultivated varieties, of many plant species, all with monstrously enlarged petals and double flowers, in which anthers and sepals have been converted into petals. These varieties are unable to reproduce sexually and have to be multiplied by methods such as taking cuttings. We humans have exaggerated their sexual parts to such an extent that for them, sex is now impossible.

There is another side to this process. Without human intervention, orchids have evolved wondrous flowers, complex and colourful. But orchids tend to be rare, growing in remote forests in the angles between the stems of vast trees, or in tiny patches at the edges of dangerous marshes. Humans, admiring the flowers without wanting to modify them, have used a different technique to make them available, to transcend nature. They have developed a variety of sophisticated methods to multiply plants without sex, including tissue culture, by which almost any part of a plant can be made to grow into a whole little plant.

The result is a deluge of orchids. They have been multiplied to the point at which it is possible to buy living orchid plants for a few pounds at any nursery. Left to their own, in their rare habitats, these plants would not have had any significant impact on humanity. Only a few botanists would ever have heard of them. But today we see them everywhere, in huge quantities; in bridesmaids' corsages, on restaurant tables and on windowsills. Human cultural capital, this time in the form of know-how, has caused these orchids to exist.

The same goes for trains, cars and aeroplanes. And electrical distribution systems. And washing-up detergents. And the most grotesque weaponry. We all live among the products of this cultural capital, even those of us who live 'in the wild', on mountains or in jungles (except for a few indigenous peoples who have hardly any contact with the outside world). Part of being a twenty-first century human is that nearly all of our surroundings have been 'caused' by previous investment, by cultural capital, be it artefacts or knowledge. We have taken over the natural world, and are remaking it in our own image. Nearly all of the causality that surrounds us depends on cultural capital.

In this way, we have remade our world in the image of narrativium. There is lots of hidden wiring behind the scenes, but it is *deliberately* hidden, so that we don't need to understand it to work our world. If you needed a PhD to log onto Facebook, the internet would have remained what it originally was when Tim Berners-Lee invented the world wide web: a research tool for particle physicists.

Things happen 'by magic' because we have made them work like magic. If we want something to happen, it does.

Like turning the light on, or buying an orchid for a few pounds.

SEVEN

AMAZING GLOBE

 Miss Marjorie looked so uncertain that Ridcully helped her out.

'Well, here in Unseen University we take the view that sufficiently advanced magic is indistinguishable from technology. However, as I understand it, you seldom need to say a mantra to get some engine to work … though I rather suspect that some people do.'

Despite everything, Marjorie was finding this weird looking-glass world rather amusing and bemusing at the same time, and as a good librarian she noted the fact, and wondered if there could be a 'cemusing' when you couldn't believe your eyes. She said, 'As a matter of fact, Archchancellor, I used to have a very old Morris Minor, bequeathed to me by my father, who had polished it every Sunday, religiously, and berated it in Latin if it went wrong. I still have the vehicle, and I myself have found that it can sometimes be persuaded to start by singing to it a few verses from *Hymns Ancient and Modern*; a few bars of "All Things Bright and Beautiful" often does the trick, even on frosty mornings. My father was a vicar, and I think he truly thought that you could find a semblance of life in the most unlikely things.'

'Ah yes; the quasi-pagan God of the English, who like their psalms to be full of references to nature, living creatures and growing things – a god of the green and the green-fingered. We have studied your world quite considerably – I told you this – but perhaps I left out one or two significant facts?' A thoughtful look appeared on his face. 'I think, madam, that it is time for me to show you *your* world as it seems to us. Please be so kind as to follow me; I think you will find the experience ... enlightening.'

It seemed to Marjorie Daw that this so-called Unseen University was huge and sprawling everywhere, *especially* down. The progress was slow, and the corridors filled with leaking heating pipes and more scurrying people – and if her eyes had not deceived her, at least one squid. But after a while, Ridcully knocked on a door that was liberally *plastered* with nameplates for professorial roles. She noticed a large number of buckets filled with coal in the corridor outside before they stepped in, and at the same time in*to*, whatever was in there, which turned out to be a rather grubby middle-aged man. The room itself was steaming hot.

A look of panic began to widen on the man's face when he saw Marjorie, causing the Archchancellor to *harrumph!* with amazing force. 'Professor Rincewind, Miss Daw wishes to see Roundworld. *Please* don't tell me that you've mislaid it *again*, will you?'

Rincewind retorted, 'That wasn't my fault, sir, really! They sign it out, then forget what they did with it, then remember that they loaned it to another student without telling me. Honestly, only last week I traced it to a pawnshop on Pigsty Hill! Students? Give me strength! I've got it back though, and haven't let a student have it since. But if that wasn't enough, Archchancellor, only today we've had *another* demand for it from the Omnians. Not from the almost likeable ones either – you know, like the Sanitary Army, an amiable bunch. No! It's that new lot – the ones who would like to go back to Vorbis if they could; they are becoming rather *testy*, sir, if you get my drift.' He looked sideways at Marjorie Daw in a way that suggested he didn't want to.

Ridcully stepped between them, saying, 'Professor Rincewind, Miss Daw is indeed a woman; you really must have been in close proximity to a woman before, unless you were built by somebody with a kit of parts? Moreover, she is my guest. Now, please give Roundworld to your Archchancellor, if you would be so good. After all, *I am your Archchancellor!*' His hand moved to his beard …

Rincewind nodded hurriedly, and said, 'Yes, of course, sir. Ponder Stibbons has told me you want me to go into Roundworld again; is that right?'

'Of course! I want you and the Dean, when he gets here, to have a look around in the flesh, as it were. The onlooker sees more of the game and so forth. Don't look so scared! It's pretty safe at the moment – no dinosaurs, one or two little wars, a little bit of global warming, nothing very dangerous at all; after all, this young lady has just come from there.' As Rincewind gave Marjorie a look that told her he really wished that she would go back there as soon as possible, the Archchancellor finished with, 'Mister Rincewind, you *will* give me Roundworld – now!'

Shortly afterwards, Mustrum Ridcully sat down at his desk and pushed some extremely high pieces of paperwork off it; these fluttered away and settled like snow. Marjorie watched him then put down the bag that the Rincewind creature had given to him *without* asking for a signature; quite possibly he had thought that it was the safest way.

The bag itself was green baize, very padded. She took a seat that Mustrum pulled out for her, and then watched him take out of the bag … the Earth!

She said, 'My word, that is an amazing globe of the Earth you have there; it seems just like those pictures taken from space! Personally I dislike people who call anything even vaguely interesting "marvellous"; but now I'm going to say it! Marvellous!'

'As I mentioned, Marjorie, we can't get you home yet, but we can let you see just about anything you want to see … and if I might suggest a few items of interest? Mister Stibbons only a few days ago showed me a wonderful display of sea creatures in the uttermost depths of the sea.' He pointed towards an area clearly consisting mostly of sea, a sea moreover that he was implying was now literally teeming with interesting lives. 'I don't always see eye to eye with the Dean,' he said, 'but I do believe he did surpass himself when he created your planet out of raw firmament. I rather suspect, though, that there could be a template somewhere, and quite possibly even a passing fly might have triggered *Roundworld*.'

'A fly … Roundworld?' Marjorie managed.

Ridcully chuckled. 'That's what we call it. We wizards are pretty good on magic, but somewhat uncreative when it comes to making up names.' Then he stared at Marjorie and added, 'I must congratulate you, madam, on your composure in this matter. I am sure many people would, at this point, be telling themselves that it wasn't happening, and – like your world's fictional Alice, who you will doubtless know of – will assume they would shortly wake up. Quite possibly at the entrance to a rabbit hole. It seems that you, as a librarian, are excellent at assessing data. Cataloguing and indexing in your mind. All very impressive.'

'Well, I did go to Roedean, and that counts for something … And if *I* were Alice, Mr Archchancellor, Wonderland would most certainly have shaped up, in no short measure.' Miss Daw's voice faltered, and she went on, 'You know *everything*, don't you?'

'Certainly not. But because what you call Earth lies in a subordinate plane, we can by accident or intent find a way into the place, sometimes in the flesh, but mostly via a variety of devices: crystal balls and so on. It is not intrusive – we may not be good at names, but we are very good at surreption, and we use such instruments sparingly. Excuse me, come!'

This was in response to a knocking on the door, the sound level of which had caused bits of plaster and miscellaneous debris to settle gently to the floor; indeed, a scattering of dust tumbled onto the Earth itself, causing Marjorie to giggle.

EIGHT

BEMUSING GLOBE

Roundworld is called Roundworld because, er, it's round.

From outside. As the wizards perceive it.

From inside ... well, that's a good question.

In the *Science of Discworld* series, the name does double duty for our planet and our universe. The planet is indeed round – ish – though at various times in history and in various cultures this was not appreciated and other shapes were favoured. The universe ... well, we don't really know what shape that is. Round is an obvious possibility, perhaps too obvious. If you not only have a point of view, but *are* one, and you can see equally far in every direction, the entire visible world automatically looks round. With *you* at the centre! Amazing.

In the absence of narrativium, Roundworld *does not know what shape it ought to be.* Somehow the actual shape, of planet, universe, and everything else for that matter, has to be a consequence of those mysterious rules. But there isn't a rule that says 'make planets round'. There isn't even a rule that says 'make planets'. The rules as we currently conceive of them say obscure things like $i\hbar\partial\Psi/\partial t = \hat{H}\Psi$.* This perverse lack of human focus in the rules drives the

---

* This is Schrödinger's equation, the one that says a cat can be both alive and dead. Do you see why? Isn't it obvious? Oh, since you insist. Let $\Psi = A$ (alive) to deduce that $i\hbar\partial A/\partial t = \hat{H}A$. Then let $\Psi = D$ (dead) to obtain $i\hbar\partial D/\partial t = \hat{H}D$. Add these two equations and rearrange to get $i\hbar\partial(A+D)/\partial t = \hat{H}(A+D)$. That's a cat that's alive *and* dead, and *it satisfies the same equation.* (To preserve unitarity, a few $1/\sqrt{2}$'s are also needed ... but you know that.)

wizards mad. Though they do like the fancy symbols, which are obviously magical.

Even worse: the rules are not written down. They are not even implicit in narrativium, since there is none, not until human beings invent it for themselves. The rules operate (we think) behind the scenes; an occasional truly sapient human can draw back the veil and glimpse nature's cogwheels spinning. So the creatures that live in or on Roundworld (that's us) play a lengthy guessing game in which they make up rules that seem to work, and then argue about whether they really do. This game has gone by many names: religion, philosophy, natural philosophy, science, or just The Truth. We are still playing it.

In this chapter, we'll deal with the shape of our planet. The answer is common knowledge, so we'll focus on the imaginative alternatives that have at times been proposed, the processes that led to the current answer, and the lengths to which some people have gone to deny it. We'll leave the shape of the universe to chapter 16. That's a much harder problem, in part because we can't stand outside the universe and look at it. However, until the 1960s we had the same problem concerning our planet, and that did not stop scientists pinning down its shape and size. Also how old it is, although the accepted scientific figure for the age of the Earth remains contentious in some quarters because some people don't like the answer, and of course that is all you need to prove it must be wrong.

The ancient Greeks started out thinking the world was flat, but they revised their opinion when they began to appreciate indirect evidence to the contrary. Like several earlier cultures, they were aware that the Moon is a sphere. Superficially, it may look like a flat disc viewed sideways on, but because of its phases, simple geometry reveals that it must be roughly spherical. The Sun, which is difficult to look at without blinding yourself, is a disc that seems to be almost exactly the same shape and size as the Moon, so presumably that, too, is a sphere. Eventually the Greeks concluded that the Earth is a sphere as well – a bit of a surprise because it doesn't look like one. If you live in mountainous regions the world looks bumpy; if in a desert, away from big sand dunes, it looks flat. But if you look really carefully, you will see ships slowly disappearing below the horizon as they leave harbour, so the *sea* is curved. Other clues, such as the Earth's shadow on the Moon during an eclipse, also indicate that the Earth is round. To the Greek worldview, a mix of human-centred and universe-centred thinking, that made narrative sense: a sphere is a perfect geometric form, so of course the gods would have used it to make the world.

After 250,000 years or more of the evolution and cultural development of modern humans, preceded by millions of years of our hominin ancestors, we have developed our own kind of narrativium, in which things happen because we tell each other stories about them, and then become inspired to *make* them happen. Having told ourselves innumerable stories about the shape of the Earth, most of them wrong, we have finally managed to gain a pretty accurate picture of the shape of our home planet. It is, as previously mentioned, a potato. The potato is very close to a spheroid of rotation, like a beach ball that someone has sat on. A spheroid is not too far away from a sphere. The Greeks did an amazing job for their time.

A spherical shape makes even more sense once you realise that we live on a planet that is similar to the other planets of the solar system, and once you have telescopes revealing that Mercury, Venus, Mars, Jupiter, Saturn, Uranus and Neptune (not to mention Pluto, Ceres, Titan, and many other bodies that are not classed as planets) are round. As above, so below. However, all this relies on logical inference, and it is only relatively recently that we have possessed the technology to look at the Earth from outside. The famous 'Earthrise' photo taken from lunar orbit in 1968 by astronaut William Anders of

Apollo 8 shows a gibbous Earth, predominantly blue and white but with shades of green and brown, rising above a sterile, grey, mountainous lunar landscape. (The first manned lunar landing, Apollo 11, happened a year later.) This image dramatised our world's fragility as it sailed through space, forever changing the associations of the word 'Earth'. Ironically, the astronauts weren't supposed to have taken it. NASA transcripts include an exchange between Anders and mission commander Frank Borman, who had previously taken a black and white photo of the Earth rising:

> *Borman*: Oh my God! Look at that picture over there! Here's the Earth coming up. Wow, is that pretty!
> *Anders*: Hey, don't take that, it's not scheduled.
> *Borman*: You got a colour film, Jim?*
> *Anders*: Hand me that roll of colour quick, will you!

The rest was a triumph of astronautical narrativium over managerial mission schedules.

Even though we now know the world is round, some diehards still refuse to accept the evidence. They 'know' that the Moon landings never happened; they were all faked in Hollywood studios. There is no question that this is possible *now*; movie-makers routinely use computer-generated imagery to create far more complicated things – among them the movie *Apollo 13*, made 25 years later, with highly realistic special effects. It's doubtful that the imagery existed *then*, but of course secret guv'mint projects were concealing technological advances that they only made public much later ... Though not, apparently, the relatively straightforward engineering technologies needed to put a man on the Moon. The theory that the Moon landings never happened makes perfect sense provided you think it is possible to sustain a global conspiracy ultimately involving millions

---

* Command Module Pilot James Lovell.

of people, prominent among whom were the Russians, who were trying to beat the Americans to their lunar prize.

We don't want to dissect conspiracy theories, or make any further attempt to convince you that Neil Armstrong and Buzz Aldrin really did land on the Moon in 1969, or, for that matter, that they didn't. Instead, we want to examine one of the reasons why many people used to believe, and a fair number still believe, that the Earth is flat. Or some other shape that is not the nice round globe of the Earth we encounter in geography lessons.

This reason is the role of inference, as opposed to direct observation. Inferences are always open to interpretation, and there is often enough wiggle-room to permit apparently logical escape routes. Devotees of a flat Earth have used this wiggle-room to devise more-or-less plausible explanations for most of the usual arguments that it is round. Explaining away one piece of evidence for a round Earth often conflicts with explaining away some other piece of evidence, but in a point-scoring debate, few in the audience notice. We, your humble authors, actually have a totally convincing proof that the Earth is round, which does not depend on photos from space, but we'll save it until the end of this chapter.

Before the 1960s, even the most technologically developed nations could not observe our planet from any vantage point higher than a plane could fly or a balloon could rise. In earlier times, the available evidence was limited to what a groundhog could observe with its own senses, and *Pan narrans*'s insatiable need to tell explanatory stories led to some imaginative proposals.

One of the earliest cosmologies that we know something about is that of ancient Egypt in the early dynastic period, around 3000 BC. It remained surprisingly unchanged for much of the next three millennia, although new elements came in from time to time and fashions changed. The basis for Egyptian cosmology seems to have been informal observations of natural phenomena, laced with imagination and thickly coated in religious imagery.

Egyptian thinking was strongly influenced by their natural coordinate system, which provided four very clear cardinal directions, each having a deep meaning. Egypt was the 'black land' sandwiched between two regions of 'red land': a thin fertile strip between wide deserts – though early on the desert areas were more like savannah than the arid expanses they are today. The Nile ran roughly from south to north, and the prevailing wind went the other way. The extent to which this axis was embedded in Egyptian thinking can be gauged from the hieroglyphs for south (a boat with its sails raised) and north (a boat with sails furled). The Sun – considered a god from predynastic times – rose in the east and set in the west.

In Egyptian mythology, the Earth was flat, with a sort-of square aspect because of the importance of the cardinal directions. It was associated with the god Geb. The goddess Nut formed a gigantic arch above the Earth, corresponding to the sky and the heavens. In between was the air god Shu. Various features of the night sky echoed those on the ground; in particular, the Milky Way, a bright, dramatic band of light in the night-time desert sky, corresponded to the Nile. Since the Sun disappeared from the sky in the west and reappeared in the east, it obviously passed under the Earth, through the solid body of the ground. During the night, the Sun god Ra battled with the demons and gods of the underworld, emerging victorious – or at least, as a survivor – each morning. Thanks, you appreciate, to the strenuous efforts and rituals of the priesthood.

Cosmology, you will recall, is the theory of the form of the universe, and it goes hand in hand with cosmogony, its origins. The Egyptians had several creation myths, originating in different regions of the country, and different myths were often combined in a mix-and-match way. A common element in most versions was mentioned earlier: the emergence of the Earth when the primal mound rose from the sea of chaos. The triangular shape of the pyramids is thought to represent, among other things, this primal mound. It has long been known that the Temple of Karnak in present-day Luxor had a ritual function as a representation of this primal mound, but there may be more to it than that. Recently archaeologist Angus Graham has been making geophysical surveys; using electrical resistivity tomography to detect the former course of the Nile through the silt it deposited, he has shown that in ancient times Karnak was located on an island in the middle of the Nile. As the annual floods receded, it would have re-enacted the emergence of the primal mound literally, not just symbolically.

Despite their religious interest in the night sky, the Egyptians seem not to have made a systematic study of astronomy for its own sake. For that, we must turn to another ancient culture: Babylon.

Babylon was one of a variety of civilisations in the Mesopotamian region, the fertile lands between the Tigris and Euphrates rivers. Today this area comprises Iraq, plus parts of Iran, Syria and Turkey. The city of Babylon was in central Mesopotamia, about 80 km south of present-day Baghdad.

During the Bronze Age, Mesopotamia included the empires of the Old Babylonians, Sumerians, Assyrians and Old Akkadians. The New Babylonian and New Akkadian empires followed in the Iron Age. The Sumerians invented cuneiform writing, triangular marks in clay made by a stick, around 3500 BC. They studied the heavens, were aware of the 'wandering stars' that we now call planets, and worshipped them as gods. An ancient Sumerian tablet refers to seven heavens and seven Earths.

Babylonian history is usually divided into two periods. The city-state of Babylon became a regional power when the sixth king, Hammurabi, took charge in 1792 BC, and the Old Babylonian period dates from then until about 625 BC. The New Babylonian period followed when Nabopolassar took control following a civil war triggered by the death of the Assyrian king Ashurbanipal. Many more cuneiform astronomical texts survive from the New period than from the Old, but there are enough Old Babylonian texts to demonstrate that their study of the heavens was systematic and organised. The Old Babylonian astronomers produced the first known star catalogue around 1200 BC, but many of the star names are Sumerian, so Sumerian astronomers must have made systematic studies of the heavens even earlier.

The Babylonians paved the way for modern astronomy, and possibly science as well. They observed the motions of celestial bodies, especially the planets, carefully and accurately. Then they looked for patterns, using mathematics to analyse the data. They discovered that many astronomical phenomena are periodic: they repeat at fairly regular intervals. There is a tablet that records how the amount of daylight changes over the year, and a series of tablets called the *Enûma Anu Enlil* contains the Venus Table of Ammisaduqa, a 21-year record of the motions of Venus and the earliest known discovery of periodic events in planetary motion. This tablet, made around 700 BC, is a copy of an older one, possibly from the early part of the Old Babylonian era.

The Babylonians were assiduous observers, but they had no great interest in theoretical explanations, and we know little about their cosmology. Tablets contain phrases such as 'the circumference of heaven and earth', suggesting that they imagined the Earth and the cosmos united in a single round object. The two components were of equal importance, and both revolved in circles. The Babylonians did not link their scientific studies of the planets to their religious views of the cosmos, and they seem not to have thought that the planets themselves move in circles.

After 400 BC, the centre of natural philosophy in the ancient world shifted to Greece. Philolaus, a member of the cult founded by Pythagoras, viewed the cosmos as a central fire, around which the Sun, Moon, Earth and planets all revolve in circles. We don't notice the fire because it is hidden by the bulk of the Earth. Around 300 BC, Aristarchus of Samos came up with perhaps the first heliocentric cosmology, by the simple expedient of replacing the central fire by the Sun.

The novel idea that the Earth revolves around the Sun received a general thumbs-down from almost everyone else, including virtually all early Greek philosophers. Thales thought that a flat Earth floated on water. Anaximander thought it was a thick disc with a flat top. Anaximenes held that a flat Earth rode on air like the other celestial bodies. Xenophanes maintained that we lived on the flat top of a semi-infinite cylinder, extending downwards for ever (shades of 'turtles all the way down'). Anaxagoras accepted that the Earth was flat, but Archelaus insisted it was saucer-shaped, which is why we don't all see the Sun rising and setting at the same time.

Most ancient natural philosophers preferred the theories of Aristotle and Ptolemy, who placed the Earth where any sensible person naturally would: at the centre of things. Plutarch, in a work about the Man in the Moon – the apparent face formed by the darker regions – wrote that the head of the Stoics, Cleanthes, urged that Aristarchus should be called to account for lack of piety towards the gods. Why? Because he had dared to set 'the hearth of the universe' (Earth) in motion, and suggested that the heavens are static whereas the Earth rotates in 'an oblique circle' and – even worse – spins on its axis.

The heliocentric theory found favour with just one of Aristarchus's successors, Seleucus of Seleucia, a hundred years later. By then, the Greeks were aware that the Earth is round, and Eratosthenes obtained a fairly accurate estimate of its size by observing the altitude of the midday Sun at Alexandria and Syene, present-day Aswan.

One variant Egyptian creation myth, the Ogdoad, replaces the primal mound by a cosmic egg. The Milky Way emerged from the ocean of chaos as a mound, associated with the goddess Hathor. A heavenly goose laid an egg on the mound, and inside it was Ra. Later, when the cult of the god Thoth rose to prominence, the goose mutated into an Ibis, an aspect of Thoth.

The image of the cosmos as an egg is common to many cultures. Typically either the universe or important deities come into existence when the egg hatches. The egg may be all that initially exists, or it may rest on a primal ocean. In Hindu mythology the *Brahmanda Purana*, a Sanskrit religious text, describes the cosmic egg at length. Here *brahm* means either 'cosmos' or 'expanding' and *anda* means 'egg'. The *Rig Veda* refers to *hiranyagarbha*, 'golden womb'. This floated in nothing until it fragmented into two parts, heaven and Earth. In Chinese Buddhism, Taoist monks told of a god called Pangu, born inside the cosmic egg, who broke it into heaven and Earth when he emerged. In Japanese mythology, a cosmic egg floats in a vast sea.

The Finnish epic *Kalevala* has a novel slant on creation, which it attributes to a duck that laid fragments of an egg on the knee of the air goddess Ilmatar:

One egg's lower half transformed
And became the Earth below,
And its upper half transmuted
And became the sky above.
From the yolk the Sun was made,
Light of day to shine upon us;
From the white the Moon was made,
Light of night to gleam above us.

This extract exemplifies a common feature of many myths: they are human-centred. They explain the vast, enigmatic cosmos in terms of a familiar everyday object. An egg is round, like the Sun and the Moon. A living creature emerges from it, so the egg functions as a symbol for the source of all life. Crack one open, and you see two main colours: yellow yolk, and white. These just happen to be the colours of the Sun and the Moon. It is no wonder that images of this kind became so widespread. It just takes a certain combination of logic and mysticism, akin to the Egyptian association between the Sun god and a dung-beetle because both pushed a ball around.

The same combination is characteristic of Discworld narrativium; it is why so much on Discworld 'makes sense' even though it is about wizards, witches, trolls, vampires, elves and magic. All you need is a small amount of 'suspension of disbelief', as they say in science fiction circles. After that, everything is perfectly sensible. The main difference in ancient times was that there was very little disbelief to suspend. The universe-centred way of thinking was confined to a few deep thinkers in a few cultures.

As Greek civilisation became subsumed under the Romans, the main centres for the study of the natural world moved to Arabia, India, and China. Europe entered a lengthy period often referred to as the Dark Ages, a name that suggests (correctly) that we know very little about them, and also (incorrectly) that this is because nothing much happened on an intellectual level. There was a lot of scholarly effort, but most of it went into theology and rhetoric. What we now consider to be fledgling science struggled.

It is often claimed that in medieval times the Earth was thought to be a flat disc, but the evidence is ambiguous, except very early on. Around AD 350 St John Chrysostom deduced from the Bible that the Earth floated on the waters below the firmament of heaven, a view shared by St Athanasius at much the same time. In about AD 400 Bishop Severian of Gabala considered the Earth to be flat. Unusually, he also believed that the Sun did not travel beneath it during the hours of darkness, but instead nipped back round to the north, hidden from view. By 550 Cosmas Indicopleustes, an Egyptian monk, was doggedly following Egyptian tradition and offered theological arguments for a flat Earth, but with a new twist: the shape was that of a parallelogram surrounded by four oceans.

Many medieval writers definitely knew the world was round, although many believed that no humans lived on its underside, the antipodes. The important regions of the world formed a hemisphere, and in drawings and text it was easy to confuse this with a flat disc.

A famous case is the seventh century AD Bishop Isidore of Seville, who wrote in his *Etymologiae*: 'The mass of solid land is called round after the roundness of a circle, because it is like a wheel. Because of this, the Ocean flowing round it is contained in a circular limit, and it is divided into three parts, one part being called Asia, the second Europe, and the third Africa.'

At first sight, 'round' here seems to mean a flat disc, not a sphere. Maps of the period, known as T and O, T-O, O-T, or *orbis terrarum* maps, draw a round O outside a capital T. This divides the O into three parts: Asia above the horizontal stroke, Europe and Africa to the left and right of the vertical stroke. Rotate it through a right angle and it looks much like a modern map, though distorted. The oceans all join up and there is a complete ring of water surrounding the land. However, the map could be a projection into the plane of a hemisphere, and that seems to be the prevailing opinion among scholars today. On the other hand, the statement that the oceans are 'contained in a circular limit' is difficult to reconcile with a round Earth, especially since the reason is stated to be 'it is like a wheel'. Do the scholars protest too much?

Be that as it may, there are many references from early Christian times indicating knowledge of a round Earth, but that raised a more difficult theological issue. A round Earth requires the existence of antipodal regions, diametrically opposite to the geographical regions that were then known to Europeans. The existence of these regions wasn't a problem, but there was general disbelief that they were, or could be, inhabited. The objection was not that people would fall off, but that no one had been there to see whether there was any land – and if there were, whether there were *people*. It was a perfectly scientific objection: the problem was lack of evidence. Shortly after the sack of Rome in 410, Saint Augustine of Hippo addressed the issue in his *City of God*:

... as to the fable that there are Antipodes, that is to say, men on the opposite side of the Earth ... that is on no ground credible ... Although it be supposed or scientifically demonstrated that the world is of a round and spherical form, yet it does not follow that the other side of the Earth is bare of water; nor even, though it be bare, does it immediately follow that it is peopled ... Since these people would have to be descended from Adam, they would have had to travel to the other side of the Earth at some point ... It is too absurd to say, that some men might have taken ship and traversed the whole wide ocean, and crossed from this side of the world to the other, and that thus even the inhabitants of that distant region are descended from that one first man.

Full marks for geography, then.

The history of flat versus round Earth is complex, open to many divergent interpretations, and littered with myths. A common one is that Columbus had to overcome a widespread belief that the Earth was flat in order to persuade the Spanish royal family to allow him to try to sail westwards to India. Actually, the main obstacles were twofold: the correct belief that the round Earth was too big for this to work according to Columbus's schedule, and the cost.

Columbus fudged the figures.

Educated people seriously began to wonder whether the Earth really might be flat, or at least not the conventional spheroid, in the Victorian era, around 1850. Paradoxically, the new spirit of scientific enquiry was encouraging some people to question well-established observations of the shape of our planet. It is worth remembering that this was also a period when belief in the spirit world flourished. It wasn't just Biblical creation that was coming under fire from science. Although no reputable scientists seem to have reverted to believing in a flat Earth, several prominent figures in society did. What motivated them was often a fundamentalist attitude to the Bible, coupled with naive or idiosyncratic interpretations of its contents.

One of the most celebrated flat-Earth disputes was the Bedford Level experiment. The Bedford Level is a long stretch of the Old Bedford River in Norfolk, remodelled as a straight canal. If the theory that the Earth is round has any merit, it ought to be possible to observe the curvature by sighting along the surface of the river. In 1838 Samuel Birley Rowbotham did just that, wading into the river with a telescope and watching a boat as it rowed the six miles to Welney bridge. He reported that the boat's mast, five feet tall, remained in view the entire time: clear evidence for a flat Earth.

Rowbotham led a colourful life. He was an organiser of an Owenite commune in the Norfolk Fens, which practised the socialist utopian views of the reformer Robert Owen. After allegations of sexual peccadillos, Rowbotham travelled the country giving lectures about why the Earth is flat and science had got it wrong. At a lecture in Blackburn, a member of the audience asked why ships disappear from the hull up when they sail out to sea, until only the tops of the mast remains visible. Unable to answer, Rowbotham fled the lecture hall, but he learned from the debacle, improved his debating skills and found plausible counters to the usual arguments for a round Earth. He published his views in 1849 in a pamphlet called *Zetetic Astronomy*. Later he put them in a second pamphlet, *The Inconsistency of Modern Astronomy and Its Opposition to the Scripture*, whose title hints at a possible motive.

Public scepticism ran high, and he was repeatedly asked to carry out proper experiments, but he always refused. By 1864, however, the pressure had become so intense that he set up an experiment on Plymouth Hoe, an open area of ground where Sir Francis Drake memorably played bowls in 1588 while waiting for the tide to turn so that he could attack the Spanish Armada.* If the Earth were round, then only the top of the Eddystone lighthouse, 14 miles away, would

---

* This tale is probably untrue, but it's a good story, so it survives – much like the story of a flat Earth. Never underestimate the power of narrativium.

be visible through a telescope; if it were flat, the entire lighthouse would be visible. The result was decisive: only half of the lantern was visible. Rowbotham resorted to a standard pseudoscientific response to contrary evidence: ignore it and claim the opposite. Under the name 'Dr Samuel Birley' he allegedly sold cures for all human diseases and claimed the ability to prevent ageing. His patents include one for a life-preserving cylindrical railway carriage. In 1861 he married his laundress's sixteen-year old daughter, and they had fourteen children.

In 1870 John Hampden wagered that he could show, by repeating Rowbotham's Bedford Level experiment, that the Earth is flat. He encountered a formidable opponent: Alfred Russel Wallace, who had trained as a surveyor. We met Wallace in *The Science of Discworld III: Darwin's Watch*. On 1 July 1858 his paper 'On the perpetuation of varieties and species by natural means of selection' was read to the Linnaean Society, along with a very similar work 'On the tendency of species to form varieties' by Charles Darwin. In his annual report the President of the Society, Thomas Bell, wrote: 'The year which has passed has not, indeed, been marked by any of those striking discoveries which at once revolutionize, so to speak, the department of science on which they bear.' The two papers had announced the theory of evolution by means of natural selection.

At any rate, Wallace accepted Hampden's wager. His surveyor's training allowed him to avoid the errors of the preceding experiments and he won the bet. Hampden published a pamphlet alleging that Wallace had cheated, and sued for his money. Several lengthy court cases ensued, and eventually Hampden was jailed for libel.

Rowbotham was not to be silenced. In 1883 he set up the Zetetic Society, a forerunner of the Flat Earth Society, with himself as president. It had branches in England and the United States. One of his supporters, William Carpenter, published *Theoretical Astronomy Examined and Exposed – Proving the Earth not a Globe* using the pseudonym Common Sense. He followed it with *A Hundred Proofs the Earth is Not a Globe.* One was the observation that many rivers flow for long distances without descending more than a few feet, an example being the Nile, which drops one foot in a thousand miles. 'A level expanse of this extent is quite incompatible with the idea of the Earth's convexity. It is, therefore, a reasonable proof that Earth is not a globe.'

It pays to check the facts. The Nile is fed from Lake Victoria, although there are other rivers that run into the lake so it is technically not the source. It flows more than 6,500 km to the Mediterranean Sea. The lake is 1,140 metres above sea level. So the river drops, on average, slightly under one metre for every six kilometres of its length. Over a thousand miles, it drops about 900 feet, not one.

People with extreme religious beliefs, who adopt a human-centred view of the world despite attributing its creation to an all-powerful deity, tend to have problems with universe-centred thinking. Lady Anne Blount was a Biblical literalist, and a rather unimaginative one to boot. Not only did she view the Bible as the sole source of reliable information about nature; she had no doubt that it states that the Earth is flat. Convinced that no true Christian could believe in a round Earth (so much for Augustine), Lady Blount set up a magazine, *Earth not a Globe Review*. In 1901 she founded another, called simply *Earth*.

That was the year when the geographer Henry Yule Oldham repeated the Bedford Level Experiment using a better experimental design. He placed three vertical poles in the river, at the same height above the water. When viewed through a theodolite, the middle pole was almost three feet above the other two, a result that is consistent with a round Earth of the correct diameter. Until the Earthrise photo became available, this experiment was widely taught in schools to demonstrate that the world is round. Lady Blount's response was to hire a photographer, Edgar Clifton. In 1904, using a telephoto lens placed two feet above the river, he took a picture looking back from Welney bridge to where Rowbotham had started it all by wading into the river, six miles distant. The photo showed a large white sheet, touching the surface of the water. Apparently the result surprised him: he knew the sheet should not have been visible. Lady Blount gave the picture a lot of publicity.

How did Clifton get his photo? Was it a fraud? That would be easy to arrange. Take the photo from much closer, then switch plates when performing the actual experiment in the public eye. Or place the sheet or camera higher than claimed. Alternatively, Lady Blount might have got lucky: the result could have been a mirage. Temperature differences in air bend light, in ways that depend on which regions are hotter and which colder. A 'superior image' mirage would have led to similar results.

Even in these allegedly enlightened times, belief in a flat Earth survives, remarkably unaffected by a wealth of contrary evidence, though it is definitely a minority view. The *International Flat Earth Research Society*, usually referred to as the *Flat Earth Society*, was set up in 1956. The Society's most recent proposal for the shape of the Earth is a disc centred at the North Pole, surrounded by a 150-foot wall of ice at its rim (Antarctica). As evidence, the Society cites the logo of the United Nations, which depicts exactly this arrangement except for the ice wall. The logo is based on an azimuthal equidistant projection centred on the North Pole, which is one standard mapmaking method for turning a round Earth into a flat map.

Given the attitudes of the religious right and other pressure groups in America to issues like evolution and climate change, and Young Earth Creationism – which believes that the Bible proves the Earth is at most 10,000 years old* – it wouldn't be a great surprise to read in

---

* Archbishop James Ussher's scripture-based calculation that the Creation dates to the night before Sunday, 23 October 4004 BC is a little bit too recent because of archaeological records that are hard to dismiss. A retreat by 4000 years neatly avoids the issue. Ussher's date is so precise because he figured that Creation happened *exactly* 4000 years before the birth of Christ. Why the deity is so obsessed with decimal reckoning in multiples of one planetary orbit is not explained.

tomorrow's papers that some school board in Boondocks Mississippi is insisting that science lessons should 'teach the controversy' about the shape of our world, by giving equal time to the proposition that it's flat.

We now come to the most curious twist in the story of the Bedford Level Experiment. A few years earlier, in 1896, the American newspaper editor Ulysses Grant Morrow carried out a similar experiment on the Old Illinois Drainage Canal. But he wasn't trying to emulate Rowbotham and prove that the Earth is flat. Morrow intended to prove that it's curved. In the experiment, his target, just above water level eight kilometres away, was clearly visible. Morrow concluded that the surface of our planet is curved, but not like a ball. Instead of the world being convex, it is concave, like a saucer. This claim makes more sense once we appreciate who sponsored Morrow's research: the Koreshan Unity Society, founded by Cyrus Teed in the 1870s.

Teed, a doctor, was fascinated by alchemy. He carried out numerous experiments, often using high voltage electricity, and in 1869 he gave himself a severe electric shock. He claimed that while he was unconscious a spirit had contacted him, telling him he was the Messiah. He changed his name to Koresh, Hebrew for Cyrus, and set out to save the soul of humanity. Teed's reformulation of our planet's shape stemmed from this experience. It went much further than merely proposing a hollow interior. According to his Cellular Cosmogony, we are inside the Earth, a hollow ball with the Sun at its centre. Gravity does not exist; instead, we are pinned to the planet's surface by centrifugal force. The Sun is operated by batteries, and the stars are distorted images of it.

Koreshanity attracted adherents, and Teed preached celibacy,* reincarnation and communism, as well as weird science. A foray into

---

* A poor choice for any cult. The most effective way of spreading a belief is to tell adherents to teach it to their children.

politics led to an assault by his opponents, and the injuries led to his death in 1908. With its leader gone, the cult faded away.

Now, there is a rather trivial sense in which Teed is right. A solid Earth surrounded by the rest of the universe can be transformed into a hollow Earth, surrounded by an infinite expanse of rock, whose interior contains the rest of the universe. All laws of nature, equations of mathematical physics and so on, can be transferred into the transformed coordinates. They will (usually) look different, but the two realisations match perfectly, are logically equivalent, and are physically indistinguishable. As far as mathematicians are concerned, they are 'the same'.

To obtain a hollow Earth, use a geometric transformation invented by Ludwig Magnus in 1831: inversion. Choose a point in space as the origin; then transform a point distance d along a radius to the point that is distance $1/d$ along the same radius. This transformation leaves the sphere of unit radius unchanged, because $1/1 = 1$, but it swaps the inside and outside of the sphere, because if d is bigger than 1 then $1/d$ is less than 1. The centre of the sphere goes to infinity; infinity goes to the centre of the sphere. Do this with the origin at the centre of the Earth and you get a hollow planet with the rest of the universe inside it, surrounded by an infinite expanse of rock.

You can play this game with any description of nature. You can use it to argue that the United Nations logo is the true shape of the Earth. You can rewrite astronomy in an Earth-centred frame of reference. If you transform every law of nature to match, no one can contradict you. There is a sensible way to play the game: some transformations take precedence because they lead to simpler equations. But Hollow Earth theories that use inversion as justification apply meaningless transformations that tell us nothing new about reality.

Some kind of world existing inside our planet, that is, underground, is a common element of many religions. We've already encountered the ancient Egyptian belief in the underworld. The Judaeo-Christian

vision of Hell, until a few centuries ago, had elements in common.
The Hindu *Puranas* tell of an underground city called Shamballa,
and the same story occurs in Tibetan Buddhism. However, none of
these myths suggests that the Earth is a hollow ball.

In 1692, the astronomer Edmond Halley, a leading scientist of the
period, famous for a comet, was trying to explain why compasses
don't always point towards magnetic north. He suggested that the
variations in direction could be explained if the Earth were a series of
concentric spherical shells: a surface shell 800 kilometres thick, two
smaller shells within it, and a solid ball in the middle. He thought
that they were separated by atmospheres, rotated at different speeds,
and had their own magnetic poles. Escaping gas at the poles glowed
to create the auroras. It was a kind of magnetic version of Ptolemy's
crystal spheres, and like that theory, it explained a great deal and was
completely wrong.

Pseudoscience got in on the act in a big way in 1818, when John
Symmes advanced a similar model, in which the outer shell was 1300
kilometres thick with huge circular openings at both poles. Inside
were four more shells, also with polar apertures. You have to remember that this was seventy-seven years before the Norwegian explorers
Fridtjof Nansen and Hjalmar Johansen reached latitude 86° north in
1895, and ninety-one years before Robert Peary reached the North
Pole in 1909 – or, as now seems plausible, got very close but maybe
didn't quite make it. Symmes agitated for a polar expedition, and his
follower James McBride seems to have convinced the US President
John Quincy Adams to authorise and fund it. But the incoming President Andrew Jackson put a stop to the idea.

In 1826 McBride published *Symmes' Theory of Concentric Spheres*,
and a flurry of similar theories and books quickly followed. Among
them were the 1906 *Phantom of the Poles* by William Reed, which
abolished the secondary shells inside, and Marshall Gardner's 1913
A Journey to the Earth's Interior which sported an interior Sun. As
late as 1964 the (probably pseudonymous) Dr Raymond Bernard's

The Hollow Earth proposed that our planet's open interior is the source of UFOs. It also explained what happened to Atlantis, and indeed was where the Atlanteans fled to when their continent disappeared. Rather desperately, the book referred to the Ring Nebula as proof that hollow worlds exist. This structure, just over one light year across and 2300 light years away, is an expanding shell of gas expelled by a red giant star on its way to becoming a white dwarf.

Mapmaking can't distinguish the geometry of the interior of a sphere from that of the exterior, although differences arise as soon as the surface extends into the third dimension. The peaks of mountains would be closer together if they were inside the Earth. Not surprisingly, there are some big problems with Teed's theories. Many can be resolved by special pleading, such as strange refractions of light, but these extra features come very close to reformulating conventional physics in an inverted frame of reference, and have no serious substance. Centrifugal force doesn't work as a substitute for gravity, because it always acts at right angles to the planet's axis of rotation. The perceived force would be zero at the poles, and only at the equator would it act in the observed direction, at right angles to the surface. The oceans would migrate to form circular pools at the poles, hundreds of kilometres deep. A central Sun would lead to rapid overheating. A large open interior would block seismic waves from earthquakes, contrary to observations. Smaller caverns would not be a problem in this regard, though. Satellite measurements of gravity wouldn't work, and neither would satellite orbits.

Fiction is unconstrained by mere facts, and there are many fictional depictions of a hollow Earth. An early example is *Niels Klim's Underground Travels*, published by Ludvig Holberg in 1741. The hero falls through a hole in the Earth while caving, and lives on the inside of the outer shell of the planet, and on a separate central ball. In 1788 Giacomo Casanova wrote a five-volume blockbuster *Icosaméron* about a brother and sister who discover a race of hermaphrodite dwarves inside a hollow Earth. Symmes's pseudoscience found a fictional outlet in Captain Adam Seaborn's 1820 *Symzonia: a Voyage of Discovery*. The most familiar story of this subgenre is Jules Verne's 1864 *Journey to the Centre of the Earth*, which has inspired a number of movies, only loosely related to the original. The novels that come closest to a genuine hollow Earth are those in Edgar Rice Burroughs's *Pellucidar* series, beginning with *At the Earth's Core* in 1914, where the Earth's surface is an 800 km thick shell illuminated by a central Sun, with numerous species of quasi-intelligent and intelligent beings living on the inside surface. The hero ends up in Pellucidar when his mechanical mole refuses to turn and burrows directly downwards into the Earth.

In recent times, hollow worlds have turned up in the media and in computer games.

We promised an unorthodox but solid proof that the Earth is round. Not satellite photos: those are fakes, you understand – NASA never managed to get satellites in orbit, or if they did, their photos of a planar planet are being suppressed, along with secret transcripts from visiting aliens and the true pictures of the Face on Mars.

No, the proof lies in airline schedules.

We can all get on the internet and book flights. The information on airline websites has to be correct, barring a few accidental errors, because millions of passengers – including conspiracy theorists – would have noticed if it weren't. Websites list innumerable flights every day, and you can work out the travel times. Commercial jet aircraft, used on the major routes, all travel at much the same speed – let's say 800 kilometres per hour in round figures. The exact figure doesn't matter; the point is that it's fairly uniform. It has to be: commercial pressures would put any airline that flew significantly slower than the rest out of business. Anyway, most long-haul aircraft are made by the same small number of companies.

It is therefore possible to draw up a reliable list of approximate distances (which are proportional to the times) between selected cities: say Cape Town, Honolulu, London, Los Angeles, Rio de Janeiro and Sydney. Simple geometry – you can draw triangles with a ruler – reveals that if the world is a plane, then Honolulu, Rio de Janeiro, Cape Town and Sydney (in that order) must lie along a path that is very close to a straight line. The travel times along that path are 13, 8 and 14 hours respectively, a total of 35 hours. Since the path is almost straight, and distances are proportional to times, that total time must be pretty close to the time it should take to travel directly from Honolulu to Sydney.

However, the actual figure is 14 hours.

Even allowing for minor errors in the approximations, the discrepancy is far too large, so the hypothesis of a flat planet must be rejected. The figures can't lie: not even the most dedicated conspiracy theorist would suggest that global corporations are conspiring to lose large sums of money.

NINE

UNHOLY WRIT

 The door was opened by Ponder Stibbons, a busy young man who seemed to be central to just about everything that was happening in the university. He was, Marjorie considered, one of those most useful people: a housetrained *near*-nerd, conscientious to the point of insanity but not any further, *apparently*.

'It is the Omnians again, Archchancellor. They have issued a writ against us for ownership of Roundworld since, they say, it is clearly bound up with their religion. They are rather acerbic on the subject, Archchancellor,' said Ponder, looking nervously at Marjorie. He added, 'They are demanding the artefact and are hinting at dire action if it isn't handed over to them.'

Ponder stayed silent then, because Ridcully himself had remained silent, and if you are a wizard you can apprehend the subtle signs of the volcano stirring. He carefully took a few steps backwards, just in case, and when the Archchancellor spoke it was almost a sullen growl.

'Mister Stibbons, turn the writ over to Mister Slant, will you? And then make it clear to him, as our legal representative in the mundane world, that wizards react somewhat erratically when it comes to threats. *Acerbic* is only a beginning. Thank you, Mister Stibbons, and you may go.'

Marjorie had been watching all this with a kind of weird fascination. This place was certainly magical; occasionally you saw the wretched squid somewhere about the place, and candles were lit with a wave of the hand, though curiously enough created mundanely

115

by servants. The magic was *there* but apparently like, for example, a really good bank balance: ready for use if required, and otherwise barely noticed.

As Ponder Stibbons rushed off, she drew breath and said, 'Mustrum, since I am your guest, do you not mind telling me what that just now was all about? It sounded deeply interesting!'

'My dear Miss Daw …'

Before Mustrum could articulate a further word, Marjorie said in a friendly voice, 'I really do not mean any offence, but I am not *your* dear. I have a number of gentlemen friends – and occasionally others not so gentle – but I belong to none of them; I am indeed my own woman. I thank you for your hospitality, albeit because you accidentally dropped me here – and may I say I wouldn't miss this for worlds – but I'm sure you understand that the important thing in life is to know *exactly* who you are. And I'm mine. No offence taken; just more of a heads up.'

'Alas, Marjorie,' the Archchancellor replied, dusting off the globe on his desk with one hand as he spoke, 'I feel my head is down in presumptuous guilt. However, a word to the wise is enough, and since I perceive by the glint in your eye that we might still be friends, I shall send out for some coffee and a small snack, then spill the beans on this new development.'

There appears to be no such thing as a snack in Unseen University. Indeed, the term was *used*, but you could probably stave off starvation for a week on a university 'snack'. So shortly afterwards three trolleys were wheeled into the room by some servants, and the contents of the trolleys were like the biggest picnic imaginable.

When Marjorie said so, the Archchancellor just laughed and said, 'Anything that isn't eaten is given to the students. *They* will eat everything. Please help yourself.'

A bell was rung, a servant came with a further trolley wobbling under the weight of coffee pots and cups and saucers, then left, and Ridcully said, 'Oh my, what can I tell you about Omnianism, which is now uppermost in my mind to the extent that I rather wonder if your accidental arrival here has something to do with this wretched Omnian situation. In my experience, very little happens by chance. Ever since the beginning we have had a great many gods in our world, and they are mostly gods of phenomena and places and even func-tions – such as Anoia, the goddess of things which stick in drawers; that is wooden drawers, of course – the fabric type presumably have a different goddess. Among these was a reasonably decent religion known as the Church of Om, which eventually became extremely warlike and aggressive towards other faiths for the glory of their god. Then one day a decent man by the name of Brutha – possi-bly the ghost of a shamed god – changed everything about the way Omnianism worked, making it more based on helping others rather than repeatedly telling an all-seeing god how good he was.* Which, I should imagine, must have been boring him to bits, yes?'

Marjorie had an unsettled look, and then she said, 'You know, don't you, that this is quite similar to what many believe to have happened on my own world? Which, if you don't mind me telling you, you have just defiled a little with a drop of mayonnaise … Is it likely that people back on Earth will see an asteroid of dairy products hurtling through the sky over their heads?'

Mustrum smiled. 'It can easily be removed. Besides, the connec-tion between Roundworld and Discworld isn't quite as simple as that. But they are linked by narrativium, one of the most powerful forces in the multiverse. It tells causality what to do next; or what *not* to do if the journey is not to come to an end so bleak that not even darkness itself could find a space, and after that there is only empty and screaming despair.'

After a pause in which the air in the room seemed itself to be chok-ing while the firmament crumbled and the mayonnaise dribbled down the side of the globe, the Archchancellor completely spoiled

* See *Small Gods*.

the effect by brightening up with a big grin and saying, 'But there is no need to worry, of course, because we are always keeping an eye on things! That's what human beings are for, you see? If the multiverse isn't watched, it would cease to exist. The dogs and cats and sea urchins and orangutans and oysters and locusts and so on take their share of the work, but mostly it's left up to us to do what you might call the heavy psychic lifting, because we observe, and *know* we are observing, and we think not only about what we see but also *about the way* we think. As a reward we somehow come across even more interesting things to think about, especially when the thinking leads on to interesting new discoveries and so on.'

Marjorie went to say something, but a look in the Archchancellor's eye made her lean forward and take another cake instead.

'We realise, of course,' Ridcully continued, 'that in truth we know very little compared to what we *don't* know, and somehow that is good for us – all things must strive, and because we know how ignorant we actually are then we must strive hardest of all.' He took a deep breath and said as it were a valedictory: 'We will not give up Roundworld to meddlers!'

'Meddlers?' Marjorie managed.

'Yes, indeed!' Ridcully confirmed. 'The Church of the Latter-Day Omnians has become a combative and philosophically greedy organisation, declaring that only *it* knows what is true!' Marjorie saw his knuckles whiten. 'Not even *we* know everything that is true, and I strongly suspect that if everything in the universe becomes true, the whole business could start over again. The Omnians do not see reason even with a telescope – and without reason there can be *nothing*. Those who wish to tell us how we should think, and sometimes that we shouldn't even think at all, must be ignored. The glowing message that came to light in the time of Brutha, the most enlightened Omnian priest, was clear: all men are brothers – or sisters of course as appropriate – and subject to their conscience and the golden rule.'

Suddenly Ridcully looked smaller; his face was red and he was sweating profusely, to the extent that Marjorie silently handed him a large glass of water, which appeared to her to steam as it touched his lips.

He thanked her, and she said carefully, 'Do you know that some people in what you call Roundworld refuse to believe that it is indeed a sphere, despite the fact that it has been proved by, among other things, the Apollo Moon landings? They assert that these were forgeries, despite *actual footprints* on the Moon. In fact, I'm sorry to say that in my own library the other day we had one of those rather nervous gentlemen who declared that the Moon mission was nothing but a hoax. You get all sorts of people in the library, and the librarian gets it all; by the way, Mustrum, just then you looked like a preacher. No offence meant.'

'My brother Hughnon is a priest, not me,' said Mustrum. 'And even he is having difficulty with the modern Omnians. They are insisting that children are not told that this world survives on the back of an enormous turtle!' He smiled at her and said, 'I saw your face just then, Marjorie; but in fact the turtle *is* real – plucky explorers have seen it. Of course, it's real in this reality; other realities may vary. And then there is Roundworld, which we suspect may originate from a universal template, unlike Discworld which we believe was bespoke. Both, however, have narrativium … yes, what is it?'

The door opened to admit Ponder Stibbons again, smiling for once. 'Good news, Archchancellor; and you too, Miss Daw. Our little problem has been solved, and access to Roundworld is now easily negotiable.' Ponder hesitated for a moment and added, 'But if I were you I would wipe the mayonnaise off it first.'

WHERE DID *THAT* COME FROM?

 As the Archchancellor remarks, Discworld runs on narrativium, which tells causality what to do. The same goes for Roundworld, from the outside; that is, as seen by the wizards. But from inside, Roundworld did not have any narrativium until humans evolved and started inventing stories to 'explain' all of the puzzling features of the natural world: why it did or did not rain, how a rainbow forms, what causes thunder and lightning, why the Sun rises and sets. We have already seen how these storytelling explanations, often involving heroes, monsters and gods, appeal to a human-centred viewpoint, and how they fail – often dismally – from a universe-centred one.

Many of the greatest questions about causality concern origins. How did plants, animals, the Sun, the Moon, even the world itself, come into existence? We storytelling apes are fascinated by origins. We are not content just to see trees, stones or thunderstorms; we want to know what gave rise to them. We want to see the acorn that makes the oak, to understand the geological story that underlies the stone, and to delineate the electrical genesis of the storm. We want our own special type of narrativium: stories that explain how such things get started, as well as how they work. This wish for simple stories makes us expect simple answers to questions about origins. However, science shows us that our love of stories misleads us. Origins are extremely tricky concepts.

The acorn and the oak have a superficially simple story, which we all understand: plant the acorn, water it, give it light, and it grows into the oak. However, that simple story cloaks a really difficult explanation of an immensely complex development: it is, in fact, much the same account as getting you from an egg. And there's another complication: not only does the oak come from the acorn: the acorn's origin is the oak. This is exactly like the chicken and egg cliché. The important question, though, is not 'which came first?'. That's a silly question, because they are both part of the repeating system. It's clear that the chicken is only the egg's way of making another egg. Before chickens, the same egg lineage used jungle fowl instead to make more eggs; long before that, it used little dinosaurs to make its eggs; and long before that, it used ancient amphibians.

The big problem with 'turtles all the way down' as an explanation is not the ludicrous mental image, amusing though that may be. Each turtle is indeed supported by the one beneath. The problem is how and why an entire infinite pile of turtles should exist. What matters in recursive systems is not which part came first, but the origin of *the whole system*. For eggs and their chickens, that story is mainly an evolutionary one, a sequence of developments that change progressively, so that now we have chickens when previously we had jungle fowl or dinosaurs. In this case, the origins of the system go all the way back to the first eggs, the first multicellular creatures that used embryonic development from eggs as part of their reproductive process. In that same way, the acorn is the modern version of a seed that used to produce early seed plants, and prior to that produced tree-ferns ... all the way back to the origins of multicellular plants.

What we mean by 'immensely complicated development' also takes a bit of explaining. It's clear that the acorn doesn't *become* the oak tree, any more than the egg that generated you became you. The oak tree is mostly made from carbon dioxide extracted from the air, water from the soil and minerals, including nitrogen, also from the soil. In trees, those ingredients mainly make carbohydrates, cellulose and lignin, along with proteins for the working chemical machinery. The amount of material contributed by the acorn is minuscule. Similarly, almost all of the baby that (in a very restricted sense) became you, was built from a variety of chemicals obtained from your mother through the placenta. The tiny egg contributed very little by way of materials ... but an awful lot by way of organisation. The egg functioned to recruit the chemicals that your mother provided, initiating and controlling the succession of stages – blastocyst, embryo, fetus – that led to your birth. Similarly, the acorn is already an embryo, and it has a very complex organisation, beautifully crafted to drive a root down into the soil, to extend leaves up into the air, and to start the business of becoming a tiny oak.

It's that word 'becoming' that we all have trouble with. Jack, on a hospital ethics committee, once had to explain how an embryo → fetus → baby → *becomes* human. It's not like switching on a light, he explained; it's more like painting a picture, or writing a novel. There isn't one paintbrush-stroke or one word that completes the task; it's a gradual becoming. 'That's fine,' a lay member of the committee replied, 'but how far into a pregnancy is it before you have a human being, not just an egg?' We seem to need to draw lines, even when nature fails to present us with tidily distinguished stages.

So let's not start with complex development, like acorns and eggs, when thinking about origins. Let's start with something genuinely simpler: a thunderstorm. Before the storm, there is a time of cool, clear skies, clouds moving with the wind, probably a weather front. What we don't see, because it's invisible, is the static electricity building up in the clouds. Clouds are masses of water droplets, billions of tiny spheres of liquid water in a mass of water vapour: a saturated solution of water in air. The droplets and vapour rise to the top of the cloud; then they fall back through the cloud, not quite dropping out as rain, and the cycle repeats. Many do drop out as rain when the storm starts, of course.

Clouds are very active structures, with massive circulations. They look gauzy and simple, but internally they are a mass of water-droplet and ice-particle currents. Each droplet and particle carries a tiny electric charge, and the cloud as a whole also acquires an electric charge, for much the same reason that your nylon underwear acquires an electrical charge opposite to that of your body. So the cloud has the opposite charge to that of the hills it passes over, a clear recipe for trouble. As the charge builds, the electric potential between the cloud and the ground gets bigger. Eventually it becomes big enough for lightning to make its own path between cloud and ground, following a trail of lower-resistance ionised air. Metal spikes sticking up from the ground, or on the top of tall buildings like churches, provide particularly good targets. In the absence of those, a person walking on a hill might be the unlucky Earth-end of a strike.

A thunderstorm seems simpler than an acorn becoming an oak, because it doesn't need lots of intricate organisation. But even a thunderstorm is not as simple as we tend to imagine: we don't know how the electric potential builds. There are 16 million thunderstorms each year on Roundworld, but we're still not really sure how they happen. No wonder we have trouble understanding how an acorn becomes an oak.

As for the *origin*, the beginnings of a storm, the beginnings of anything … To explain thunderstorms, do we have to explain clouds? The constituents of the atmosphere? Static electricity? The elements of physics and physical chemistry? The origin of anything lies in the interactions of multiple causes. In practice, in order to explain the origin of a storm, or anything else, both the person providing the explanation and the one on the receiving end must have a lot of knowledge in common, covering many different areas. Unfortunately, it may not be present.

You might be an English teacher, an accountant, a housewife, a psychologist, a merchant, a builder, a banker or a student. The chances are that you will not have come across one or more phrases such as 'saturated solution' or 'particle carries a tiny electric charge'. And those phrases are themselves simplifications of concepts with many more associations, and more intellectual depth, than anyone can be expected to generate for themselves.

You might be a biology teacher, a mathematician, or even a science journalist, with a more extensive mental database in such areas. Even so we'd still have difficulty explaining the origin of storms, because *we* don't understand it in enough depth. None of us is a meteorologist. And even if we were, we *still* wouldn't be able to generate enough depth of understanding for you to be able to say, 'Ah, yes – I understand that now.' Jack is an embryologist, and understands eggs and acorns in some depth; he would have the same problem for the same reason, even for those examples. The origin of absolutely anything on Roundworld – of it, off it, all the way up to everything that exists – is a complicated mesh involving enormously many factors that we know very little about.

One way to duck out of this issue is to appeal to divine creation. If you believe in a creator god, you can invoke supernatural intervention to explain the origins of anything, from the universe to thunderstorms. Thor does a great job with his hammer: job done, thunder explained. Or don't you think so? We don't find that a very satisfactory explanation, because you then have to explain how the gods came to be, and where their powers came from. Maybe it's not Thor at all, but Jupiter. Maybe it's a giant invisible snake thrashing its coils. Maybe it's an alien spacecraft breaking the sound barrier.

Some quite sophisticated creation stories exist, as mentioned in chapter 4, but none of them are genuine explanations. The same form of words 'explains' absolutely anything, and would equally well appear to explain a lot of things that don't happen at all. If you think the sky is blue because God made it that way, you would be equally happy if it were pink, or yellow with purple stripes, and would offer exactly the same explanation. On the other hand, if you explain the colour of the sky in terms of light being scattered by dust in the upper atmosphere, and discover that the intensity of the scattered light is inversely proportional to the fourth power of the wavelength, then you will understand why short-wavelength blue light will dominate compared to the longer wavelengths of yellow and red. (The fourth power of a small number is very small indeed, and *inverse* proportionality means that small numbers are more important than big ones – just as one tenth is bigger than one hundredth.) Now you've learned something useful and informative, which you can apply to other questions.

However, this type of explanation only goes so far: it doesn't explain where the dust came from, or more difficult things like why blue light looks blue. If you want complete explanations of anything at all, creation is the way to go. Theology really does have all the answers. Indeed, the myriad religions and creeds on the planet offer a huge choice of answers, any one of which will keep you happy if what you really want is a reason to stop asking why the sky is blue. Attributing it to a deity is just a roundabout way of saying 'it just is'.

Asimov pointed out that when churches adopted lightning-conductors, they promoted science above theology. Following that way of thinking, we are trying to present scientific – or at least rational – explanations for origins, indeed for many other issues. Ponder Stibbons is the most rational of the wizards, yet even he is fighting an uphill battle. On the whole, though, he's winning, explaining Round-world without magic, even though magic – the mechanism behind most Discworld phenomena – is his default viewpoint.

Many, perhaps most, human beings are not rational in their beliefs. Essentially they believe in magic, the supernatural. They are rational in many other respects, but they allow what they want the world to be like to cloud their judgment about what it *is* like. In the run-up to the American Presidential elections in 2012, several Republican candidates who had previously accepted basic science ended up denying it. A prominent Republican supporter opposed any kind of regulation of the markets on the grounds that this was 'interfering with God's plan for the American economy'. More extreme figures on the political right oppose taking steps to mitigate climate change – not because they think it doesn't exist, but because the quicker we wreck the planet, the sooner Christ's second coming will happen. Armageddon? Bring it on!

One reason for trying rational approaches first is that most phenomena here on Roundworld have turned out *not* to be magical. More strongly, many that used to seem magical now make a lot of sense without any appeal to the supernatural: thunder, for instance – though not the American economy, which baffles even economists. So in this book, our explanations of origins will, so far as we can manage, stick to the rational, however complicated it is. But we do wonder whether Christian Scientists, who believe it to be sinful to transplant organs, or even to transfuse blood – because they have been taught that this defies God's wishes – use lightning-conductors.

Even today, we understand less about thunderstorms than you might imagine.

Two decades ago, astronauts on the space shuttle Atlantis placed a satellite in orbit, the Compton Gamma Ray Observatory. Gamma rays are electromagnetic waves, like light, but of much higher frequency. Since the energy of a photon is proportional to its frequency, that makes them very energetic. CGRO was designed to detect gamma rays from distant neutron stars and remnants of supernovas, and it seemed clear that something was horribly wrong, because the observatory was reporting long bursts of gamma rays, emanating from … the Earth.

This was ridiculous. Gamma rays are produced when electrons and other particles are accelerated in a vacuum. Not in an atmosphere. So something was obviously going wrong with CGRO. Except – it wasn't. The observatory was functioning perfectly. Somehow, the Earth's atmosphere was generating gamma rays.

At first, these rays were thought to be generated about 80 kilo-metres up, well above the clouds. It had just been discovered that strange glowing lights, known as sprites and resembling huge jelly-fish, existed at that height. They are thought to be an unexpected effect of lightning in thunderclouds below. At any rate, it seemed clear that sprites must be producing the gamma rays, or at least, asso-ciated with them. Theoreticians produced several explanations; the most plausible was that avalanches of electrons produced by light-ning were colliding with atoms in the atmosphere, generating both the sprites and the gamma rays. The electrons could move at almost the speed of light and create a chain reaction in which each electron could kick others out of atoms.

From 1996 onward, physicists added bells and whistles to this theory, predicting the energy spectrum of the gamma rays. Data from CGRO fitted these predictions, and confirmed that the rays originated at very high altitudes. It all looked pretty good.

Until 2003.

That year, Joseph Dwyer was in Florida, on the ground, measur-ing x-rays from lightning, and he observed a huge burst of gamma rays from the storm clouds overhead. The burst had exactly the same energy spectrum as those that were thought to come from much higher. Even so, no one really imagined that the rays that CGRO was detecting came from thunderclouds: they were much too energetic. The energy needed to propel the rays through an atmosphere was too large to be credible.

In 2002 NASA had launched a satellite called RHESSI (Reuven Ramaty High Energy Solar Spectroscopic Imager) to observe gamma rays from the Sun. David Smith hired a student, Liliana Lopez, to look through the data for evidence of gamma rays from the Earth. There was a burst every few days, far more often than CGRO was detecting. This new instrument provided far better information about the energy spectrum, and it showed that these gamma rays had traversed a lot of atmosphere. In fact, they originated at altitudes of about 15-25 kilometres – the tops of typical thunderclouds. As new evidence piled up, it became ever harder to deny that thunderstorms generate gamma rays in huge quantities. Sprites, on the other hand, do not.

How do thunderclouds produce such energetic radiation? The answer is straight out of *Star Trek*: antimatter. When ordinary matter and antimatter come together, they annihilate each other in a burst of energy – almost total conversion of mass to energy. Antimatter powers Starfleet's vessels. Its commonest form is the positron, the anti-electron, which is naturally produced by radioactive decay and is routinely used in medical PET scanners (Positron Emission Tomography). However, naturally produced antimatter is rare, and thunderclouds are not renowned for their radioactive atoms. Nevertheless, there is strong evidence that gamma rays from thunderclouds involve positrons.

The idea is this. The electric field inside a cloud is negative at the bottom and positive at the top. This field can sometimes generate runaway electrons with high energies. Being negatively charged, these electrons are repelled by the field at the bottom of the cloud and attracted by that at the top, so they go upwards. They then hit atoms in air molecules and create gamma rays. If such a ray hits another atom, it can produce a positron-electron pair. The electron keeps going upwards, but the positron, having a positive charge, goes *downwards*, attracted by the field at the bottom of the cloud. On the way down it bumps into an air atom and knocks out new electrons … and the process repeats. Again there is a kind of chain reaction, which spreads sideways, across entire banks of storm clouds.

It's a bit like a naturally formed laser, in which cascades of photons shuttle to and fro between mirrors, triggering the production of ever more photons as they do so – until they get so energetic that they escape through one of the mirrors. The mirrors are the top and bottom of the cloud, but instead of bouncing photons to and fro, the cloud sends electrons up and positrons down. By 2005 this theory was pretty much firm. The Fermi Gamma-ray space telescope has now detected beams of charged particles, produced by thunderclouds and travelling thousands of miles along the Earth's magnetic field lines. A substantial proportion is positrons.

This discovery puts thunderstorms in a new light. Not only is Thor's hammer creating sparks (lightning) and noise (thunder): it is creating antimatter. It's not the sort of discovery you make by trotting out facile explanations in terms of the supernatural. It depends on repeated scientific questioning of the known 'facts'.

Even familiar origins lead to new stories as time passes. In its search for rational explanations of origins, science often changes paradigm in response to new evidence or a new idea. The origin of the Earth and the Moon is a good example, with some curious twists. One of them being a short-term failure to change the paradigm in response to new evidence.

In this case, the main problem is too much evidence, rather than too little. We can examine the structure of the Earth, look at the record written in the rocks, and travel to the Moon and bring back specimens. But in some ways this wealth of evidence makes the problem more complicated. What does it all mean? We're trying to work out what happened, about 4.5 billion years after the event. At that time the universe had already been around for about 9 billion years (according to the Big Bang theory, and even longer according to the main alternatives). In all cosmological theories, the state of the universe gets more complicated as time passes. So by the time our solar system came into being, there was a lot of stuff around.

We have to infer, from what we can observe today, how that stuff aggregated to make the Earth/Moon system. Those observations include data from asteroids, from the Sun and the other planets, and from detailed knowledge of the structure of the Earth and the Moon. (We say 'the' Moon, but according to a recent suggestion perhaps there were two or more moons at one stage.) It is clear that there was a time before Earth existed, and then the Earth came into being. The Moon turned up a few hundred million years later. Their origins are intertwined, and we can't explain one while ignoring the other.

The central problem of the Moon's origin and Earth's genesis is that Moon rock is very similar, in subtle chemical detail, to Earth's mantle. This is the thick layer of rock immediately below the continental and oceanic crust, above the iron core. In particular, the proportions of different isotopes of several elements are the same in rock from either source. This coincidence is too improbable to be compatible with earlier theories of the formation of the Moon, such as the two bodies condensing independently from a primal dust cloud surrounding the Sun, or the Earth's gravitational field capturing the Moon as it was flying past. George Darwin, one of Charles Darwin's sons, suggested that the Moon was spun off from a rapidly rotating Earth, but the mechanics – such as energy and angular momentum, a measure of spin – don't work out correctly. Moreover, the Earth and Moon did not just condense from dust. Astrophysicists and geophysicists now think that the Earth aggregated from many tiny planetesimals, which formed part of a great disc with the burgeoning Sun at its centre. Our telescopes are now good enough to observe several such discs around young suns in neighbouring star systems, and many of these have been found, so that theory seems to hold up.

Between 2000 and the middle of 2012, astrophysicists and geophysicists mostly agreed that the Moon resulted from an enormous collision between an early Earth and an object about the size of Mars. They named it Theia, after the mother of the lunar goddess Selene. This collision vaporised much of the Earth, and nearly all of Theia. Most of the vapour condensed again in lunar orbit, coming together to make the Moon. The rest of it became Earth's mantle, hence the similarity. The same theory explains the large angular momentum of the Earth/Moon system, a gratifying bonus.

As time passed, problems with the Theia theory began to emerge. It would have produced very high temperatures on Earth's surface, so pretty much all of the water should have boiled away. This seems incompatible with Earth's present-day oceans. So extra assumptions were needed to save Theia. Perhaps a few ice asteroids fell on the early Earth and put the water back; perhaps the vaporised water fell back to Earth anyway. However, some very ancient Australian rocks seem to testify to the presence of a lot of water on our world about four billion years ago, which seems to be too soon after the Moon's origin for such an enormous collision to have occurred.

We described the Theia theory in *The Science of Discworld* in 1999, but by the second edition in 2002 we were no longer convinced. The biggest problem came from newer computer models of the collision. The first such models, the ones that had established the Theia theory, showed a large chunk of the Earth splashing off; then that chunk split. One part formed the Moon, and the rest fell back to Earth to form the mantle. Theia got mixed up with both of them, but in similar proportions, so anyone could see why both the Moon and the Earth's mantle had the same composition.

However, the simulations that led to this conclusion took a lot of computing time, and only a few scenarios could be explored. As computers improved, the mathematical models became more sophisticated and their implications could be worked out more quickly and more easily. It turned out that in most of them the bulk of Theia was incorporated into the Moon, while very little went into the mantle.

How can both Moon and mantle be virtually identical, then?

The proposal that was accepted until 2012 was: Theia's composition must have been very similar to that of the former Earth's mantle.

This of course is the problem that the whole theory was trying to solve. *Why should the compositions be the same?* If we can answer that for Theia by declaring 'they just were', then why not apply the same reasoning to the Moon? The Theia theory had to assume the same coincidence that it was supposed to explain.

In the second edition of *The Science of Discworld*, we described this as 'losing the plot', an opinion that Ian repeated in *Mathematics of Life*. This view seems to have been vindicated by the recent (July 2012) discovery of a similar but different scenario by Andreas Reufer and colleagues. This also involves an impactor, but now the body concerned was much larger than Theia (or Mars), and moved much faster. It was a hit-and-run sideswipe rather than a head-on collision. Most of the material that was splashed off came from the Earth, while very little came from the impactor. This new theory agrees with the angular momentum figures, and it predicts that the composition of the Moon and the mantle should be even more similar than had previously been thought. Some supporting evidence for that already exists. A new analysis of Apollo lunar rock samples by Junjun Zhang's team* has found that the ratio of isotope titanium-50 (50Ti) to isotope titanium-47 (47Ti) on the Moon is 'identical to that of the Earth within about four parts per million'.

That's not the only possible alternative. Matija Ćuk and colleagues have shown that the observed chemistry of Moon rocks could have arisen from a collision if the Earth was spinning much faster at the time – one rotation every few hours. This changes how much rock splashes off and where it comes from. Afterwards, the gravity of the Sun and Moon could have slowed the Earth's rotation down to its present 24-hour day. Robin Canup has obtained similar results using simulations in which the Earth was spinning only a little faster than it is now, but the impactor was bigger than the Mars-sized body originally suggested.

This is a case where *Pan narrans* became so committed to an appealing story that it forgot why the story was originally invented. The coincidence that it was supposed to explain faded from view, and a new narrative took over in which the coincidence took back

* Junjun Zhang, Nicolas Dauphas, Andrew M. Davis, Inigo Leya and Alexei Fedkin, The proto-Earth as a significant source of lunar material, *Nature Geoscience* 5 (2012) 251-255.

stage. But now the storytelling ape is rethinking the entire story – and this time it is paying proper attention to the plot.

The biggest origin question, philosophically speaking, is that of the universe, which we'll come to in chapter 18. That aside, the most puzzling origin, a much more personal one, is that of life on Earth.

How did we get here?

Our own inability to create life from scratch, or even to understand how 'it' works, makes us imagine that nature had to do something pretty remarkable to produce life. This conviction may be correct, but it could well be misplaced, because a complex world need not be comprehensible in simple terms. Life might be virtually inevitable once the mix of potential ingredients becomes sufficiently rich, without there being some special secret that can be summarised on a postcard. But explaining natural phenomena requires a convincing human-level story. That's what 'explain' means to *Pan narrans*. However, the stories scientists tell about the origin of life are generally difficult and complex, especially when it comes to filling in details. What happened probably can't be turned into a story. Even if we could go back and see what happened, what we observed might not make a great deal of sense.

Nevertheless, we can seek stories that provide useful insights.

Most scientific thinking about the origin of life considers two phases: pre-biotic and biotic. Often the problem is simplified further, to inorganic chemistry before life appeared, and organic chemistry afterwards. These are the two great branches of chemistry. The latter concerns itself with the massive and complex molecules that can be formed using lots of atoms of carbon, and the former concerns itself with everything else. And life, as it now exists on Roundworld, makes essential and ubiquitous use of organic chemistry. However, there is no good reason to imagine that the origin of life fits neatly into this convenient but rather arbitrary pair of categories. Organic molecules almost certainly existed before there were organisms to use them. So trying to understand the origin of life as some kind of sudden switch from inorganic chemistry to organic chemistry is a mistake, confusing two different distinctions.

Yes, there was a time before there was life, and a time when life was beginning. But there wasn't a sudden origin like turning a light on. There was a period, perhaps quite a long one – hundreds of millions of years – of what has been called mesobiosis. This is chemistry, both inorganic and organic, *becoming* life: the journey, not the starting point or the destination.

A large number of alternative pathways by which life might have originated have been proposed. In the 1980s Jack counted thirty-five plausible theories, and there must be hundreds by now. It is sobering to realise that we may never know which pathway actually happened. Indeed, this is quite likely. The pathway that occurred could well have been one of thousands that we haven't yet thought of. For some of us, an account which starts in chemistry and finishes in simple biochemistry is sufficient; others will want to see bacterial-grade life produced artificially in the laboratory before being convinced that the sequence of steps can work. Yet others will want to see an artificial elephant, synthesised from chemicals in bottles, and would still insist that someone cheated.

Many of you will be convinced that life is so different from the non-living, even from the freshly dead, that no account of a more or less continuous series of steps can be plausible. In part, this conviction arises from our neurophysiology: we use different areas of our brains for thinking about living or inorganic entities, mice or stones. So it is difficult for us to construct thought-chains leading from stones to mice, or even from school chemistry to 'germs'. Instead, we come up with concepts like the soul, which makes a clear distinction between our thinking about a living person, and the very different way we think about a dead body.

We'll summarise some of the plausible accounts of life's origins, so that you may enjoy the various ideas on offer and the different ways of thinking about the problem that they illustrate. We have written about the origins of life several times in the *Science of Discworld* series, so we will try to make this account a little different. The virus story at the end of this section, for instance, is quite new. It was sitting quietly behind the scenes around 2000, but in 2009 a review paper by Harald Brüssow opened it up for discussion. To put it in context, we need to look at some of the earlier proposals.

The most important early experiment was that of Stanley Miller, working in Harold Urey's laboratory in the 1950s. He imitated the effects of lightning on a reasonable approximation to Earth's early atmosphere: ammonia, carbon dioxide, methane and water vapour. Initially, he got several noxious gases, like cyanide and formaldehyde, both notable poisons; this encouraged him, because 'poison' is not an inherent property – it describes an effect on living organisms. Most gases don't get involved with life at all. Further runs of the experiment produced amino acids, some of the most important chemicals for life, because they aggregate into proteins. He came up with a variety of other small organic molecules as well.

Understanding how these molecules came into existence would be very complicated, but the experiment shows that nature can achieve the result without making any special effort. There is no reason to suppose that anything beyond standard chemistry, obeying the usual physical and chemical rules, is involved in Miller's experiments. We can tell plausible chemical tales about reasonable ways for the atoms and molecules to combine and change. It happens all the time; this is why the subject 'chemistry' exists. Reasonably detailed models would capture the main steps – but the reality is almost certainly more complicated than those models. This is an important principle: what seems complicated to us may be easy for nature.

Workers repeating this experiment with different reasonable atmospheres have obtained many other organic compounds, such as sugars, and even the bases that link up to make DNA and RNA, key molecules of terrestrial life. We've already mentioned DNA and its double helix, and in any case it's very well known nowadays. RNA, which stands for 'ribonucleic acid', is less well known: it is like DNA, but simpler. With a few exceptions, RNA forms a single strand instead of two intertwined ones. Specific forms of RNA play vital roles in the development of an organism.

These two molecules could easily have been present in the early seas on our planet; indeed, they were probably unavoidable. In addition, we now know that meteorites contain many of these simple organic compounds; indeed, they can form in empty space. So that's another sensible source of organic chemicals. In short, small organic molecules were around, in quantity, for reasons that have nothing to do with living organisms.

This simple chemistry, though a promising start, isn't enough. The key molecules in organisms are far more complicated, involving vastly more atoms arranged in fairly specific ways. Graham Cairns-Smith suggested that clay molecules would be ideal catalysts for turning simple organic compounds into polymers of the kinds found in living things: linking amino acids into peptides and proteins, and possibly linking bases with phosphorus and sugars to form short strings of nucleic acids including RNA and DNA. Again, nothing beyond standard chemistry is required to achieve this, and the processes do not involve living creatures. So it would be surprising if there were *not* many polymers in the early seas. Getting complex molecules is not a problem. We may have trouble coping with their complexity, but nature just follows the rules; from this, a sort of complexity unavoidably follows.

However, polymers aren't alive. They don't reproduce, or even replicate, except in very special situations. (Replication is the making of exact copies; reproduction is the making of inexact copies which nevertheless can themselves reproduce, which is more flexible, but even harder to understand.) Replication or reproduction seem to require not just complexity, but organised complexity, and it's difficult to see where the organisation can come from. However, some of these special situations can occur entirely naturally with certain clays, which themselves exhibit replication. In a watery environment, little slabs of clay can make stacks of almost identical copies, without any help.

Since the late 1990s many things have changed. At that time, in *The Science of Discworld*, we paid particular attention to the ideas of Gunther Wächtershäuser. His proposal differed from the by then conventional Miller-Urey primeval soup, which spontaneously produced replicating nucleic acids, the first heredity. Instead, Wächtershäuser proposed that the first thing to happen was metabolism: working biochemistry. He suggested that this might have occurred where there was plenty of sulphur, iron oxide and iron sulphide, plus a suitable source of heat to drive the chemistry. One possible location that possesses these ingredients is an undersea hydrothermal vent, known as a black smoker, where molten rock from the mantle makes its way to the surface through cracks where the ocean floor is spreading. Less dramatically, underwater volcanic vents do the same. Using this kind of iron-oxygen-sulphur chemistry, Wächtershäuser came up with a set of chemical reactions that closely mimicked the Krebs cycle, a central biochemical system in nearly all living things.

In laboratory experiments, his scenario performed reasonably well, though not perfectly. So the theory of the origin of life turned into a kind of primeval pizza, with molecules dotted around on a surface, rather than a primeval soup sloshing around in pools or the open sea. In 1999 we liked this idea because it was different from heredity-first systems: we couldn't see why they would necessarily replicate – what was in it for them. Moreover, Wächtershäuser was a lawyer as well as a biochemist, and it's unusual to get good original scientific ideas from a lawyer.

However, since then a different idea, the RNA world, has really taken off. RNA and DNA are both nucleic acids, so named because they are found in the nuclei of cells. There are many other kinds of nucleic acid; some are much simpler than DNA and RNA, and some are much more complicated. Both are long chains formed by joining together four smaller molecular units, called nucleotides. Nucleotides are combinations of bases, which in turn are specific molecules that look like complicated amino acids, linked together by sugars and phosphate. Does that help? We thought not. You can look up all the details in many sources, but for present purposes we just need convenient words to keep straight which bits we're talking about.

The great trick that nucleic acids exploit is their ability to form double-chains, each half encoding the same 'information' in related ways. The DNA code letters, the four bases, come in two associated pairs, and the sequence of bases on one chain consists of the partners of the bases on the other chain. This makes possible the key feature of these pairings: each chain determines what happens in the other chain. If they split apart, and each chain acquires a new partner, by sticking on the complementary bases ... lo and behold: originally we had one double-chain, and now we have two of them, each identical to the first. The molecule not only can replicate: it does, given enough unattached bases to play with. It would be hard to stop it.

RNA has other tricks. It can function as an enzyme, a biological catalyst; it can even be the catalyst for its own replication. (A catalyst is a molecule that promotes a chemical reaction without being used up: it gets involved, helps things along and then ducks back out.) And it can also catalyse other chemical reactions that are useful to life. It's a universal fix-it molecule for living organisms. If it were possible to explain how RNA could appear in the absence of life, it would constitute a wonderfully useful step from non-living chemistry towards a primitive kind of life form. Unfortunately, it turned out to be very difficult to see how RNA could turn up in the primeval soup without any assistance. For many years, the RNA world theory was missing one of its most vital features.

This is no longer an obstacle. In recent years, many different solutions to this problem have been found, including several that work experimentally as well as theoretically. The chains of bases involved were initially fairly short – a chain of six is easy, but now there can be fifty or more bases in a chain. This is getting close to the length found in real biological enzymes, which usually have 100-250 bases. So there is real hope that long RNA chains must have been present in that ancient soup. More plausibly still, fatty membranes, which closely resemble cell membranes, have been synthesised in circumstances very similar to those that are thought to have existed on the primitive Earth, and RNA gets linked to these in useful ways. Moreover, it has recently been suggested that the RNA chains could repeatedly be broken apart – unzipped – by high temperatures in black smokers and reassembled at lower temperature in cycling convection currents. This is a lovely idea, exactly like the way DNA is multiplied in systems that analyse its sequence using the polymerase chain reaction, where alternating high and low temperatures break the chains apart and then permit them to build complementary chains, repeatedly doubling the number of copies. RNA could be replicated by this natural physico-chemical process.

For these reasons and many others, the RNA world has now become a respectable image for the earliest stages of life on Earth. It may not be what actually happened, but it provides a plausible scenario. And even if life did not arise in that way, the RNA world shows that there is no compulsion to invoke the supernatural. In the primitive seas, probably around smokers but perhaps on tidal beaches where pools were concentrated – and irradiated – in sunlight, and diluted when the tide came in, or under the influence of volcanoes or earthquakes, RNA strings were growing and being copied.

The copying process wasn't always perfectly accurate, but that was a positive advantage, because it led, without any special interference, to diversity. If random variation of this kind could be coupled to some kind of selection, favouring sequences with specific features, then RNA could – had to – evolve. And selection wasn't an issue; the big problem would have been to prevent it. As special sequences with particular properties appeared, competition between them for free nucleotides, and probably for interactions with particular fatty membranes, eliminated some sequences and encouraged others to proliferate. This led to longer chains with even more special properties.

Natural selection had begun ... and the system was *becoming* alive.

In this view, not only does evolution by natural selection explain how life diversified: it is part and parcel of what brought it into being in the first place. Copying errors, if they occur, though not *too* often, can be creative, in the context of a sufficiently rich system.

The RNA world is not the only game in town. The latest proposals for the origin of life hinge upon viruses. Viruses are long DNA or RNA chains, usually surrounded by a protein coat that contrives to inject them into other organisms, especially bacteria and animal and plant cells. Most viruses rely on the DNA/RNA copying machinery of the organism they infect to replicate them. Then the new copies are usually sprayed out into the environment when that cell, or the organism, dies.

Since the work of Carl Woese in 1977, taxonomists – scientists who classify life into its innumerable related forms – have recognised three basic kinds of life form, the largest and earliest branches of the tree of life. These 'domains' comprise bacteria, archaea and eukaryotes. Creatures in the first two domains are superficially similar, being micro-organisms, but each domain had a very distinctive evolutionary history. Archaea may trace back to the earliest organisms of them all; many live in strange and unusual environments: very hot, very cold, lots of salt. Bacteria, you know about. Both types of organism are prokaryotes, meaning that their cells do not clump their genetic material together inside a nucleus, but string it from the cell wall, or let it float around as closed loops called plasmids.

The third domain, eukaryotes, is characterised by having cells with nuclei. It includes all complex 'multicellular' creatures, from insects and worms up to elephants and whales. And humans, of course. It also includes many single-celled organisms. RNA sequences imply that the first big split in the tree of life occurred when bacteria branched away from ancestral archaea. Then that branch split into archaea and eukaryotes. So we are more closely related to archaea than we are to bacteria.

Viruses are not part of that scheme, and it is controversial whether they are a form of life because most of them can't reproduce unaided. It used to be thought that viruses had two different origins. Some were wild genes that escaped from their genomes and made a living by parasitising other creatures and hijacking their gene-copying equipment. The others were desperately reduced bacteria or archaea; in fact, they were reduced so far in their pursuit of a parasitic lifestyle that all they had left were their genes. Occasionally it was supposed by lay people, physicists or maverick biologists – who should have known better – that, being so simple, they were relics of ancient life. This incorrect line of thinking stems from the same, mistaken, principle as the one that considers *Amoeba* to be ancestral because it looks simple. Actually, there are many kinds of amoeba, and some have 240 chromosomes, bodies in the cell that contain the genes. We have a mere 46 chromosomes. So in that sense an amoeba is more complex than we are. Why so many? Because it takes a lot of organisation, in a very small space, to get all of an amoeba's functions to work.

Brüssow, in 2009, wrote a review called 'The not so universal tree of life *or* the place of viruses in the living world'.* In it he pointed out that Darwin's tree of life, a beautiful idea that derives from a sketch in *The Origin of Species* and has become iconic, gets very scrambled around its roots because of a process called horizontal gene transfer. Bacteria, archaea and viruses swap genes with gay abandon, and they can also insert them into the genomes of higher animals, or cut them out. So a gene in one type of bacterium might have come from

---

* Harald Brüssow, The not so universal tree of life *or* the place of viruses in the living world, *Philosophical Transactions of the Royal Society of London* B **364** (2009) 2263-2274.

another type of bacterium altogether, or from an archaean, or even from an animal or a plant.

The major agents of this swapping are viruses, and there are lots of them on the planet, probably ten times as many virus particles as all other forms of life added together. Now, it might appear that with all this swapping, it would be virtually impossible to work out lineages, the heredity of individual bacteria. Even more so, it would seem impossible to work out the lineages of the viruses doing the swapping. Surprisingly, this is not the case; well, not altogether. There are clues in the order in which specific genes appear in many viruses, and there are useful clues as to which organisms the viruses parasitise. Some parasitise both bacteria and archaeans, suggesting strongly that they have been doing so since before these groups diverged. Moreover, these are viruses with RNA genetics. So Brüssow proposes quite convincingly that these particular viruses may be relics of a former RNA world. Going further: infection by ancient DNA viruses could have imported DNA into the heredity of all of the familiar creatures whose genomes we now make such a fuss about. So some of the mavericks, and physicists, might have been right all along, even if it was for the wrong reasons.

If that is the case, we need to look with new eyes at all the ways in which RNA is involved in modern life forms. According to the standard story, which has not changed for some time, RNA serves as a humble messenger that carries the all-important DNA sequence to the ribosomes, huge molecular structures in which proteins are assembled. There are also small RNAs that transfer amino acids to the ribosomes for protein assembly. Ribosomes in turn are made of several kinds of RNA, and several people have suggested that they are the central mechanism of protein construction in cells, their most important function.

This story may soon have to change.

There has been a revolution in nucleic acid biology over the last ten years, and almost all of it has been about RNA. Messenger

RNA and transfer RNA are merely the most prosaic jobs that RNA performs in cells. But RNA does many more important – perhaps having said 'prosaic' we should now say 'poetic' – jobs too. When DNA was considered the most important molecule in the cell, and protein construction the most important function (many textbooks still think so), strings of DNA that specified proteins by transcribing messenger RNA were called *genes*. The strings of DNA upstream and downstream, which did not specify proteins, were mostly thought to be 'junk DNA' of no importance to the organism. Junk DNA was just there as an accidental by-product of past history, but because it didn't cost much to replicate it, there was no evolutionary reason to eliminate it.

Indeed, there are plenty of remnants of old genes, and quite a lot of sequences from ancient viral attacks, which really might be junk. However, it turns out that although it doesn't specify proteins, nearly all DNA between genes does transcribe RNA molecules. These RNA molecules form the main control system of cells: they control which genes are activated and when, and how long different messenger RNAs last before destruction. In bacteria they also control genes, but a subset of them protects the bacterial cell against attack by viruses. This is a simple kind of immune system. So DNA may be the soloist, but RNA is the orchestra.

With that established, we can return to ribosomes, the molecular factories that assemble proteins. They are tiny particles, mostly of RNA. In bacteria, archaea, animals, plants and fungi, every cell has its own complement of ribosomes; moreover, much the same RNA occurs, though with different proteins, right across the span of life.

Marcello Barbieri is a leading exponent of biosemiotics, a relatively new science concerned with the *codes* of life. You have probably heard of the genetic code, the way in which triplets of DNA nucleotides are turned into different amino acids in proteins – by the ribosome. Barbieri has pointed out that there are hundreds of other codes; they range from insulin anchoring itself to receptors on the cell surface and causing different effects in the cell, to a smell (technically a pheromone) in male mouse urine that affects the oestrous cycle of female mice. All such effects are the results of translating one chemical language – hormones, pheromones – into a different language – physiological effects. So the genetic code is not alone: there are codes everywhere in biology. From this viewpoint, the crucial element in protein formation is not the DNA that prescribes it, or the messenger RNA that transmits the prescription: it's the ribosome. Which, to complete the analogy, is the pharmacist that makes up the prescription.

It also seems clear that this very ancient piece of machinery, so central to all living function, pre-dates the bacteria/archaea split, so it probably derives fairly directly from the RNA world. Something back then formed a relationship, a translation, probably from nucleic acid to protein. The ancestor of today's ribosomes, probably not very different from today's range of RNA structures, did the trick. So at the beginning of life, we find the translation of one kind of chemistry into another, by a structure that has come down to us almost unchanged.

Before the ribosome, there was just chemistry. Complicated chemistry, to be sure, but complication alone isn't quite the point. What matters is complexity, which in this context means 'organised complication'. Every cook knows that heating sugar with fats, two fairly simple chemical substances, produces caramel. Caramel is enormously complicated on a chemical level. It includes innumerable different molecules, each of which has thousands of atoms. The molecular structure of caramel is far more complicated than most of the molecules you're using to read this page. But caramel doesn't do much, aside from tasting good, so mere complication isn't enough to make interesting new things happen. Similarly, mixing dilute solutions of amino acids, sugars, bases and so on with particular clays generates long, very complicated, polymers. But, like caramel, they're not very interesting. However, as soon as transactions between those molecules came about, via the earliest ribosomes, complexity took over from complication.

Here, 'complexity' refers to *organised* complication. In a complicated system, such as a car, the individual bits – brakes, steering wheel, engine – behave in much the same way outside the system as they do when they're part of it. Mostly, they just sit there unless they're pushed, or pulled, or operated, by something else. But you, a fly, or an amoeba, are different. Their components behave differently when they are part of the system compared to what they do on their own. The parts interact more closely, changing their nature in the context of the system.

A bridge linking an island to the mainland is a complex system in this sense. In order to do its job, it doesn't much matter what the bridge is made of: it could be rope, steel or concrete. It could even be made of nothing (or air) if it's a tunnel. The important property is not what it's made from, but that it links the two ends effectively. That linkage is an *emergent property* of the bridge. That is, it's not inherent in any of the materials used. It arises because of their relationships to each other and to the local geography. Moreover, once the bridge is in place, the local geographical function is changed. The river that the bridge spans is no longer an obstacle to vehicles, even though they can't float or travel underwater. Crucially, you won't understand how that change occurs by studying the materials that made the bridge.

When the two ends of the bridge are linked, and only then, the local geography changes dramatically. So the real origin of a bridge occurs *when the ends are linked*. For some purposes, this is when the first rope crosses the divide; for other purposes it's when the first car makes the crossing; for yet other purposes it's when the Customs Office is set up.

Similarly, a ribosome in a cell is very different from an isolated one. It has a specific but complex job to do, reading messenger RNA and constructing proteins according to the genetic code. We wonder whether the chemical transactions made possible by early ribosomes in effect constructed bridges between several different kinds of chemistry, providing energy and materials for the ribosome to replicate itself. It's mostly RNA, after all.

Indeed, if we had to point to a single innovation that marked biotic from pre-biotic, it would be the ribosome, the translator supreme. Barbieri thinks the ribosome is central to life, and so do we. DNA is simply the rather prosaic, boring text. The ribosome is the orator; the other RNAs are the poetry. Once the ribosome emerged, the future became a living future, and in many ways this step marks the true origin of life.

Most origins also involve more subtle forms of emergence: the beginning of a storm, the acorn's origin as a bud on the oak, the origin of the Earth. Each of these origins is a quantitative-to-qualitative transformation, an emergent event that localises a real beginning. The first stroke of lightning, the first pair of leaves, the generation of heat that melts the core inside the Earth's mantle: these are emergent events that can label beginnings of new structures. The 'becoming' has divided into two issues, before and after the emergence.

If a phenomenon is emergent, it transcends all that has gone before. It does something that its bits and pieces could not have done on their own, or partially assembled, or assembled with some extra scaffolding that gets in the way. This transition is often the best stab we can make at assigning an origin. An emergent phenomenon does not originate in the bits and pieces that led to it: it originates when it emerges.

The emergence of the first lightning strike marks the beginning of the storm. The cell divisions that mark the acorn's difference from the other buds around it are the emergent oak. The cell divisions and relationships that promoted the egg that later became you orchestrated the emergent event that began you. The universe is complicated because emergent events – quantitative differences becoming qualitative differences – have occurred so many times.

Bridges like ribosomes have been built, and the Moon now circles the Earth.

These links have joined separate events into a web of causality that is the most notable property of the world around us. A story, however, is not a web. It has a linear structure, because both speech and writing proceed one word at a time. Even hypertext, used on the internet, is determined by a linear programme written in hypertext mark-up language (html). And that is why storytelling – human narrativium – finds origins to be so difficult and puzzling, and sometimes looks for simplicities where none exist.

ELEVEN

A VERY INTERESTING CASE

Mustrum looked at Miss Daw with a slightly sorry expression, which burst into a smile. 'Going home, then? Well now, isn't that good news? I'm sure your people there will be wondering what has happened to you, though of course you needn't worry – we can put you back right at the point where and when you left. Such a pity you couldn't stay longer; it is always useful to talk to somebody who knows how to talk.' Ridcully sighed. 'It isn't easy being Archchancellor. Very few people will talk to you as if you are a human as opposed to a very large hat; you just have to hope that there is somebody ready and willing to tell you when you are making a bloody fool of yourself.'

He sighed again, and Marjorie said, 'Would you mind if I stayed a little longer, then? I mean, if you can send me back home as if this never happened, well, it's a long time since I've had a holiday, and I'm fascinated by what is happening here. After all, it appears that there is going to be a major court case to see who owns my planet. So excuse me if I demand a ringside seat, since I am a sitting tenant, as it were. I could earn my keep too; although I say it myself, I am well versed in all aspects of library practice. But *really*, surely some representative of the population of the world in question should in all fairness be allowed to at least follow the proceedings.'

Ponder Stibbons glanced at the Archchancellor and said, 'She might have to wear a beard, Archchancellor; it *is* laid down by statute.' The air thickened a little, and he kept a weather eye on Ridcully's face.

Slowly the Archchancellor said, turning over every letter like some delicate and precious thing, 'It would seem, Mister Stibbons, that you have forgotten ... the codicil.'

'The codicil, Archchancellor?'

'*Yes*, Mister Stibbons, the *codicil* which directs that the sex of a librarian is immaterial.'

Theoretically, Ponder Stibbons was at this point treading on dangerous ground, were it not for the fact that he had both tenure and an encyclopaedic knowledge of the university that was second to none. And so he theoretically girded his theoretical loins and said, 'Archchancellor, there *is* no such codicil. Believe me, sir, I am aware of all relevant university statutes and guidelines.'

He was expecting a certain amount of noise about this and had stepped back a little before Mustrum Ridcully beamed at him and said, 'My dear boy, there is a *de facto* codicil; surely if an orangutan – albeit one who has travelled *through* humanity on his way to a higher calling – can be our Librarian, and indeed the best librarian we have ever had apart from being the cheapest to feed, then a librarian who is also a lady can *certainly* work in our library *beardless*! After all, the convention that you do not need to be a human male to be a librarian is there in place *irrevocably*.'

After the thunder had died away, Marjorie said, as cheerfully as possible, 'Is it true you *have* an orangutan librarian? I knew it! I've seen him before – and so have others, although it is seldom openly discussed, just in case. The first time was when I had to go down to the stacks, and he must have been surprised because he handed me a fresh banana skin and disappeared. The head librarian told me not to mention it to younger librarians, and whispered, "You are lucky if it happens once in a lifetime." And the second time—'

'*Twice* in a lifetime, Miss Daw?' Ridcully beamed. 'Let us make it three. I'll take you to meet him shortly, but first, alas, I must go and have a chat with Mister Slant, who is our lawyer. I can hardly wait! *The game is afoot!* Yes, Mister Stibbons, you have a point?'

'I do, Archchancellor. In a case like this I am sure that Lord Vetinari himself will want to be the adjudicator, to ensure fairness.'

'What! But we *made* the Roundworld; it belongs to us as it is our creature. It's not as if we just pulled it out of the air ...'

Ponder fell on that statement like a chess player taking the opponent's Queen. 'But pulling it out of the air was *exactly* what we did, Archchancellor. Exactly! You could say that it was *immanent* in the air, but whose imminence? It's going to be a very interesting case ...'

'This is a very interesting case,' said Mister Slant, the foremost lawyer in Ankh-Morpork, and indeed the most dead – at least, the most dead person who could tell you that he *was* dead. He rustled the papers in front of him, or possibly – since Mister Slant was the hardest-working zombie in Ankh-Morpork – they were his hands. He looked over the table at Ridcully and his face looked ... well, *grave* ... and his voice crackled; regrettably, there was no other way of putting it.

'You see, Archchancellor, this isn't just a squabble over a horse or a house; it goes beyond the occult into unknown regions – *expensive* regions. I am aware that the Church of the Latter-Day Omnians is seeking support from other religious groups, and it is no secret that some of them don't have all that much love for wizardry; they think of it as trespassing.'

Ridcully was outraged. 'Trespass!?'

Mister Slant gave a chuckle, which ended, as ever, as a crackle. 'If I judge the temperature in the ecclesiastical circles, they find the Omnians dangerously old-fashioned and lacking any understanding of compromise; in short, the Omnians simply *know* they are right – and that, Archchancellor, is that. Incidentally, I heard this afternoon that Lord Vetinari is prepared to take this case under his wing, as he is the highest temporal power, which means that his word will be law.'

He crackled through the papers on his desk again. 'Ah, he can find time on Thursday.'

The next day, Marjorie Daw was awakened by Mrs Whitlow with a bowl of bowel-scouring muesli, a teapot full of Earl Green tea, two hard-boiled eggs, and a copy of what turned out to be the *Ankh-Morpork Times*. On the front page, in big letters, was the headline: THE CHALLENGE OF ROUND WORLD. There was of course also an editorial, but like so many scribblings of that ilk it soft-pedalled when talking about things like faith and gods; it chose instead to hurry hastily towards such anodyne old favourites like seeing everybody's point of view, since religion was clearly a source of comfort for many people, and without respect for the other's point of view there can be no debate.

She called it vamp-till-ready journalism, hanging back until the public position was overwhelming; in that way, nobody would get into trouble with the public, or have nasty letters in their in-tray. What the editor called *Vox Populari* was a lot of fun, however, certainly for those who got their fun by looking sideways at the world. The wizards' absolute determination not to turn over Roundworld to the Omnians was causing people to think, sometimes without adequate equipment, which was signalled by such phrases as 'I reckon'.

Marjorie was of the opinion, after years of working in libraries, that any philosophical remark that begins with 'I reckon' was probably unlikely to come up with a world-shattering insight or even a new un-shattered one.

She couldn't help it; she had three degrees, a doctorate and could *think* in Greek – an excellent language for dealing with ideas. Latin, she thought, was … well, quite useful; but Greek had that extra *je ne sais quoi*, and so did French, when you came to think about it. So *while* you were thinking that you could be entertaining seditious arguments against democracy, she couldn't help sometimes finding herself annoyed that the system allowed the deliberations of somebody who explored a great deal of the background of the talking point in question to have the same value as that of a man who buys his newspapers because they have naked women in them.

She'd had many arguments with her mother about that, and her mother had taken the view that it all worked out in the end, pointing out that some of the most renowned and intelligent people could be guilty of the most stupid and even homicidally dangerous ideas. She said that stupid *clever* people do much more damage than stupid untutored morons.

Marjorie tossed the paper away and there was a knock, a nervous one. She opened the door to see the wizard known as Rincewind; he was dwarfed by an orangutan – a large one, but a very amiable-looking one who knuckled his way into the room.

Rincewind said, 'Excuse me, miss; the Archchancellor would like you to meet the Librarian. He used to be as human as you or me but now, after a bit of an accident in the library, he is ... *more so*, if you see what I mean ... You don't look surprised?'

'You know, Mister Rincewind, I am *not* surprised, not really. We librarians don't often talk about it, of course, but everybody knows about the banana skins that turn up overnight when a book you desperately need is found exactly where it ought to be, even though you might swear that place had been empty for months. We all have *experience* – we know he's out there; sometimes upside down. I personally have already briefly met the gentleman on two previous occasions.'

She held out her hand to the Librarian; it felt like shaking hands with a delicate ladies' glove. He winked at her, then Rincewind broke the spell by saying, 'He will understand everything you say. After a while you find yourself *knowing* what he is saying; it sort of seeps in ... what's the word?'

'Osmosis,' said Marjorie without thinking, and she was rewarded with a very large 'Ook!'

'The Archchancellor has decreed that you have the run of our library, which of course holds a copy of every book ever written since the concept of writing began. You might like the contents of the library of Alexandria – we got everything out while it was burning – and … let me see, yes – the library of Atlantis. There weren't any humans there, of course, but the Librarian – with help from friends – has deciphered the language of a most sapient species of lobster-like creatures that wrote on stone slabs about the creation of the world. It is just a shame that they were so *tasty*.'

Marjorie stood with her mouth open while Rincewind chattered on, 'The Archchancellor told me you might like to see around while everybody is getting ready for the case on Thursday; it's the talk of the city! So now, a grand tour of the Library. Strictly speaking, it should take more than one million billion years, but we can take short cuts.'

In fact, Marjorie didn't get back until dinner time on Wednesday – sated of books, but not so much that she wouldn't have wanted another foray the following day. There would be no chance of that, however; the day was going to be tied up with lawyers.

The Archchancellor had agreed with her request to be in the law chamber, but since she was in Discworld by accident her origins would not be mentioned, just in case; and in whose case it was, she didn't know.

But nobody said she couldn't talk, or watch the case like a hawk, moreover like a hawk with extremely acute eyesight. She had found time from gloating over the books to read the papers, and it seemed that most of the population weren't really interested in the outcome at all or even aware of the stakes.

They were much more interested in the fight.

TWELVE

LONG ARM
OF THE LORE

Discworld has a Guild of Lawyers, even though it has no systematic legal system. This is only to be expected: lawyers never let little things like that get in their way. It does have a traditional method for settling legal disputes, however: a tribunal, over which Lord Vetinari, Patrician of Ankh-Morpork, is entitled to preside, should he so wish. On Discworld, as in many parts of Roundworld, disagreements about the law, or alleged infringements of it, are subjected to formal procedures, often involving a written body of legislation, precedents from other (often totally unrelated) cases, arguments, counter-arguments, expert witnesses and … oh, yes, evidence.

What, though, counts as evidence?

On Roundworld, even in countries that consider themselves to be democratic, a surprisingly large part of the legal process involves one or other party trying to arrange for key evidence to be excluded or included, doing its best to rig the jury in its client's favour, plea-bargaining, and generally subverting the process of obtaining a fair trial. Law trumps justice.

This tendency is universal among lawyers on both worlds.

Roundworld, however, also has laws of another kind. Its inhabitants optimistically call them 'laws of nature', by which they mean the rules according to which their world operates. Human laws can be broken;

nature's laws cannot. They are not regulations made by people, but statements about how the universe behaves. The law-court of science also judges evidence, but for a different purpose. Instead of deciding the guilt or innocence of the accused, scientific evidence decides the truth or falsity of *the law*.

If only it were that simple.

That's what we used to think, back in the heady days when gravity really did seem to fall off inversely as the square of distance, light was a wave, and time was independent of space. God was a mathematician and the universe was clockwork. But now, alongside the T-shirt bearing the equations of relativity, we find others that read 'I used to be uncertain, but now I'm not so sure'.

That pretty much sums up the current status of physical law among scientists. Today, we expect longstanding 'laws' of nature to be occasionally overturned when better observations become available, or when new contexts for the laws arise. The laws of chemistry do not allow base metal to be transmuted into gold, but the laws of nuclear reactions do. What we call 'laws' seem to be recurrent patterns in the physical world, which we can approximate very closely using mathematical equations, in limited contexts. We often call them 'models' or 'rules' instead, but on the whole we still use 'laws' for the deepest and best supported among them.

This rejection of certainty makes science stronger, because it gives scientists the opportunity to revise their views when the evidence proves them wrong. But people *like* certainty, and many seem unable to understand why informed doubt is a strength. This opens up a huge opportunity for the storytelling ape, who insists on courtroom drama and the struggle between prosecution and defence. The case may pit one scientist against another, because individuals have their own ideas about what nature's laws *are*. Or it may pit science against anti-science in the court of public opinion – lung cancer *v* the tobacco industry, evolution *v* intelligent design, climate change *v* scepticism and denial.

Now nature's laws, and humans', start to look much more similar, because once again what determines the outcome is not the evidence as such, but whether it is allowed to be taken into account, and how it is interpreted. In place of humans united in a quest to find out how nature works, we find some who want that, but others who think they already *know* how nature works, and will use any trick in the book to ram their answer down everybody else's throats. Scientific doubt provides the latter with a useful weapon: it opens science up to the criticism that it doesn't actually *know* anything.

Scientists do not make laws, or enforce them, or try to wriggle out of them. They do not, as social relativists and postmodernists seem to imagine, get together, decide what laws will suit their purposes and then declare them to be correct. Instead, the scientists of Roundworld, and their predecessors – the natural philosophers – have always spent much of their time investigating the potential consequences of hypothetical versions of natural law, hoping either to support theories or to demolish them. Being human, they tend to prefer support for their own theories and demolition of the opposition's, but most of them make a genuine effort to avoid that kind of bias if the evidence that they are wrong becomes sufficiently strong.

A topical example is Richard Muller, leader of the 2009 Berkeley Earth Project and (until July 2012) a prominent climate change sceptic. In an analysis aimed at refuting claimed evidence of man-made global warming, the Project (funded by groups that support lobbying to resist action on climate change) made a fresh analysis of historical data on the Earth's temperature over the last two hundred and fifty years. In the event, the study was entirely in line with, and strengthened, the existing evidence in favour of man-made global warming. The analysis showed that during that period, the Earth's average land temperature increased by 1.5°C. Nearly two thirds of that rise occurred in the last fifty years.

Muller promptly* announced that his previous concerns about possible errors of data collection and analysis had proved unfounded. 'Last year,' he said, 'I concluded that global warming was real and that the prior estimates of the rate of warming were correct. I'm now going a step further: humans are almost entirely the cause.'

That's the difference between scepticism and denial.

There are two big philosophical problems about laws of nature. What are they? Where do they come from?

To complicate matters, the phrase itself can mean several different things. The philosopher Thomas Hobbes, who published *Leviathan* in 1651, proposed essentially God-given laws: 'The first law of nature is that every man ought to endeavour peace, as far as he has hope of obtaining it' – which determined what humankind should do. Another usage was that of John Locke, an early Fellow of the Royal Society, who cheerfully assumed that God had ruled against slavery: 'The state of nature has a law of nature to govern it, which obliges every one: and reason, which is that law, teaches all mankind, who will but consult it, that being all equal and independent, no one ought to harm another in his life, health, liberty, or possessions.' Fine: consult reason and produce a system with liberty for all. That's all right to start with, perhaps. But then you must make exceptions: for witches, of course; or for children caught stealing bread; or for malefactors in general. For a given value of 'mal'.

Laws of nature in these senses were much nearer to human laws than is our common usage today, physical law. Examples are the law of gravity and Ohm's law about the relation between voltage, current and resistance in electrical circuits. This meaning seems much closer to 'how things work', and it will be our starting point.

---

* A little too promptly for some scientists, who complained that the results were announced before being peer-reviewed for journal publication.

In *The Nature of Physical Law*, Richard Feynman wrote that in order to discover a law of nature, we start with a hypothesis, like Newton's theory of gravitational attraction. Then we do some calculations, to see if examples fit our hypothesis. If all goes well, we call it a theory and try it out on many other examples. To the extent that these examples get wider and wider – from the famous apple* to the Moon, to planetary orbits, then to the discovery that large heavy spheres attract each other very slightly in the laboratory, *and* that galaxies seem to have gravitational interactions with each other over vast distances – we can then elevate the theory to the status of a law.

That brings us back to the Large Hadron Collider and its dramatic discovery of the Higgs boson, a long-sought fundamental particle that sorts out the masses of the other sixteen particles in the 'standard model' of particle physics. What was once wild surmise has now become respectable orthodoxy, and the standard model has now taken a giant leap towards becoming a law of nature. However, it hasn't yet attained that status, because the current state of knowledge leaves some alternatives open.

At the end of 2011, if you were an optimist, the Higgs was barely visible, a statistically insignificant bump on a graph at an energy of about 125 GeV (billion electronvolts). By the middle of 2012, the same bump had achieved five-sigma significance, meaning that the chance that it was spurious was less than one in two million. On 4 July 2012 CERN, the European laboratory that administers and runs the LHC, announced the existence of the Higgs.

Well, *a* Higgs. Higgs-like. Sort of Higgsy. (A theory called supersymmetry, currently popular among mathematical physicists,

---

* Although often thought to be a myth, this story has some basis. Newton often said that he had been inspired by the fall of an apple. *Wikipedia* states: 'Acquaintances ... such as William Stukeley, whose manuscript ... has been made available by the Royal Society, confirm the incident, though not the cartoon version that the apple actually hit Newton's head.'

predicts at least *five* Higgses. Maybe this is just the first.) The observations did fit the predicted behaviour of *the* Higgs, a specific theoretical construct, but some key properties of the real particle have not yet been measured. No one can be certain that those will fit too, until suitable data have been collected. But now the particle physicists know where to look.

Journalists, true to form, insisted on referring to the Higgs as the God particle, for no very sensible reason except sensational headlines. The name comes from the book *The God Particle: If the Universe Is the Answer, What Is the Question?* by Nobel prize-winning physicist Leon Ledermann. However, he wanted to call the Higgs the goddamn particle because of all the trouble it was causing. His publisher brought God into it.

This is always a dangerous tactic. It is presumably why some people with religious objectives imagine there is a link between the Higgs and their concept of God – just as some previously imagined that Stephen Hawking's use of 'the mind of God' in *A Brief History of Time* was a theological statement rather than a metaphor. The 'God particle' name must surely be what inspired some hopeful doorstep missionary to claim (as reported in *New Scientist*) that scientists now believe in God. The evangelist's reason – 'They've found Him in the Large Hadron Kaleidoscope' – is a dead giveaway.

Pity about 'kaleidoscope', of course, but that slip pales into insignificance compared to the claim that scientists now believe in God because they've observed the Higgs. It's like citing the photon to prove they've seen the light.

Ian, being a mathematician, rather likes the standard model cake with Higgs icing, although he'd have been even happier if the Higgs had turned out not to exist, as Hawking once predicted. That would have been much more exciting. Jack, a biologist, has more misgivings. He is worried that the evidence for all fundamental particles depends on specific *interpretations* of the data, and the manner by which they are obtained. It's not easy to observe a new particle: you don't just look for it and see it, like in the old days. In particular, you spot a Higgs by the company it keeps. It doesn't hang around long enough to be observed in its own right; instead, it decays into a complicated shower of other particles. So you have to look for the kind of shower that a Higgs would produce, and infer the presence of a Higgs.

By analogy, consider a piano, as observed by pianologists: creatures that have great facility with sound, but can't see a piano or feel what shape it is. How would they find out what this musical instrument is made of?

Let's allow them the ability to throw things at it. Hurling small stones would be rewarded, from time to time, by a musical note. We know this occurs when a stone hits a key, but pianologists would detect only the music. By collecting data, they would find a range of notes, with a nice mathematical structure. Clearly a piano is made from twangons of various frequencies. Experiments at higher energy would reveal a new and rather different 'pianicle': the slamon. (We understand that you get this by slamming the lid shut.) Now it's got more complicated. Soon the pianino has joined the list, along with the muano, the tauano and much else.

Instead of making everything simpler, new data at higher energies has just muddied the waters. So how do pianologists propose to resolve the many theoretical issues involved? They obtain large government grants to create collisions of even *higher* energy. This requires erecting an LHC (Large Hotel Collapser) forty storeys high, and pushing the piano out of a top-floor window in the time-honoured fashion of visiting rock stars. The results are impressive, but hard to interpret. Careful analysis decomposes the resulting sound into a cacophony of a hundred or so different twangons, several variants of the slamon … and a bit left over. This bit, obtained by deducting from the overall sound every known component, is of course the long-sought proof of the existence of the Bigg Bashon – which journalists insist on calling the Thud pianicle, a name given to the sound created when a piano encounters a hypothetical field … or maybe a car park.

This proves that a piano has mass.

Because the procedure that confirms the new pianicle is so complex and error-prone, several billion pianos need to be launched into oblivion before the results become statistically significant. They are, and the discovery is published, months after the first experiment hit the headlines.

The big question here, which is where Ian and Jack tend to differ, though not by a lot, is whether particle physicists are misinterpreting the nature of matter in a similar way to pianologists resolutely failing to understand a piano. Bashing things to see what happens *can* break them into constituent parts, but it can also excite new modes of behaviour that can't sensibly be thought of as components. Are particle physicists really finding out what matter is made of, or are they just causing it to behave in ever wilder ways?

Less facetiously, think about how we analyse sounds themselves. Scientists and engineers like to break a complex sound into simple 'components', sinusoidal vibrations with specific frequencies. 'Sinusoidal' refers to the mathematical sine curve, the simplest pure sound. This technique is called Fourier analysis, after Joseph Fourier, who used it to study heat flow in 1807. The sound produced by a clarinet, for example, has three main Fourier components: a vibration at the dominant frequency (the note that it sounds like), a slightly softer vibration at three times that frequency (the third harmonic), and an even softer vibration at five times that frequency (the fifth harmonic). This pattern continues with only odd-numbered harmonics, until the components reach such a high pitch that the human ear can't hear them.

The sound of a clarinet can be synthesised, digitally, by adding together all of these Fourier components.* But do those components 'exist' as physical *things*? That's a moot point, even though we can

---

* For a dominant frequency ω, the combination $\sin(\omega t) + 0\cdot75 \sin(3\omega t) + 0\cdot5 \sin(5\omega t) + 0\cdot14 \sin(7\omega t) + 0\cdot5 \sin(9\omega t) + 0\cdot12 \sin(11\omega t) + 0\cdot17 \sin(13\omega t)$, going as far as the 13th harmonic, is pretty convincing to the human ear.

pull the sound apart into those 'things' and reassemble them. On the one hand, we can detect them by applying the right mathematics to the sound that the clarinet emits. On the other hand, a clarinet does not emit pure sinusoidal tones at all, at least not without an awful lot of fiddling about to damp out unwanted components – in which case it's not exactly a clarinet any more. Mathematically, a clarinet's vibrations are best described by a nonlinear equation, which generates the complex waveform *only*, not its individual Fourier components. In that sense, a clarinet does not generate the components and then add them together. Instead, they come as a single, indivisible package.

You can learn a lot about the sound a clarinet makes from these mathematical constructs – but that doesn't imply that the constructs are real, just that the mathematical technique is useful in its own right. A similar method is used to compress the data in digital images, using grey-scale patterns in place of sound waves – but in the real world the image is not formed by adding these components.

Are physicists just picking up mathematical constructs – in a sense, creating them by the way they analyse their data – and *interpreting* them as fundamental particles? Are fancy high-energy particles real, or artefacts of complex excitations in something else? Even if they are, does this make any important scientific or philosophical difference? Now we are venturing into questions about the nature of reality, of which the most crucial is whether such a thing exists at all. We aren't sure of the answers, so we'll content ourselves with raising the questions. But we suspect that several different interpretations of the same physics may be equally valid,* and which one is best depends on what you want to do with it.

---

* In the science fiction novel *Light* by M. John Harrison, aliens living around the Galactic Core have invented six different space drives, each based on a different theory of fundamental physics, several of which are known to be wrong. All of the drives work fine. In Roundworld, our theories of aerodynamics are approximations that ignore atomic-scale structure, yet aircraft fly perfectly well. Lies-to-children often *work*.

Evidentially, the Higgs is a small bump on an otherwise smooth curve. With the mind-set and traditions of particle physics, it is interpreted as a particle. What's interesting to us is how the bump becomes the object of attention, while the much larger quantity of data representing the smooth curve is relegated to the background.

A more familiar example has the same features. Our view of the solar system, with all the planets, all the asteroids and comets, behaving as they should, would be upset if we spotted a spaceship rocketing about but thought it was just another regular body. It would be a malefactor, not obeying the law of gravity. Indeed, the law tells us what is natural, so the spaceship becomes an anomaly.

Think of all the fuss about the Pioneer anomaly, an unexplained deceleration discovered when observing the spacecraft Pioneer 10 and Pioneer 11. These were the first space probes to reach the outer planets of the solar system, from Jupiter to Neptune. Because of the gravitational pull of the Sun, their speed continually decreased, but they were travelling fast enough to escape the solar system entirely, given enough time. However, when they were at about the same distance from the Sun as Uranus, observations showed that they were slowing down a little bit faster than gravity alone could explain – by about one billionth of a metre per second per second. After much head-scratching, an analysis published in 2011 showed that this effect could be accounted for by the way the craft were radiating heat, which created very small pressure effects.

Here, the underlying physical law, that of gravity, sets up the scenery: the backdrop against which the spaceship becomes a story. *Pan narrans* cannot help but see the spaceship as the most interesting item, because it doesn't fit the story – it seems not to obey the law.

Our minds seem to have evolved to place extra weight on exceptions. The prolific science fiction and popular science author Isaac Asimov wrote: 'The most exciting phrase to hear in science, the one that heralds new discoveries, is not "Eureka" but "That's funny ..."' Law-abiding planets and comets are banal, unable to catch our attention. In the same way, we find the law-abiding mass of humanity essentially boring, so our stories are about witches and malefactors. Among Discworld's characters, the witch Granny Weatherwax and the sweeper and history monk Lu-Tze catch our attention. It's the *exceptions* to the law that make the law useful.

Are laws like that of gravity unique, special statements that are in some sense universally true? Would aliens come up with a theory like gravity, or is there something peculiarly human about falling apples, which leads our peculiar minds on to lunar orbits and solar systems? Is there perhaps a quite different way to describe solar systems?

Similarly, when Thomson started playing with cathode ray tubes, he had no idea that he was separating a beam of electrons, breaking up atoms. If we had started from some *other* particle than an electron, and we had gone on to find a zoo of others, would we have described the same zoo? Or would we have come up with a different zoo, which nevertheless describes the 'real world' as accurately as the one we've got?

Physicists, by and large, think not; they believe that there really *are* these particles out there, and that any scientific endeavour would find the same zoo. But the zoo you find depends on the theoretical model you use to direct the search. Ten years ago they had a different zoo, and in ten years' time …

To expand on that point, consider the development of quantum mechanics. The relevant law here is the Schrödinger equation, which describes the state of a quantum system as a propagating wave. However, it seems to be impossible to detect this wave, as such, experimentally. Observations of a quantum system give specific results, and once you've made one observation, you've interfered with the hypothetical wave. So you can't be sure that the next observation refers to the same wave. This apparently inherent indeterminacy has led to some extra interpretational features of the theory: that the quantum wave is a wave of probabilities, telling us what the state might be, and how likely any given choice is, but not what the state *is*;

that measurements 'collapse' the wavefunction to a single state, and so on. By now this interpretation has become close to received gospel, and attempts to find alternatives are often dismissed out of hand. There is even a piece of mathematics, Bell's theorem, which allegedly proves that quantum mechanics cannot be embedded within a broader deterministic local model, one that does not allow instant communication between widely separated entities.

All of the above notwithstanding, *Pan narrans* has problems with quantum indeterminacy. How does nature *know what to do*? This is the thinking behind Einstein's famous remark about a (non-) dicing deity. Generations of physicists have become accustomed to the problem – the mathematics says 'it's just like that', and there's no need to worry about interpretations. But it's not quite that simple, because working out the implications of the mathematics requires some extra bolt-on assumptions. 'What it's like' could be a consequence of those assumptions, not of the mathematics itself.

It's curious that we and Einstein use, as our icon for chance, the image of dice. A die (singular) is a cube, and when it is thrown, and bounces, it obeys the deterministic laws of mechanics. In principle, you ought to be able to predict the outcome as soon as the die leaves the hand. Of course there are modelling issues here, but that statement ought at least to be true of the idealised model. However, it's not, and the reason is that the corners of the die amplify tiny errors of description. This is a form of chaos, related to the butterfly effect but technically different.

Mathematically, the probabilities of the die landing on its various faces derive from the dynamical equations as a so-called invariant measure. One chance in six for each face. There is a sense in which the invariant measure is like a quantum wavefunction. You can calculate it from the dynamical equations and use it to predict statistical behaviour, but you can't observe it directly. You infer it from a repeated series of experiments. There is also a sense in which an observation (of the final state of the die) 'collapses' this wavefunction. The table, and friction, force the die into an equilibrium state, which might be any of the six possibilities. What determines the observed value of the wavefunction is the secret dynamics of a rolling die, bouncing off a table. That's not encoded in the wavefunction at all. It involves new 'hidden variables'.

You can't help wondering whether something similar is happening in the quantum world. The quantum wavefunction may not be the whole story.

When quantum mechanics was introduced, chaos theory didn't exist. But the whole development might have been different if it had existed, because chaos theory tells us that deterministic dynamics can mimic randomness *exactly*. If you ignore some very fine detail of the deterministic system, what you see looks like random coin tosses. Now, if you don't realise that determinism can mimic randomness, you can't see any hope of connecting the apparent randomness observed in quantum systems with any deterministic law. Bell's theorem knocks the whole idea on the head anyway. Except – it doesn't. There are chaotic systems that closely resemble quantum ones, generate apparent randomness deterministically and, crucially, do not conflict with Bell's theorem in any way.

These models would need a lot more work to turn them into a genuine competitor for conventional quantum theory, even if that's possible. The Rolls-Royce problem raises its head: if the test of a new design of car is that it has to outperform a Roller, innovation becomes impossible. No newcomer can hope to displace what is already firmly established. But we can't help but wonder what would have happened if chaos theory had appeared *before* the early work in quantum mechanics did. Working within a very different background, one in which deterministic models were not seen to conflict with apparent randomness, would physicists still have ended up with the current theory?

Maybe – but some aspects of the standard theory don't make a lot of sense. In particular, an observation is represented mathematically as simple, crystalline process, whereas a real observation requires a measuring device whose detailed quantum-mechanical formulation is far too complicated ever to be tractable. Most of the paradoxical features of quantum theory stem from this mismatch between an *ad hoc* add-on to the Schrödinger equation, and the actual process of observing, not from the equations as such. So we can speculate that in a re-run of history, our 'law' for quantum systems really could have turned out very different, giving Schrödinger no reason to introduce his puzzling cat.

Whether our current physical laws are special and unique, or a different set would work just as well, there is something more to say about laws in general. And about their exceptions, and especially about transcending them. By that word we don't mean that the laws are disobeyed. We mean that they become irrelevant because of a change in context, like the way a jumbo jet transcends gravity by using air-flow past its wings.

We'll take Ohm's law as an example, because it appears to be simple.

Matter is basically of two kinds with regard to electricity: either it's an insulator, or it's a conductor. If it's a conductor, Ohm's law applies: current equals voltage divided by resistance. So, for fixed resistance, a greater current requires a greater voltage. However, resistance need not be fixed, and this possibility lies behind some natural anomalies, like the way that lightning changes the insulating gas of the atmosphere into a conducting ionised path for the lightning strike, or ball lightning, which essentially folds up into the surface of a sphere. Being anomalies, these phenomena are automatically interesting. We can also play tricks with variable conductors of electricity, starting with thermionic valves (vacuum tubes) in the 1920s and continuing with semiconductors like transistors. The computer industry is built upon this trick.

The discovery of superconducting alloys – *no* electrical resistance – near zero Absolute temperature was a very interesting anomaly, which, as new alloys have been found that exhibit no resistance at higher and higher temperatures, promises to give us a whole new energy technology. The interesting items are those that *differ* from the Ohm's law picture: the witches, the spacecraft.

Ohm's law is intimately involved with stories about electricity distribution. By describing these problems, and their solutions, we can show how leaving the law to 'work its will', but changing the context, can completely alter the situation. From there we can go from Feynman's position – that laws determine the context as well as the content of natural events – to a more progressive view.

Electricity distribution to households is made difficult by the resistance of the cables, which causes a lot of electrical energy to be dissipated from the transmission lines as heat. Ohm's law implies that the same amount of power can be transmitted, with lower losses, by making the voltage higher and the current lower. However, this would supply homes with very high-voltage electricity, and accidents would be fatal.

The trick is to use alternating current, back and forth fifty or sixty times a second. Transformers can change the voltage of alternating current, so it can be high for transmission and then reduced to not-very-lethal values when it gets to our homes. Today we could stick to direct current, using modern electronics to change the voltage, but that option wasn't available when the distribution system was being created. We've now invested so much in alternating current systems that we can't easily change them, even if that turned out to be a good idea. This trick dodges the Ohm's law problem of resistance, hence energy loss. Even now, more than a third of the energy can be lost in long transmission lines, but that's still far more efficient than the 70% loss delivered by the low-voltage direct current systems of the 1920s. By changing the parameters, by going to low-current high-voltage alternating current, we can to some extent change the rules.

Too many physicists seem to have a mind-set that considers physics to be *all of reality*, simply because it is concerned with all the basic structure of matter. In *The Character of Physical Law*, Feynman says:

The same kinds of atoms appear to be in living creatures as in non-living creatures (*sic*); frogs are made of the same 'goup' as rocks, only in different arrangements. So that makes our problems simpler; we have nothing but atoms, all the same, everywhere.

In the same book, he says:

Probably the most powerful single assumption that contributes most to the progress of biology is the assumption that everything animals do the atoms can do, that the things that are seen in the biological world are the results of the behaviour of physical and chemical phenomena, with no 'extra something'.

Like Feynman, we don't think that there's an 'extra something', an *élan vital* ('life force') that drives life. No, it's much simpler than that. Organisms have *evolved*, and whereas at the outset of life they were very limited, mostly 'doing what their atoms did', as Feynman would have it, they acquired new properties, like cell division. They got a workable heredity, they acquired eyes and the nervous systems to use them. They moved up *out* of physico-chemical systems, just as we've moved up *out* of the law of gravity. Organisms have new tricks, exploiting new contexts. For instance: birds, despite being heavier than air, can fly.

We're not saying that what birds do is inconsistent with the 'fundamental' physical laws for the matter out of which they are made. That would be very close to making Descartes's error, postulating that mind and matter are two different things. In fact, flight is entirely consistent with physical law. The force of gravity, acting on the atoms that make up the bird, must be counteracted by the lifting forces generated by the wings as they move through the air. If not, the bird won't fly. Ditto jumbo jets. Our point is that flight is not something that you can naturally deduce from the fundamental laws. Molecules can't fly, but birds – made from molecules – can. A molecule can fly if it's included in a bird. Context makes a big difference. Life has acquired a multitudinous list of complex systems, each resulting from natural selection, to lift organisms out of ancient incompetences into new competences.

The goup in a frog isn't a bit like the goup in a rock. The atoms may be much the same, but the different arrangements, to use Feynman's words, completely change how you expect frog goup to behave. Similarly, the atoms in a person or a penguin or a packet of soap powder are in different arrangements. To understand the bird, the frog, or the soap powder, it's not enough to know about the underlying atoms or subatomic particles. It's *how they are arranged* that matters. In fact, they could be made of rather different stuff, but if it were arranged to carry out similar functions, you'd still end up with effective birds, frogs and soap powder.

It's the arrangements that make the magic, not the goup.

Atoms in different arrangements have different properties: an atom in a piece of rock is probably one of millions in a crystal array, and is essentially a permanent part of that array. An atom in a living creature is probably part of a very complex network, changing atomic and molecular partners all the time. Moreover, this changing system is not typical of the unaided activities of matter obeying the fundamental laws, despite being consistent with those laws. It has been selected over many generations so that it works, so that it *does* something. And the something that it does, while not having any 'extra something' in Feynman's sense, contributes to the life of the organism that it's part of. It may even be part of a virus, destroying the organism, but it's still enmeshed in all the processes that make up life.

Life has lifted itself out of the simple laws of nature, where it started, and is now a whole complex world, at least as different from that origin as a modern aeroplane is from a flint axe. The scene at the beginning of the film *2001*, where the ape throws up a thighbone and it morphs into a space station, is a lovely illustration of just that kind of evolution. And that transformation is minor, compared to how life has transcended its origins.

Let's look at it from a different perspective. The material world, the world of physics and chemistry, has many continuing processes, from the unimaginable physics in the middle of stars to the freezing and thawing of ethane and methane on Saturn's moon Titan. Stars explode, scattering the elements that have formed within them into the cosmos, and planets condense from that mixture, according to the laws of physics and chemistry. Then, perhaps in the deep ocean near the rift in the ocean floor from which highly reduced compounds are pouring, some anomalous chemistry sets up a hereditary system. It may be a mixture of chemical processes that is in some sense heritable, it may be RNA, it may be a pre-metabolic system ... But it's the beginning of a *story*, a narrative that has lifted itself out of the frame of the laws, and is about to transcend them. Spaceships and witches are in its future.

As life first starts, it's not remarkable. It proceeds more or less according to the rules of physics and chemistry, according to the laws. Then it begins to compete, perhaps for space, or for particular chemicals, or for membranes that are fatty layers on clay. Those systems that work better lift themselves out of the laws, into a tiny simple narrative that says 'A does a little bit better than B or C, so there's more of it in the future ...' Come back in a million years, and the oceans are full of A, while there's no C to be found. And by then, A has diversified into A1 and A2 and A3. Now, lurking – a good narrative word – in the depths is Q, which loves to include A3 in its system. So later we have QA3XYZ, and the system is well started.

It's all gone according to the laws, for sure; but there's a mite of competition, selection of this over that. Come back in a million years, or perhaps six weeks, and there will be a bacterial cell that has lifted itself into a story ...

The laws facilitate such changes, but they don't direct them. They are merely history, with all the living stuff transcending them in every direction. Come back in 3000 million years, you'll find a mess of Burgess Shale organisms. Come back 580 million years later still, and you'll find a physicist denying that any of this is important. But the action transcends the laws: it's the spaceships and witches that drive the narrative.

Life originally emerged from non-living systems, with laws, but it has gone on to complicate itself out of all recognition. Biology isn't just physics and chemistry with knobs on. It's a whole new world.

Within that world, one of its beasts has acquired language, imagination, and a penchant for stories: a special, wholly new thing in the cosmos. Narrativium has escaped from Discworld into Roundworld; now some things *do* happen because there is a creature that wants them to.

Perhaps there are many such creatures, all over the place; perhaps as many as one species per hundred million stars. But we should be very careful indeed, just in case we're the only one.

Just one *story* in the whole cosmos.

Everywhere else, only laws.

THIRTEEN

RINCEWIND'S ADVENTURES IN ROUNDWORLD

The arrival into Roundworld was always a hit-or-miss business these days, Rincewind knew. The people in the Inadvisably Applied Magic group had a word for it – or, more accurately, a number of equations, which you would see on the walls, being drawn and then subsequently redrawn by the next researcher, or survivor. But the Dean said that he knew what he was doing, and landed them in the middle of London; regrettably during a race, which Rincewind inadvertently won; and he had to submit to multiple slaps on the back, admiration for his wizard's outfit, and many thanks from the organisers for helping the Orangutan Foundation to raise so much money.

He was surprised, as well, when someone he had thought was the Librarian turned out to be a young woman in an outfit, which led to hilarious misunderstanding as a result of which both he and the Dean had to run a little further.

They found a pleasant park with trees, and ducks in the pond, and considered their circumstances. After a while Rincewind said, 'I told you about the automobiles, didn't I? Terrible waste of resources. Honestly, is this really *Homo sapiens*? Horses breed other horses, eat grass and you get fertiliser as well; don't you remember the street cries of "Tuppence a bucket, well stamped down"?'

'Yes,' said the Dean. 'I also remember "gardyloo", and it wasn't very pleasant. I must admit, though, that they have progressed in this era – but I think at enormous cost, which most of them don't recognise, although right now I see people in very decent health: lots of colour, no heads on railings … all in all, if you don't think too hard … though *we* know what's coming their way.' Then the Dean pointed to a building in the distance and said, 'Fairly big place there; I'm sure I've seen it before.'

'You have,' said Rincewind. 'You remember the Great Fire of London? We helped Mister Pepys to bury his Parmesan cheese.'

'Oh, right. I wonder if the fellow got it back again?'

'No,' said Rincewind. 'I asked him where he put it, and I couldn't remember either, so I went back to the moment when he buried it and doubled up myself; if you remember, Mrs Whitlow was very happy to see it. I figured that since he was going to forget the cheese *anyway* … well, it would be such a wicked shame to let it go to waste.'

'It was a bad move,' said the Dean. 'Causality, you see.'

'Don't talk to me about causality,' said Rincewind. 'It hasn't done me that many favours, what with one thing and another. But since we are here and chatting, I have to ask: well, what did you *do* to *make* this place? I mean, you say you just put your hand in some firmament and, if I may quote, you "wiggled it about". I must say, I can understand that in a slightly not understanding way, but what about the continents and all that? There's an awful lot of fine detail, like squirrels and creatures and fish, and amazing things on coral reefs; seriously amazing things. And while we're on the subject, full marks for putting the Moon in the right place to get tides. Tides in, tides out: *very* clever idea – not only a beach-cleaning service, but also making it easier for crawling things to come out of the sea. I would take off my hat to you, if I ever took my hat off; well done, I say!'

They strolled a little further towards the dome-shaped place in the distance, and at last the Dean said, 'Rincewind. Indeed, *Professor* Rincewind, I understand that you are a very learned head when it comes to Cruel and Unusual Geography. Egregious Professor of it, indeed! But I feel I must tell you this.' The Dean cleared his throat, as if for a statement of enormous moment and worth. 'I didn't do a thing. I didn't plan a thing. I didn't frame the fearful symmetry of the tyger, of which it appears there are now all too few. No! It all just *happened*.'

'But you—' Rincewind began.

'Oh, of course I take an interest in the place – it would be remiss of me to do otherwise,' the Dean continued, adding, 'but I've never tried it again. I wouldn't like to take the responsibility.' They strolled on a bit and he said, 'I'm quite getting the hang of this era, and my feet hurt. Let's take a cab; at least these days you no longer have to scrape the horse dung off your boots.'

He snapped his fingers and a cab halted so quickly that the driver was nearly thrown out; still bemused, he watched as the two figures got in and two seat belts miraculously strapped themselves up.

Without even looking at the driver, the Dean said, 'You will drive us to the place under the dome over there; you will have had an indecently high tip, and when we get out of your moving apparatus you will totally forget that we were ever in it. Thank you so much.'

When the wizards stepped into St Paul's, the Dean sighed. 'Most excellent work. I've always thought it worth a fire or two, and for that matter some Parmesan cheese: wonderful architecture, intelligent design! Old Bill got it right, didn't he: "What a piece of work is a man." I do not claim the credit, but these people have done some wonderful things, you must admit. With our help, of course – the occasional nudge here and there ...'

'No,' said Rincewind. 'I've explored Roundworld all too often, one way or the other, and let me tell you, my friend, nudges or no nudges, that it is a good job I can run fast. But I'll tell you what: let's go up to the Whispering Gallery and tell the Americans there is a prize for the loudest noise – how about that?'

'Americans?' said the Dean.

'Yes, great travellers in Roundworld, which they secretly think belongs to them; but salt of the Earth, even so – bearing in mind that salt occasionally gets under the skin. Mind you, we must remember that *they* were the ones who persevered in the attempt to get to the Moon. In my book that shows the right attitude, yes! What is it you want?'

This was directly to the person who was suggesting to the Dean and Rincewind that they pay him fifteen pounds each to go to the Whispering Gallery, and Rincewind hissed to the Dean that they should have gone invisible, as usual.

But the Dean, once called pig-headed by Mustrum Ridcully, said, 'My dear sir, do you know to whom you speak? I brought this little world into being! I really do not believe that *I* have to pay to go *anywhere.*' Rincewind grabbed the Dean's hand and tugged, but the Dean raised his voice and added, 'It's a matter of principle.' A phrase that in any area of conflict had something of the overtones of the *Titanic* – it would sink you every time.

Rincewind managed to convince the staff and subsequently the constabulary that the Dean, although bellowing his celestial *bona fides*, had been recently hit on the head by a piece of falling masonry and would never do it again. And he, that is to say Rincewind, would see to it that he, the Dean, got home – although Rincewind took both of them to Australia, just because he liked the place.

As they sat addressing a bucket of Oysters Kilpatrick, the Dean said, 'You know, I'm getting annoyed. People: they think it's all about *them*!'

'Well,' said Rincewind, 'one of their most important holy books tells them that this is so; indeed, there are some people who seriously believe that their *job* is to use up everything on the planet so that their god will make them another one. When I read that, I thought, *Oh dear me, aren't we going to be surprised!*'

'It sounds to me like toxic advice,' said the Dean, 'but surely they have brains? I mean, we *know* they do; though there is politics of course, and mercantile greed – monkey stuff. And surely there will be a lot of wise men, as opposed to wise guys, even though wise guys have *money* behind them. No wise man could sell that kind of bad news, though, even if it *is* important; it would take a fairly brave person to stand up and say that no matter what is in their particular holy book there are certainly some parts that need re-evaluation.' He sighed. 'Alas, apparently belief in a god gives a believer the right to have their views taken seriously. It's superstition – you don't want to upset a god.'

'Well, I've managed to upset several,' Rincewind said. 'I think it keeps them on their toes. You know how it is; you can get quite stale unless you are occasionally tested.' He added, rather gloomily, 'It happens to me quite a lot.'

But the Dean wasn't listening. 'It's not all bad, though, or for that matter all that stupid,' he continued. 'Science works and is *seen* to work – we made sure of *that* – even though there are still those who believe, for example, in a holy book written in the Iron Age by a committee of old men. Admittedly, it was right in some parts.'

Rincewind butted in. 'The tiny little swimming things did come first, and after that the fish, which wasn't a bad guess. I know! I was there!'

The Dean helped himself to the last oyster and said, 'Do you think I should materialise in one of their important places and very carefully tell one of them what they are doing wrong? I can't help but feeling some responsibility, silly though it sounds.'

'Don't,' said Rincewind emphatically. 'You will only get nailed to something; although from what I can find out, the nails nowadays have become a lot more subtle – they'd give you a very big prize and a hearty handshake, and subsequently tell one another that as an academic you are out of touch with reality, despite wading through the wretched stuff for your whole long career.'

'Nothing can be done, then?' said the Dean.

'No, not really. Small things in the sea and underground will survive, but at the rate the resources of the planet are being destroyed, I can't see any room for civilisation again. Maybe it would be a good idea to come back in a million years' time. There may be something left.'

The Dean was not one to take no for an answer, and tried again. 'Or, of course, innocence will prevail!'

'Yes,' said Rincewind gloomily. 'It might. And *I* might prefer horses, but I suspect the automobiles are breeding faster ...'

FOURTEEN

A BETTER MOUSETRAP

Rincewind has a soft spot for horses – which unfortunately leave soft spots for everyone else. Even so, he prefers horses to automobiles. You don't have to *make* a horse – they make themselves from previous horses.

Cars are made individually, by people. They are designed to serve a purpose, which was present in the designer's mind before the cars were made, and indeed *caused* it to be made. Without people, you could leave the Earth on its own for a billion years and it wouldn't produce a car. But it did produce a horse, without human intervention, in a rather shorter period.

Scientists believe that horses evolved. The proof includes an iconic series of fossils, showing exactly *how* they evolved, between 54 million and a million years ago. The sequence begins with a horse-like mammal a mere 0.4 metres long. This genus was originally given the poetic name *Eohippus* ('dawn horse'), but has now been renamed *Hyracotherium* because of the rules of taxonomy, which in this case managed to deliver a silly result.* It moves on to *Mesohippus*, 35 million years old and 0.6 metres long; then *Merychippus*, 15 million

---

* In 1841 Richard Owen, a leading palaeontologist, found an incomplete fossil that he thought was a hyrax (because of its teeth) and assigned it to a new genus, *Hyracotherium*. In 1876 Othniel Marsh discovered a complete skeleton, obviously horse-like, and assigned it to another new genus, *Eohippus* (dawn horse). Later it became clear that the two fossils belonged to the same genus, and by the rules of taxonomy, the name that was the first to be published won. So the evocative 'dawn horse' was lost, and a scientific misconception was preserved.

years old and 1 metre long; then *Pliohippus*, 8 million years old and 1.3 metres long; and finally (so far) *Equus*, essentially the same as the modern horse, 1 million years old and 1.6 metres long.

Taxonomists can track, in great detail, the sequence of changes that occurred in this lineage of ancient horse ancestors; for example, in the animal's teeth and hooves. They can also track the timing of these changes, because rocks can be dated. So now evidence from geology can be thrown into the mix. It would take only one fossil species in the wrong stratum of rock to cast doubt on the evolutionary story. The succession of rocks, their ages as determined by a variety of different methods, the evolutionary sequences of fossils, and the DNA of horses and modern relatives – all agree, to a remarkable extent.

There is similar evidence that humans evolved from ape-like ancestors, but the story is not as neat and tidy, with many potentially coexisting species. These ancestral hominins evolved from other mammals, which evolved from reptiles, which evolved from amphibians, which evolved from fish.* Rincewind knows how land animals evolved: he was there. Roundworld's inhabitants weren't, which is one reason why they argue about what happened.

Both William Paley, in his *Natural Theology* of 1802, and modern creationists, believe that horses and humans were designed by God, and that these creatures' modern forms are exactly those given to them at the moment of their creation. The hypothesis of intelligent design attempts to infer the existence of an unspecified cosmic designer (we all know who, but it would be unscientific to say so ...) from the existence of complex structures in living organisms. Darwin argued that design in this sense is neither necessary, nor plausible: instead, living creatures evolved. Almost all biologists agree. Neo-Darwinism underpins those ideas with genes.

---

* Since 1881, fossil discoveries have inserted a whole series of intermediates between fish and amphibians: *Osteolepis, Eusthenopteron, Panderichthys, Tiktaalik, Elginerpeton, Obruchevichthys, Ventastega, Acanthostega, Ichthyostega, Hynerpeton, Tulerpeton, Pederpes, Eryops.*

Evolved, or designed?

Maybe the difference isn't as great as most of us think.

When design is presented as an alternative to evolution, there is an unstated assumption that the two are very different. Design is a conscious process carried out by a designer who knows what result he, she, or it is aiming at, and whose purpose is to achieve it. Evolution selects, from a lot of random variants, changes that lead to some kind of improvement in survival prospects; then it makes lots of copies of the successes. It has no aims and no purpose. It is not 'blind chance', a description that creationists often use, forgetting (we are being charitable) the crucial element of selection. But the process of evolution is exploratory, not goal-seeking.

On closer examination, however, design and evolution are much more similar than most of us imagine. Technology appears to be designed, but mostly it evolves. Improved technology is selected because it works better, and it then displaces earlier technology. This process is analogous to the way that natural selection causes organisms to evolve, so it is reasonable to speak of technology evolving. (The analogy is loose and should not be taken to extremes. Technical drawings or CAD designs are poor analogues of genes.) Selection of technology may appear to be by human agency, but it is highly constrained. Success is decided by vote, and voters vote with their wallets. The inventor's intentions are almost irrelevant. Just as in biological evolution, the main constraint is *what works*.

Because of the difficulties inherent in the simple-minded approach to design that Paley proposed – because designers don't go straight from idea to design to product – we should look carefully at just how designs appear in technology. That changes our attitude to 'design' in nature too.

Most human designs don't work the first time round. Most jugs still don't pour well. It's cheaper to invent a new type of jug, even if it's no good, than it is to pay licensing fees for one that works. The better mousetrap, even when it is genuinely better, is a minor variation on hundreds of previous mousetraps. Usually.

Mousetrap evolution is a coherent process, not just a succession of unrelated gadgets. The same goes for bicycles, cars, computers, even jugs. Each new capability causes a particular technological path to branch, leading to new roads. Stuart Kauffman, one of the founders of complexity science, introduced the term 'the adjacent possible' to mean the possible behaviours of a complex system that are just a short step away from wherever it currently is. The adjacent possible is a list of what potentially might develop. In a sense, it *is* the system's potential.

Organic evolution proceeds by invading the adjacent possible. Invasions that fail aren't invasions at all, and nothing much changes. Successful invasions don't just change the system that does the invading; they change the adjacent possible of *everything*. When insects first took to the air, the ones that stayed on the ground were suddenly in danger of predation from above, even though they hadn't changed at all. Likewise, technology advances by continually invading the adjacent possible. Technological evolution is faster than organic evolution because human minds can use their imaginations to jump into the adjacent possible and see if it works, without actually doing it. They can also copy, which organic evolution does only rarely, aside from reproducing near copies of organisms. These are processes that generate paths and histories, and contexts in which some evolutionary trajectories are viable, but others are not. Only a few select trajectories work. In contrast, thinking in terms of innovations that generate products makes the design process work like magic.

There are a few useful analogies between technological evolution and organic evolution, and a lot of misleading ones. Comparisons between organic evolution and economics abound in the literature, and nearly all of them are misleading, from social Darwinism to the 'cost' of reproduction. Some evolutionary trajectories, however, can usefully be compared to biological ones. Examples include telegraph

→ telephone, especially international with undersea cables as investment, pens → word processors, and rockets → space elevators, which
we'll come to shortly. These changes get rid of old constraints at each
subsequent recursion.

There are biological precedents, in which evolution did *not* lead
to increased complexity (as measured by DNA information), but
the reverse. One is the evolution of mammals. Mammals have *less*
DNA than their 'more primitive' amphibian ancestors, a trick that
can be pulled off because mother mammals control the temperature of their developing embryos by keeping them inside their own
bodies. Amphibians need huge quantities of genetic instructions to
plan for many different contingencies, as their embryos grow in a
pond, subject to the unpredictable vagaries of the weather. Mammals
dispense with this excess baggage by investing in temperature control.

With the expanding possibilities of the chemical/physical universe
as a substrate, and organic evolution as a model for an emergent
phase space, we should be asking 'What are the constraints on
technology, if any?' rather than 'What is the pattern of technological advance?' Sometimes there are persistent patterns. Moore's Law
states that computing power doubles every eighteen months. It has
worked for decades, even though (indeed, because) technologies
have changed dramatically. Some experts think that the increase in
power will shortly have to slow down, but others remain convinced
that new ideas, often already visible, will keep it going.

Our culture sometimes seems to follow evolutionary trajectories too. As individuals, we respond to the cultures in which we live,
and we are conducted into our technological future as it changes
progressively. As far as cultures go, this is an evolutionary process.
From a human viewpoint, however, such progressive change looks
like the development of a more complex living system, a socio-
dynamic. Is technology cancerous, born of mutation as it burst out
of its hunter-gatherer background, as it evolves into new forms? Or
is it developmental, exploiting new organisations as it invents them

but maintaining an adaptable but stable path, just like a developing embryo? An embryo destroys many organised structures, and kills many of its cells, as it develops. It builds scaffolding and throws it away when it is no longer needed.

From the point of view of the individual human, caught up in a technological rat race, this stress is clearly a symptom of social pathology, as Alvin Toffler argued in *Future Shock*. In contrast, looked at culturally, it is natural development. This difference of viewpoint resembles the two ways to describe a thinking mind: nerve cells and consciousness. More generally, not only can every complex system be described in several non-overlapping ways: it can also be described on several levels ... as concrete or as a bridge; as an architectural bridge or as a weak point for an enemy invasion.

Human evolution occurs on two levels: embryological development and cultural development. Neither process is preformational, with all necessary ingredients already present. Neither is a straightforward blueprint: make it like *this*. In both, evolutionary changes occur through complicity between several programmes, each of which affects the future of the others. As time passes, each programme not only affects its own future by its own internal dynamics: it also changes its future by the changes it causes in the other programmes.

To what extent are those changes predictable or accidental? There is a difference here between two modern viewpoints, one associated with the palaeontologist Simon Conway Morris in *Life's Solution: Inevitable Humans in a Lonely Universe*, and the other with the late Stephen Jay Gould in *Wonderful Life*. This difference is crucial to the issue of design in evolution.

Gould made great play of the variety of the animals represented by the fossils in the Burgess Shale, deposited at the start of the Cambrian period about 570 million years ago. These fossils had been described by previous biologists, but Morris reworked and reconstructed them. He classified these fossils into a wide range of morphological types; in fact, many more basic kinds of animal design ('phyla') than had been assigned previously. Gould used this wide range of body designs, only a few of which have descendants among present-day creatures, to argue that life can do almost anything by way of morphology, even in its fundamental or basic structure, and that the organisms that now exist are accidental survivals from the much vaster range that existed at the start of the Cambrian.

Morris, however, has come to believe the opposite, namely: because some of the many themes have converged to produce similar beasts, some specific designs must be winners, no matter how they are realised. Therefore any wide array of different body structures will necessarily evolve to generate much the same spectrum that we observe today, automatically selected because those are the body-plans that work best. The fossil record contains many cases of this kind of convergence:[*] ichthyosaurs and dolphins have evolved to look like sharks and other carnivorous fishes, because that's the shape that's most efficient for a fishy predator. In short, Morris believes that if we were to find living creatures on a similar planet to Earth, or if we were to run Earthly evolution again, then much the same range of animal designs would appear. Aliens on a world like ours would be much like us, even if their biochemistry were totally different.

In contrast, Gould believed, as we do,[†] that in such a rerun the resulting spectrum of life forms would not resemble the current ones at all. Different designs, fundamentally different body forms, would be just as likely as the ones that happen to exist now. The current body-plans are just a contingent, accidental collection that happened to survive. Aliens, even the highest ones, would most likely be very different in design from us, whatever world they evolved on. Including a reboot of ours.

---

[*] Jack recalls a bright Irish student who, in an exam question about convergent evolution, defined it as 'where the organs of two descendants are more alike than they were in the common ancestor'.

[†] See Jack Cohen and Ian Stewart, *What Does a Martian Look Like?*

The old view of the role of genes in Darwinian evolution emphasised mutations: random changes to DNA sequences. However, at least in sexual species, the main source of genetic variability is actually recombination: mix-and-match shuffling of gene variants from the parents. New mutations are not needed to innovate; new combinations of existing genes are sufficient. The diversity of available gene variations can be traced back to much older mutations, but you don't need a mutation *now* to change an organism.

All biologists now agree that the body-plans of organisms are not built up piece by piece, mutation by mutation, but have been selected by recombination. Instead of mutations to new genetic variants, we find recombinations of many ancient mutations. These are sorted from kits of compatible parts in every generation, not put together higgledy-piggledy and expected to work. If, as seems plausible, only a few developmental trajectories can lead to larvae that can feed and grow into working adults, compared to the huge number that can't, then it is to be expected that the successful designs are all separated, without intermediate forms bridging the gaps. 'Missing links' need not be missing – or links – because continuous variation is not required in a discontinuous process.

By looking at so-called *r*-strategists, animals like plaice and oysters whose larvae comprise only a few developmentally competent ones among a majority that aren't, we can see how this is achieved today. What it does not tell us – what distinguishes the Morris and Gould views – is whether the successful designs are out there in some Platonic organism-space, waiting to be found, or whether the organisms have all invented their own, unpredictable, designs as they went along. Morris, a Christian, believes the former: the appearance of design is the revelation of transcendental attractors in God's design-space of possible organisms. We, however, believe that there are so many possible ways of being a successful organism, so many effective designs, that the drunkard's walk of evolution keeps finding them, even though they are sparsely embedded in the vast majority of failures.

In particular, we think that intelligent design focuses too narrowly on the evolution of *specific* structures found today, such as the precise molecular configuration of haemoglobin or the bacterial motor. In retrospect, these structures seem highly improbable; if nature were to aim for them again, it would almost certainly miss. But evolution selected these structures when it encountered them. What matters is how likely it is that evolution could find *some* such structure, not that *specific* one. If there are many suitable structures, then a process that automatically homes in on anything that seems to be an improvement has a good chance of finding one of them.

Think how improbable *you* are. If two genomes had not combined just so, if that egg and that sperm had not come together, if your father hadn't met your mother at the dance, if the wartime bomb in the harbour had hit your grandfather instead of being a hundred metres away, if Napoleon had won the Battle of Waterloo, or if victory had gone the other way in the American War of Independence, if the nascent Earth had not acquired an ocean, or the ripples in the Big Bang had been slightly different … you wouldn't be here.

The odds that you exist are infinitesimal.

No. The odds that you exist are certain, *because you do.*

The processes that led to you are robust, and at each stage would have led to something similar, albeit different, if run again. No complex process ever produces the same result twice. But if it produces a similar result instead, that makes its consequences certain, not utterly unlikely. Only fine details will be different, second time around. The lottery of life is quite different when seen through the eyes of the eventual winners, rather than those of a random competitor before the contest has happened.

It's tempting to assume that the evolution of technology can tell us about organic evolution, or vice versa, but these processes lead to apparent design in very different ways. However, there is a grand overall similarity in how we *think* about both systems, particularly how our thinking has changed over the last few years. The appearance of design is the most dramatic element in both systems. Although its provenance is different in the two cases, we are no longer surprised by it. We have realised that the universe is *not* doomed by increasing entropy to an eventual 'heat death', a traditional but somewhat misleading term which actually means that the universe will end up as a structureless lukewarm soup. Instead, the universe 'makes it up as it goes along', and what it makes up are designs. In that sense, at least, the appearance of new design in both technical and organic systems can be considered comparable. But it's important not to stretch the metaphor too far.

Cultures can also be seen as evolving. In many ways, cultural evolution sits between organic and technological evolution. Advanced human societies make their members different and varied. All societies produce numerous distinct roles, from those limited by sex and age, such as childbearing or going to school, to those that seem to be chosen by the individual: warrior, accountant, thief. There is a division among sociologists that is comparable to that between Morris and Gould. Some believe that the roles are in some sense transcendent or universal; they look for proto-accountants in 'primitive' hunter-gatherer societies. Carl Gustav Jung's theory of archetypes, such as the persona, the shadow, and the self. In his view, these were extremely ancient common images derived from humanity's collective subconscious, which affected how we interpret the world. Others, however, believe that some roles in different societies, even though they look similar and the names translate similarly, can be fundamentally different: a Japanese car worker has a different worldview from that of his English equivalent, and occupies a different societal slot.

Both sociological viewpoints can provide useful insights: different societies, like different ecologies and different cultures, provide diverse roles for their members. The cultural invention of generic occupations is comparable to the organic invention of things like chordates, trilobites, muscles and nests. It is also comparable to the technological inventions of – say – bicycles, the internal combustion engine, wheat and rope. Money in human societies is usefully analogous to the way cells produce and exchange energy, using the molecules ADP and ATP (adenosine di- and tri-phosphate). Indeed, ATP is often called the unit of molecular currency. The appearance of new designs in organic evolution, in cultures, in technology, and even in language, can usefully be compared. Even so, such comparisons must be made very carefully and not pushed beyond reasonable limits.

The idea that technology evolves is not the orthodox view, wherein design and evolution are considered to be opposites. Design in technology is usually seen as being invented, not as having evolved. This assumption lies at the core of Paley's famous analogy between a living creature and a watch. Watches are intricate devices, designed and made by an intelligent agency. Therefore, if you find something equally intricate in living creatures, it must also be designed, and the creatures must have been made by an intelligent agency. Therefore there must have been a cosmic designer, QED. The same assumption motivates the current hypothesis of intelligent design, which is basically Paley's argument restated using examples from modern biochemistry.

However, analysis of the history of nearly all inventions shows them either to be developments of previous technology, that is to say adaptations, or perversions of some technology in a different sphere. (A few do seem to come out of thin air, with no significant precursors.) The biological term for such things is 'exaptations', a word introduced by Gould and Elizabet Vrba in the 1980s. It refers to an organic or a technological development that arises from an entirely different structure or function. An example is the use of feathers for flight. Feathers first appeared in dinosaurs, but their skeletal structure shows that the early feathered dinosaurs didn't use their feathers to fly. We can't be certain what they did use them for, but the most plausible functions are for warmth or for sexual display. It may well have been both. Later, feathers turned out to be useful for wings and flight, and birds evolved. Nature is an opportunist. A technological example of exaptation is the use of disc-recorded sound for music. Edison originally developed the phonograph for a more serious purpose, to record for posterity the last words of famous men and the historical speeches of politicians. He greatly deplored its use for frivolities like music, but accepted payments gracefully, nevertheless.

Exaptation is one of the less obvious tricks that evolution has up its sleeve, and is often the solution to evolutionary puzzles, in which a particular function can occur only when several interrelated structures apparently have to appear simultaneously, but none of them can perform that function on its own. Although it's tempting to deduce that such structures can't evolve at all, they can if exaptations occur. Then the structures concerned initially perform different functions.

A classic instance is the bacterial flagellum, a structure that proponents of intelligent design argue cannot possibly have evolved by any conceivable route. The flagellum allows some bacteria to move of their own volition. Its most important component is a tiny molecular motor, which causes the flagellum to rotate, much as the motor of a boat turns the propeller. The bacterial motor* is made from a large number of different protein molecules. Until recently, evolutionary biologists could offer no convincing explanation of the origin of such a complex structure by natural selection.

In 1978 Robert MacNab wrote: 'One can only marvel at the intricacy, in a simple bacterium, of the total motor and sensory system ... What advantage could derive ... from a "preflagellum" [meaning a

---

* We say 'the' motor, because everyone does, but different bacteria have different motors. Darwin was puzzled why the deity would design hundreds of very similar barnacles, all of different species; we may similarly wonder why an intelligent designer would intervene in the normal process of evolution to equip dozens of bacteria with individually designed motors.

subset of its components], and yet what is the probability of "simultaneous" development?' In 1996 Michael Behe, a biochemist and leading proponent of intelligent design, repeated MacNab's worries in *Darwin's Black Box*, together with several similar evolutionary puzzles. He concluded that while many, indeed most, features of living creatures have evolved, some cannot possibly have done so because they are irreducibly complex: if you remove any component, they cease to function.

It's a genuine puzzle, but before invoking some unspecified genie-of-the-lamp, without independent evidence that it exists, we ought to make sure that conventional evolutionary processes definitely can't hack it. Intelligent design doesn't just argue that some specific evolutionary route is wrong: it claims a proof that *in principle* no such route can exist. If you're going to invoke a general principle of this kind to assert the existence of a supernatural being or a highly advanced cosmic designer, you need to close any loopholes in your logic. Otherwise your entire philosophy will be built on sand, whatever actually happened. The Book of Genesis could be true in every detail, but your supposed proof would still be nonsense if its logic were defective.

In response to intelligent design, biochemists have taken a closer look at the proteins in the bacterial motor and the associated genes. The most prominent components of these motors are rings of proteins, which are very common in evolution. What use is a ring? It has a hole. Holes are amazingly useful to a bacterium or a cell, because they can function as pores or sockets. Pores let in molecules from the outside world, or expel molecules into the outside world. Different-sized pores deal with different-sized molecules. That's something that natural selection can work on: a mutation in the DNA that codes for the protein can lead to one with a similar, but slightly different, shape or size. As soon as a pore does a useful job, evolution can find a pore that is better at doing that job, if there is one.

Sockets allow bacteria or cells to attach new structures, either inside or outside the cell membrane. Many different molecules can fit into the same socket, and again, evolution has plenty of opportunities to work with. What began as a pore can become a socket if something happens to fit into it. When the two modules come together, their function may change. Exaptation demolishes irreducible complexity as an obstacle to evolution. You don't even have to prove exactly how a given structure evolved, because irreducible complexity allegedly rules out not just the actual route, but *any conceivable one.*

So let's conceive.

A number of biologists have attempted to deduce a plausible or likely evolutionary route to a bacterial motor, from DNA and other biochemical evidence. This turns out not to be especially difficult. Many details are still provisional, as is all science, but the story is now sufficiently complete to disprove the contention that the motor exhibits a type of complexity that rules out *all* evolutionary explanations. Agreed, that doesn't prove that the current evolutionary explanation is correct. That must be confirmed, or denied, by further scientific investigations. But it's quite different from asking whether, in principle, any such explanation can exist.

The most fully developed synthesis of these proposals, put together by Nicholas Matzke, starts with a general-purpose pore. This evolves into a pore with more specific functions. At this early stage, the structure is not a motor, but it already has a very useful, entirely different, function: it can transport molecules out of the cell. In fact, it is recognisable as a primitive version of so-called Type III Export Apparatus, which exists in modern bacteria, and DNA sequences support this. Further changes, in which the pore's function is successively improved, or changed by exaptation, provide an entirely plausible evolutionary route to the bacterial motor, increasingly supported by DNA evidence.*

---

* N.J. Matzke, Evolution in (Brownian) space: a model for the origin of the bacterial flagellum, www.talkdesign.org/faqs/flagellum.html.

Yes, if you take away enough parts of the bacterial motor, then it might not be a very good motor any more. But evolution didn't know it was supposed to be making a motor.

So 'design' isn't what it is often thought to be, even for human technology, let alone biology. Each innovative step may be driven by human intentions, but what works, and what passes on to later technology, evolves. To some extent, cars evolved from horse-drawn carriages, and a ballpoint pen is the lineal descendant of a quill made from a feather. We can legitimately compare these developments to mammals evolving from a Devonian fish that came out of the water onto land, or to our little middle-ear bones being the lineal descendants of bony gill structures in that fish.

Evolution is not efficient. It throws an awful lot of things away. Innumerable land vertebrate species have gone extinct. Similarly, most human designs don't work. From the enormous number on offer, only a few develop into sophisticated structure/function niches. We are all bound by tradition, as well as by functional constraints that require any new development to fulfil the same functions as its ancestor. There's a classic example: Apollo rockets were moved to their launching-pads on rails that were much too close together for stability, because the gauge of America's railways came from mine railways that were two horses wide. So the Moon project was jeopardised by horse's asses.

To be specific, let's think about better mousetraps. Mousetrap evolution is a process, not just a succession of models; it branches into the future. The pattern that has a metal bar coming down and (one hopes) breaking the mouse's neck, has expanded into dozens of different models, some computer-controlled. Those that trap the mouse in a metal tube, or a cage, are more like descendants of lobster-pots, but these too have performed what biologists would call an adaptive radiation: we found seven different kinds, with sprung doors or elastic apertures for entry.

The same goes for bicycles, cars or computers: they all adaptively radiate into the future. Each new ability, such as computer control – a logic chip – on a particular technical road branches into new roads. Think of the familiar cat flap, now available in versions that allow your own cat, wearing its magnetic collar, in or out, but exclude foreign cats. Or fancy electronic ones that verify your cat's ID. Full-body scanners to detect terrorist cats carrying exploding mice cannot be far away. Just as in organic evolution, the adjacent possible is continually being invaded: possibilities just one step away from current practice are tried, rather unoriginally.

We usually think of this as technical development, not innovation, unless it is in an unexpected direction: Teflon used for non-stick frying-pans, or penguins' wings used for swimming. Most aquatic vertebrates, unlike these birds that have become secondarily aquatic, use their tails, not their fins, for propulsion. Such more original changes of direction are best thought of as exaptations rather than adaptations. Or, to use a less biological term, genuine innovations.

Among those who accept evolution as a reasonable metaphor for many examples of progress in technology, it used to be thought that the major difference between technical and organic evolution is that technological evolution is Lamarckian – named after the French naturalist Jean-Baptiste Lamarck, a contemporary of Darwin – whereas organic evolution is Darwinian. In Lamarckian evolution, acquired characteristics can be inherited – if a blacksmith acquires strong arms because of his work, his sons should also have strong arms. In Darwinian evolution, that's not possible. Neo-Darwinism illuminates the difference: heritable characteristics are those that are determined by genes.

Lately, this distinction has become a bit blurred, and each mechanism has acquired features that were thought to be characteristic of the other. Technical development has borrowed a trick from evolution to construct so-called genetic algorithms for the development of new products. Digitised designs are shuffled, by analogy with recombination, the way biological reproduction shuffles gene variants from both parents. The next technological generation to survive this process combines the more useful features of previous generations. Sometimes it has new emergent properties, which are selected if they prove useful, and are retained. Often the final design is incomprehensible to a human engineer. Evolution need not obey human narrativium.

The phenomenon of genetic assimilation, which is entirely Darwinian, can look very Lamarckian. Changing a population progressively by selecting genetic combinations that work can change the thresholds at which particular capabilities come into play. As a result, effects that originally depended on some environmental stimulus can happen without that stimulus in later generations. For example, the skin on the soles of our feet gets thicker when we walk regularly, an acquired characteristic; however, genetic recombinations that provide babies with thicker skin on their feet from the start make this process more effective, and so are selected for. Any new feature, acquired or not, that *works* – that improves the chances of surviving to reproduce – reveals a feature that Darwinian evolution could blunder into and exploit. Genetic assimilation may indeed be the usual way that originally responsive adaptations get built in to the developmental schedule.

In particular, the old distinction between Lamarck and Darwin has lost its power to distinguish technical from organic evolution. But that doesn't imply that there are no significant differences. It's tempting to think that one obvious aspect of technological evolution surely can't apply to Darwinian evolution: *imagining* a possibility before designing a technique or gadget to implement it. Human technology is born in the imagination of a series of inventors or discoverers: 'What would happen if … ?' is a theoretical exploration of Kauffman's adjacent possible. Much of the time, imagining possibilities leads to hypothetical new inventions being rejected without bothering to make them or test them: they wouldn't work because ... *or* no one could use them because ... *or* they would be too expensive ... *or* they wouldn't perform well enough to displace the widget that already does the job very well.

It doesn't seem possible that this imaginative process could have an organic analogue – but it does. In 1896 the psychologist James Mark Baldwin wondered whether animals carrying out behavioural experiments might be drawn into the evolutionary process, in effect by imagining what would happen if they could perform some new task that was actually beyond them. For instance, an okapi is like a giraffe, but its neck and legs are of normal length. Suppose that an adventurous okapi, for example, kept reaching up in an attempt to browse on the lowest branches of trees, despite repeated failure. *Because* it failed, this would be analogous to imagination. But occasional success could favour okapi with slightly longer necks and legs, leading to a giraffe. This process is often called the Baldwin effect.

A few years ago, we observed some animal behaviour that could well become the root of such an evolutionary trajectory – an exaptation in the making. Plecostomid catfish ('plecs') are common scavengers in larger aquariums, cleaning algae off the glass with their sucker-like mouths. In the wild, they can hold tight to smooth rocks as they glean the algal film; they also have effective armour with barbed bony supports in their dorsal and pectoral fins. In aquaria, these characteristics give them an entirely different ability, which we saw a plec exploiting in the Mathematics Institute common room at the University of Warwick. This plec's natural abilities made it much better than other fish at garnering floating pellets of food. It did this using a method quite alien to wild plecs: it turned on its back and used its sucker-mouth to take in soggy pellets, while its spiky fins kept off the competition. So a catfish mouth, adapted for taking food from rocks, can be exapted to take food pellets from the water surface, especially if the fish concerned has effective defences, and the food is soft.

Future genetic assimilation could easily build this kind of exapted behaviour into the genes of the plec population. It could be selected for, and then adapted along an evolutionary trajectory, so that a plec would take food from the surface *normally* in just this way.

In fact, something of the kind has probably happened already – though not in descendants of the Mathematics Institute plec, which had none. The fish in question is the upside-down catfish *Synodontis nigriventris*,* which takes insects from the surface of the water in the wild using a similar technique. We have, then, both ends of a plausible evolutionary trajectory. It starts, perhaps, with a hungry catfish alerted to a food mass on the surface, near it in shallow water; perhaps a rotting, floating insect carcass. The catfish turns over in its attempts to get its mouth near to the tempting morsel, and even if it mostly makes a hash of this, any occasional success is rewarded. It will now be sensitised to this source of food, and might haunt the shallows for more of them. Its offspring, growing up in the same environment, are then more likely to be selected for similar behaviour if genetic changes can make it more effective.

This scenario contradicts Stephen Jay Gould's assertion in *The Flamingo's Smile* that adaptations like the upside-down feeding of the flamingo, scooping up crustaceans from saline lakes, must involve a single radical departure from the normal use of the beak. Animals can try out little behavioural experiments, and if they are rewarded, these can become built into their subsequent behaviour. Then, if the reward is as important as a new source of food or novel access to mates, natural selection can improve it.

Technical evolution can avoid such time-wasting, progeny-wasting, and new-function-wasting aspects of organic evolution in two ways. The first, we have discussed already: human minds can attempt to

---

* The name means 'dark belly', because when it swims upside down, its back has become light like most fishes' bellies, and its belly dark.

jump into the adjacent possible and see if it works 'in the imagination'. Can we imagine an aeroplane ten times the size, and what would need to be changed for it to work? If we exaggerated the length of a bicycle frame and had the cyclist lean back, how could he see the road? Do we then want him on his front? Both have been tried, and are excellent examples: technical results of our imagination playing in the adjacent possible.

The other trick that minds can do to improve technology is to copy: to take a technical trick used in one invention and to spread its use to others. That trick, except for a few cases where genes have achieved horizontal transfer between species, is impossible for organic evolution: each lineage must invent for itself. A recent spread of this kind has been the use of digital switches in a variety of machines from toasters and children's toys to automobiles. The big one before that was the use of plastics to replace metals in the nursery, kitchen and laboratory. Before that, transparent plastics, mostly acrylics, had been used to replace glass in many applications. The progressive use of semiconductor technology is giving us solar panels, tiny refrigerating or heating elements, and a new family of very efficient light bulbs: white-light LEDs. Banks of coloured LEDs can now be tuned to give different lighting conditions; bright white light is not conducive to sleep and can be replaced with softer tones. Flexible television/computer screens, which can be rolled up like paper, already exist in the laboratory, and are not far from commercial production. An entire book has just been encoded in DNA, and a human face has been printed on a human hair.

In biological evolution, it used to be thought that environmental 'niches', such as predatory behaviour, were already available and waiting to be occupied, rather as though some cosmic script had already written down all the possible things that an organism might do. Now it is thought that organisms construct niches as they evolve; for instance, you can't occupy the dog-flea niche until there are dogs.

Even taking copying into account, the analogous questions of competition and niche-construction in technology are as important as they are in the natural world, and they too force the evolution of new products. A good example was the colonisation of the market-place in the 1970s by VHS videotapes, even though its rival Betamax was much better in several respects. As in natural ecologies, it often happens that a less-adapted, often foreign, invader exploits the ecosystem more effectively, forcing the demise of well-established local species. The grey squirrel, for example, carries a disease that decimates indigenous red squirrels, much as the Spanish invaded South America and destroyed Inca and Maya empires. The red squirrel was better-adapted to its original environment, but the arrival of the invading grey squirrel changed that environment; in particular, it now included grey squirrels and their disease organisms. The change was sudden, biological warfare rather than the usual sedate pace of natural selection in a slowly changing environment.

In the technical world, then, there do exist processes resembling those of organic ecosystems. Many of them are recursive, affecting their own development: supermarkets make their own ecosystem of consumers, just as dogs create a new niche for dog-fleas. This makes questions about the design of technology much more difficult, because there are few real innovations, but many exaptations, copyings and adaptational trajectories. Only a few really novel tricks can be claimed to have a human designer in a non-evolutionary sense.

There is a trajectory of development for a technological product: a car starting from carriages and an engine, steam or internal-combustion; a radio starting from a crystal set and headphones; a bicycle starting as a penny-farthing and evolving through the sit-up-and-beg still seen all over China and India to the mountain bikes and lie-down versions of the latest adaptive radiation.

These are paths through our cultural history, and they make their own contexts as they evolve. The car creates vast and important areas of our cities where cars are built, where auto workers live, where the suppliers of parts have some of their factories and warehouses. When we give little Johnnie a bicycle on his seventh birthday, we introduce him to a new world that has grazed knees, gears, punctures, comparison with Fred's bike … When the transistor radio erupted into Western culture in the 1960s, it changed the relationships of teenagers to each other and to pop stars, though nothing like as much as the mobile phone has changed all of our lives in the last few years. Alexander Graham Bell, on a promotional tour of his invention the telephone, so impressed one city's mayor that he is said to have declared: 'What a wonderful invention; every town should have one.'

Artefacts evolve, and the functions they perform get better, wider, cheaper. But they also change the society around them, so that their 'improved' next generation already has the ground prepared for it. The Ford Model T would not have been viable without gas stations, which had appeared to service the much more expensive previous generation of automobiles. In turn, the Model T and other similar affordable automobiles with privacy in the back seat changed much of the sex life of the young men and women who had access to them. Society's rules change as the Ford Model T, the transistor radio, central heating, subway travel and mobile phones affect their context, and the context in turn constrains or directs the further evolution of the product.

Nearly all inventions don't follow that kind of successful path; like nearly all species of organisms, they prosper for a little while but then die out. The few that do survive find a trajectory that takes them into the future. Frequently they move into a whole new phase space of possibilities, where their original design is effectively useless, but the new world now has an *improved* design. Like a genuine Stone-Age axe that's had its handle and blade changed several times, we find a new world with a new artefact and a new function.

In *The Science of Discworld III* we described how apparently rigid limitations on the energy needed to put a person or cargo in orbit around the Earth could, in principle, be overcome by changing the context. If you use a rocket, the amount of energy needed to get a 100-kilogramme man up to synchronous orbit can be calculated using Newton's laws of motion. It is the difference in potential energy caused by the planet's gravity well. You can't change that, so at first the limitation seems foolproof.

In the mid-1970s, however, a wholly new suggestion was made: the space bolas. Essentially this is a giant Ferris wheel in orbit. The traveller gets into the cabin as it swings past the upper atmosphere, and gets out again when it approaches the furthest point from Earth. A succession of such gadgets can deposit him in synchronous orbit a few weeks later.

A third step in the ladder of technology, not practical yet but already being discussed by engineers, is the space elevator. The science fiction writer and futurologist Arthur C. Clarke was one of several people who had this idea: take a 'rope' up to synchronous orbit and let it down to an equatorial landing-strip. The result would be a material link from a point in synchronous orbit to the ground. Once this is set up, a system of cabins and pulleys-and-weights like those used in skyscraper elevators could take a person up to orbit very efficiently. Counterweights, or another man coming down, would reduce the cost to that of the energy required to override friction.

The point is not whether we can do this yet. We can't; even carbon-fibre 'rope' is too weak. But the space elevator shows how a design trajectory can take a function away from its earliest, primitive constraints, so that a whole new set of rules applies, and the old limitations become ... not invalid, but irrelevant.

More familiar examples of this 'transcendent' process are writing and telecommunication. The first attempts at writing probably involved scratches on rock or bark, and these matured in two directions – pictorial and phonetic writing. Pictorial writing, such as ancient Egyptian hieroglyphs and modern Chinese, has found it difficult to move up the technological ladder. They are not even at the rocket stage; fireworks, perhaps. Phonetic writing was more suitable for printing – the space bolas stage of the technology. This was improved as far as the great newspaper printing presses of the twentieth century and the electric typewriter. Then came the space elevator stage, word processing by computer. Ironically, this may just have saved Chinese ideograms, now easily typeset by computer, from oblivion. A further stage is starting to appear with eBooks and iPads. Eventually, all writing might be virtual, encoded in physically tiny memories until it needs only to be actualised on screens and in minds.

Communication at a distance started with semaphore and chains of watch-fires on hilltops. Navies developed coded systems of flags for communication between ships. Discworld inventors developed the clacks, a mechanical telegraph with repeaters at limit-of-sight, aided by telescopes, while we used a signal-box and mechanical linkages to signal to trains miles from the box. With electricity came the ability to send signals via cables, and the telegraph was born. Several different coding systems for commercial transactions, and a primitive fax machine, were in commercial use before 1900. All these were rocket-ships. Then came the telephone, which uses sound waves to modulate an electrical signal. Much capital investment went into wiring the countryside and undersea cables to connect the continents. These heroic ventures were comparable, in technical difficulty, with putting up a space bolas now. Meanwhile 'wireless' began to be used: radio, and later television. With mobile phone technology, depending upon billions of pounds of investment in immensely sophisticated base stations and in research to improve and develop the handsets, we are now beginning the space elevator stage of telephone technology.

We can compare these technical innovations to developments in organic evolution. We analyse the development of mammals on two scales, to show how the evolutionary process outgrows its initial constraints and achieves new properties and functions as the trajectory changes direction. We choose the two scales to emphasise that this is not a description of what actually happens during organic evolution.

We have already met the question of the extent of diversity in the animals of the Burgess Shale, and the differences of opinion between Gould and Morris. Among these animals from the Cambrian explosion, several were early chordates, ancestral to our own group of animals, including today's fishes, amphibians, reptiles, birds and mammals, as well as a diversity of modern oddities like sea squirts and lampreys. The Burgess Shale fossil *Pikaia* is the best-known early chordate, but there are others in similar Australian and Chinese fossil beds.

The early chordates produced a great adaptive radiation, firstly of jawless armoured fishes, then of a substantial number of jawed forms, including sharks, rays and bony fishes. Some of the latter, in the Devonian period, came out onto the land as early amphibians. These aquatic forms are/were the rocket-ship phase of chordate existence. The amphibians, and their diverse reptilian descendants, such as dinosaurs, birds and mammal-like reptiles that included our ancestors, constitute the next step up, the chordate space bolas. The third stage was achieved separately, and rather differently, by birds and mammals. Birds specialised in warm-bloodedness and efficient lung ventilation for flight, so that they had to provide food for their young, caring for them in nests until they could adopt the very demanding lifestyle of their parents. Mammals became turbo-powered by maintaining a stable high body temperature, and invaded many more habitats than birds, from burrowing and swimming to flying. Which they now do nearly as well as birds, but without flow-through lung ventilation. From a wide-screen chordate viewpoint, mammalian design is their space elevator.

Within that last step, we can find a similar series of invasions of the adjacent possible, in which terrestrial ecosystems were themselves changed by the presence of large land animals. Grassland such as savannah and steppes, arctic birch, lichen and moss tundra are all maintained by continuing interactions with large herbivorous mammals. Vast numbers of small rodents – mice, rats, voles, lemmings, hamsters – live in and under these grasslands. They eat more of the vegetation than their larger cousins do, and they contribute more to those ecosystems. Some interactions between mammals and their environment are familiar: rabbits making warrens, badgers excavating setts, deer ringing trees. We have to visit zoos to see the full adaptive radiation, including those strange rodents of the South American pampas: pacas, capybaras and cavies (guinea-pigs). And bats. And porpoises, dolphins, toothed whales and filter-feeding baleen whales. And all of the primates, including us. So mammals, like insects among the invertebrates, are the big terrestrial success story.

In terms of our space-exploration analogy, the mammal-like reptiles of four hundred million years ago, and today's monotremes (egg-laying oddities like the echidna and the duck-billed platypus) are the rocket-ships. The marsupial mammals – kangaroos, potoroos and opossums – are the space bolas. The placental mammals – most of today's mammals, including cows, pigs, cats, dogs, hippos, elephants, monkeys, apes and humans – are the space elevator.

Any evolutionary series can be presented as a ladder of emergent properties, new ways of being that obey new rules and have effectively discarded the old constraints. This vision is as appropriate to mammals as it is to writing tools or radio receivers. It is a general property of our self-complexifying planet in its self-complexifying universe. As time passes, more different things happen in more ways, with new rules and new functions.

That vision, of the multifarious universe knotting itself into patterns that themselves build upon previous patterns, is almost perfectly opposite to the twentieth-century view of ever-increasing entropy leading to heat death. Can this self-complication continue infinitely? We don't know, but it is as sensible a view as its opposite, and there is considerable evidence for it. Does that mean that *anything* not possible now will necessarily be possible in future? Of course not. At each step upwards, there is selection among possibilities.

This selection process is what mathematicians call symmetry-breaking: more possibilities seem to be available beforehand than are actualised at the next stage, yet paradoxically there are more possibilities afterwards than before. If advancement is the rule, and it seems to be, then contingency and selection are making up the future by evolving from rocket-ships into future space elevators, almost everywhere. We should perhaps be surprised that Moore's Law has worked for so long, but when we examine the changes in computing technology over the last decades we see that, just as in the recent mammal story, the improvements were always inconceivable at the earlier step.

This is why blinkered applications of laws of nature, such as conservation of energy or the second law of thermodynamics, can be misleading. As well as content, laws have contexts. A law of nature may appear to pose an insuperable barrier, but if you have applied the law in an inappropriate context, you may have left a way for nature to sneak round it. And it will.

FIFTEEN

CASE FOR THE PLAINTIFFS

The Great Hall in the palace had been opened to all-comers with, of course, a podium for Lord Vetinari and desks for the lawyers. A number of guards surrounded his Lordship, and everyone heard him tell them loudly, 'No, I am in my own palace, in a court of law at the moment, and since we are not talking about a murder or a dreadful crime I see no reason to introduce weaponry into what is, when all is said and done, a philosophical debate.'

Marjorie watched the unhappy hangers-on disappear into the body of the hall, and then was further impressed by the way Lord Vetinari achieved *silence*. It was a masterclass; he simply sat silent and immobile with his hands spread out in front of him, oblivious to all the laughter, chattering, gossiping and arguing. It seemed that the air was just full of fragments of nothing whatsoever, fractured words breaking up and fading, until the final chattering fool suddenly found a great hush filling the room, in the centre of which there was his last stupid, idiotic remark, evaporating in his Lordship's dreadful, patient silence.

'Ladies and gentlemen, I cannot conceive of a more interesting case than the one we have today. The dispute is over a mere artefact: shiny, I grant you, and attractive in its way. I am given to believe by the wizards and natural scientists of Unseen University and elsewhere that, reasonably small though it be, it is in fact larger by many orders of magnitude than all of our own world.

'I intend to seek evidence of this during the deliberations of this very *unusual* tribunal, which has been brought into being because there are two parties who both profess to believe that the artefact is theirs. For my part, I intend to test this assumption.' Lord Vetinari sighed, and said, 'I rather fear the term "quantum" will make an appearance; but these are, after all, modern times.'

Marjorie had to put her hand over her mouth to stop giggling; his lordship had said *modern times* like a duchess finding a caterpillar in her soup.

Lord Vetinari looked around at the crowd, frowned at the desks in front of him, and said, 'Mister Slant, who is a foremost arbiter of the law, will assist me and advise me on aspects as relevant.' He raised his voice and continued, 'This, ladies and gentlemen, is not a criminal court! Indeed, I am slightly at a loss as to what kind of court it *is*, since the law works in the temporal sphere with its feet firmly on the ground. Therefore, with the two parties in this case planning to engage a number of, shall we say, experts in the celestial, as well as in the mundane sphere—' Lord Vetinari looked around and said, 'Shouldn't I have a gavel? You know, one of those things judges bang on the table. I feel quite naked without one.'

A gavel was acquired from somewhere at speed and handed to his Lordship, who banged it once or twice in a kind of happiness.

'Well, this seems to work; and now I call the counsel for the plaintiffs. Over to you, Mister Stackpole; you have the floor.'

Marjorie craned to see Mister Stackpole, but could only make out the top of a head. The voice emanating from it had a curious tone, as if its owner was actually vibrating. He said, 'A small point, my Lord, but I am a priest of the Omnian faith, and generally addressed as "Reverend".'

Lord Vetinari looked interested and said, 'Really. I shall make a note of that. Please continue, Mister Stackpole.'

Marjorie really wished she could see the face of the Reverend Stackpole. Her father, when he was alive, had quite liked being called

'Mister'; he once told her that he could never think of himself as 'Reverend' – he never *felt* like a 'Reverend', but was just happy in his job at St John's-on-the-Water where everybody knew him and he knew everybody.

She looked up out of the mist of memory, because the *Reverend* Mister Stackpole was making his opening statement.

'My Lord, we of the Latter-Day Omnian faith know that the world is *round*, and the discovery of Roundworld vindicates our faith. The ridiculous notion that the world travels on the back of an enormous turtle is entirely false. How can it exist in the vastness of space? How can it feed? Where did it come from? Fantasy, my Lord, nothing but fantasy! Unseen University's custody of Roundworld is indefensible: it constitutes a serious violation of the theological property rights of the Church of the Latter-Day Omnians! The concept of a round world has been central to our faith for centuries.' He took a deep breath and continued, 'Justice *demands* that Roundworld should be in the possession of my brethren – and, of course, sistren – who are undoubtedly more capable of looking after it than the so-called wizards, who profess to know all the secrets of the multiverse, yet do not even know the true form of their own world! I appreciate that they can occasionally be of some *practical* use, but wizards should not be allowed to engage in celestial or ecclesiastical matters. They acquired this artefact by accident, and they have no right to retain it. In their hands it is a blasphemous caricature of our own *round* world, as created by the great god Om!'

Lord Vetinari glanced at the paperwork in front of him and said, 'Mister Stackpole, I am a little puzzled here: enlighten me if I am wrong, but surely did we not, several years ago at great expense, send a dragon-powered flying machine known as the *Kite* on a mission initially to reach the home of the gods? It was designed and captained by Leonard of Quirm, was launched over the edge with extra momentum given by a number of swamp dragons, and subsequently landed on the Moon where a few samples were taken of the flora and fauna such as it turned out to be. Ultimately it crashed at the triumphal end of its mission – fortuitously without any fatalities – but the crew saw the turtle from every direction. It certainly existed, and Leonard himself produced quite a number of paintings – *lifelike* paintings. The three people who accompanied him on the voyage also testified about what they had seen.

'I'm curious: do you believe that this *did not happen*? I'm perplexed. I am also aware that on many occasions explorers have climbed to the edge and seen the turtle, and indeed the elephants. Granted, their presence is unlikely, but unlikely things happen all the time – so they are in fact quite likely, which is the reason for things happening. Mister Stackpole, all the evidence says the world is on the back of an enormous turtle. Unlikely, yes: an unlikely turtle, but nevertheless the turtle in front of us, or rather below us. And it is therefore the truth, surely?'

Watching him carefully, Marjorie thought she recognised the Reverend Stackpole now; he was one of the *left-ear people* who you often got in libraries – people who talked *at* you while staring at your left ear and who would never, it seemed, look one directly in the eye. At the same time they willed you to believe, as an example, that the government was poisoning the water supply because of over-population. The worst of them, if you couldn't shake them off, were the ones who at some point used the word 'Aryan' and declared that the master race was already in orbit around Jupiter, just waiting for the Chosen. Library rules forbade physical violence, but sometimes she wanted to go and have a wash afterwards, apologising to her ears for what she had made them hear, and to her fists for clenching them red.

In this world, she had no idea if she was somehow on the back of a turtle or not; but from her reading she recalled that it was a very long time before humanity knew that it even *lived* on a planet, and even then the concept took some time to permeate. As did concepts like looking after said planet. She remembered her grandmother saying,

'I take all my bottles to the bottle bank to help save the planet,' and Marjorie had for a moment rejoiced that in some way or other a new message was getting through even to a confused old lady.

Right now, she wondered if Lord Vetinari, by phrasing his points as questions, was being kind to the man, or was simply trying to ascertain the depths of his delusions.

But Mister Stackpole was not giving in; in fact, he was fighting back. 'My Lord, we look at the sky and see round things; for example the Moon is round, and the Sun is round. *Sphericality*, surely, is everywhere. Don't you think it is trying to tell us something?'

The Reverend got applause from some quarters of the room for this.

Lord Vetinari, on the other hand, had not allowed his expression to change by one iota. Once the noise had subsided, he banged on his gavel and said, 'Thank you, Mister Stackpole. Please be so good to go back to your seat.' The gavel struck again and the Patrician said, 'There will now be an adjournment of fifteen minutes; refreshments for all are available in the black gallery.'

Every wizard's face brightened immediately. Free food – well, *that* was worth coming along for. The sound of the gavel had barely faded away before Marjorie found herself alone on the bench. The wizards had stampeded – in a genteel way – to the gallery.

SIXTEEN

SPHERICALITY SURELY IS EVERYWHERE

 The Reverend Stackpole's appeal to the ubiquity of round objects strikes a chord. The storytelling ape has a strong preference for neat, simple geometric forms. Circles and spheres featured prominently in early theories of planetary motion, such as those of Ptolemy and his successors: see chapter 22. To some extent today's science, with its neat, simple mathematical laws, derives from an ancient tradition in which particular shapes and numbers have mystical significance. Stackpole appeals to the sphericality of several objects that are *not* Discworld to argue that the Disc must also be spherical. He is using a ploy that is all too common among people trying to promote some belief system: introducing 'evidence' that undeniably exists, observing that it is consistent with his beliefs but skirting quietly round a big logical gap. Namely: is the belief system the *only* possible explanation for the evidence concerned, or is it consistent with alternatives?

When it came to the shape of the universe, the cosmologists of the early twentieth century were a bit like Stackpole. They *assumed* that the universe should be spherically symmetric – behave the same way in all directions – to keep the sums easy. When they put that assumption into the equations, and did the sums, the mathematics spat out a spherical universe. This shape quickly became the perceived wisdom. However, there was very little independent evidence to support their original assumption. The logic was – well, circular.

What shape *is* the universe, then?

It's a big question. We somehow have to work out the shape of everything that exists, from one location on the inside. It sounds impossible. But we can make significant progress by borrowing some tricks from a fictional square and an ant.

In 1884 the Victorian headmaster, clergyman and Shakespearean scholar Edwin Abbott Abbott* published a curious little book, *Flatland*. It remains in print to this day, in numerous editions. Its protagonist, A. Square,† lives in a world shaped like the Euclidean plane. His universe is two-dimensional, flat, and of infinite extent. Abbott made a few gestures towards figuring out plausible physics and biology in a two-dimensional world, but his main objectives were to satirise the rigid male-dominated class structure of Victorian society, and to explain the hot topic of the fourth dimension. With its mixture of satirical fantasy and science, *Flatland* has to be considered a serious contender for *The Science of Discworld 0*.

Abbott's scientific aims were accomplished through the vehicle of a dimensional analogy: that a three-dimensional creature trying to comprehend the fourth dimension is much the same as a two-dimensional creature trying to comprehend the third. We say 'the' for convenience: there is no reason for a fourth dimension to be unique. However, *Flatland* was, in its day, almost unique. There was one other tale of a two-dimensional world, Charles Howard Hinton's *An Episode on Flatland: Or How a Plain Folk Discovered the Third Dimension*. Although this was published in 1907, Hinton had written several articles about the fourth dimension and analogies with a two-dimensional world shortly before Abbott's *Flatland* appeared.

There is circumstantial evidence that the two must have met, but neither of them claimed priority or was bothered by the other's

---

* Yes, two Abbotts. His father was Edwin Abbott. So was his son.
† Abbott never said what the 'A' stood for. One theory is that $A^2 = AA = $ Abbott Abbott. In Ian's modern sequel *Flatterland* it is 'Albert'. Google 'Albert Square'.

work. The fourth dimension was very much 'in the air' at that time, emerging as a serious concept from physics and mathematics, and attracting a variety of people ranging from ghost-hunters and spiritualists to hyperspace theologians. Just as we three-dimensional beings can gaze upon a flat sheet of paper without intersecting it, so a fourth dimension is an attractive location for ghosts, the spirit world or God.

In Abbott's narrative, A. Square strenuously denies that a third dimension is possible, let alone real, until a visiting Sphere bumps him out of his planar world into three-dimensional space. Inference didn't do the trick; direct personal experience did. Abbott was telling his readers not to be unduly influenced by what the universe appears like to unaided human senses. We should not imagine that every possible world must be just like our own – or, more precisely, what we naively believe our world to be. In terms of Benford's dichotomy – human-centred thinking, or universe-centred thinking – Abbott takes a universe-centred view.

The spaces considered in *Flatland* obey the traditional geometry of Euclid – a topic that Abbott encountered as a schoolboy, and didn't greatly enjoy. To remove this restriction on the shape of space, we require a more general image, which seems to have originated with the great mathematician Carl Friedrich Gauss. He discovered an elegant mathematical formula for the curvature of a surface: how bent it is near any given point. He considered this formula to be one of his greatest discoveries, and called it his *theorema egregium* – 'remarkable theorem'. What made it remarkable was a striking feature: the formula did not depend on how the surface was embedded in surrounding space. It was intrinsic *to the surface alone*.

This may not sound terribly radical, but it implies that space can be curved without being curved *round* anything else. Imagine a sphere, hovering in space. In your mind's eye, it is visibly curved. This view of curvature comes naturally to the human imagination, but it depends on there being a surrounding space, somewhere for the sphere to be curved *in*. Gauss's formula blew this assumption out of the water: it showed that you can discover that a sphere is curved, without ever leaving its surface. The surrounding space, rather than being necessary for the surface to have some direction in which to bend, is irrelevant.

According to his biographer Sartorius van Waltershausen, Gauss had a habit of explaining this point in terms of an ant that was confined to the surface. As far as the ant was concerned, nothing else existed. Nevertheless, by wandering around the surface with a tape measure (Gauss didn't actually use that instrument, but let's not be *too* purist) the ant could *infer* that its universe was curved. Not curved round anything: just curved.

We all learn at school that in Euclid's geometry, the angles of any triangle add up to 180°. This theorem is true for a flat plane, but false on curved surfaces. For example, on a sphere we can form a triangle by starting at the north pole, going south to the equator, going a quarter of the way round the equator, and returning to the north pole. The sides of this triangle are great circles on the sphere, which are the natural analogues of straight lines, being the shortest paths *on the surface* between given points. The angles of this triangle are all right angles: 90°. So they add up to 270°, not 180°. Fair enough: a sphere is not a plane. But this example suggests that we might be able to work out that we are *not* on a plane by measuring triangles. And that's what Gauss's remarkable theorem says. The universe's metric – the way distances behave, which can be determined by analysing the shapes and sizes of small triangles – can tell the ant exactly how curved its universe is. Just plug the measurements into his formula.

Gauss was immensely impressed by this discovery. His assistant Bernhard Riemann generalised the formula to spaces with any number of dimensions, opening up a new branch of mathematics called differential geometry. However, working out the curvature at every point of a space involves an awful lot of work, and mathematicians wondered if there might be a simpler way to get less detailed information. They tried to find a more flexible notion of 'shape' that would be easier to handle.

What they came up with is now called topology, and it led to a qualitative characterisation of shape that does not require numerical measurements. In this branch of mathematics, two shapes are considered to be the same if one of them can be continuously deformed into the other. For example, a doughnut (of the type that has a hole) is the same as a coffee-cup. Think about a cup made from some flexible substance that can easily be bent, compressed, or stretched. You can start by slowly flattening out the depression in the cup to make a disc, with the handle still attached to its edge. Then you can shrink the disc until it has the same thickness as the handle, forming a ring. Now fatten everything up a bit, and you end up with a doughnut shape. In fact, to a topologist, both shapes are a distorted form of a blob to which one handle has been attached.

The topological version of 'shape' asks whether the universe is a spherical lump, like an English doughnut, or a torus, like an American doughnut with a hole in it, or something more complicated.

It turns out that a topologically savvy ant can deduce a great deal about the shape of its world by pushing closed loops around and seeing what they do. If the space has a hole, the ant can wind a loop of string through it, and it is impossible to pull the loop away, always remaining on the surface, without breaking it. If the space has several holes, the ant can wind a separate loop through each, and use them to work out how many holes there are and how they are arranged. And if the space has no holes, the ant can push any closed loop around, without it ever leaving the surface, until it all piles up in the same place.

Ant-like thinking, which is restricted to the intrinsic features of a space, takes a bit of getting used to, but without it, modern cosmology makes no sense, because Einstein's general theory of relativity reinterprets gravity as the curvature of spacetime, using Riemann's generalisation of Gauss's remarkable theorem.

Until now, we've used the word 'curvature' in a loose sense: how a shape *bends*. But now we must be more careful, because from an ant's-eye view, curvature is a subtle concept, not quite what we might expect. In particular, an ant living on a cylinder would insist that its universe is *not* curved. A cylinder may look like a rolled-up sheet of paper to an external viewer, but the geometry of small triangles on a cylinder is exactly the same as it is on the Euclidean plane. Proof: unroll the paper. Lengths and angles, *measured within the paper*, do not change. So an ant living on a cylinder would consider it to be flat.

Mathematicians and cosmologists agree with the ant. However, a cylinder is definitely different from a plane in some respects. If the ant starts at a point on a cylinder, and heads off in just the right direction in what it considers to be a straight line, then after a time it gets back to where it started. The line wraps round the cylinder and returns to its origin. That's not possible with a straight line on a plane. This is a topological difference, and Gaussian curvature cannot detect it.

We mention the cylinder because it's familiar, but also because it has an important cousin called a *flat torus* – an oxymoron if ever there was one, since a torus is shaped like a doughnut with a hole, which is deliciously curved. But the name makes sense nonetheless. Metrically, the space is flat, no curvature; topologically, it's a torus. To make a flat torus we conceptually glue the opposite edges of a square together, and squares are flat. This construction is analogous to the way computer games connect opposite edges of a screen together, so that when a monster or an alien spacecraft falls off one edge, it instantly reappears in the corresponding position on the opposite edge. Game programmers call this 'wrapping round', which is what it feels like, but exactly what you do not attempt to do literally unless you want to create a big mess of broken screen. Topologically, wrapping the vertical edges round converts the screen into a cylinder. Wrapping the horizontal edges round then joins the ends of the cylinder to make a torus. Now there's no edge and the aliens can't escape.

The flat torus is the simplest instance of a general method used by topologists to make complicated spaces from simpler ones. Take one or more simple shapes, then 'glue' them together by listing rules for which bit attaches where. It's like flat-pack furniture: lots of pieces and a list of instructions like 'insert shelf A into slot B'. But mathematically, the pieces and the list are all you need: you don't actually have to *assemble* the furniture. Instead, you think about how it would behave if you did.

Until humanity invented space travel, we were in the same position as the ant with regard to the shape of the Earth. We still *are* in the same position as the ant with regard to the shape of the universe. Like the ant, we can nevertheless infer that shape by making suitable observations. However, observations alone are not enough; we also need to interpret them in the context of some coherent theory about the general nature of the world. If the ant doesn't know it's on a surface, Gauss's formula isn't much help.

At the moment, that context is general relativity, which explains gravity in terms of the curvature of spacetime. In a flat region of spacetime, particles travel in straight lines, just as they would in Newtonian physics if no forces were acting. If spacetime is warped, particles travel along curved paths, which in Newtonian physics would be a sign that a force is acting – such as gravity. Einstein threw away the forces and kept the curvature. In general relativity, a massive body, such as a star or a planet, bends spacetime; particles deviate from a straight line path because of the curvature, not because a force is acting on them. If you want to understand gravity, said Einstein, you have to understand the geometry of the universe.

In the early days of general relativity, cosmologists discovered a sensible shape for the universe, one that was consistent with relativity: a hypersphere. Topologically, this is like an ordinary sphere, by which they mean just the surface. A sphere is two-dimensional: two numbers are enough to specify any point on it. For example, latitude and longitude. But a hypersphere is three-dimensional. Mathematicians define a hypersphere using coordinate geometry. Unfortunately, it's not a shape that lives naturally in ordinary space, so we can't just make a model or draw a picture.

It's not just a solid ball – a sphere plus the material of its interior. A sphere has no boundary, so neither should a hypersphere. Discworld, for instance, does have a boundary, where the world *stops* and the oceans fall off the edge. Our spherical world is different: it has no edge. Wherever you stand, you can look around you in all directions and see land or ocean. An ant, wandering through its spherical world, would not encounter a place where it runs out of universe. The same should be true of a hypersphere. But a solid ball does have a boundary: its surface. An ant that could travel at will through the interior of a ball – as we move through space unless something gets in the way – would run out of universe when it hit the surface at the other side.

For present purposes, all we really need to know about a hypersphere is that it's the natural analogue of a sphere, but with one extra dimension. For a more specific image, we can think about how an ant might visualise a sphere, and beef everything up by one dimension – the same trick that A. Square uses in *Flatland*. A sphere is two hemispheres glued together at the equator. A hemisphere can be flattened out to form a flat disc: a circle plus its interior, and this is a continuous deformation. So a topologist can think of a sphere as two discs glued together along their edges, like a flying saucer. In three dimensions, the analogue of a disc is a solid ball. So we can make a hypersphere by conceptually gluing the surfaces of two solid balls together. This can't be done in ordinary space using round balls, but mathematically we can specify a rule that associates each point on the surface of one ball with a corresponding point on the surface of the other ball. Then we pretend that corresponding points are the same, much as we 'glued' the edges of a square together to get a flat torus.

The hypersphere played a prominent role in the early work of Henri Poincaré, one of the creators of modern topology. He operated around the turn of the nineteenth century, and was one of the top two or three mathematicians of the day. He came perilously close to beating Einstein to special relativity.* In the early 1900s, Poincaré set up many of the basic tools of topology. He knew that hyperspheres play a fundamental role in three-dimensional topology, just as spheres do in two-dimensional topology. In particular, a hypersphere has no 'holes' analogous to the hole in a doughnut, so in a sense it is the simplest three-dimensional topological space. Poincaré assumed, without proof, that the converse is also true: a three-dimensional topological space without holes must be a hypersphere.

In 1904, however, he discovered a more complicated shape, the dodecahedral space, which has no holes, but *isn't* a hypersphere. The existence of this particular shape proved that his assumption was wrong. This unexpected setback led him to add one further condition, which he hoped would fully characterise the hypersphere. In two dimensions, a surface is a sphere if and only if every closed loop can be pushed around until it all piles up in the same place. Poincaré conjectured that the same property characterises a hypersphere in three dimensions. He was right, but it took mathematicians almost a century to prove it. In 2003 a young Russian, Grigori Perelman, succeeded in proving Poincaré's conjecture. This entitled him to a million-dollar prize, which he famously declined.

Although a hyperspherical universe is the simplest and most obvious possibility, there's not a great deal of observational evidence for it. A flat plane used to be the simplest and most obvious possibility for the Earth's surface, and look where that got us. So cosmologists stopped tacitly assuming that the universe must be a hypersphere, and started to think about other possible shapes. One of the most widely publicised suggestions, for a short time, appealed to the news

---

* Some mathematicians think he did, but the physicists didn't notice because he wasn't a physicist.

media because it indicated that the universe is shaped like a football. (For US readers: soccer ball.) Editors loved it, because although readers might not know much cosmology, they sure know what a football is.*

It's not a sphere, you understand. A football – at that time, and not for long – had abandoned the old shape of eighteen rectangular panels sewn into a sort of cube, and adopted a snazzy new shape, twelve pentagons and twenty hexagons sewn or glued into a truncated icosahedron.† This is a solid that goes back to ancient Greece, and with a name like that, it's a good job you can refer to it as a football. Except that – well, actually it's not a truncated icosahedron at all. It's a three-dimensional hypersurface bearing a loose relationship to a truncated icosahedron. A football from another dimension.

To be specific, it is Poincaré's dodecahedral space.

To make a dodecahedral space, you start with a dodecahedron. This is a solid with twelve faces, each a regular pentagon; like a football without the hexagons. Then you glue opposite faces together – something that is not possible with a real dodecahedron. Mathematically, there is a way to pretend that distinct faces are actually the same, without bending the thing to join them together, as we saw for the flat torus; topologists, however, insist on calling it 'gluing'.

The dodecahedral space is an elaborate variation on a flat torus. Recall that we make a flat torus by taking a square and gluing opposite *edges* together. To get the dodecahedral space, which is not a surface but a three-dimensional object, we take a dodecahedron and glue opposite *faces* together. The result is a three-dimensional topological space. It has no boundary, just like a torus, and for the same reason: anything that is in danger of falling out through a face

---

* So do the wizards: see *Unseen Academicals*.
† By the 2006 World Cup it was made from 14 panels: six dumbbell-shaped ones and eight like the Isle of Man's triple running-legs emblem. The underlying symmetry was again that of a cube. If you think that analysing symmetries of footballs is nerdy, look up the literature on symmetries of golf balls.

reappears inside at the opposite one, so there's no way out. It has finite size. And, like a hypersphere, it has no holes, so if you are a slightly naive topologist you might be tempted to think it passes all the tests needed to be a hypersphere – but it *isn't* a hypersphere, not even topologically.

Poincaré devised his dodecahedral space as a piece of pure mathematics, exposing a limitation of the topological methods available in his day – one that he set out to remedy. But in 2003 the dodecahedral space acquired brief notoriety and a potential application to cosmology when NASA's Wilkinson Microwave Anisotropy Probe (WMAP) satellite was measuring fluctuations in the cosmic microwave background, a persistent hiss detected by radio telescopes that is interpreted as a relic of the Big Bang. The statistics of these tiny irregularities provide information about how matter clumped together in the early universe, acting as a seed from which stars and galaxies formed. WMAP can see far enough in space to, in effect, see back in time to about 380,000 years after the Big Bang.

At the time, most cosmologists thought that the universe was infinite. (Although this conflicts with the standard description of the Big Bang, there are ways to accommodate it, and 'universes all the way out' has the innate appeal already noted for 'universes all the way back' – which, ironically, is not what the Big Bang indicates.) However, the WMAP data suggested that the universe is *finite*. An infinite universe ought to support fluctuations of all sizes, but the data did not show any large waves. As a report in *Nature* said at the time, 'you don't see breakers in your bathtub'. The detailed data provided further clues about the likely shape of our breakerless bathtub universe. Working out the statistics of the fluctuations for a variety of potential shapes, the mathematician Jeffrey Weeks noticed that the dodecahedral space fitted the data very well, without any special pleading. Jean-Pierre Luminet's group published an analysis showing that if this were correct, the universe would have to be about 30 billion light years across.* This theory has since fallen out of favour thanks to further observations, but it was fun while it lasted.

We human ants can use another trick to infer the shape of space. If the universe is finite, some rays of light will eventually return to their point of origin. If you could look along one of these 'closed geodesics' (a geodesic is a shortest path) with a sufficiently high-powered telescope, and if light travelled infinitely fast, you would see the back of your own head. Taking the finite speed of light into account, patterns should occur in the cosmic microwave background, forming matching circles in the sky. The way these circles are arranged would provide information about the topology of space. Cosmologists and mathematicians have tried to find such circles, so far with no convincing successes. If the universe is finite but too big, we wouldn't be able to see far enough to spot the circles anyway.

So the current answer to the question 'what shape is the universe?' is very simple. We don't know. We don't know whether it's a hypersphere or something more elaborate. The universe is too big for us to observe it all, and our current understanding of cosmology, indeed of fundamental physics, wouldn't be up to the task even if we could.

Some of the difficulties surrounding cosmology stem from a mix-and-match approach in which relativity is invoked at some stages and quantum mechanics at others, without recognising that they contradict each other. Theorists are reluctant to discard the tools they are accustomed to, even when those tools don't seem to be working. But the shape of the universe is a problem that really requires a combination of these two great physical theories. And that brings us to the search for a unified field theory, or Theory of Everything, to which Einstein devoted many years of thought – without success. Somehow, relativity and quantum mechanics have to be

---

* J-P Luminet, Jeffrey R. Weeks, Alain Riazuelo, Roland Lehoucq and Jean-Philippe Uzan, Dodecahedral space topology as an explanation for weak wide-angle temperature correlations in the cosmic microwave background, *Nature* **425** (2003) 593.

modified to produce a consistent theory that agrees with each of them in the relevant domain.

Today's front runner is string theory, which replaces point particles by tiny multidimensional shapes, as we discussed in *The Science of Discworld III*. Some versions of string theory require space to be nine-dimensional, so spacetime has to be ten-dimensional. The extra six dimensions of space are thought either to be curled up so tightly that we don't notice them, or inaccessible to humans – in the same way that A. Square could not travel out of Flatland unaided, but needed a shove from the Sphere to push him into the third dimension. The formulations of string theory currently in vogue also introduce new 'supersymmetry' principles, predicting the existence of a host of new 'sparticles' to match the known particles. So an electron is paired with a selectron, and so on. So far, however, this prediction has not been confirmed. The LHC has looked for sparticles, but so far it has found precisely none of them.

One of the latest unification attempts, refreshingly different from most that have gone before, takes us neatly back to Flatland. The idea, common in mathematics and often fruitful, is to take inspiration from a cut-down toy problem. If unifying relativity and quantum mechanics is too hard using three-dimensional space, why not simplify the problems by looking at the non-physical but mathematically informative case of two-dimensional space? Plus one of time, naturally. It's clear enough where to start. In order to unify two theories, you have to have two theories to unify. So what would gravity look like in Flatland, and what would quantum mechanics look like in Flatland? We hasten to add that Flatland, here, need not be A. Square's Euclidean plane. Any two-dimensional space, any surface, would do. Indeed, other topologies are essential to get anything interesting.

It's straightforward to write down sensible analogues of Einstein's field equations when space is a surface. It's very close to what Gauss did when he started the whole thing off, and his ant would have no trouble in devising the right equations, since they're all about curvature. There are obvious analogies to follow; all you do is replace the number three by the number two at key points. In Roundworld, the Polish physicist Andrzej Staruszkiewicz wrote such equations down in 1963.

It turns out that gravity in two dimensions differs significantly from gravity in three. In three dimensions relativity predicts the existence of gravitational waves, which propagate at the speed of light. But there are no gravitational waves in two dimensions. In three dimensions, relativity predicts that any mass bends space into a rounded bump, so that anything that passes nearby will follow a curved path, as if it were attracted by Newtonian gravity. And an object that was at rest will fall into the gravitational well of the mass concerned. In two dimensions, however, gravity bends space into a cone. Moving bodies are deflected, but bodies at rest simply remain at rest. In three dimensions massive bodies collapse under their own gravitation to form black holes. In two dimensions, this is impossible.

These differences are things we can live with, but in three dimensions, gravitational waves are a useful way to link relativity to quantum theory. The absence of gravitational waves in two dimensions causes headaches, because it means there is nothing to quantise – nothing to use as a starting point for a quantum-mechanical formulation. Gravity should correspond to hypothetical particles called gravitons, and in quantum theory particles have ghostly companions – waves. No waves, no gravitons. But in 1989 Edward Witten, one of the architects of string theory, ran into other quantum problems involving fields that do not propagate waves. Two-dimensional gravity is like that, and it opened his eyes to a missing ingredient.

Topology.

Even when gravity can't travel as a wave, it can have a huge effect on the shape of space. Witten's experience with topological quantum field theories, where just this ingredient arises, suggested a way forward. The humble torus, in many ways the simplest non-trivial topological space, plays a key role. We've mentioned the flat torus, in which we glue together the opposite edges of a square. Squares are nice because they can be fitted with grids of smaller squares, which have a quantum feel to them because they are discrete – they come in tiny lumps. But you can make flat tori from other shapes too, namely parallelograms.

The shape of the parallelogram can be captured by a number called the modulus, which distinguishes long thin parallelograms from short fat ones. A different modulus gives a different torus. Although the tori obtained in this manner are flat, they have different metrics. They can't be mapped into each other while keeping all distances the same. The effect of gravity in Torusland is not to create gravitons: it is to change the modulus, the shape of space.

Steven Carlipp has shown that in Torusland, there is an analogue of the Big Bang. But it doesn't start with a *point* singularity. Instead, it begins as a *circle*: a torus with modulus zero. As time passes, the modulus increases, and the circle expands into a torus. Initially this looks like a bicycle tyre, and corresponds to a long thin parallelogram; it is heading towards a square, the standard model for a flat torus, which when curled up looks more like a bagel. So the long-term goal of the Flatland Big Bang turns out to be A. Square. Crucially, Carlipp quantised this entire process; that is, he formulated a quantum-mechanical analogue. That let theoretical physicists explore the relationship between quantum theory and gravity in a precise mathematical context.

Torusland sheds a great deal of light on the process of quantising a gravitational theory. One apparent casualty of this process, however, is time. The quantum wave function of Torusland does not involve time at all.

In *The Science of Discworld III* Chapter 6, we discussed Julian Barbour's *The End of Time*, which proposes that time does not exist in a quantum world because there is only one universal wavefunction, not involving time. The book was widely interpreted as telling us that time is an illusion. 'There can only be once-and-for-all probabilities,' Barbour wrote. We argued that alongside the universal wavefunction, our universe has another basic quantum-theoretic feature, which describes how likely transitions between different states are. These transition probabilities show that some states are closer together than others, and that lets us arrange the events in a natural order, restoring a sensible notion of time.

Torusland supports this idea, because it has several sensible notions of time, even though its quantum wavefunction is timeless. Time can be measured using Torusland's equivalent of GPS satellites, by using the lengths of curves between its version of the Big Bang and 'now', or by the current size of the universe. Torusland is not timeless at all. You just have to look at it in the right way. In fact, Torusland time leads to an intriguing thought: perhaps time is a consequence of gravity.

Another idea that Torusland casts doubt on is the holographic principle. This says that the quantum state of the entire observable universe can be 'projected' onto any black hole's event horizon – the point of no return from which nothing can escape – so the universe's three spatial dimensions can be reduced to just two. It's like taking a photograph, with the startling property that the photograph faithfully represents *all* aspects of reality. In Roundworld, if someone shows you a photo of a field with a dozen sheep lying down, you can't tell whether there are lambs hiding behind some of the sheep. But in this event-horizon photo of the universe, nothing can be hidden. The behaviour in two dimensions corresponds perfectly to that in three. The laws of physics change, but everything matches up.

This is a bit like the way a two-dimensional hologram creates a three-dimensional image, which is why this idea is called the holographic principle. It suggests that not only is the dimension of the universe an open question: it may not be well defined – the answers 'two' and 'three' may both be true at the same time. This idea has led to some advances in the way string theory represents gravity, and also to articles in the press stating '*You are a hologram!*'

Physicists began to suspect that a similar principle works in any number of dimensions. But it turns out that in Torusland, there is no holographic principle. A. Square may be flat, but he's not a hologram. So maybe we're not holograms either. Which would be nice.

Some even more radical ideas about the shape of our universe have just surfaced, threatening to overturn many deep-seated assumptions in cosmology. Instead of being a gigantic hypersphere, or a flat Euclidean space, the universe might be more like an etching by the Dutch artist Maurits Escher.

Welcome to the Escherverse.

A hypersphere is the iconic surface with constant positive curvature. There is also an iconic surface of constant negative curvature, called the hyperbolic plane. It can be visualised as a circular disc in the usual Euclidean plane, equipped with an unusual metric, in which the unit of measurement shrinks the closer you get to the boundary. Escher based some of his etchings on the hyperbolic plane. A famous one, which he called 'Circle Limit IV' but is usually referred to as 'angels and devils', tiles the disc with black devils and white angels. Near the middle these appear quite large; as they approach the boundary they shrink, so that in principle there would be infinitely many of them. In the metric of the hyperbolic plane, all devils are the same size, and so are all angels.

String theory tries to unify the three quantum-mechanical forces (weak, strong and electromagnetic) with the relativistic force of gravity, and gravity is all about curvature. So curvature plays a key role in string theory. However, attempts to marry string theory to relativistic cosmology tend to come to grief, because string theory works best in spaces with negative curvature, whereas positive curvature works better for the cosmos. Which is a nuisance.

At least, that's what everyone thought.

But in 2012 Stephen Hawking, Thomas Hertog and James Hartle discovered that they could use a version of string theory to write down a quantum wavefunction for the universe – indeed, for all plausible variations on the universe – using a space with constant negative curvature. This is the Escherverse. It's terrific mathematics, and it disproves some widely believed assumptions about the curvature of spacetime. Whether it will also work out as physics remains to be seen.

So what have we learned? That the shape of our universe is intimately related to the laws of nature, and its study sheds some light – and a lot more darkness – on possible ways to unify relativity and quantum theory. Mathematical models like Torusland and the Escherverse have opened up new possibilities by showing that some common assumptions are wrong. But despite all of these fascinating developments, we don't know what shape our universe is. We don't know whether it is finite or infinite. We don't even know for sure what *dimension* it is, or even whether its dimension can be pinned down uniquely.

Like A. Square, trapped in Flatland, we are unable to step outside our world and view it unobstructed. But, also like him, we can learn a lot about the world despite that. On Discworld, creatures from the dungeon dimensions are only an incantation away; in Flatland a helpful Sphere may pop into view to help the story along. But Roundworld doesn't run on narrativium, and an extra-universal visitor from hidden dimensions seems unlikely.

So we are stuck with our own resources: imagination, ingenuity, logic and respect for evidence. With these, we can hope to infer more about our universe. Is it finite or infinite? Is it four-dimensional or eleven-dimensional? Is it round, flat or hyperbolic?

For all we know right now, it might be banana-shaped.

SEVENTEEN

THE WIZARD FORMERLY KNOWN AS THE DEAN

 The black gallery wasn't as black or foreboding as Marjorie had expected; it was just filled with pictures of long-deceased people with no indication of how they had become deceased, these facts lost now to memory as well as to life.

The wizards went into a huddle, and she heard the Archchancellor say, 'Look! We have always known we were not your average planet; after all, we have sometimes passed other more *ordinary* planets as the turtle has moved, and often as you know by occult ways and means. I think the opposition will try to say that *we* are somehow on a freak world. I am debating with myself whether or not to allow them to feel that is the way forward. What do you say, Mister Stibbons?'

Ponder nodded. 'A sensible plan, Archchancellor. If we live in a freak world, then surely we are all freaks; though somehow I do not think this will sit well with the population at large, especially the dwarfs who take offence at that sort of thing.'

'Offending small people as well, then? Capital!'

Ponder shuddered, then very carefully said, 'Very droll, Archchancellor, but I fear that little codicil might just do more harm than good, sir. Oh, and the Dean has arrived from Pseudopolis, and has made that inspection tour of Roundworld that you told Rincewind to arrange. He will be happy to testify. I thought you should know, Archchancellor.'

Ponder edged away a little; the subject of the Dean, or more accurately the person *formerly* known as the Dean, generally had the same effect on Mustrum Ridcully as the dropping of a hint in a game of chess – you did it at your peril. On the other hand, the Archchancellor could be mercurial at times, one of these times fortunately being *now*.

'Henry! So he did get my message then. That's nice of him, but of course he secretly yearns for the old *Alma Pater*.'*

Ponder sighed with relief. Relationships with Pseudopolis University had been rather dire after the Dean had left to become Archchancellor there; there had been much muttering about there being only one *arch* Chancellor on Discworld. But time had healed as it proverbially does, and relationships between the two universities were back to the standard for universities everywhere – which is to say they were keeping a friendly eye on the opposition, while politely and privately misleading them if necessary, but always *smiling* whilst doing so.

The Dean, still recovering from his visit to Roundworld, arrived in the gallery, breathless. He shook hands with Ridcully, who said, 'You will have to be my ace in the hole, Henry. So happy that you could come in time.'

'Don't mention it, Mustrum! Nobody can tell wizards what to do – except of course *other* wizards! And even then they will argue and find fault, hurrah!'

'Hurrah! Indeed, Henry! We test, test and test again – we are extremely testy people, and we would argue with our own grandmother if we thought she was wrong. "*Nullius in verba*": we take *nobody's* word for anything – including our own. The truth does not distil out of the air; it has to be thought – pursued, in fact!'

---

* Generally speaking, centres of learning are almost always referred to as feminine; rather surprising considering the length of time it took for any woman to get into one of them for a purpose higher than scrubbing the floors. Unseen University, of course, still marches to a different drum; it is a broken drum, but it is *their* drum, and they won't have it any other way.

'Yes indeed, old chap, and that at some cost. Faith can move mountains, but only as a metaphor, and the gods, if they exist, exist as bystanders.'

'Hang on a minute, old fellow. What about Anoia, the goddess of things that get stuck in drawers? I myself was disembogued of a particularly difficult ladle by her, thanks be – but of course this is hardly worship: it is a simple mercantile matter. She keeps our drawers rattle-free, and our belief keeps her going. *Quid pro quo*, but without the quid.'

The Dean was enjoying the argument immensely. 'But we must remember, Mustrum,' he pointed out, 'that Discworld and Roundworld are entirely different things, albeit that – as has been said – they have quite a lot in common. Well, when you forget about the turtle and if you ignore that terrifying core of overheated iron. Then you don't really notice any difference, apart from the trolls, and so on. As Lord Vetinari says, sooner or later it all comes down to people and the commonality of mankind.'

The two Archchancellors were suddenly aware of the silence in the large room; they were the centre of attention and it seemed that everybody, some even holding teacups, was staring like people might if they saw two lobsters having a dance for no other reason than *joie de vivre*. There was even some applause, sprinkled with little spurts of laughter.

Marjorie didn't join in, but watched the wizards carefully. The Archchancellor had told her about the origins of Roundworld, and had seemed, at the time, to be almost apologetic. He had also been very surprised when she laughed.

It was a strange world, this turtle world, but it didn't *seem* outlandish when you were on it. As for the religious connotations, she couldn't help thinking of the day her mother had died, which had been unpleasant, for all that the hospice had been able to do. Her father had taken off his clerical collar and dropped it in a waste basket without saying a word, and she had helped him with such things as

231

probate and the sundry unpleasant hoops the bereaved must jump through to satisfy the temporal powers. But he had grieved, and for weeks afterwards he would barely talk to her beyond the niceties of please and thank you – those stayed with him, courtesy even where courtesy was not forthcoming, since he was that kind of a man.

She had spoken to him some months afterwards, worried that after years and years of growing doubt he might have now lost his faith, triggered by the death of his wife so unfairly. She understood that, she understood *him*, though she had never understood his bishop, who in her presence was pernicious, stupid and condescending.

Right in front of her – yes, she who had read the Bible by the time she was seven and who by the time she was twenty-five had decided that it had by rights to be put on the fantasy and science fiction shelf – he had talked at length, without a *shred* of evidence, about her mother now being 'in God's embrace'. He wouldn't have been alone, either; there were many people who would *insist* that what he said was true when to her it manifestly was not. Yearning for a truth they had already declared was solid and immutable, they demanded – *demanded* – that their brand of fiction should be treated as fact.

She remembered a dreadful tidal wave that had almost devoured a small country, and she remembered how men and women all over the planet had found their way to the island and scrabbled in the ruins of stricken houses until they heard faint cries from below … The newspapers had called it a miracle; she had gone ballistic, screaming to the world at large: *It wasn't a bloody miracle!* A miracle would have been the appearance of God and all His angels, coming to the rescue. But it wasn't, not even close; it had been people – everyday people – helping other people, acknowledging them as people like themselves: a triumph for the commonality of mankind and the knowledge, slewed into our genes, that the person who you helped today might be the person who would pull you out from under a burning car tomorrow.

Support the clan. If one man tries to fight a mastodon, he is a dead man; a whole clan fights the mastodon, and everybody gets to eat for a week. And if enough of the clan work together, a couple of surprised former monkeys eventually land on the Moon …

And yet, as she had grown up and worked, building her career, she could all too easily spot those who thought that being a believer gave them power. She could see the shine on their faces, the determination never to let go – sometimes never even to think again for themselves.

After all, it had all been done for them already.

Right from the moment their God created their world in His own image. Which probably wasn't that of a turtle …

EIGHTEEN

BYE-BYE BIG BANG?

 Viewed from Discworld, Roundworld is a puzzle. It sits neatly on a shelf in Rincewind's office, but the wizards know that its outside has to be far smaller than its inside, because Rincewind (among many others) has visited the inside in person. Indeed, the whole of the inside is absolutely gigantic. The wizards have a theory about how this can be. Roundworld runs on mysterious rules, and its shape, size, and even its origin seem to be consequences of those rules. But the rules apply only on the inside. On the outside, magic takes over.

In chapter 16 we examined how Roundworld's rules affect not just the answer to the question of its shape, but what we mean by the question itself. Now we turn to its origins.

When the Archchancellor told Marjorie about the origins of Roundworld, he naturally did so from the wizards' perspective, in which the entire human universe is somehow located inside a small sphere, about the size of a football. And was brought into being by HEX saving Discworld from annihilation, and the Dean poking an exploratory finger into the resulting magical containment field.

What about the perspective of its inhabitants? Since ancient times, they have wondered how (or whether) their world began, but until recently their answers were resolutely human-centred: mainly stories about creator gods. In contrast, today's scientific theories of the origins of the universe are (surprise!) universe-centred. They are based not on stories about gods, but on the rules that the universe seems to obey.

Since the rules are not written down in a book of magical spells, the wizards have to infer the rules from what Roundworld does. Roundworld scientists are in the same position, but their difficulty is compounded, being stuck inside the thing and confined to the present. Even so, they have outperformed the wizards by working out many of the rules that govern their world and their universe.

When it comes to the origin of the universe, what we really need is a time machine. Despite some hints at the frontiers of today's physics, discussed in *The Science of Discworld II* and *III*, no practical time machine exists, or is likely to. But that doesn't stop us wanting to know exactly how the universe began, or taking a serious stab at working it out from the evidence it left behind.

The origin of the universe is a weighty philosophical question, leading to profound scientific and mathematical ideas. Mathematics, after all, is humanity's best-developed and most powerful system of logical inference, and if you can't go back to the distant past to take a look, you have to remain in the present and infer.

We've already seen that questions of shape and origin tend to go hand in hand. That is especially true of the universe, because it is dynamic: what it looks like now depends on what happened to it in the past. So cosmology and cosmogony are intimately intertwined, just as they were in ancient mythology. The current theory of the origins of the universe is of course the Big Bang, which emerged unexpectedly from astronomical observations that were intended to sort out its size and shape. So before we examine the universe's origins, we'll take a quick look at these observations and what they led to.

In ancient times, the world and the universe were pretty much identified. The Sun, Moon, planets and stars were little more than added decoration in the sky; the world on which we lived dominated everything else. Now we realise that our planet is a very tiny lump of rock in a universe so huge that we find it hard to comprehend.

Humanity first caught a glimpse of the sheer vastness of the universe in 1838, when the astronomer Friedrich Bessel measured the distance to the star 61 Cygni. Until then, people who did not believe that the Earth goes round the Sun could offer a fairly plausible argument to show that the Earth had to be fixed. If it moved round the Sun, then the nearer stars would appear to move slightly against the background of more distant stars, an effect called parallax. But they didn't. Bessel found out why: even the nearest stars are a tremendous distance away, making this apparent motion too small to detect. He used a sensitive new telescope to observe the star 61 Cygni. This had been nicknamed the 'flying star' by Giuseppe Piazzi in 1804 because its apparent motion across the sky, though very small, was unusually large compared to that of most other stars. This suggested that the star might be unusually close to the Earth. Bessel discovered that it is 11.4 light years away, roughly 10^{14} (one hundred trillion) kilometres. The modern figure is 11.403, so Bessel was spot-on.

The diminution of humanity had barely begun. As well as twinkling points of light, the night sky boasted a glowing river of light, the Milky Way. In fact it is a disc of stars, most of them too far away to be resolved as individuals, and we are inside it. We now call such a disc a galaxy. Hints that other galaxies might exist appeared when astronomers detected distant nebulas, fuzzy wisps of light. In 1755 the philosopher Immanuel Kant called such nebulas 'island universes'; eventually they became known as galaxies, from the Latin for 'milk'. Charles Messier compiled the first systematic catalogue of nebulas (a few were genuine wisps, not galaxies) in 1774. A prominent one, in the constellation of Andromeda, was the 31st in his list, and it was therefore designated M31. It showed no parallax, so it was presumably a long way away. The big question was: how far?

In 1924 Edwin Hubble showed that M31 lies far beyond the Milky Way, thanks to some brilliant work by Henrietta Leavitt, a human 'computer' hired to carry out the repetitive task of measuring and cataloguing how bright the stars were. At that time astronomers were looking for a 'standard candle' – a type of star whose intrinsic brightness could be inferred from other observations. This could then be compared to its apparent brightness, and the way brightness decreases with distance could be used to calculate how far away the star was. Leavitt was observing Cepheid variables – stars whose light output changes in a periodic cycle – and in 1908 she discovered that the light output of a Cepheid is related to the period of its cycle. Therefore its intrinsic brightness can be calculated from observations, so it can be used as a standard candle. In 1924 Hubble observed Cepheid variables in M31, and calculated that this galaxy is a million light years away. The current estimate is 2.5 million light years.

Most galaxies are much further away than that; so distant that there is no prospect of distinguishing Cepheids, indeed any individual stars. However, Hubble overcame this obstacle too. Vesto Slipher and Milton Humason discovered that the spectra of many galaxies were shifted towards the red end of the spectrum. The most plausible explanation was the Doppler effect, in which a wave changes frequency if its source moves. It is most familiar for sound waves: the pitch of a police car's siren gets lower when it passes, changing from moving towards us to going away from us. The Doppler effect implies that the galaxies concerned must be receding at significant speeds. Hubble plotted the amount of redshift against estimates of distance for forty-six galaxies in which Cepheids had been spotted. The graph was approximately a straight line, suggesting that the velocity of recession (deduced from redshift) and distance were proportional. In 1929 he formulated this as a formula, which we now call Hubble's law. The constant of proportionality, Hubble's constant, is currently thought to be about 21 km/s per million light years. Hubble's initial estimate was about seven times as big.

It is now realised that the Swedish astronomer Knut Lundmark had the same idea in 1924, five years before Hubble. He used the apparent sizes of galaxies to infer how far away they were, and his figure for the 'Hubble' constant was within 1% of today's – far better than Hubble's. However, his work was ignored because his methods had not been cross-checked using independent measurements.

These developments tied the size of the universe and its dynamic behaviour together, and led to a surprising inference. If all of the galaxies are moving away from us, then either the Earth is near the centre of some expanding region, or the entire universe is getting bigger.

Astronomers were already aware that the universe might be expanding. Einstein's field equations, the basis of general relativity, predicted it. In 1924 Aleksandr Friedmann derived three types of solution of the field equations, depending on whether the curvature of space is positive, zero or negative. Mathematicians working in non-Euclidean geometry had already discovered such spaces: respectively, they are said to be elliptic, Euclidean or hyperbolic (like the Escherverse). Elliptic space is finite, a hypersphere – like the surface of a sphere but three-dimensional. The other two are of infinite extent. (The Escherverse is like Roundworld: from the outside it appears to be finite, but from inside, measured using its own metric, it is infinite in extent. That's how it can contain infinitely many angels or devils, all the same size.) The field equations specified a range of shapes for the universe, but did not pin the shape down uniquely.

The field equations also allow the shape of the universe to change as time passes. In 1927 Georges Lemaître derived an expanding universe from Einstein's field equations, and estimated the rate of expansion. His 1931 paper 'A homogeneous universe of constant mass and growing radius accounting for the radial velocity of extragalactic nebulae' went largely unread, because he published it in an obscure Belgian journal, but eventually it became a classic.

Lemaître's solution conflicted with the prevailing cosmological wisdom, but the popular (and populist) astronomer Sir Arthur Eddington believed that Lemaître's theory solved many of the major problems in cosmology. In 1930 he invited Lemaître to a meeting in London about physics and spirituality. By then, Lemaître had realised that if you ran the universe's expansion backwards, every-thing converged to a single point some lengthy period into the past.* He called this initial singularity the primeval atom, and published the idea in the leading scientific journal *Nature*. A huge controversy ensued. Lemaître may not have helped his cause by referring to the idea as 'the Cosmic Egg exploding at the moment of the creation'.

Much later Fred Hoyle, by then a leading advocate of the steady-state theory – that the universe is in equilibrium, aside from local fluctuations, and it has always been that way – dismissed Lemaître's theory as the 'Big Bang'. The name stuck. So did the theory, to Hoyle's discomfort. Hoyle had developed the steady-state theory in 1948, aided by Thomas Gold, Hermann Bondi and others. It required matter to be continuously created, gently, particle by particle, in the voids between the stars, to prevent the density of matter decreasing as the universe got bigger. The necessary rate of production was low, about one hydrogen atom per cubic metre every billion years.

Unfortunately for Hoyle, indirect evidence against the steady-state theory, and in favour of the Big Bang, kept piling up. The smoking gun was the discovery of cosmic background radiation in 1965 – a sizzle of random radio noise that we now think originated when the universe first became transparent to radio waves, shortly after the Big Bang. Moreover, its temperature agreed with theory. Hawking has called this observation 'the final nail in the coffin of the steady-state theory'.

Einstein, in private, was unimpressed by Lemaître's expanding-universe solution. He accepted the mathematics, but not the physical reality. But when Hubble's results were published two years later, Einstein immediately changed his mind and gave Lemaître strong public support. In 1935 Howard Robertson and Arthur Walker proved that every homogeneous, isotropic universe – one that is

---

* Actually, Lemaître's doesn't, not in its original formulation. Instead of a point singularity at a finite time in the past, it has a hyperspherical singularity infinitely far in the past.

the same at every point and in every direction – corresponds to a particular family of solutions of Einstein's field equations. The resulting universes could be static, expanding or contracting; their topology could be simple or complex. The family is called the Friedmann-Lemaître-Robertson-Walker metric, or the 'standard model of cosmology' if that's too big a mouthful. It now dominates mainstream cosmological thinking.

Narrativium now took over, and led many cosmologists into the realms of scientific mythology. The correct statement that 'there exist solutions of Einstein's field equations corresponding to the classical non-Euclidean geometries' transmogrified into the false statement 'these are the only possible solutions of constant curvature'. The mistake may have arisen because mathematicians weren't paying enough attention to astronomy and astronomers weren't paying enough attention to mathematics. Robertson and Walker's uniqueness theorem proves that the *metric* is unique, and it is easy to imagine that the space must also be unique. After all, doesn't the metric define the space?

No, it doesn't.

The metric is local; the space is global. Both infinite Euclidean space and the flat torus have the same metric, because the geometry of small regions is identical. The computer screen remains flat; what changes are the rules about going off the edge. But globally, the flat torus has special geodesics – ones that form closed loops – whereas Euclidean space does not. So the metric does not define the space. But cosmologists thought it did. In 1999, writing in *Scientific American*, Jean-Pierre Luminet, Glenn Starkman, and Jeffrey Weeks, wrote: 'The decades from 1930 to 1990 were the dark ages of the subject. Most astronomy textbooks, quoting one another for support, stated that the universe must be either a hypersphere, an infinite Euclidean space, or an infinite hyperbolic space. Other topologies were largely forgotten.'

In fact, more than one topology is possible in each of the three cases. Friedmann had said as much in his 1924 paper, for negative curvature, but this remark somehow became forgotten. Finite spaces of zero curvature had already been discovered, the most obvious being the flat torus. Elliptic space was finite anyway. But even that space was not the only possibility with constant positive curvature, a fact known to Poincaré in 1904. Unfortunately, once the misconception had set in, it was very hard to root it out again, and it obscured the question of the shape of the universe for decades.

However, at that time cosmologists were after bigger game: the origin of the universe. According to the Big Bang solution of the field equations, both space *and time* sprang into existence from nothing, and then evolved into today's universe. Physicists were ready for this radical theory because quantum mechanics had already softened them up for the idea that particles can arise spontaneously from nothing. If a particle can do it, why not a universe? If space can do it, why not time?

Looking back at Einstein again. He could even have *predicted* an expanding spherical universe, but he got it into his head that the static one was the right one. To obtain a static solution, he modified his field equations to include an extra term depending on a 'cosmological constant'. By choosing this constant suitably, the universe could be rendered static. Precisely *why* the cosmological constant would have that value was less clear, but the new term in the equations obeyed all of the deep symmetry principles that drove Einstein's philosophy of how the universe ought to behave. It would actually take a lot of special pleading to eliminate that term. When telescopic observations of the spectra of galaxies revealed an expanding universe, Einstein decided that including the cosmological constant had been his 'biggest blunder'. If he had left it out, he could have predicted the expansion.

Well ... that's the standard story, but it requires an unstated assumption. In order to derive a formula for how the shape and size of the universe changes over time, the mathematical physicists of the early twentieth century looked only for spherically symmetric solutions of Einstein's field equations. This assumption reduces the spatial variables from three to one: the distance from the centre. As a bonus, it simplifies the Einstein field equations, which can now be solved by an explicit formula. Although there is a hand-waving justification of spherical symmetry, 'the universe should be the same everywhere', it doesn't have a solid basis. Einstein had insisted that the *laws* should be the same everywhere, but that doesn't imply the same *behaviour* everywhere. Both planets and the vacuum obey the same laws, for example.

With the advent of computers, it turned out that the Einstein field equations have zillions of solutions – infinitely many, depending on the choice of initial conditions – almost all of which are not spherically symmetric. Space might expand in some regions, contract in others, or swirl round and round. It could change its behaviour as time passed. So although an expanding universe is one possible solution of the Einstein field equations, it no more constitutes a prediction of an expanding universe than the *possibility* of rain tomorrow, as a solution of the weather equations, constitutes a firm forecast of rain.

A few years ago, all was sweetness and light. The Big Bang fitted all the important observations. In particular, it predicted that the cosmic microwave background radiation should have a temperature of about 3 degrees absolute. Score one to the Big Bang.

As research continued, however, difficulties emerged. Today's universe has a lot of large-scale structure – vast skeins of galaxies surrounding even vaster voids, like the foam in a glass of beer, with galaxies forming on the surfaces of beer bubbles, and voids corresponding to the air inside them. Backtracking from its present state and using current theories, the universe should be about 13.5 billion years old. On the one hand, that's too short a time to explain the current clumpiness of matter. On the other hand, it's not long enough to explain the current flatness of space.

A second difficulty emerges from the observed 'rotation curves' of galaxies. Galaxies do not rotate like a rigid object: stars at different distances from the centre move with different speeds. Stars in the galaxy's central bulge move quite slowly; those further out are faster. However, the stars outside the central bulge all move with much the same speed. This is a puzzle for theorists, because both Newtonian and Einsteinian gravity require the stars to move more slowly in the outer reaches of the galaxy. Virtually all galaxies behave in this unexpected manner, which conflicts with numerous observations.

The third problem is the 1998 discovery that the expansion of the universe is accelerating, which is consistent with a positive non-zero cosmological constant. This was based on the High-z Supernova Search Team's observations of the redshift in Type Ia supernovae, and won the Nobel Prize for Physics in 2011.

The prevailing cosmological wisdom deals with these problems by bolting on three additional assumptions. The first is inflation, in which the entire universe expanded to a huge size in an extraordinarily short time. The figures are shocking: between 10^{-36} and 10^{-32} seconds after the Big Bang the volume of the universe multiplied by a factor of at least 10^{78}. The cause of this rapid growth – an explosion far more impressive than the wimpy Big Bang that started it all – is, we are told, an inflaton field. (Not 'inflation field': an inflaton is – well, a quantum field that causes inflation.) This theory fits many observations very well. The main snag is the absence of any direct evidence for the existence of an inflaton field.

To solve the problem of galactic rotation curves, cosmologists propose the existence of dark matter. This is a form of matter that can't be observed by the radiation it emits, because it doesn't, not in any quantity that can be observed from here. It's entirely reasonable that a lot of the matter in the universe might not be observable, but what we can infer indirectly leads to the conclusion that whatever dark matter may be, it's not made from the fundamental particles that we know about on Earth. It's a very alien form of matter, which mainly interacts with everything else through the force of gravity. No such particles have ever been observed, but there are several competing suggestions for what they ought to be, the front runner being WIMPs (weakly interacting massive particles). Despite a lot of theorising, the precise nature of dark matter is up for grabs.

The acceleration of the expansion of the universe is attributed to 'dark energy', which is little more than a name for 'stuff that makes the expansion accelerate' – though, to be fair, supplemented by detailed analyses of what kind of effect this stuff must have, and suggestions for what it might be. One possibility is Einstein's cosmological constant.

Until recently, these three *dei ex machina* resolved most significant discrepancies between the naive Big Bang theory and increasingly sophisticated observations. The introduction of these three items of novel physics, all produced out of a hat and without much independent observational support (other than what they were invented to explain), could be justified pragmatically: they worked, and nothing else seemed to. But there is now a growing realisation that the first of those statements no longer holds, but unfortunately the second still does. A growing minority of cosmologists suspect that three *dei ex machina* is at least two too many for comfort.

It is now realised that if an inflaton field exists, it doesn't conveniently switch on once and then cease to operate, which is assumed in the usual explanation of the structure of our universe. Instead, the inflaton field can swing into action anywhere, and at any time, repeatedly. This leads to a scenario called eternal inflation, with our region of the universe being just one inflated bubble in a bubble-bath of cosmic foam. A new period of inflation might start in your living room this afternoon, instantaneously blowing up your television set and the cat by a factor of 10^{78}.

Another problem is that almost all inflationary universes fail to match ours, and if you restrict initial conditions to get the ones that do, then a non-inflationary universe that performs just as well is vastly more probable. According to Roger Penrose suitable initial conditions not requiring inflation outnumber those for an inflationary universe by a factor of one googolplex – ten to the power ten to the power one hundred. So an explanation not involving inflation, although it requires an extraordinarily unlikely initial state, is massively more plausible than an explanation that does involve inflation.

A few mavericks have been devising alternatives to the standard model all along, but now mainstream cosmologists are also having to rethink the theory. There is no shortage of ideas. In some, there is no Big Bang; instead, there is a kind of revival of the steady-state universe, in which a suitably clumpy distribution of matter can survive for hundreds of billions of years, perhaps indefinitely. The redshift is not caused by expansion, but by gravity. Dark matter is not needed to explain rotation curves: instead, relativistic inertial dragging, in which rotating matter carries space along with it, might do the job.

Perhaps more radical is the proposal that either our theory of gravity, or our theory of motion, need to be modified slightly. In 2012 the particle physicist and Nobel prize-winner Martinus Veltman, when asked 'Will supersymmetry explain dark matter?', replied: 'Of course it won't. People have been looking for this stuff since the 1980s and are just talking ballyhoo. Isn't it more likely that we don't understand gravity all that well? Astrophysicists believe in Einstein's theory of gravity with a fervour that is unbelievable. Do you know how much of Einstein's theory has been tested at the distances of galaxies where we "see" dark matter? None of it.'*

The best known proposal here is MOND, Modified Newtonian Dynamics, suggested in 1983 by Mordehai Milgrom. The basic idea is that Newton's second law of motion may not be valid for very small accelerations, so that acceleration is not proportional to the force of

---

* Martinus Veltman, coming to terms with the Higgs, *Nature* **490** (2012) S10-S11.

gravity when that force is very weak. There is a tendency to assume that MOND is the only alternative to general relativity; the correct statement is that it is the most extensively explored one. Robert Caldwell,[*] in a special issue of a Royal Society journal devoted to cosmological tests of general relativity, wrote: 'To date, it appears entirely reasonable that the observations may be explained by new laws of gravitation.' In the same issue Ruth Durrer[†] pointed out that the evidence for dark energy is weak: 'Our single indication for the existence of dark energy comes from distance measurements and their relation to redshift.' The rest of the evidence, she says, merely establishes that distances estimated by redshift measurements are larger than those expected from the standard cosmological model. Something unexpected is going on, but it might not be dark energy.

Our confidence that we know how our universe began is being shaken. Some modified version of the Big Bang may well be correct – but then again, maybe not. When new evidence comes along, scientists change their minds.

Though perhaps not quite yet.

---

[*] Robert R. Caldwell, A gravitational puzzle, *Philosophical Transactions of the Royal Society of London* A (2011) **369**, 4998-5002.
[†] Ruth Durrer, What do we really know about dark energy? *Philosophical Transactions of the Royal Society of London* A (2011) **369**, 5102-5114.

DOES GOD WIGGLE HIS FINGERS?

 Marjorie had been lost in her furious thoughts for an unmeasured length of time which, as it turned out, was about five minutes. These were broken into by Mustrum Ridcully, who had given her an appropriate nudge. She shook herself, stood up straight (which she generally did anyway) and said brightly, 'This is going to be round two; yes?'

Ponder Stibbons hurried over, detected a certain look in her eye, and said, 'Really, Miss Daw, please leave it all to the Archchancellors. After all, it is *our* business.'

Marjorie smiled: not the smile she had for a good book well read and catalogued and subsequently handed to the appropriate reader – a process she thought of as carrying *the flame*.*

The chamber was buzzing as people poured in, chattering. Lord Vetinari, apparently refreshed, was ascending the stairs to the podium. The gavel dropped like thunder and, almost immediately, so did the noise.

---

* At this point it must be said that Marjorie also had a smile for a gentleman known as Jeffrey, who travelled the world inspecting, reviewing, cataloguing and pricing – and *in extremis* also restoring – the libraries of a very large number of people and organisations across the world. The two of them had an understanding, and understood quite a lot, especially about Bliss. In case anybody is now thinking of librarian pornography, this is an alternative way of cataloguing books: a system created by Henry E. Bliss (1870–1955), still in use in America and specialised libraries.

'Ladies and gentlemen, I ask the wizards of Unseen University to defend their ownership of the Round World, although it appears to me that *stewardship* might be a better and more appropriate term. It also occurs to me that I haven't even *seen* this curious thing. It is apparently reasonably small, so I will have it on my podium right now, so we can all visualise what is at the centre of today's little escapade. It will be brought to me *at once.*'

Ponder Stibbons was dispatched in haste to the university and returned, breathless, carrying the padded baize bag. Against a background of laughter, giggles and outright tittering, he gently put the contents of the bag on a tripod in front of the Patrician, who himself seemed somewhat amused by what had been placed before him.

There was a twinkle in his eye as he said, 'Excuse me if I seek for clarity, gentlemen, but could this indeed be a living world with a population of millions? Over to *you*, Archchancellor. I must say I am all agog!'

'In fact, your Lordship, I will delegate this job firstly to Ponder Stibbons, head of the Inadvisably Applied Magical facility. What he does not know about quantum – yes, I am afraid we *must* use the term, my Lord – just isn't worth knowing. Mister Stibbons—?'

Ponder cleared his throat. 'My Lord, Roundworld came into being several years ago when we were experimenting with raw firmament. The Dean experimentally put his hand in the container and wiggled it about …'

Ponder's voice faded as he saw Lord Vetinari's expression. The Patrician was writing notes on his papers on the desk in front of him, and now he looked up, blinked, and said out loud, 'Wiggled it about? May I ask whether he intends to wiggle anything today?' A titter ran around the room as Lord Vetinari added, 'Shouldn't he be wearing gloves? I have no real ambition to be transmogrified!'

Ponder Stibbons, after he stopped laughing, rose to the occasion. 'It is unlikely, sir: we've tried and it only works with raw firmament, and *that* is very difficult to get hold of these days. If I may continue … ?

The firmament in this case reconstituted itself as a universe, somewhat similar to our own, though happily using up only local firmament supplies. It is our belief, based *on experimentation*, that Roundworld picked up some aspects of our own world, but alas with rather less firmament. Nevertheless, it turned out to be quite small but ingeniously formed in most respects and, I might say, punching above its weight.

'We have explored other universes by various occult means, and frankly, my Lord,' he added, 'so many of them are rather drab – just a few stars banging together occasionally and with planets where there is little or no life at all. And such as it is, life there is snivelling and grovelling underground, or at the bottom of the sea, if the planet has even been lucky enough to have one of those!'

'Mister Stibbons, in your opinion, when the Dean – who I believe we shall hear from shortly – "wiggled his fingers" in firmament, did he then become a *god*?'

'Not at all, my Lord. He was nothing more than a random event, turning an instability into coherence – the same as a last snowflake just before an avalanche. Not the best way of putting it, but I think it will suffice for now. However, as a result, the whole business left certain effects in both Discworld and Roundworld; for example, Roundworld has traditions of wizards, unicorns, trolls and dwarfs; not to mention zombies, werewolves and vampires. Our research shows that although these things don't appear in Roundworld, the *concept* of them is shared by both worlds.'

Ponder took a deep breath and continued, 'The idea of gods has permeated cultures in both worlds. In our world gods are not only acknowledged but also, occasionally, *seen*. Although there are claims that they *have* been seen on Roundworld as well, the evidence is generally patchy, and sometimes simply wishful, thinking.'

'Really,' said Lord Vetinari. 'I am surprised. Gods have their uses and a part to play, and I often thank Saponaria when getting into the bath; she generally arranges the very best of suds – wonderfully fine, smooth and plentiful. Of course, I never neglect a candle for Narrativia before I embark on a lengthy memoir. It would also appear that the small gods, the household gods, survive very well. I take leave to wonder what went wrong in Roundworld?'

Marjorie's self-control finally snapped. 'Such concepts of the gods as there were on Roundworld didn't work!' she cried. 'Proud people and smart people started to put their ideas into the mouths of the gods, and shamefully it has not been unusual for two countries, ostensibly both running on the rules of the same one sacred God, to nevertheless engage one and another in combat such as never been seen on *this world* – the deliberate destruction of whole cities and even attempts to slaughter whole races. Today, many of those who saw the name of God invoked as part of this dreadful pantomime have stepped back and very much prefer reason to faith, because it is self-checking.'

Lord Vetinari sat for a moment taking this in. Then he stared at Marjorie like a cat assessing an amazing new type of mouse, and said, 'I do not believe I know your name, *madam*, or your occupation; be so good as to enlighten me, will you?'

TWENTY

DISBELIEF SYSTEM

 Roundworld has its own home-grown Omnians. We're not referring to the great majority of religious believers, who are entirely normal people who happen to have been brought up in a culture that has its own distinctive set of beliefs in things that lack objective evidence. Neither are we referring to Roundworld's equivalent of mainstream Omnians, who since the overthrow of the extremist Vorbis and his rerun of the Inquisition (see *Small Gods*) have been decent-enough sorts and kept themselves to themselves.

No, it is the Vorbises of Roundworld who cause all the trouble. Believers with a capital B. These are the people who not only *know* that their worldview is The Truth – the sole truth, the only truth, the truth revealed from the mouth of God himself – but are intent on forcing it onto everyone else, whether they want it or not, at any cost.

Most sane, rational human beings learn quite early on that you feel just as certain even when you're wrong: the strength of your belief is not a valid measure of its relation to reality. If you have scientific training, you may even learn the value of doubt. You can certainly have religious beliefs and still be a good *scientist*; you can also be a good *person* and understand that people who disagree with your beliefs need not necessarily be evil, or even misguided. After all, most of the world's people – even the religious ones – probably think your beliefs are nonsense. *They* have a different set of beliefs, which *you* think are nonsense.

But religious extremists seem unaware of the human tendency towards self-delusion, and decline to take even the simplest steps to counteract it. When the British Humanist Association hired a bus to tour the UK with the advert 'There's probably no God. Now stop worrying and enjoy your life' on its side, the immediate response from some religious authorities was: 'They don't seem terribly confident about it.' No, what they did with the 'probably' was to try not to let opponents score an easy point by criticising them for being dogmatic. Being too confident of their view. More practically, they were also worried about potentially breaching the Advertising Code. Another response from some of those of a religious persuasion was synthetic outrage and claims of persecution.

But Humanists are just as entitled to put their views on the side of a bus as tens of thousands of churches worldwide are to stick 'The wages of sin is death' on their walls. That's why the Humanists hired the bus – one small voice crying out against the multitudes, many of whom were clearly intolerant.

Belief is a very odd word, and it is used in several ways. 'Belief that' differs greatly from 'belief in', which is again different from 'belief about'. Our belief *about* science, for example, is that it's simply our best defence against believing (in) what we want to. But we may also have, to some extent, a belief *in* science, as distinct from belief in a religion or a cult: we believe *that* science can find ways out of humankind's present difficulties, ways that are not available to politics, philosophy or religion.

There is also a different usage of 'belief' altogether, one that we suspect is not always appreciated. Suppose that a scientist says 'I believe that humans evolved', and a religious person counters with 'I believe humans were created by God'. On the surface, these are similar statements, and it's easy to conclude that science is just another kind of religion. However, in religion, once you believe something, then you consider it to be an immutable truth. In science, the same word means 'I'm not very sure about this'. As we might say 'I *believe* I left my credit card in the pub', when we haven't a clue where it's gone.

Ponder Stibbons believes that Roundworld is a construction whose genesis was events on Discworld. We, and you, believe the converse: that Discworld is a construct, created by Terry Pratchett in Round-world. It's just possible for both of these beliefs to be true – for a given value of truth. We all have beliefs of one kind or another. Let's look at how we get them, and how we might judge them.

Do newborn babies have beliefs? Surprisingly, the answer seems to be 'yes'. They are very primitive, ill-formed beliefs, and they are consid-erably refined even in the first six months of life, but a few behaviours, even of newborns, suggest that a lot of wiring-up of the brain has gone on in the womb. The baby is far from being a blank slate on which anything can be written – a stance that Pinker argues persua-sively in his book *The Blank Slate*. The baby is especially responsive to the sight of its mother, and can become very disturbed if she simply disappears from view. It responds to music that is similar to what it heard while in the womb in the later stages of its development; it can distinguish jazz from Beethoven or folksong by attentively 'listening' for familiar sounds. It has a whole suite of beliefs about suckling, about breasts and what they're for. These things are beliefs in the sense that the baby's brain already holds some model of mother, and of music, and it prefers things that fit this model.

Soon, the baby begins to smile in response to a smile; even to a drawing of a smile. Is that a belief too? The answer depends on, but also illuminates, what we mean by a belief. The baby acts in particu-lar ways – smiles, or suckles – because of the way its brain is wired up, because of programmes in its brain that could be otherwise, and, in occasional babies, *are* otherwise. Mostly, these are pathologies; apart from different musical preferences, there are few normal differences between baby brains. But very soon, because of a mother's behaviour, whether the baby is swaddled or carried on a bare back into the fields, or left out on a mountainside, or has its feet bound, babies *diverge*. And very soon, they are inducted into the Make-a-Human-Being kit that is characteristic of, and specific to, each human culture.

There are several ways to look at how a baby interacts with its surroundings. When the baby throws out toys from its pram, for example, this can be read in at least two ways. On the one hand, we might simply assume that it cannot retain a good grasp of the toy, which falls. However, observing the radiant smile with which it welcomes the return of the toy, we might conclude that the baby is teaching its mother to fetch. Such apparently minor interactions have a strong effect on the baby's future, and they complicate it in ways that often reinforce the culture concerned. They include little songs and stories; learning to walk, to talk, and to play. We say 'learning' here, but these processes are like birds learning to fly. Many features of the ability are already wired into the brain, but now they have to be adjusted in a kind of dialogue with the real world. 'If I stretch this bit out, and pull it back, what happens?' So these abilities *mature*: they are not learned from scratch.

In *Unweaving the Rainbow*, Dawkins likens juvenile humans to caterpillars, voracious in their uptake of information, especially from parents: Father Christmas, Heaven, fairies, what food to eat at festivals. He points out how credulous we *must* be as juveniles, to avoid obstacles to learning; but also how we should become more sceptical as adults, and that too many adults fail to do so, hence, alas, astrologers, mediums, priests and the like.

We can see just how indiscriminately juveniles pick up information through something that happened to Jack. He ran an extramural class in animal-handling for about thirty years, and became very impressed by the distribution of animal phobias (although he did realise that this was a very peculiar group of students in that respect). About a quarter of the students had a spider phobia, rather fewer had snake phobia (which, if bad, included worms). Some had a phobia for rats and mice. A few reacted badly to birds, feathers or bats. It seems likely (but we can't document it in this instance) that these phobias came about by cultural infection: Mother screamed when she found a spider in the bath, or a television series depicted snakes as poisonous. (Less than 3% actually are, but it might be wise to assume lethality as a default, for solid evolutionary reasons.) Rats are often depicted as being dirty, and the same goes for mice. Jack never worked out what gave rise to phobias about birds and feathers, but it certainly passes on in families, and it's much more likely to be learned rather than genetic. It might be a great example of how beliefs can pass from brain to brain like a computer virus, in this case not transmitted verbally. But we can see how useful these phobias would have been when we were much nearer to nature. They let us learn what creatures to avoid, instantly. And while it didn't much matter if we occasionally avoided an animal that was actually harmless, the same mistake the other way round could be disastrous.

Beliefs are formed through interactions between an individual's brain and his or her environment, especially other people but also the natural world (spiders!) So it's worth taking a general look at interactions.

If A acts on B, we call this an action; but if B also (re)acts on A, we say that A and B are *interacting*. A baby and its mother are like that. But most interactions are not just some sort of exchange, and they have a deeper effect: A and B are, to a greater or lesser extent, *changed* by the interaction. They then become A' and B'; then they interact again, and again, and are changed still more. After several changes of this kind, A and B have become quite different systems.

For example, the actor walks out onto the stage, and the audience reacts; the actor reacts to this, and the audience in turn reacts to the actor's new persona … and so on. In *The Collapse of Chaos* we called this deeper kind of interaction 'complicity', giving a familiar word a technical meaning that is not too far removed from the usual one, but also hinting at a mix of complexity and simplicity. The complicity between child and mother, later between child and teachers, then with sports teams, then with the whole adult world, is the Make-a-Human-Being kit we talked of earlier. We also need a word for this cultural interaction, and have suggested 'extelligence'. Individuals are *in*telligent; there are useful ideas and abilities somehow represented, remembered and readied for use, inside their brains. But most of a culture's collective knowledge is outside any given individual, forming a body of information that is not in any one brain, but *outside*; hence *ex*telligence. Before the invention of writing, most of a culture's extelligence resided in the entire collective of brains, but when writing came along, some of it – often the most important to the culture – didn't need a brain to contain it; only to extract and interpret it. Printing boosted the role of this type of extelligence, and modern technology has led to its dominance.

Where do our beliefs come from? From complicity between our intelligence and the extelligence that surrounds it. This process continues into adulthood, but its greatest effect occurs when we are children. St Francis Xavier, co-founder of the Jesuits and a missionary, is quoted as saying 'Give me the child until he is seven and I'll give you the man'. A trawl of today's premier extelligence, the internet, will haul up an almost endless range of interpretations of that phrase, from benign to malign, but their common ingredient is the malleability of human intelligence at an early age, and its fixity thereafter.

Until fairly recently, almost all people were religious believers. The majority still are, but the proportions depend on culture in a dramatic way. In the United Kingdom, about 40% say they have no religion, 30% align themselves with one but do not consider themselves in any way religious, and only 30% say they have significant religious beliefs. An even smaller proportion attends some kind of place of worship regularly. In the United States, over 80% identify with a specific religious denomination, 40% say they attend services weekly, and 58% say that they pray most weeks. It's an intriguing difference between cultures that have such a lot in common.

Most religious activity, for the last few thousand years, is based on belief in a god or gods that acted to create the world, human beings, the beasts of the field, plants – everything. We discussed some of these creator gods in chapter 4; they used to resemble human beings or animals, but nowadays they are often abstract and ineffable; either way, they have supernatural powers. They are believed to be in daily contact with the world, making thunderstorms, providing good and bad luck for individual people, acting as a source of wisdom and authority through oral tradition (maintained by a shaman, a priest, or a priesthood). And, in the last few thousand years, Holy Books. Such theist beliefs contrast with deist beliefs, in which there is no overt anthropomorphic god, but some entity, or process, looks after the whole caboodle in deep background.

Such beliefs can be very powerful, and they form the basis of most people's views of the world and of our lives. In the seventeenth and eighteenth centuries there was a strong movement among intellectuals to reform the structure of society, by basing it on reason, rather than on faith and tradition. This movement, known as the Enlightenment or the Age of Reason, was highly influential throughout Europe and America. It played a role in the formulation of constitutional declarations of human rights, among them the American Declaration of Independence and the French Declaration of the Rights of Man.

Since then, the proportion of non-believers has increased throughout the Western world, especially among those who are well educated and well heeled financially (as a survey in the United States has clearly shown, for example). Such people, among whom we count ourselves, agree with Dawkins, though perhaps not so publicly: they maintain that there is no god, or God, out there: it's all done by laws of nature, sometimes 'transcended' by changing the context for those laws.

Good and bad 'luck' come from our own actions and the general cussedness of nature; there's no supernatural entity that consciously affects our lives.

Why do so many people believe in a god? Dennett's *Breaking the Spell* is an attempt to examine that question, for Christian fundamentalists, Islamic teachers, Buddhist monks, atheists, and others. He begins by pointing to the commonality of pre-scientific answers in groups of people: 'How do thunderstorms happen?' answered by 'It must be someone up there with a gigantic hammer' (our example, not his). Then, probably after a minimum of discussion, a name such as 'Thor' becomes agreed. Having successfully sorted out thunderstorms, in the sense that you now have an agreed answer to why they happen, other forces of nature are similarly identified and named. Soon you have a pantheon, a community of gods to blame everything on. It's very satisfying when everyone around you agrees, so the pantheon soon becomes the accepted wisdom, and few question it. In some cultures, few dare to question it, because there are penalties if you do.

J. Anderson Thomson Jr's book *Why We Believe in God(s)* devotes each chapter to a different reason for the existence of beliefs. It makes a good case for a Dennett-style system, and is persuasive enough that we'd expect aliens, if they have anything like the kind of social life we have, to have believed in god(s) during at least the early growth of their culture. The aliens would have to have had nurturing parent(s), tribes with a big alien as boss, and so on, but that's a reasonable expectation if they are extelligent.

People in all cultures grow up and acquire a set of beliefs. One way of looking at this is to call the beliefs that are inherited 'memes'. Just as 'genes' code for hereditary traits, so memes are intended to show the inheritance of individual items, rather than a whole belief system. A tune like 'Happy Birthday', a concept like Father Christmas, atom, bicycle or fairy – all are memes. A whole slew of memes that forms an interacting whole is called a memeplex, and religions are the best examples, which at various times and in various cultures have had, or still do have, many linked-up memes like 'There is Heaven and there is Hell …' and 'Unless you pray to *this* God you'll go to Hell' and 'You must teach this to your children …' and 'You must kill those who don't believe in this …' and so on. You will have some familiarity with other religions, and you will appreciate that we're not saying that *your* religion is like that. It's all the others, the mistaken ones …

We should look at a few belief systems, to see how they worked and whence they got their authority. We'll choose some relatively un-familiar ones, where it's easier (for most of us) to set aside our own beliefs. If you're a Jewish Cathar Scientologist, skip this bit.

The Cathars were an odd group of Christians, existing from about 1100 until they were massacred around the period 1220 to 1250, initially by barons of Northern France empowered by the Pope, but then by the Inquisition. They believed that the material world was essentially evil, and that only the spiritual world was good. They deplored sex in general; indeed their bonhommes, or perfecti, wouldn't eat meat because it was the result of sexuality. Fish was all right: they didn't know about underwater sex – or plant sex, for that matter. They were totally celibate, and deplored sex even in marriage. There was a ceremony, prescribed for attainment of the perfectus state, a single sacrament, the consolamentum or consola-tion. It involved a brief spiritual ceremony to remove all sin from the credente, or believer, and induct them into the next higher level as a perfectus. It was commonly performed as death approached, so that the believer was not condemned. Belief in its effectiveness, however, was by no means universal.

Presumably their anti-sex views would weigh against having children, so that any such belief system would be likely to lose its adherents as time passes, but that seems not to have happened. They were remarkably successful in Languedoc, perhaps mostly through conversion. In this they were the cultivated roses of religion, prop-agated not through sex but by taking cuttings. Considering the practices of Catholic priests, whose behaviour at that time was a distinct contrast, it's not surprising there were many conversions. That is probably why they had to be annihilated.

The Jews of Poland in the late Middle Ages were mostly confined to ghettos, and restricted to a few trades including usury – money-lending. Their beliefs were complicated. Males learned *Torah* (Old Testament, Five Books of Moses) from a very young age, and then graduated to *Talmud*, a compilation of commentaries on the *Torah* by mostly-Babylonian rabbis. After the Bar Mitzvah cere-mony at about age thirteen, which included reciting, and usually singing, a piece from *Torah* and commenting on it, they continued to study Jewish texts, especially the *Talmud* and the *Gemara* (addi-tional rabbinical comments).

Boys who continued to study were frequently maintained by general ghetto funds, such as they were (even today in Israel, boys of Orthodox clans are allowed not to do national service). Females had to learn to keep a kosher household, which involved a whole complex of issues, not simply having kosher meat, but also separating milk dishes from meat dishes, keeping separate cloths and cutlery as well as dishes, and cleaning house, particularly for the Passover, which required a different set of menus. The reward system was not, basi-cally, Heaven or Hell; it was simply that doing these things led to a good life, consonant with what God (Jehovah, but his name must not be said) wanted for man, and to some extent woman.

In the 1550s the rules were collected into a great composition, the *Shulchan Aruch*, by a Sephardic rabbi in Israel, or possibly Damascus. They became the greatest compendium of Jewish law, especially for the Ashkenazi communities of middle-Europe (Sephardi and Ash-kenazi are two separate streams of Jewish culture). This belief system has continued, with much evolution, to the present day. Jack's rabbi has said that he's the best atheist in her congregation.

Scientology evolved from L. Ron Hubbard's earlier invention, Dianetics. L. Ron ('Elron') was a fairly successful science fiction author, but his entry into belief systems was distinctly more successful. Few scientists would agree with his claim that Dianetics was a science, but it sold a lot of books; he had audiences of thousands, and after the editor John W. Campbell described it in *Astounding Science Fiction* it really took off. Martin Gardner's claim that science fiction fans were very gullible seems to have been true. However, in the longer term Dianetics failed, and Hubbard produced Scientology, which has gone from strength to strength on the basis of a set of beliefs not very different from those of Dianetics.

Basically, the idea is that a set of 'engrams' is induced in people by their experiences (including when they were an embryo, before the nervous system develops). Engrams are records of bad experiences, especially very bad ones, which have to be erased for people to become clears – a step upwards on the evolutionary ladder from ordinary humans. People have souls, thetans, that have jumped from alien to alien over billions of years. The important issue for questions about belief is that this system derived from the imagination of one man, who failed to sell Dianetics. It now has tens of thousands of adherents, at least; it claims millions.

These are just three examples. Here are some others to consider, since people seem to pick up sets of beliefs terribly easily.

Rosicrucians, for instance, believe that a set of mystical instructions will enable them to achieve telepathy, success in their jobs and instantaneous travel anywhere, including other planets. The cost of this instruction is considerable, but eventually it gets you into the central core of the sect, where anything is possible. Atlanteans believe that every so often the Earth tilts, flooding all the present continents and exposing new ones; if you find an Atlantean, note where he buys his next house. There are hundreds of such belief systems, and the people who subscribe to them – often paying large sums of money –

get all kinds of benefits, especially being privy to the real truth about life, the universe, and everything.

Other belief systems are not so wild. We have in mind systems like Count Alfred Korzybski's general semantics, which produced wise little gems like 'the map is not the territory', Ludwig von Bertalanffy's general system theory, and the many systems of mind training such as Esalen, with which Gregory Bateson was associated. There are thousands of 'mind training' hits on Google, most of them based in California. It is easy to understand the feelings, the beliefs, that send people into these systems of self-improvement. We subscribe to some ourselves – devotion to explanations involving 'complexity', promoted by the Santa Fe Institute for Complex Systems and the New England Complex Systems Institute (whose acronym, NECSI, has enabled Jack to promote himself as a necsialist, if not quite a nexialist*).

However, the variety of these beliefs – most of which seem very strange to outsiders – is amazing. How can so many belief systems, differing so radically from the common experience of humanity, be accepted by so many people? For each individual belief system, the majority of us consider at least some of the beliefs to be absurd. So why is the absurdity not apparent to everyone? Can it be that people in general are so ignorant of reality nowadays that they will buy into anything that promises a better or more interesting life?

There was also a system advertised not that long ago which forecast that 2012 would be a year of financial collapse *and* the beginning of World War III – which wouldn't of itself have been a great surprise given some of the conflicts. However, the forecast was based on rather strange reasoning: not as a result of the antics of greedy bankers and the armaments industry, but because the ancient Mayan calendar ran out in 2012.[†] The Mayans themselves mostly ran out in

---

* Science fiction author A.E. Van Vogt coined the term in *Voyage of the Space Beagle*. He defined a nexialist to be someone who is good at joining together, in an orderly fashion, the knowledge of several fields of learning.

† It didn't, anyway. The period concerned was just the first of an even vaster series of calendar cycles.

the 1600s, because of the diseases which the Spaniards brought, not because of Spanish military prowess. So it's difficult to see what their calendar had to do with us. The calendars on many kitchen walls this year – and most years – run out on 31 December … Hallelujah! It's the apocalypse!

In 2012 *Scientific American** reported a psychological study carried out by Will Gervais and Ara Norenzayan, under the title 'How critical thinkers lose their faith in God'. It was a follow-up to a 2011 investigation by Harvard researchers, who concluded that what we believe is closely linked to how we usually think. Intuitive thinkers, who come to conclusions instinctively, tend to have religious beliefs. Analytic thinkers tend not to. Encouraging people to use intuition rather than logical analysis increased their belief in God.

Gervais and Norenzayan wondered whether the underlying distinction could be understood in a slightly different manner, as a difference between two ways of thinking that are both useful in suitable circumstances. System 1 thinking is 'quick and dirty', relying on simple rules of thumb to make decisions rapidly. If an early human on the savannah spots a patch of orange behind a bush, it makes good sense to assume that it might be a lion, and take avoiding action. A more analytical System 2 assessment might subsequently discover that the orange patch was a bunch of dried leaves, but the processes involved would be slower, and involve more work. In this case, System 1 thinking does little harm if it later turns out to be mistaken, but System 2 could kill you if there really is a lion and you waste time trying to decide.

On the other hand, there are many occasions on which System 2 saves lives, but System 1 does not. Thinking about past forest fires, and deciding not to build your village in an area surrounded by dry

---

* Daisy Grewal, How critical thinkers lose their faith in God, *Scientific American* **307** No. 1 (July 2012) 26.

vegetation, trumps an intuitive assessment that the location has ample building materials. Avoiding floodplains, even though it is easy to build houses on them and they are currently unoccupied, can prevent complete destruction of your property when the river rises. There is a *reason* why they are currently unoccupied.

Teasing out the workings of the human brain is tricky, but psychologists have developed techniques that help. In this case, participants were first interviewed to determine the extent of their religious beliefs. Sometime later, the main experiment was carried out, in two different ways. In the first, participants were given a randomly re-arranged five-word phrase – such as 'speak than louder words actions' – and were asked to rearrange the words to make sense. Some of them were given scrambled phrases containing many words related to analytical thinking; the rest were not. After this exercise, they were asked whether they agreed that God exists. The group whose training period involved words related to analytical thinking were more likely to disagree. Moreover, this tendency remained, even when their prior beliefs were taken into account. The second version of the experiment relied on previous research, showing that asking people to read something printed in a hard-to-read font promoted analytical thinking, perhaps because they have to proceed more slowly and puzzle out the meaning of the letters. Subjects that completed a survey printed in a semi-illegible font were less likely to agree that God exists than those given the same material in a legible one.

The magazine article summed up the study: 'It may help to explain why the vast majority of Americans tend to believe in God. Because System 2 thinking requires effort, most of us tend to rely on System 1 thinking processes whenever possible.'

There is a loose relationship between System 1/System 2 and Benford's distinction between human-centred or universe-centred thinking. Intuitive thinking mainly takes a human-scale view of the world, and often places emphasis on quick decisions based on little more than hunches. Many people, finding it difficult to weigh up electoral candidates' manifestos because political issues are often complicated, rely on instant judgments – System 1. 'His eyes look too close together.' 'I like that smart suit he's wearing.' 'Anyone who's for/against a free market gets my vote.' Universe-centred thinking is necessarily analytical, System 2. Humans have to train themselves to think inhuman thoughts. It takes conscious effort, and education, to reject a human-centred view.

Of course, there is no reason to suppose that these two ways of distinguishing thought processes have to match up, and they probably don't, not in detail. Moreover, the psychological experiments only scratch the surface of human motivations and beliefs. Even if the conclusions are correct – and it is relatively easy to raise objections – they demonstrate an association, not a cause. But the results correspond to other observations of religious belief, for example that it is much rarer among scientists and well-educated people than it is among the poorly educated. And it is the common experience of atheists and rationalists that people who embrace extreme versions of religion tend not to be good at critical thinking. Especially about their own beliefs.

Psychologists study the whole human brain; neuroscientists look at the brain's detailed workings, in particular how it controls the movements of the body. Many think that this is why the brain evolved to begin with, and sensory information-processing came later, along with all of the other subtler functions of the brain. Engineers, aiming to build better robots, are borrowing tricks from the brain. One of the fundamental features of the brain is how it deals with uncertainty.

Our senses are imprecise, and their inputs to the brain are subject to 'noise' – random mistakes. The workings of the brain, being evolved wetware (the organic material of the nervous system) rather than carefully engineered hardware or software, are also subject to errors. The signals that the brain sends to the body suffer from unavoidable variability. Try to sink a golf ball with a ten-metre putt, a hundred times. You won't get it in the hole every time. Sometimes you may succeed, sometimes you'll miss by a small amount, but occasionally you'll miss by more. Professional golfers are paid a lot of money because they are marginally better at reducing this kind of variability than the rest of us.

The same variability comes into play, usually in a more exaggerated form, when it comes to social and political judgments. Here the noise-to-signal ratio is even higher. Not only do we need to take into account all of the information that is being provided: we have to decide which of it is sensible and which is rubbish. How does the brain juggle all of these conflicting factors and come to some kind of decision? A theory that currently explains a great deal, and has a lot of experimental support, is that the brain can be well modelled as a Bayesian decision machine.

It's a mistake to say that any natural phenomenon is *the same as* some formal mathematical model, if only because mathematics is a system of human thought, and nature isn't. Bayesian decision theory is a branch of mathematics, a way of formulating probabilities and statistics. The brain is an interconnected network of nerve cells, whose dynamics depend on chemistry and electrical currents. Bearing this in mind, it seems that over the megayears our brains have evolved networks that mimic the mathematical features of Bayesian decision theory. We can test whether such networks exist, but as yet we have little idea of how they actually work.

In the 1700s, the Reverend Thomas Bayes unwittingly started a revolution in statistics when he suggested a new interpretation of probability. At the time this was a hazy concept anyway, but there was broad agreement that the probability of some event can be defined as the proportion of trials on which that event happens, in the long run. Pick a card at random from a pack, billions of times, and you will get the ace of spades about one time in 52. The same goes for any other specific card, and the reason is that there are 52 cards, and it's hard to see why any particular one should turn up more frequently than any other.

Bayes had a different idea. There are many circumstances in which it is not possible to repeat a trial many times. What, for example, is the probability that God exists? Whatever our views, we can't generate billions of universes and count how many of them have a deity. One way to handle such problems is to decide that such probabilities have no meaning. But Bayes argued that in many contexts, you could assign a probability to a one-off event: it was the degree of belief in the occurrence of that event. More strongly, if there was some genuine evidence, it was the degree of *confidence* in the evidence. We make this kind of snap judgment all the time, for example when thinking that Spain's football team has roughly a 75% chance of winning the UEFA Europa League football championship, or that the chances of rain today are low.

What Bayes did, sometime in the mid-1700s, was to find a mathematical formula, allowing these 'prior probabilities' to modify solid information obtained by other means. A friend of his published the formula in 1763, two years after his death. Suppose you know that Spain's record of winning big football tournaments is only 60% (a figure we pluck from a hat for illustrative purposes), but you also have a hunch that this year they are playing a lot better than usual. Put the two together, and you will assess their chances as being higher.

Bayesian inference can put numbers to all of this, and provide a rational system for calculating the probabilities concerned – except for prior probabilities, which are plugged into the formulas but are not consequences of them. So the method is a 'worlds of if' approach: *if* the prior probability is such and such, *then* the consequences of new data will be so and so. The formula does not justify any particular prior probability; however, its consequences may let us test the accuracy of the prior probability, by comparison with observations. Bayesian inference often outperforms more 'rational' methods. Although we may not be certain that we've assessed the prior probabilities correctly, it may still be better to make a guess, rather than ignoring such influences altogether.

In conventional statistics, a statement being tested – a hypothesis – should be accepted (or at least not rejected) if the evidence agrees with it. In the Bayesian approach, however, the hypothesis should be rejected, despite the evidence, if its prior probability is very low. Indeed, it may be reasonable to reject the alleged *evidence*, on the same grounds.

For example, suppose the hypothesis is the existence of UFOs, and the evidence is a photograph of one. The photo supports the hypothesis, but if you believe that the chance of UFOs existing is extremely small, then the evidence is not convincing. The photo might be a fake, for example; but even if you don't know whether it is genuine, you are justified in rejecting the hypothesis … unless, of course, it turns out that your prior probability is wrong. So Bayesian inference does not disprove the existence of UFOs: instead, it quantifies the view that 'extraordinary claims require extraordinary evidence'. And a photo isn't extraordinary enough.

Anyway, the neuroscience theory holds that the brain operates by generating beliefs about the world. Here a belief is defined to be what the brain decides about some event or phenomenon, so it is hard to deny that the brain operates by generating such things. The theory says something less tautologous, however: it asserts that the brain combines two distinct sources of information: memory and data. It does not just *assess* incoming sensory data as such; it *compares* them to what's already stored in memory.

Experiments carried out by Daniel Wolpert and his team support the view that the results of these comparisons correspond very closely to Bayes's formula. The brain seems to have evolved an effective and fairly accurate way to combine its existing knowledge with new information, thereby modifying what it holds in its memory.

The experiments look at how we move our limbs to perform some task. Suppose we want to pick up a cup of coffee. There are many ways to do this, and most end in disaster. If we tip the cup too far, for example, the coffee will spill. The response of our muscles is affected by inherent random fluctuations in the motor system, and some strategies for picking up the cup are less error-prone than others. Optimal choices, determined by Bayesian decision theory, generally agree with the actual motions observed.

We repeat, this doesn't imply that the brain carries out Bayesian calculations the way a mathematician would consciously do using pencil and paper. On the contrary, the brain has evolved neural networks that produce the same general results. The choices indicated by Bayesian decision theory are the choices that best fit reality, assuming that memory and data are being combined. This fit provides an evolutionary advantage – on the whole, those choices work better. So the neural networks that control how we walk, run, hold or throw objects, have been selected to mimic the results of Bayesian decision theory – our way to formalise mathematical rules that describe whatever nature is actually doing.

More generally, we can speculate that similar neural networks control our snap judgments about social or political matters. Again, there are two ingredients: prior beliefs already in memory, and new data. Crucially, the Bayesian model shows why beliefs may override data. If you are certain that global warming is a hoax – for whatever reasons, good or bad – the Bayesian decision machine in your head will reject new evidence that global warming exists, whatever that may be, and stick to your existing beliefs. It may even lead you to reject all such evidence on the grounds that it has to be part of the hoax. If you don't have strong beliefs either way, new evidence may cause you to modify your views. If you are already convinced about global warming, you may accept new evidence even if it is questionable.

The same goes for religious beliefs. What we might call the epidemiology of religion shows that most people get their beliefs from their parents, close relatives, teachers (if of that persuasion), and priests. By the time they reach an age where they are capable of questioning what they have been taught, they may have built up such a strong system of beliefs that it is proof against any contrary evidence.

So we use two ways of thinking, Systems 1 and 2. That's suspiciously like Benford's distinction. Are human-centred and universe-centred thinking related to the two components of Bayesian decisions – memory and data? It's always tempting to line up dichotomies, assuming they carve things up in the same way, but in this case they don't. Both memory and data are part of a quick-and-dirty intuitive decision process; they are different components that together drive System 1 thinking. System 2 is different, a much more conscious, deliberative analysis, assessing the evidence and *trying* – not always successfully – to ignore inbuilt prejudices. It's not Bayesian.

What does this tell us about belief? First, it explains why people have beliefs at all. They are a vital part of System 1 thinking, which has evolutionary survival value when snap judgments are essential. On the other hand, it also shows that this type of thinking may have deep flaws, whereby our beliefs override important data. If a snap judgment is not needed, it is better not to make one. Instead, we can employ System 2 thinking – often described as 'rational' or 'analytical' – and allow the data to change our beliefs if they fail to match reality.

There is also the knotty question of belief versus disbelief. A UFO believer, for example, may argue that not believing in UFOs is merely another kind of belief. Namely, a belief that UFOs don't exist. However, when virtually all of the alleged 'evidence' for UFOs turns out to be mistaken, or false, the contrary position isn't a matter of belief at all. Zero belief in UFOs is not the same as 100% belief in the nonexistence of UFOs. Zero belief is an *absence* of belief, not an opposed form of belief. Similarly, science sets up a framework in which human beings consciously try to override their innate tendency to use System 1 thinking, because they know it can often be misleading. Scientists actively try to disprove the things they would like to be true.

That's not a belief system. It's a disbelief system.

TWENTY-ONE

THE TURTLE MOVES!

 Marjorie drew breath.

'My name, sir, is Marjorie Daw, and I am chief librarian for the borough of Four Farthings in London, England, er, on Earth. I am fluent in Latin and Greek, also in French, of course; and well versed in the patois of Essex … *whatever*. Today, I am also rather proud to have learned the library cataloguing language of Ook – a great revelation!'

As she spoke, Marjorie was aware of the double doors at the end of the room swinging open, causing a susurrus among the audience. All eyes turned towards a tall white-haired man who looked rather like a farm worker; although, Marjorie thought, a farm worker would never walk with such presence, regardless of how many pigs he had. Moreover, the man strolling towards Lord Vetinari had a large hand-axe, which was attached to his body by a careful arrangement of leather strips.

Lord Vetinari was watching the oncoming man with a smile on his face, while behind Marjorie the susurration had died away into silence, which was somehow a lot noisier by the time it hit the brain, where it thundered. The Patrician was on his feet as the interloper reached him; he held out his hand in welcome.

'Pastor Oats!* I thought that my envoys hadn't been able to track you down. Do please take a seat.'

---

* The Quite Reverend Mightily-Praiseworthy-Are-Ye-Who-Exalteth-Om Oats, a mainstream Omnian priest.

'You know me, Havelock; I travel at the speed of an ass, and thank you, but I will stand – I've spent far too much time on my ass as it is.'

Nobody tittered, nobody laughed; Pastor Oats held the floor, and when he began speaking you could *hear* the listening.

He looked around the room and said, 'The Church of the Latter-Day Omnians has, in my opinion, no claim whatsoever to the orb known as Roundworld, and neither do the sapient species on Roundworld itself. After all, however unlikely, *they* didn't make it; *it* made *them*, with a little deference to the multiple, tireless and curiously inventive processes that altogether made it what it is today – a decent paradise for those who approach it in the right state of mind, and ultimately a charnel house for those who do not.'

Marjorie sat back and listened intently. She wasn't sure about being described as a 'sapient species', but you didn't argue with a man with an axe, no matter how wise he seemed. Not if you wanted to continue to have fingers to turn the pages of the books you loved, anyway.

'Intelligence helps,' Pastor Oats continued, 'but it must be informed intelligence and I am sorry to say that the Latter-Day Omnians possess neither. The turtle moves! And that is a truth, but certainly not the whole of the truth, because it doesn't move for Roundworld, a world that more or less moves for itself. It will take *real* stupidity to stop it doing so, and that kind of stupidity begins when facts are denied.'

This was food and drink to Marjorie. She *liked* facts.

'Lord Vetinari, you sent for me to ask my advice, and I have given it to you,' the pastor concluded. 'Allow the wizards to be stewards of Roundworld. Admittedly, they are often proud, and wrong, but ultimately they search for the truth, by trial and error, and this is how it should be. The search for truth might be flawed, but the search itself is *priceless*!'

Vetinari nodded and reached for his gavel.

'My Lord!' Stackpole objected. 'That is merely one man's opinion. I can call a dozen expert witnesses to refute it. Among them persons of the highest—' Dramatically, he fell to his knees in an attitude of prayer and continued, 'As Om is my witness! I call upon the great god ...'

There was a ripple in the world, followed by the appearance of an imposing figure in full morning dress and sporting an exquisite hairstyle. He glanced at Mister Stackpole and said, 'Oh, it's you ... *again*. I am indeed your witness, Mister Stackpole, but you don't call me – *I* call *you*. There are rules, you know.'

Later, there was some discussion as to whether the appearance of the great god in, as it were, the flesh, caused a kerfuffle or merely a very large stir. A small, but pernicious argument about this point continued for some considerable time among the audience.

Mister Slant, raising his voice over the hubbub, or possibly tumult, said, 'For the record, I ask the witness to state his name, address, and profession.'

The great god raised an eyebrow at Mister Slant.

Mister Slant returned the raised eyebrow and said, 'As you say, sir, there *must* be rules.'

'Oh, all right,' said Om. 'Om. No fixed abode. Great god. Now get on with the questions – I have a swanky dinner to attend in Valhalla.'

Mister Stackpole spluttered in anger. 'Mister Slant can't ask him questions! It's *my* job to interpret the ways of God to Man! We'd all be out of a job if He just comes down here and tells us all what to do – talks to *anyone*!'

'I can do *anything* I want,' said the great god. 'The agent cannot transcend the principal. Now, what's all this nonsense about the Disc being round? *Roundworld* is round. The Disc is flat. Believe me, I know. I know *everything*, for a given value of everything and, if it comes to that, a given value of *know*.'

Vetinari again reached for his gavel.

Stackpole, dredging up a shred of resistance, said, 'It is a test of my faith ... I must ... My Lord, what concerns the court is not truth. It is belief. And once there is no belief, there is nothing.'

'Since when should belief trump truth, Mister Stackpole?' asked Vetinari.

'This case does not depend upon the *actual* shape of the so-called Disc, my Lord. The substance of the Church's case is that Unseen University has infringed our theological property rights to the *concept* of a spherical world. They have committed blasphemy.'

'If they have,' said Om, 'I can deal with it myself. I don't need your help. Personally, I don't see a problem. The turtle moves. Get used to it.'

Ignoring his god, Stackpole ploughed on, 'The Church claims custody of the Round World. The true shape of the Disc is irrelevant to our case.'

Vetinari moved as if to replace his gavel.

'You misunderstand, Mister Stackpole,' Om countered. 'I was not referring to the true *shape* of the Disc; I was referring to the origin of your *belief* that the Disc is round.' He turned towards Ponder Stibbons. 'Mister Stibbons, I was present, extra-dimensionally, when you switched on your recent experiment in quantum thaumodynamics – your Great Big Thing. But you neglected One Tiny Little Thing.'

The Librarian gave Ponder a sharp glance. 'Ook?'

'Of course,' cried Ponder. 'You're absolutely right! I assumed that when narrativium propagates through L-space, it doesn't interact with librarium! But if we invoke Crumbworthy's Perpetually Overlooked Constraint, an otherwise negligible interaction could weaken the fabric of L-space and create a chronoclastic fistula! Then the thaum would spontaneously split, and mythons would leak one way and antimythons the other way. I ... er ...'

'Mythcalculated,' said Om. 'Since L-space links libraries across all of space *and time*, the concept of a flat Disc leaked into the distant past of Roundworld. And the concept of a round world leaked the other way, into the distant past of Discworld – where it became a central feature of the old Omnian religion.'

'Discworld reality became a Roundworld myth, and Roundworld rules became a Discworld belief!' said Ponder.

Marjorie jabbed the Archchancellor in the ribs. 'So, Unseen University *didn't* get the idea of a round world from the ancient roots of Omnianism!'

'No,' said Ridcully. 'They got it from *us*.'

'Game, set and myth,' said the Dean. 'Done and dusted.'

Ridcully looked sceptical and continued, 'I wouldn't count on that. In my experience, fanatics don't change their minds whatever the evidence. Even if their own god were to appear before them and tell them they were wrong, they would still—'

'Om is not mocked! That is to say that our concept of the true being of Om is not mocked!' yelled Stackpole. 'The Disc *is* round! The turtle does *not* move! There is *no* tur—'

'Oh, do shut up, you horrible little man,' said Om. 'And I don't want any more of this, or I'll start again and give ants a try.' He vanished.

'Well, that's *one* dissenting opinion ...' Stackpole began, picking himself up from the floor.

Vetinari picked up his gavel with a hopeful expression. 'The case is closed. My judgment is that the Church of Latter-Day Omnians' claim to custody of the Round World has no merit, and it shall remain in the care of Unseen University, in perpetuity.' He banged the gavel, then glared at Ridcully, raising his eyebrow without twitching a muscle, just to show them. 'I hope you look after it with more care than you have in the past, Mustrum.'

'O Great God Om!' All eyes turned on Stackpole as he threw himself prostrate, yelling and frothing at the mouth. 'Help your true believers in their hour of need! Confound the lies of the infidels!'

'He's wasting his time,' said the Dean. 'His god has already pronounced judgment. Why can't he just accept—?'

But Stackpole took no notice. 'We will not stand for this! We will continue fighting! There is a truth even higher than the truth!'

Suddenly a small group of hooded figures was in the room at speed, taking the onlookers by surprise and gathering around Lord

Vetinari, who in the circumstances appeared to be unflustered, only thoughtful. One of the hooded men grabbed Roundworld from its tripod and ran with it back towards the entrance, and a voice by Marjorie rang out, 'If our demands are not met, his Lordship and the precious Round World will both be destroyed! Death to the tyrant!'

Marjorie was impressed at her own presence of mind, but a librarian must be prepared for any eventuality, including terrorists. *When in doubt strike first, making certain no valuable volumes are harmed*, she reminded herself. Then she sank to her knees in front of the hooded man and pleaded for her life: 'Oh, sir, please don't kill me, sir, please, sir, I'm on my knees!'

That ringing plea was then echoed by a black figure that had suddenly been punched in the groin. One small blow for a librarian; one giant step for Roundworld, Marjorie thought, gratified to hear a crunch. And mere seconds after this first challenge, she was pelting down the aisle after the retreating bandit carrying her home. *Her library* and all of the planet surrounding it was accelerating away to only God – or more likely Richard Dawkins – knew where.

Being the fastest track and field runner in Roedean School helped. The fleeing bandit hadn't had her training, and certainly didn't have her stamina, and was flagging as he zigzagged through streets that were quite alien to Marjorie. She had to keep him in sight; she would be completely lost if he got away, so she girded her loins, metaphysically speaking, gulped for breath and sped on. Now it was beginning to look as if the wretched miscreant was weakening – she was sure of it – and this reassurance gave her wings.

She could hear the sounds of hue and cry dwindling behind her. And then the figure stopped dead, turned round, screamed something incoherent and flung the globe directly at her head.

TWENTY-TWO

FAREWELL, FINE-TUNING

 They didn't make it; it made them.

Pastor Oats, a truly wise man, has put his finger on a deep, often unappreciated, truth, which illuminates the misty borderland where science and religion meet. Here lie some of the most perplexing riddles of modern cosmology, where the austere workings of fundamental physics collide with the richness of human experience.

At the heart of this collision is an astonishing coincidence: universes that can sustain living creatures are extraordinarily unlikely. This coincidence violates, in the most dramatic manner possible, the Copernican principle that humans aren't special.

Before Nicholas Copernicus published *On the Revolutions of the Celestial Spheres* in 1543, with a few honourable exceptions, almost everyone viewed humanity as the centre of the universe. This was so obviously true that it seemed ridiculous to deny it. Look around you. Everything else trails off into the distance, and you are smack bang in the middle. Your own senses prove that the stars and other celestial bodies revolve around the Earth. The natural shape for their orbits must surely be a circle, a perfect geometric figure; its perfection provides yet more evidence that everything was created for us, and that we are located at the heart of creation.

However, ancient astronomers were excellent observers, and when they looked at what the universe was actually doing, they realised that circles don't fit. But they could save the 'perfect form' theory, because *combinations* of circles agree very closely with observations. In the second century AD, Claudius Ptolemaeus (Ptolemy) wrote the *Almagest* ('the greatest'), which represented the movements of the Sun and planets around a stationary Earth. To match the complex trajectories observed, he employed several geometric constructions, involving spheres rotating on axes that are supported by other spheres. In a simplified form, the most important features of the Ptolemaic system were epicycles: circular orbits whose centres themselves revolved in circular orbits. If necessary, those centres might also revolve in circular orbits, and so on. In total, Ptolemy needed more than eighty spheres, but the resulting system was very accurate. Especially at a time when Earth was not recognised as a planet. That term referred to wandering stars, and the Earth was neither a star, nor a wanderer. It was *fixed*.

We are special.

Copernicus was clearly a contrarian, and he realised that everything makes a lot more sense if we're not special, and the Earth is not at the centre. This is an instance of the mediocrity principle: as a working heuristic, it is best to avoid assuming that any given phenomenon has unusual, special features, or violates the laws of nature. One feature of Ptolemy's system that may have led Copernicus to this view was a suspicious coincidence. The numbers associated with most of the epicycles – size, speed of rotation – were rather haphazard, with no clear patterns. But Copernicus noticed that identical copies of one particular set of epicycle data occurred many times over: in the motion of the Sun and of all the planets. He could cut the number of epicycles down from Ptolemy's eighty to a mere thirty-four by transferring this one to the Earth. The Sun then became stationary, and everything else (bar the Moon) revolved around it – Earth included. By adopting an Earth-centred frame of reference, Ptolemy had been obliged to transfer the Earth's motion round the Sun to *every other body*, by adding a single extra epicycle to all of them. Remove this common epicycle, and the description would be much simpler. But then you are faced with a radical change to the theory: among the many celestial bodies, only the Moon revolves around the Earth. Everything else revolves around the Sun.

That statement is open to challenge, on grounds discussed for flat Earths in chapter 8. You can represent the universe in any frame of reference you wish. There is nothing to stop you choosing a coordinate system in which the Earth is stationary, and you can even decide – depending on your assessment of your own importance in the scheme of things – that *you* are at the origin. It is entirely straightforward, for those who play this kind of game, to rewrite all of the laws of nature within that you-centred frame of reference. So there is a sense in which what's in the middle and what goes round what is entirely arbitrary.

However, another philosophical principle, Occam's razor, suggests that this freedom to choose is not terribly meaningful. William of Occam (or Ockham) is credited with the philosophical principle 'entities should not be multiplied beyond necessity'.* This tends to be interpreted as 'simple explanations are better than complex ones', but that goes beyond what William actually said. His point was that it is silly to include features that can be removed without making any significant difference. Complex explanations are often better than simple ones, but only when simpler ones won't do the job. Interpreting Occam's razor either way, lots of copies of an epicycle are trumped by just one copy, even if it has to be attached to a different body.

In a frame attached to the Earth, the laws of motion become extraordinarily complicated. The nearest major galaxy, M31 in Andromeda, about 2.6 million light years away, has to whiz all the way round the Earth once every 24 hours. More distant objects – the current record is about 13.2 billion light years – must undergo

---

* This phrase is not found in his extant writings; it probably originated with the Irish theologian John Punch. The closest phrase in Occam's work is 'Plurality must never be posited without necessity' in the *Sententiarum Petri Lombardi* of 1495. Not as pithy.

even more outlandish gyrations. In contrast, if we choose a frame of reference centred on the Sun, making it stationary relative to the average positions of the stars, the mathematics becomes far simpler and the physics and metaphysics far more reasonable. Ignoring the gravitational influences of any other bodies, the Sun and Earth *both* orbit their mutual centre of gravity in ellipses. But because the Sun is so much more massive than the Earth, that centre lies well inside the Sun. So ... the Earth goes round the Sun. We foolishly *think* the Earth is stationary because it is, relative to us. (Sorry, still too human-centred: make that 'we are stationary, relative to it'.)

Lesson learned – after several centuries, a few burnings and a lot of fuss and bother. But that was just the warm-up act. When astronomers realised that distant blobs of light were galaxies – swirling masses composed of billions of stars – it eventually dawned on them that the familiar Milky Way's river of light is no accident: it is our own galaxy seen edge-on, from inside. Naturally our Sun will be at the galactic centre ... Well, no, it is actually in a very nondescript region about two thirds of the way towards the rim: 27,000 light years from the galactic core, close to one of the galaxy's spiral arms, the Orion Arm. The glorious Sun is merely one star (and a pretty feeble one at that) among thousands in the Local Fluff, which itself lies inside the Local Bubble. The Sun is not even in the galactic plane, though it's fairly close – about sixty light years.

After several centuries in which every successive attempt to portray humanity as special was debunked, the Copernican principle became embedded in fundamental physics as a generalisation of Einstein's basic principle of relativity: there is no such thing as a privileged observer.

We said earlier that a major motivation behind the scientific method is a conscious awareness that people tend to believe things because they want to, or have been socially brainwashed into wanting to. Religions exploit this tendency by making faith paramount: strength of belief trumps contrary or absent evidence. Science deliberately tries to counteract it by demanding convincing evidence. The Copernican principle is one extra reminder about what not to assume. It doesn't always apply, but it punctures our sense of self-importance.

Broad quasi-philosophical principles like those of Copernicus and Occam are guidelines, not hard-and-fast rules. And, wouldn't you just know it: as soon as we started to get used to the idea that in the vast scheme of things we are pretty ordinary, evidence began to turn up that this wasn't a done deal. Maybe we *are* special. Maybe the Earth *is* in a privileged position, or a privileged state. Maybe it has to be.

By the time this line of reasoning had run its course, we seemed to be so special that the entire universe must somehow operate in precisely the manner that can give rise to ... us. It is as though the universe were created with humanity in mind.

To those of a religious persuasion, this was hardly news, and they welcomed the partial conversion of the scientific world with open arms. But even atheists were coming round to the idea that if the universe were even slightly different from what it is, we wouldn't be here. There's even a general principle, a distinctly non-Copernican one, that can be used to justify these claims. It's called the Anthropic Principle.

There are two flavours. The Weak Anthropic Principle states that the universe has to be of a kind that can give rise to creatures like us, because if it weren't, we wouldn't be here to ask awkward questions. The Strong Anthropic Principle states that the universe was in some sense *designed* for us. We are not just an accidental by-product; we are what it's all *for*. In 1986 John Barrow and Frank Tipler compiled an impressive, highly technical, analysis: *The Anthropic Cosmological Principle*. It discussed the view that in several respects our universe – as opposed to innumerable conceivable alternatives – is uniquely fine-tuned for life to arise. Many scientists and most cosmologists now seem to accept that.

A common image dramatises the point. Take a shiny metal rod and a sharp knife. Rest the rod on the knife's edge, and try to balance it. You can't. Unless the rod's centre of mass is *exactly* above the edge of the blade, the rod will slip, then slide and fall to the ground.

Life is balanced on a cosmic knife edge.

Less metaphorically: the laws of nature are exquisitely finely tuned. Change any of the fundamental constants of nature by the smallest amount, and life's delicate cycles will fail. Poise humanity one micron away from cosmic perfection, and it will topple.

Alongside this human-centred view of the universe goes a human-centred view of humans. Forget all those weird and wonderful aliens that infest science fiction, living in the hydrogen-helium atmospheres of gas giants, or the frigid cold of worlds so far from their suns that the temperature is barely above absolute zero. It's much simpler than that. The only viable aliens will be just like us. They will live on a rocky world with oceans and plenty of oxygen in its atmosphere; it will need to be just the right distance from its sun. The world will need a strong magnetic field to keep radiation at bay, a large companion like our Moon to keep its axis stable, and a gas giant like Jupiter to protect it from comets.

The aliens' sun will also have to be special. Remarkably like ours, in fact. Not just in its spectral type, its general shape, size, and the kind of nuclear reaction it uses, but in its location. The sun needs to be reasonably far away from any of its galaxy's spiral arms, because the process of star formation creates a lot of radiation, and most stars form in the spiral arms. On the other hand, it can't be *too* far away, as our own Sun demonstrates. Moreover, the aliens' sun must be near enough to the galactic centre for there to be enough heavy elements to provide the planet with a rocky core, but far enough from the centre to avoid being subject to intense radiation, which would destroy life.

Well, carbon-based life, like ours … but that's the only kind that can exist. The element carbon is unique: it forms the complex molecules required to make living creatures. Carbon is a key element in the claim that life anywhere on the universe has to be much like life on Earth. But in the cosmic scheme of things, carbon is highly unlikely. It exists only by virtue of a remarkably precise alignment of the energy levels of nuclear reactions inside stars. So stars are special, and the reason is life.

Not just stars. The whole universe is special, finely tuned for life to exist. The basic physics of our universe, on which everything else rests, depends on about thirty fundamental constants: numbers such as the strength of gravity, the speed of light and the strength of atomic forces. Those numbers appear in the deep laws of nature, relativity and quantum theory, and there seems to be no clear mathematical reason why they might not be different. They are 'adjustable parameters' – knobs that a creator god could twiddle to any value He/She/It desired. But, tellingly, if you do the sums, it turns out that if any of these constants were even slightly different from its actual value, then not only would life be impossible: there would be no planets for life to inhabit, no stars to provide energy, and no atoms to assemble into matter.

Our universe, like life, is also improbably balanced on the finest of knife edges, and the slightest deviation would have spelled disaster.

This scenario of cosmological fine-tuning is widely viewed as one of the biggest puzzles in cosmology, a series of wildly unlikely coincidences that demands rational explanation but seems to lead only to imaginative speculations involving physics that has not yet been supported by evidence. Religious fundamentalists have seized upon it as a proof of the existence of God. It is difficult, even for atheists, not to have some sympathy with them, because the usual presentation of the science involved points unerringly towards some kind of design principle for our universe.

Fine-tuning, be it terrestrial or cosmological, makes perfect sense from a human-centred viewpoint. In contrast, it seems to pose some very difficult questions for universe-centred thinking.

Most of the scientific effort to resolve these questions starts from the premise that fine-tuning is genuine, so our universe really is virtually unique when it comes to its ability to harbour life. From here it is easy to become convinced that we are the purpose of the whole thing, or even that without us there would be no observers to collapse the quantum wavefunction of the universe and maintain its existence. Less human-centred explanations have also been offered, including a virtually endless cycle of creation and destruction of different universes, which can be noticed by their intelligent inhabitants only when they are the kind of universe that can *have* intelligent inhabitants, or a vast multiverse of parallel or independent universes in which every physical possibility is realised. Either removes the need to explain any *particular* universe. The sheer scope of the imaginative proposals that emerge from a few numbers is breathtaking.

There is, however, another way. Instead of accepting the premise of fine-tuning and trying to explain it – or explain it away – we can challenge the premise itself. For a start, it's strange that physicists can think of no other way to make a universe than to keep ours but change a few constants. It's even stranger that believers don't hesitate to impose the same restriction on their omnipotent deity's creative abilities. But even accepting this limitation, it has been clear for at least a decade that the usual description of fine-tuning is needlessly mystical, and verges on the mythical.

The issues are deep, and it is important not to avoid them by offering glib 'explanations' that miss the point. For example, the Weak Anthropic Principle – that we can observe a universe only if it is suited to our own existence – really does explain why our universe must satisfy some pretty stringent constraints. Since we exist, it has to. But that is just another way of saying 'the universe is how it is'. It's no different from reasoning from the existence of, say, sulphur, and concluding that atomic theory has to be much as we think it is. The Weak Anthropic Principle only seems different from the equally valid Weak Sulphuric Principle* because it's about us rather than a lump of yellow rock. But the Copernican principle cautions us not to imagine that there's anything special about us, and in this case, there isn't. We are just one piece of evidence. An equally convincing case can be made that the universe is uniquely finely tuned to make sulphur.

The Weak Anthropic Principle only goes so far. It doesn't explain *why* this kind of universe exists, rather than something different – especially when almost any alternative would allegedly fall apart or explode the moment it came into being, or would be so boring that only very simple structures could form. However, the Strong Anthropic Principle – that the universe was made *in order for* humans to exist – doesn't explain any of that either. We could just as readily formulate the Strong Sulphuric Principle: the universe was made *in order for* sulphur to exist.

Why us? The Strong Anthropic Principle just assumes it's obvious that we are the purpose of the whole thing. Sulphur? Don't be silly.

Let's warm up with the carbon story, which is easier to grasp. Then we'll take a look at those puzzling fundamental constants. We discussed both of these in *The Science of Discworld II: the Globe,* and we have to cover some of the same ground again before going further. We'll keep it brief.

Astrophysicists have put together a careful account of how the chemical elements formed. Combinations of elementary particles – protons, neutrons, or their more exotic precursors – came together in vast clouds to form atoms of the lightest element, hydrogen. The early universe was hot enough for hydrogen atoms to fuse together, making the next lightest element, helium. Then the clouds collapsed under their own gravity, triggering nuclear reactions. Stars were born, and within those stars new elements assembled, with atomic weights

---

* 'A universe containing sulphur has to be suitable for containing sulphur.'

up to and including iron. Subtler processes, occurring in red giant stars, put together heavier elements, as far as bismuth. Everything else required high-energy processes occurring only in supernovas – massive stellar explosions.

In 1954 the astronomer Fred Hoyle realised that there was a problem with carbon. The universe contains a lot more of it than the known nuclear reactions can explain. And carbon is the vital element for life. Carbon can form in red giants through the 'triple-alpha' process, in which three helium nuclei (atoms minus their electrons) collide, pretty much simultaneously. A helium nucleus comprises two protons and two neutrons. So three of them combined must yield a nucleus with six protons and six neutrons. This is carbon.

In the dense environment of a red giant star, nuclei collide relatively often. But it's not terribly likely that just as two of them come together, a third joins the party. So the process has to happen in two stages. First, two helium nuclei collide and fuse, making beryllium. Then another helium nucleus fuses with that. Unfortunately for this theory, the form of beryllium involved falls apart after one tenth of one quadrillionth of a second. The chance that a helium nucleus can hit such a rapidly vanishing target is much too small.

Hoyle knew this, and he also knew that there is a loophole. If the combined energies of beryllium and helium just happen to be very close to an energy level of carbon, then the nuclei can fuse much faster and the sums work out fine. Such a near-coincidence of energies is called a resonance. No suitable resonance was then known, but Hoyle insisted that it had to be there. Otherwise *Hoyle* wouldn't be there, being made from quite a lot of carbon. That led him to predict an unknown energy level of carbon around 7.7 MeV (million electronvolts, a convenient unit of energy for nuclear reactions). By the mid-1960s the experimentalist William Fowler had found such a resonance at 7.65 MeV, within 1% of Hoyle's prediction. Hoyle presented this discovery as a triumph of 'anthropic' reasoning: deducing something about the universe from the existence of humans. Without that finely tuned resonance, we wouldn't be here.

It sounds impressive, and it is when told that way. But already we see a tendency to exaggerate. For a start, the link to humans is unnecessary and irrelevant. What matters is the amount of *carbon* in the universe, not what it can make. We do not need to appeal to our own existence to know how much carbon there is. In *The Fallacy of Fine-Tuning*, Victor Stenger refers to an investigation of the history of Hoyle's prediction by the philosopher Helge Kragh. Hoyle did not initially link the resonance to the existence of life, let alone human life. The anthropic connection was not made for nearly thirty years. 'It is misleading to label the prediction of the 7.65 MeV state [as] anthropic, or to use it as an example of the predictive power of the anthropic principle,' Kragh wrote. *Pan narrans* has been at work again, and the human love of narrativium has rewritten the historical story.

Next: it's simply not true that 'without that finely tuned resonance, we wouldn't be here.' The 7.65 MeV figure for the energy of the resonance is not what's required for carbon-based life to exist. It is the energy needed to produce the amount of carbon actually observed. Change the energy, and carbon would still be produced ... but in different quantities. Not as different as you might think: Mario Livio and co-workers calculate that any value between 7.596 MeV and 7.716 MeV would generate much the same amount of carbon. Anything *up to* 7.933 MeV would generate enough carbon for carbon-based life to exist. Moreover, if the energy level dropped *below* 7.596 MeV, *more* carbon would be produced, not less. The lowest energy that would produce enough carbon for life is the ground state of the carbon atom, the lowest possible energy it can have, which is 7.337 MeV. A finely tuned resonance is not necessary.

In any case, resonances are ten a penny, because atomic nuclei have lots of energy levels. Finding one in the appropriate range isn't really very surprising.

A more serious objection arises from the calculation itself. When factors that Hoyle neglected are taken into account, the combined energies of helium and beryllium turn out to be significantly higher than the figure he used. What happens to this 'extra' energy?

It helps to keep the red giant burning.

The star burns at precisely the temperature required to compensate for the energy difference. This looks like an even more impressive coincidence. Forget carbon: something far deeper is going on. If the basic constants of the universe were different, then the precisely fine-tuned resonance would disappear, the red giant would fizzle out and there wouldn't be enough carbon to make Fred Hoyle, Adam and Eve, you or the cat.

However, this argument, too, is fallacious. Changing the fundamental constants affects the red giant star as well as the carbon resonance. In fact, because the star burns helium and beryllium fuel, the star's nuclear reactions automatically home in on the temperature that makes the fuel burn. Isn't it amazing that a coal fire burns at exactly the temperature that makes coal burn? No. If coal burns at all, then feedback ensures that the energy balance of the reaction automatically works out correctly. It may be amazing that our universe is so rich that coal can burn, or red giants shine, but that is a very different issue from fine-tuning. In a complex universe, however it may work, complex objects can arise, and they will be beautifully suited to the rules of that universe because that is how they came to be. But that does not imply that the universe was specially chosen or created to give rise to such objects. Or that those objects are improbable, or special.

The carbon resonance of a red giant, and the energetics of burning coal, are feedback systems. Like a thermostat, they automatically adjust themselves to keep going. This sort of feedback is extremely common and not at all remarkable. No more remarkable, in fact, than the amazing way that our legs are just long enough for our feet to meet the ground. Gravity pulls us down, the ground pushes us up, and the combination perches us in just the place where our feet and the ground are in exquisite alignment.

The issue of the physical constants is deeper. Today's picture of fundamental physics depends on a series of mathematical equations, all fairly elegant and neat. However, these equations also involve about thirty special numbers: things like the speed of light; and the fine structure constant, which governs the forces holding atoms together. These numbers appear to be pretty much random, but they matter just as much as the equations. Different values of these fundamental constants lead to very different solutions of the equations – different kinds of universe.

The differences are not just the obvious ones: gravity being stronger or weaker, light travelling faster or slower. They can be more dramatic. Change the fine structure constant even a little, and atoms become unstable and fall apart. Make the gravitational constant smaller, and stars blow up, galaxies disappear. Make it larger, and everything collapses into a single gigantic black hole. In fact – so the story goes – if you change any one of those constants by more than a very tiny amount, the resulting universe is so different from ours that it could not possibly support the organised complexity of life. Having lots of constants compounds this; it is like winning the lottery thirty times in a row. Our existence is not only balanced on a knife edge: it is a very sharp knife.

It's a striking tale, but it's riddled with holes. *Pan narrans* just can't stop itself.

One basic, and fatal, flaw in a large portion of the literature is to consider varying the constants only one at a time, and only by a small amount. Mathematically, this procedure explores only a tiny region of 'parameter space', the overall range of possible combinations of constants. What you find in this limited region is unlikely to be representative.

Here's an analogy. If you take a car, and change any single aspect even a little bit, the odds are that the car will no longer work. Change the size of the nuts *just a little*, and they don't fit the bolts and the car falls apart. Change the fuel *just a little*, and the engine doesn't fire and the car won't start. But this does not mean that only one size of nut or bolt is possible in a working car, or only one type of fuel. It tells us that when you change one feature, it has knock-on effects on the others, and those must also change. So parochial issues about what happens to little bits and pieces of our own universe when some constant is changed by a very small amount and the rest are left fixed are not terribly relevant to the question of that universe's suitability for life.

Some additional sloppy thinking parlays this fundamental blunder into a gross misrepresentation of what the calculations concerned actually show. Suppose, for the sake of argument, that each of the thirty parameters has to be individually fine-tuned so that the probability of a randomly chosen parameter being in the right range is 1/10. Change any parameter (alone) by more than that, and life becomes impossible. It is then argued that the probability of all thirty parameters being in the right range is 1/10 raised to the power 30. This is 10^{-30}, one part in a nonillion (ten billion billion billion). It is so ridiculously small that there is absolutely no serious prospect of it happening by chance. This calculation is the origin of the 'knife edge' image.

It is also complete nonsense.

It's like starting at Centrepoint, in the middle of London, and going a few metres westwards along New Oxford Street, a few metres northwards up Tottenham Court Road, and imagining you've covered the whole of London. You haven't even explored a few metres in a north-westerly direction, let alone anything further away. Mathematically, what is being explored by each change to a *single* parameter is a tiny interval along an axis in parameter space. When you multiply the associated probabilities together, you are exploring

291

a tiny box whose sides correspond to the changes made to individual parameters – without considering changing any of the others. The car example shows how silly this type of calculation is.

Even using the constants for *this* universe, we can't deduce the structure of something as apparently simple as a helium atom from the laws of physics, let alone a bacterium or a human being. Our understanding of everything more complex than hydrogen relies on clever approximations, refined by comparison with actual observations. But when we start thinking about other universes, we don't have any observations to compare with; we must rely on the mathematical consequences of our equations. For anything interesting, even helium, we can't do the sums. So we take short cuts, and rule out particular structures, such as stars or atoms, on various debatable grounds.

However, what such calculations actually rule out (even when they're correct) are stars just like those in this universe and atoms just like those in this universe. Which isn't quite the point when we're discussing a different universe. What other structures could exist? Could they be complex enough to constitute a form of life? The mathematics of complex systems shows that simple rules can lead to astonishingly complex behaviour. Such systems typically behave in many different interesting ways, but not in just *one* interesting way. They don't just sit there being dull and boring, except for one special 'finely tuned' set of constants where all hell breaks loose.

Stenger gives an instructive example of the fallacy of varying parameters one at a time. He works with just two: nuclear efficiency and the fine structure constant.

Nuclear efficiency is the fraction of the mass of a helium atom that is greater than the combined masses of two protons and two neutrons. This is important because the helium nucleus consists of just that combination. Add two electrons, and you're done. In our universe, this parameter has the value 0.007. It can be interpreted as how sticky the glue that holds the nucleus together is, so its value affects whether helium (and other small atoms like hydrogen and deuterium) can exist. Without any of these atoms, stars could not be powered by nuclear fusion, so this is a vital parameter for life. Calculations that vary only this parameter, keeping all others fixed, show that it has to lie between 0.006 and 0.008 for fusion-powered stars to be feasible. If it is less than 0.006, deuterium's two positively charged protons can push each other apart despite the glue. If it is more than 0.008, protons stick together, so there would be no free protons. Since a free proton is the nucleus of hydrogen, that means no hydrogen.

The fine structure constant determines the strength of electromagnetic forces. Its value in our universe is 0.007. Similar calculations show that it has to lie in the range from 0.006 to 0.008. (It seems to be coincidence that these values are essentially the same as those for nuclear efficiency. They're not *exactly* equal.)

Does this mean that in any universe with fusion-powered stars, both the nuclear efficiency and the fine structure constant must lie in the range from 0.006 to 0.008? Not at all. Changes to the fine structure constant can compensate for the changes to the nuclear efficiency. If their ratio is approximately 1, that is, if they have similar values, then the required atoms can exist and are stable. We can make the nuclear efficiency much larger, well outside the tiny range from 0.006 to 0.008, provided we also make the fine structure constant larger. The same goes if we make one of them much smaller.

With more than two constants, this effect becomes more pronounced, not less. Numerous examples are analysed at length in Stenger's book. You can compensate for a change to several constants by making suitable changes to several others. It's just like the car example. Changing any one feature of a car, even by a small amount, stops it working – but the mistake is to change just that one feature. There are thousands of makes of car, all different. When the engineers change the size of the nuts, they also change the size of the bolts. When they change the diameter of the wheel, they use a different tyre.

Cars are not finely tuned to a single design, and neither are universes.

Of course, the equations for universes might run contrary to everything that mathematicians have ever seen before. If anyone believes that, we've got a lot of money tied up in an offshore bank and we'd be delighted to share it with them if they will just send us their credit card details and PIN. But there are more specific reasons to think that the equations for universes are entirely normal in this respect.

About twenty years ago, Stenger wrote some computer software, which he called MonkeyGod. It lets you choose a few fundamental constants and discover what the resulting universe is capable of. Simulations show that combinations of parameters that would in principle permit life forms not too different from our own are extremely common, and there is absolutely no evidence that fine-tuning is needed. The values of fundamental constants do *not* have to agree with those in our current universe to one part in 10^{30}. In fact, they can differ by one part in ten without having any significant effect on the universe's suitability for life.

More recently, Fred Adams wrote a paper for the *Journal of Cosmology and Astroparticle Physics* in 2008, which focuses on a more limited version of the question.* He worked with just three constants – those that are particularly significant for the formation of stars: the gravitational constant, the fine structure constant, and a constant that governs nuclear reaction rates. The others, far from requiring fine-tuning, are irrelevant to star formation.

Adams defines 'star' to mean a self-gravitating object that is stable, long-lived, and generates energy by nuclear reactions. His calculations

---

* Fred C. Adams, Stars in other universes: stellar structure with different fundamental constants, *Journal of Cosmology and Astroparticle Physics* 8 (2008) 010. doi:10.1088/1475-7516/2008/08/010. arXiv:0807.3697.

reveal no sign of fine-tuning. Instead, stars exist for a huge range of constants. Choosing these 'at random', in the sense usually employed in fine-tuning arguments, the probability of getting a universe that can make stars is about 25%. It seems reasonable to allow more exotic objects to be treated as 'stars' too, such as black holes generating energy by quantum processes, and dark matter stars that get their energy by annihilating matter. The figure then increases to around 50%.

As far as stars go, our universe is not improbably balanced on an incredibly fine knife edge, battling odds of billions to one against. It just called 'heads', and the cosmic coin happened to land that way up.

Stars are only part of the process that equips a universe with intelligent life forms, and Adams intends to look at other aspects, notably planet formation. It seems likely that the results will be similar, debunking the almost infinitesimal chances alleged by advocates of fine-tuning, and replacing them by something that might actually *happen*.

What, then, went wrong with the fine-tuning arguments? Failures of imagination and blinkered interpretations. For the sake of argument, let us accept that most values of the constants make atoms unstable. Does this prove that 'matter' cannot exist? No, it just proves that matter identical to that in our universe can't exist. What counts is *what would happen instead*, but advocates of fine-tuning ignore this vital question.

We can ask the same question for the belief that the only viable aliens will be just like us, as many astrobiologists still maintain – though fewer of them than there used to be. The word 'astrobiology' is a compound of astronomy and biology, and what it mostly does is put the two sciences together and see how they affect each other. To analyse the possibility of alien life, especially intelligent alien life, conventional astrobiology starts with the existence of humans, as the pinnacle of life on Earth. Then it places them in the context of the rest of biology: genes, DNA, carbon. It then examines our evolutionary history, and that of our planet, to find environmental features that helped bring life, and us, into existence.

The upshot is an ever-growing catalogue of special features of our, and Earth's, history, alleged to be necessary for alien life to exist. We mentioned some of these features earlier; now we'll discuss some of them in more detail. They include the following conditions. Life needs an oxygen atmosphere. It needs water in liquid form. That implies being at a suitable distance from the Sun – the much-emphasised habitable or Goldilocks zone, where temperatures are 'just right'. Our unusually large Moon stabilises the Earth's axis, which would otherwise change its tilt chaotically. Jupiter helps protect us from comet impacts – remember how it sucked up Shoemaker-Levy 9? The Sun is neither too big nor too small, both of which make terrestrial planets less likely. Its rather dull and boring position in the galaxy – not at its centre, but out in the boondocks – is actually the best place to be. And so on and so on and so on. As the list grows ever longer, it is hard not to conclude that life is extraordinarily unlikely.

An alternative approach, which we like to call xenoscience, reverses the direction of thought. What are the possible types of habitat? We now know, as we did not until recently, that there is no shortage of planets. Astronomers have found over 850 exoplanets – planets outside our solar system – enough to provide a statistical sample that suggests that there are at least as many planets in the galaxy as stars. The physical conditions on those planets vary enormously, but that provides new opportunities for new kinds of life. So instead of asking, 'Is it like Earth?' we should ask, 'Could some form of life evolve here?'

We're not even restricted to planets: subsurface oceans on moons whose surfaces are thick layers of ice would be a good place for life, even for Earthlike life. We should take into account local conditions, but we should not assume that features that appear favourable in our solar system necessarily apply elsewhere. Without a large moon, a planet's axis may indeed tilt chaotically, but it could do so on a scale of tens of millions of years. Evolution can cope with that; it might even be enhanced by that. Life in a big enough ocean wouldn't even notice. A large gas giant may sweep up comets, but that could slow evolution down, because the occasional catastrophe adds variability. Jupiter may keep comets at bay, but it greatly increases the number of asteroid impacts on the Earth. The current best estimate suggests that Jupiter has done more harm than good, with regard to life. Some life forms such as tardigrades (commonly called waterbears or moss piglets) resist radiation better than most of those on our planet. The rest don't need to, because the Van Allen belts, regions of electrically charged particles maintained by the Earth's magnetic field, keep radiation away. In any case, if the belts hadn't been there, life could have become more tardigrade-like.

The so-called habitable zone is not the only region around a star where life might be possible. Some exotic chemical systems can make life-like complexity possible without water, and liquid water *can* exist outside the habitable zone. For example, if a world close to its star is tidally locked, so that one side perpetually faces the star and the other faces away, there will be a ring-shaped twilight zone on the boundary between the two faces, where liquid water might exist. Worlds far from the star can have liquid oceans underneath an outer coating of ice: Jupiter's moon Europa is the best-known example in the solar system, and it is thought to have an underground ocean containing as much water as all of Earth's oceans put together. The same goes for Ganymede, Callisto and Saturn's moon Enceladus. Titan – another moon around Saturn – has liquid hydrocarbon lakes and an excess of methane, hinting at non-equilibrium chemistry, a possible sign of unorthodox life.

The idea of a galactic habitable zone – the claim that alien life can exist only in the region of the galaxy with enough heavy elements but not too much radiation – is especially controversial. The Danish astronomer Lars Buchhave and his team have surveyed the chemical composition of 150 stars, with 226 known planets smaller than Neptune. The results show that 'small planets ... form around stars with a wide range of heavy metal content, including stars with only 25 per cent of the sun's metallicity'. So an excess of heavy elements is *not* required for Earthlike planets. NASA scientist Natalie Batalha remarked that 'Nature is opportunistic and prolific, finding pathways we might otherwise have thought difficult'.

And so on and so on and so on.

Life adapts to its environment, rather than the other way round. Goldilocks doesn't have the final word: Daddy Bear and Mummy Bear have valid opinions too. What is 'just right' for life depends on what kind of life. So-called extremophiles exist on Earth at temperatures below freezing and above boiling. It's a silly name. To such creatures, their environment is entirely comfortable; it is *we* who are extreme. It's even sillier to use the same name for creatures in two environments so different that each creature would consider the other to be even more extreme than us.

The second approach is far more sensible: instead of successively cutting down the opportunities for life, it explores the full range of the possible. That vast and impressive shopping list of features 'necessary' for life, making humans seem extremely special, is poor logic. Life on Earth demonstrates that the list is *sufficient* – but that doesn't make it *necessary*.

These two ways of thinking about aliens are of course yet another example of Benford's dichotomy. Astrobiology is human-centred, because it starts from us and narrows the universe down until it fits. Xenoscience is universe-centred: it keeps possibilities as broad as possible and sees where they lead. We are beautifully adapted for our environment because we evolved to be like that. This observation is much more reasonable than claiming that we humans are so special that the solar system, the galaxy, even the entire universe, was constructed in order to accommodate *us*.

Cosmic balance ...

Is life really balanced on a knife edge, then? Or have we got it all wrong?

Let us go back to our rod and sharp knife experiment. It seems undeniable. Try again to balance the rod on the cutting edge of the knife. However carefully you place it, it tips and slides to the floor. There is no question: the balance has to be extraordinarily precise.

The mathematics is, if anything, even more compelling. The masses on each side, multiplied by their distances from the knife, must be *equal.* Exactly. The slightest imbalance leads to total failure. So, by analogy, any imbalance in the laws of nature, however insignificant, would destroy the conditions required for life to exist. Change the speed of light or various other constants by a few per cent, and the delicate carbon resonance in stars would fail. No resonance, no carbon, no carbon-based life.

Maybe, though, we've accepted these arguments too readily. How relevant, how sensible, is the analogy of a metal rod and a sharp knife? Straight metal rods are an artificial product of technology. In mathematics and nature, most things are nonlinear – bent. What happens if you place a bent rod on top of a knife edge? Assume the bend is not too great, and roughly in the middle. Provided you place the rod on the knife so that it's reasonably near the balance point, as soon as you let the rod go it turns so that the free ends hang downwards. It slips sideways, but not very far, and then it stops. For a few seconds it seesaws up and down, but eventually it comes to rest.

Perfectly balanced.

Reach out a fingertip and push one end up a little. When you let go, the bent rod swings back to its original position, overshoots, reverses direction, and eventually settles back to where it was to begin with. If you push the other end down, the same thing happens.

Next, move the rod sideways on its pivot, away from the bend. The shiny metal is slippery, and the rod slides back until it balances again. It's not necessary to *arrange* for the rod to balance. It does so of its own accord. At the balance point, the forces pulling it to either side cancel out just as precisely as they would have to do to balance a straight rod, but the rod no longer falls off if the balance is wrong. It just moves a little, and finds its own balance point. The mathematical reason is straightforward. The rod seeks a state of minimum energy, where its centre of mass is lowest. Because the centre of mass of a bent rod is below the pivot, it ends up hanging in a stable position.

It's not *necessary* to fine-tune the universe.

It can fine-tune itself.

The 'knife edge' thought-experiment is rigged; the analogy with nature is false. The experiment depends on the rod being *straight*. Pretty much any other shape would be self-correcting. In fact, even a straight rod will balance on your finger. As long as the finger is close to the midpoint, the rod no longer slides off. Agreed, a finger is sweaty and sticky, and that can stop the rod sliding, but that's not the main reason why the rod balances. If one end tilts upwards, the rod rolls sideways and the point of contact with the finger moves away from the raised end. The weight of rod on the raised side is now greater than that on the other side, so the combined forces conspire to return the rod to the horizontal. If it is tilted the other way, the same thing happens. Even a straight rod will find its own balance point if the pivot is not a knife-sharp edge.

Not only is the thought-experiment rigged: so is the metaphor. A universe doesn't have to be perfectly linear, and it doesn't have to pivot on an infinitely thin line. The anthropic, human-centred mentality has unerringly homed in on exactly the wrong metaphor. It ignores the universe's tendency to respond to change by altering its own behaviour.

The triple-alpha reaction in the red giant star is just like that. An exact coincidence of energy levels is not necessary. The nuclear energy of beryllium plus that of helium is within a few per cent of one of the energy levels of carbon – but not spot-on. That's where the red giant comes in. The energies balance only if the star is at the right temperature. *And it is.* This may seem to be even further evidence of fine-tuning: the astrophysics of the red giant has to compensate precisely for the disparity in nuclear energy levels. But the star is like the bent rod. It has a nuclear thermostat. If its temperature is too low, the reaction proceeds faster, and the star heats up until the energies become equal. If the temperature is too high, the reaction proceeds more slowly, and the star cools down until the same thing happens. It would be just as sensible to admire the exquisite precision with which a wood-burning fire adjusts its temperature to be exactly that at which wood can burn. Or to be amazed that a puddle fits exactly into the dip in the ground that contains it.

The knife edge analogy depends on linear thinking – that's why it uses a straight rod. But we live in a nonlinear universe, in which anything that is stable automatically tunes itself so that it works. That's what stability *means.*

Natural systems are like your arm, not like the knife. This is how the triple-alpha process tunes itself so exquisitely, and why your legs are exactly long enough to reach the ground. It is also why we, as evolved creatures, are so neatly adapted to the universe we inhabit. Analogous beings living in different universes would *also* be exquisitely adapted to their local conditions. This is why most of the Goldilocks arguments, that life elsewhere in the universe must be just like it is here, are probably nonsense.* There are many genuine mysteries here, much to marvel at, and much yet to be understood. But there is no compelling scientific reason to believe that the universe was specially made for us.

We are faced with two alternatives. Either the universe was set up in order to bring us into being, or we evolved to fit it. The first is human-centred: it raises humanity above the universe in all its awe-inspiring vastness and complexity. The second, a universe-centred

---

* See Jack Cohen and Ian Stewart, *What Does a Martian Look Like?*

view, puts us firmly in our place: we are perhaps an interesting development, complicated enough that we don't understand exactly how it all works, but hardly the be-all and end-all of existence.

We have been around for a few million years at most, perhaps only 200,000 if you restrict attention to 'modern' humans; the universe is about 13.5 billion years old. We occupy one world orbiting one of 200 billion stars in one galaxy, which itself is one of 200 billion galaxies. Isn't it just a tiny bit arrogant to insist that the entire universe is merely a by-product of a process whose true purpose was to bring us into existence?

TWENTY-THREE

OVER-ZEALOUS ZEALOT

 Afterwards, Marjorie reflected on that aspect of the afternoon.

Roundworld was the planet Earth, in theory anyway, and surely flinging it around and sloshing it about would cause the seas to also slosh about a bit, to say the least. Nevertheless, she automatically fielded the globe, which against all reason slotted into her palm with a decisive but moderate stinging sensation, which had gone in a second.

The hooded man glared at her and drew out a curved knife. She could see the play of light on the blade and wondered how good her unarmed combat skills would prove to be against an opponent who clearly knew how to use a knife, especially since she was almost totally out of breath. The man screamed, 'Om is good!' and swung the blade at her.

Marjorie jumped backwards and a very large wolf landed in between, just as a hailstorm of bats dropped out of the sky. For a moment Marjorie stared fixedly at this tableau, and then, well, it all got quite exciting. Suddenly the wolf had the knife and the man was on the ground, and the bats had disappeared in a flurry to be replaced by a naked young woman, who looked both ways along the alleyway and said, 'Excellent work for a civilian! You ought to get a medal!'

Still clutching Roundworld like a hot water-bottle, Marjorie managed to say, 'But look! There's still a wolf!'

The wolf stood up on its hind legs, and the girl said, 'Better turn your head. Captain Angua does not like to be seen when she is – how can I put this? – well, deshabillée. Give her some space, please.'

Against all reason, Marjorie turned her back on the wolf, listened for a few seconds to what sounded like an autopsy in reverse, complete with unpleasant gurgling noises, and then a new voice said, 'I'm impressed. Some people throw up just by listening. Allow me another minute to get into this dress, and we'll be right with you.'

Indeed, only a couple of seconds later she realised that she really *was* in the company of a couple of young women – both now dressed – who showed her what looked very much like police badges. She recognised them as policemen anyway – she sometimes had to get them to call in at the library if one of the usual suspects was acting up, and policemen always looked rather out of place in the presence of literature. These two, however, seemed a whole lot smarter than the general run of the constabulary.

They cheerfully told her that they were indeed a vampire and a werewolf, the vampire introducing herself as Captain Sally and the wolf-lady as Captain Angua, before adding with a grin, 'But don't you worry, miss, we don't eat on duty.'

In Marjorie's bemused state it all seemed perfectly normal as the three of them then waited until a wagon turned up and disembogued them of their over-zealous zealot.

'I believe Lord Vetinari would like a word, miss,' the policewoman who had been a wolf then said.

'What? I distinctly heard the hooded people say they were going to kill him!'

Angua shook her head, and said, 'People *try* occasionally; sometimes he lets them live – even with all their bits if they are entertaining enough: he has what they call a mercurial sense of fun. On this occasion I can report that the group of zealous Omnians who attacked him were defenestrated.' Angua smiled and added, 'You have to hand it to his Lordship. He has style and is remarkably stronger than you might think. Lord Vetinari jumped out of the window and *refenestrated* them back into the hall!'

It was two days later when Marjorie Daw once again dined in the hall of Unseen University. In the centre of the feast, Roundworld glittered and shimmered miraculously, as became a world that could be in two places and be two different sizes all at the same time.

There were, of course, toasts and more food than was good for anybody. Lord Vetinari, who was also there, said, 'I believe, madam, that you could stay if you wish, but I understand that you have declared to the Archchancellor that you want to go back to … let me see … oh yes, the library of the borough of Four Farthings, England, wherever that may be. Are you sure?'

Marjorie smiled and said, 'Oh yes, very sure; there is no telling what the council will do if I'm not there. Probably halve the budget and fill the place with anodyne Good Citizenship displays and other idiocies. Politicians only read books they have written, or those of colleagues they suspect might have mentioned them in their text. Or they simply want to pretend that they have read the latest touted bestseller to show that they are just like "the common people", neglecting the fact that people aren't *all* common and can spot a phoney at a glance.' She paused, then added, 'Sorry for the rant, sir, but I just had to get it out of my system. I've got to get back before they replace me with a yahoo who doesn't even know where the damn word came from.'

She let Lord Vetinari refill her glass, and felt a lot better.

The following lunchtime, on the lawn in Unseen University, the Great Big Thing hung in the air, scintillating, twisting, coruscating, evaporating and gently spinning. It was, in a very strange way, alive, and yet not alive: like people are alive, and ships are alive, or even mountains – in their own strange way – are alive, but alive all the way through.

Surrounding it was the usual squash of fervent young white-robed wizards, muttering about 'thaumic energies' and 'slood derivatives' and the kind of terminology that made Rincewind's head ache. Their fingers were almost *twitching* in their eagerness to get going on the next stage of the Great Big Glitch ... oops, no, the Great Big Experiment.

Ponder Stibbons was also there, with other members of the Inadvisably Applied Magic group, and of course all the senior wizards, who would not miss something like this, even for lunch. Ponder, after all the hand-shaking, said, 'Well, Marjorie, I'm sure we are all sorry that you have to go, but I only need to press the button in front of me to put you back just where you were before you so abruptly ended up on this turf. As the Archchancellor said, it is doubtful that we will do this *particular* experiment again. Sometimes even wizards know when *not* to meddle.'

In the silence that followed, a high-pitched excitable voice could be heard from amongst the crowd of young wizards: 'You know, I think I know what we got wrong ...'

Just then the Librarian of Unseen University knuckled his way across the turf at speed. He stopped when he reached Marjorie, blew her a kiss and handed her a banana.

She blew back the kisss with an extra *s* as Ponder said, 'I have looked for a suitable sentence to speed you on your way, Marjorie, and came across a much-liked one: *What goes around comes around.* Welcome to Roundworld! It's only a page away.' Then he pressed the button. 'So, you will be back home before I have finished this senten—'

TWENTY-FOUR

NOT COLLECTING
STAMPS

Although it is widely held that faith can move mountains, it has not reliably been seen doing so. Yes, of course it's a metaphor – a powerful one, and a valid one. People have done, and will continue to do, amazing things because of their beliefs. But the main things that move mountains significantly are subducting tectonic plates, volcanic eruptions and earthquakes. Oh, and rain and cold, given long enough.

There is no denying the power that faith has over human beings, and the sometimes remarkable acts that it can motivate, but it really is a curious way for *Homo sapiens* to behave. It requires acceptance of a rather strange mixture of moral precepts and the supernatural. There is no direct objective evidence for many beliefs that are central to the world's great religions – but there are innumerable reports of miraculous events, holy people, longstanding authority and rituals that may go back thousands of years. Religions are grounded in deep culture, inculcating the present generation's values in the next. And they are often desirable values, don't get us wrong.

However, there is an evident danger if you ground your morality in authority and ineffable deities. What is moral simply becomes what is prescribed. God is good – but this can lead to the concept that *anything* can be deemed good if you can convince people that God so wills. Such as cutting off the head of an infidel, or blowing women

and children to smithereens in order to get yourself into Heaven –
typical tactics of Roundworld's own over-zealous zealots. With a few
exceptions of that kind, largely to do with who counts as a genuine
person, most of the world's religions have their prized moral values
in common. However, they are little more than the standard default
values of most human societies. Don't kill people. Don't steal. Don't
do anything that you wouldn't like done to you. Nearly all of us can
sign up to these values, be we Christians, Jews, Muslims, Hindus, Jedi
Knights … even agnostics and atheists. It is not necessary to invoke a
god to provide 'authority' for them. They are the common currency
of humanity.

That leaves the supernatural elements for us to disagree about, and
that's where the real trouble starts. Those elements matter, because
they endow a religion with its cultural significance. Anyone can sign
up to 'don't kill people', but only we Righteously Reformed Rince-
windian Roundworldists genuinely *believe* that the entire universe is
a foot across and sits on a shelf in Unseen University.

Prove us wrong.

We're sitting in the audience, and there's a debate in progress on the
stage. The protagonist is very sure of his position, has good clear
pictures, and is very clear about his story. His antagonist is different.
She is rather unsure; her pictures are sketches and cartoons, and she
is altogether more tentative.

Which do we tend to believe?

It mostly depends on who *we* are.

There are some who like certainty; they like to know just where
they are. They tend to get their knowledge, their beliefs, from author-
itative sources: the Bible, the Quran, textbooks, or the practices of
their professions. They *know* that those who disagree with them are
at least wrong, and sometimes evil. It's certainly more than sinful
for politicians to change their position on almost any topic. They
simply can't understand why someone can't see the Truth when it's

presented to them, or that someone can't appreciate the clarity of their assertions or the power of their arguments.

Over the years we have found, somewhat to our surprise, that many scientists are also like this. In private, they often acknowledge that there are difficulties with the current state-of-the-art theories in their subject area. They may even accept that some key features might have to be changed as more evidence comes in. But their public face is one of complete certainty. There are biologists who *know* that the most important feature of any organism is its DNA, and that virtually everything about living creatures is explained by their genes. There are physicists who *know* that the universe is made up of *these* particles, with *these* constants and mechanisms. They know that, ultimately, everything in the world reduces to fundamental physics. We can see that engineers can very easily adopt this position about their subject; after all, it is almost entirely man-made: gears, engines, oscilloscopes, MRI machines, LEDs, cyclotrons … But electrons? Quantum waves? W and Z particles? The Higgs boson?

Others are suspicious of such certainty, tending to say 'I don't know' quite a lot, and are unsure about lots of things. Their beliefs have come from a medley of sources, many of them quite unreliable; they tend to change their minds, even about quite important issues.

Dennett's *Breaking the Spell: Religion as a Natural Phenomenon* initially takes us back to the times when people didn't have access to information of any reliable kind. But like so many New-Agers today, they took 'information' from astrology, from myths, from gossip, from folklore – because there wasn't anywhere else to get it. Extelligence, the information outside heads, was then very disorganised; but primitive religions were an exception. They were often extensively organised, with lots of gods and goddesses, a cosmology or three, ceremonies and rituals.

Religions, in fact, were the most organised ways to run your life. As time passed, some kind of natural selection among religions went on, so that the ones that survived, the ones that gained adherents, became more effective for gaining even more. The Ten Commandments was a very good set, ensuring that there were less social problems even if most were 'More honor'd in the breach than the observance'. 'Eat rotting meat' would have been a bad one. 'Love your neighbour' was remarkably good (initially in Judaism, then in Christianity), then spreading through the next 1500 years, according to a suggestion in Pinker's *The Better Angels of our Nature* about the universal decline of human violence.

Now that extelligence has become better organised, with such things as internet search engines to help us navigate through overwhelming quantities of information, we can look back and see the beginnings of rationality among the Egyptians and the Greeks; then to some extent among the Romans and the Hebrews; then the Reformation and the Enlightenment. Rationality, and the beginnings of science, Bacon and Descartes, began to take over from theology as a way to run life, at least for a few people – those who wrote the tracts, anyway. From steam-power and canals and trains, via the industrial revolution, this led to the modern world.

However, religions remained as a backdrop to the play. Priests were always there to give their blessings, or to curse advances in rationality. Galileo, persecuted by the Church for his belief that the Earth went round the Sun, stands for thousands of such episodes. The Catholic Church has recently admitted it was in the wrong on that occasion, though rather grudgingly, and with growing ambivalence. But what about all the others, minor and major?

Among Western people, a solid proportion are now basically rational in their approach to life and its problems, but about 30% run their lives in strict accordance with religious tenets of one kind or another. Nothing like that many regularly attend churches or synagogues, but most Muslims go to mosques. The majority don't give the way they should live a lot of thought; they run their daily lives as a matter of habit, conditioned by whim … Is that really too pessimistic a statement? How many people get home from work, turn the television on and their minds off?

Mobile phones and the internet are helping, but the attitude to these is often closer to religion than rational: they are seen as supernatural, worked by demons, perhaps. You know what we mean, if you come from the era before mobile phones: they're miraculous. As Arthur C. Clarke wrote: 'Sufficiently advanced technology is indistinguishable from magic.' This was the main theme of *The Science of Discworld*, especially in Benford's alternative form 'Technology distinguishable from magic is insufficiently advanced'.

Many Cambodians, especially those in the hill tribes, are animists. They believe that spirits are everywhere: in the water, the trees, the clouds. They have shamans, tribal 'doctors'. In 2011, Ian gained an interesting insight into shamans when visiting a Cambodian village. A child was ill, and the shaman was performing a ceremony to expel bad spirits and restore her health. The interesting part was that the tribe had sent her to a conventional doctor the day before, who had put her on a course of antibiotics. Naturally, the shaman had to ratify this with the right ceremony, thereby making it possible to take the credit. The villagers presumably saw little difference between the antibiotics and the ritual – but someone in the tribe, perhaps the headman or one of his two wives, had the sense to try both. Human- and universe-centred thinking in an unholy alliance.

The world's major religions dismiss animism on the grounds that belief in several gods – polytheism – is ridiculous. The intelligent way to go is monotheism, belief in one god. (Or, in the case of Unitarianism, belief in *at most* one god.) But is monotheism the great step forward that is so unquestioningly assumed?

It has a definite attraction: unification. It assigns all of the universe's puzzling features to a single cause. Belief in one god is less off-putting than belief in dozens. It's even consistent with Occam's razor.

If you want to invoke Thomas Aquinas's ontological argument for the existence of God, in his *Summa Theologica*, monotheism is unavoidable. There, he invites us to consider 'the greatest conceivable being'. If it did not exist, then there would have to be a greater conceivable being: one that did exist. That surely is greater than a non-existent greatest being. So God exists, QED. Moreover, He is unique: you can't have two greatest beings. Each would have to be greater than the other.

Logicians and mathematicians are painfully aware, however, that this argument is flawed. Before you can use a characterisation of some entity to deduce its properties, you have to provide *independent* proof that such an entity exists.

The classic example is a proof that the largest whole number is 1. Consider the largest whole number. Its square is at least as big, so it must equal its square. The only whole numbers like that are 0 and 1, of which 1 is larger. QED. Except, 1 is clearly not the largest whole number. For instance, 2 is bigger.

Oops.

What's wrong? The proof assumes that there *is* a largest whole number. If it exists, everything else is correct, and it has to be 1. But since that makes no sense, the proof must be wrong, and that implies that it doesn't exist.

So, in order to use the ontological argument to infer the existence of the greatest conceivable being, we must first establish that such a being exists, *without* simply referring to the definition. So what the argument proves is 'If God exists, then God exists'.

Congratulations.

At any rate, whatever advantages monotheism may possess, being a consequence of the ontological argument is not one of them.

Monotheism's supposed great triumph, unification, may actually be its greatest flaw. Assigning all puzzling phenomena to the same causes is a standard philosophical error, the equation of unknowns. Asimov put it this way: if you don't understand UFOs, telepathy or ghosts, then UFOs must be piloted by telepathic ghosts. This way of thinking invents a label and attaches it to all mysteries, closing them off in the same way. It claims the same cause for all of them, which robs that cause of any explanatory force.

If you are a Cambodian animist, believing in a spirit for every natural phenomenon, you are aware that different phenomena may have different explanations. What explains water is not the same as what explains a tree. This can be a starting point for finding out more. But if you are a monotheist, offering the same explanation of *everything* you don't understand – whatever it is, and equally applicable even if it were totally different – then you are just closing down lines of enquiry, advancing the same facile answer to every mystery.

How many people, in today's scientific and technical world, have beliefs that are consonant with the kind of world they live in? How many understand about microwave ovens, why aeroplanes can stay up, about how electricity is distributed to houses (and don't expect electricity from unconnected sockets in their wall), and how milk comes from cows, not from supermarkets? What proportion of people do we need to be rational, to keep civilisation running? More to the point, these days: how many people does it take – gangsters or terrorists, bigots or zealots – to break down the workings of a civilised society? And why should (some) religions foster that kind of terrorism, aiming to do just that? It may just be extremists, but there are clearly belief systems that encourage such extremism.

There's an answer, but we would be happier if it were wrong. People live their lives, and are acquainted with all kinds of events, but for most people it's a small world. In an African tribe, there may be fasts and festivals, intimate relationships with about twenty people, mostly relatives, and a nodding acquaintance with about another hundred; just like Orthodox Jews in Golders Green, or Muslims in Bradford. Workmates, hobbyists, football supporters, pub acquaintances and friends can bring the total up to about 150. Humans seem to be able to remember about 200 faces, at most.

In consequence, the lives of all these folk are nearly all parochial, much as life is portrayed in TV soaps. The events that happen to them are mostly small. Births, marriages and deaths are rare, coronations much rarer. It is not surprising that religions, bringing order into that narrow kind of life, setting it in a much bigger frame, are popular. They provide prayer, hymns and sermons to make such lives feel more meaningful. They promise bigger things: gods, angels and life after death. Tabloid newspapers' obsession with celebrities, people everyone has seen on TV, similarly gives ordinary lives some glamour.

But there is another, darker side. Religions that preach damnation, or that predict an imminent end of everything in some kind of cataclysm, will also be attractive because what they are concerned with is imminent, now, tomorrow, happening to me and to the people I know. Relatives and friends will be damned, or caught up in the cataclysm. We must save them! Whether they want it or not.

Religion is human-centred. Though it pretends to be universe-centred, that universe is the tiny one created by their god, whether it be Odin or Jehovah or Brahma. Like the universe of *Star Trek*, it's minuscule compared to the real thing. It is a human-sized village with its own headman, blown up to cosmic proportions but not greatly changed.

Astrology, like many other 'personal' new-age philosophies, picks up on the same attraction: what matters is what happens to *me*. Such lifestyles don't even pay religious dues (maintaining the church roof, the vicar's salary, hush-money to erstwhile children assaulted by priests or celebrities). They are belief systems that pretend to knowledge of the future, *my* future – convincingly enough to have caught more than one American president – while taking no responsibility for the accuracy of those predictions. Religions whose compass includes heaven-or-damnation contrive equally to promise and threaten without any guarantee of a blissful, or terrible, afterlife. But it's an afterlife for *me* that's at stake; deeply personal, not a bit universal. No guarantee is needed if you have faith.

Contrast that with the scientific stance. It's surprisingly difficult to find science that matters, to *me*, that isn't embodied in technology. The numbers are meaningless; even that important Sun is about 150 million kilometres away; solar storms may disrupt electronics, but not (mostly) *my* electronics. There are billions of stars in the Milky Way, billions of galaxies each like our own – but what does that do for me? There are hundreds of chemicals in our foodstuffs, hundreds of kinds of plant – mostly weeds, whose particulars are not necessary for nearly everyone – in our forests and meadows. There are millions of transistors in a computer, a mobile phone or a television. But *I* don't need to know about that to operate them; just turn them on, play games on the computer, watch EastEnders on telly. Watch nature programmes, watch science programmes. Don't get involved, as there's nothing there that seems to affect *me* directly. It's all universe-related, not people-related; it's Benford's contrast again.

A story about Jack is relevant here. When he was about fourteen, he was breeding tropical fish to accumulate money for going to university. His father had been killed dumping ammunition after the end of World War II, and his mother was earning about £2 a week as a machinist: not enough to pay rent (she had only a half-pension). Jack found a mated pair of angelfish, very rare at that time, and bought them for £50. That was a lot of money: he had about £75 in the bank, from breeding other fish. Within a week, one angelfish had died. He then bought another one, for £15.

His grandfather, with whom they were living, said (and he remembers this very vividly, especially his grandfather's 'study': one corner of the living room with piles of newspapers): 'This is where we tell if you are a queen bee or a wasp.' His grandfather didn't know much biology, and Jack remembered that un-biological aspect of the remark all these years. But his grandfather did know the distinction between having global concerns or only immediate concerns, and that's the distinction he was making.

The angelfish bred, and Jack sold the first brood for £50; they bred again six weeks later, and again and again. He made a lot of money from them. The important distinction stayed with him: he became a scientist. He gave up on becoming a rabbi, which his father had intended for himself, an intention that fell on Jack's shoulders, being the only boy. He could perhaps have taken on a pet shop, but that was not to his taste. Without understanding his grandfather's distinction – he only understood it, to his shame, when writing this chapter – he was a queen bee with global concerns, not a wasp concerned only with human-centred things.

One irony of the story: Jack had thought that the fish that had died was a male, and replaced it with what he thought was another male. It turned out that both were females; the one he'd thought was female, which survived, was actually male. Even if you are a queen bee, you still need a bit of luck. Now, it becomes clear that Jack's grandfather was asking whether Jack was human-centred or universe-centred: an Omnian fundamentalist, or a wizard.

Is a science-versus-religion argument going on now? Like there was, after Darwin published *The Origin of Species*? To read the newspapers, you could easily think that scientists are up in arms, trying to destroy religions.

Without doubt, there is a desperate anti-Darwinism prejudice in the middle states of the USA, in Indonesia, and in a few other countries. This seems to have its origin in politics rather than anti-rationality, since many of its proponents, such as those promoting the hypothesis of intelligent design, claim to be putting forward a rational, scientific criticism of Darwinism. The political aim in the USA is to get round the constitutional separation of church and state, by putting religion into the schools wrapped in science's clothing. (That's not solely our view: it's what Judge John Jones concluded when presiding over *Kitzmiller v. Dover Area School District*, when he ruled that the teaching of intelligent design in school science classes was unconstitutional.) The methodology is to present an anti-Darwin stance in schools, perhaps in order to deny 'naturalism', the belief that nature can work perfectly well without gods. Alvin Plantinga and Dennett discuss this point in *Science and Religion; Are They Compatible?* This is yet another example of Benford's distinction. Believers in, and promoters of, an intelligent designer want a human-centred system of the world. They want evolution to be guided. They have completely missed Darwin's point, that a creator is unnecessary: natural selection can produce the same results without there being any human-type design.

This anti-Darwin prejudice, this wish for a human kind of design in evolution, must be distinguished from all those places in the world that haven't yet emerged from a medieval dependence on religion in people's daily lives, and where evolution isn't 'believed in'. And it must also be distinguished from an unthinking commitment to religion, hence disbelief in evolution – or in science in general – in the lives of most people even in scientific/technological societies today.

Dennett and Thomson explain the commitment to religion very well. It is irrational and faith-based, but for many people it seems almost to be a necessary part of being human. It provides a sense of identity and a shared culture. Part of the reason is that most religions have, in the course of their evolution, changed to become more and more adapted, more appropriate to the creatures they're serving. All of their organisation, and most of their practices, have been developed better to serve their practitioners. Those that didn't do so well have been lost to history. Few people now believe in Odin or Osiris.

Modern religions, with their beliefs in gods or at least in the supernatural, have all achieved congregations that seem happy with the hierarchy of senior people who determine the letters of the faith. This complicity between congregants and the hierarchy makes the belief system almost irrelevant, even though it seems to the congregants to be central. The joint activities, the singing and the praying, the individual commitments in common, give the congregants a warm feeling of belonging. From outside, each of these faiths seems a beautiful harmony, the odd spat over homosexuals or female bishops aside. It's not surprising that rationality can't edge its way in.

For decades, psychologists have been making scientific studies of religious belief; not with a view to proving or disproving the existence of any particular flavour of deity, but trying to find out what goes on inside the minds of believers. Some have concluded that belief in the supernatural is a more or less inevitable consequence of evolutionary survival value (an ironic finding, if true), because it knits human cultures together. Only recently has it occurred to a few psychologists that perhaps the thought processes of atheists also need to be investigated, since such people form a fairly large group that seems to be immune to these supposed evolutionary pressures. Comparing believers with non-believers is likely to shed more light on both.

Even if religion and other kinds of belief in the supernatural really are natural consequences of humanity's past history, built into our thought processes by evolution, there is no compulsion to continue to think that way. Our sporadic tendency towards violence, especially against each other, can also be explained in similar terms, but there seems to be a widespread (and sensible) view that this does not excuse violent behaviour. A true human being should be able to override such innate urges by an act of will. The same can be said of belief in the supernatural: by exercising our intelligence we can train ourselves to disbelieve claims for which there is no clear evidence. Of course, believers think that there *is* evidence – certainly enough to convince them – but it tends to be obscure and heavily dependent on interpretation.

An instructive example of the influence of religious belief on rational judgment occurred in 2012 when Sanal Edamaruku, founder of Rationalist International and President of the Indian Rationalist Association, was invited to examine a miracle. What follows is based on an interview with Edamaruku published in *New Scientist*, and we report what was alleged there.*

The miracle occurred at a Catholic church in Mumbai, where water was dripping spontaneously from the feet of a statue of Christ on the cross. This event was interpreted as a sign from God – a holy miracle – and flocks of believers collected and drank the water, apparently thinking that it was holy water that would cure all manner of illnesses. A television station asked Edamaruku to comment, and consonant with his position, he rejected the claim of a miracle. Since his view was at that moment purely a matter of opinion, the TV company challenged him to provide scientific proof, which of course required visiting the church and taking a look.

The church authorities gave their approval. It didn't take long to find the cause of the 'miracle'. A drainage channel from a washroom passed beneath the cross's concrete plinth. A quick look at the drain revealed that it was blocked. The walls behind the cross, and the wooden cross itself, were soaking up drainage water through capillary action. Some of the water was emerging through a nail hole and running down over the statue's feet. Edamaruku took photographs to document the cause.

Point made, you will imagine. Well, yes – but. Edamaruku had long been a thorn in the side of religious groups, and his finding caused them some embarrassment. They could have used System 2 thinking to investigate the likely causes of dripping water, or just called a plumber like most sensible people would have done when they found water dripping from places where water ought not to be. Instead, they made a System 1 judgment and plumped for a supernatural explanation. But it's not a great idea to have people drinking

* One minute with Sanal Edamaruku, *New Scientist* (30 June 2012) 27. See also http://en.wikipedia.org/wiki/Sanal_Edamaruku.

dilute sewage, even if they do imagine it's a miracle cure. The discovery probably saved the church a great deal of potential trouble, even if it debunked the miracle.

So what was the response?

The church itself did nothing. But according to Edamaruku, people from two lay Catholic associations filed charges against him under section 295A of India's penal code, which dates to 1860 and forbids 'deliberately hurting religious feelings and attempting malicious acts intended to outrage the religious sentiments of any class or community'. Edamaruku has said that he is willing to appear in court, where he is convinced the case will be thrown out – but unfortunately the law has a nasty sting in its tail. Anyone accused can be jailed, perhaps for many months, before the case comes to trial. So, as we write, Edamaruku has fled to Finland, and the Rationalist Association has set up an online petition calling for the complaints to be dropped.

Christian theologians have long worried about the paradox of *silentio dei*, the silence of God: if God exists, why does He not speak? An omnipotent, omnipresent being should have no difficulty in making His existence evident, in undeniable ways. Lined up alongside this strange absence are other problems of human existence: why a caring God permits diseases and natural disasters, for example. Theology being what it is, innumerable answers have been proposed.

There's a Jewish joke about this. (There's a Jewish joke about everything.) Three rabbis are arguing a point in theology. Two claim it was first made by Rabbi ben Avraham; the third claims it was Rabbi ben Yitzchak. 'Look, I know it was him! I studied this for my thesis!' But the others still disagree. Eventually, in desperation, the third rabbi says, 'I know, let's ask God!' So the three of them pray, and suddenly the sky splits open and God leans out, looks down, and says, 'He is right. It was Rabbi ben Yitzchak.'

After a stunned pause, the first rabbi says: 'Well, now it's two against two.'

Upon reflection, the joke works because we know it wouldn't be like that. God could solve the problem of disbelief by writing his name across the sky in letters of fire a kilometre high. But for obscure theological reasons, an omnipotent being apparently declines to exercise that particular power. The only possibility that theologians have not contemplated is that God is silent because He doesn't exist. On that particular issue all religious factions agree – and they don't accept *that* explanation.

So, if you were to take a vote, there would be a clear majority verdict: God does exist. Atheists are a definite minority. However, even if you think that questions about the universe can be decided democratically, you have to ask the question sensibly. Religious people are happy to align themselves with all of the other religions in the world when it comes to those dreadful atheists – infidels, literally people without faith. But as soon as you start to examine what different religions, or different sects within a given religion, or even different believers within the *same* sect, actually believe, common cause gives way to bedlam. The Church of England, for example, is currently split into factions over the issue of women bishops, and is perilously close to splitting into two different sects. And the Church of England itself originated in a split from the Church of Rome. There are thousands of different Christian denominations, let alone other faiths.

In this debate, we have no desire to argue for either position. We'd rather there were no bishops at all – men or women – though being realists we don't expect that to happen. What intrigues us is that good – indeed, devout and committed – Christians, people on both sides of the argument, have examined their innermost hearts, prayed to their God and been answered with a clear vision of God's wishes. There can be no doubt that that is what they sincerely believe. But, curiously, God's wishes turn out to be that (a) Women bishops should be allowed, and (b) They shouldn't. Indeed, God's wishes are remarkably similar to what those of the individuals concerned have been all along, before they consulted their deity on the matter.

From within that debate, if it can be dignified with the word, it is clear to all that one side is right and the other is wrong; one has correctly divined God's wishes, the other is deluded. Problem: which is which? From outside, we are observing an interesting experimental test of the efficacy of prayer, indeed of the existence of the kind of deity in which the Church of England believes, indeed the general concept of a belief system. *Silentio dei* is not the difficulty: God has indeed spoken to both sides – or so they genuinely believe. But He has spoken with a forked tongue. From outside, if He existed in a form consistent with the beliefs of the Church of England, then surely He would have told everyone the same thing.

So this particular religion fails a definitive experimental test, one inadvertently set up by the believers themselves. In science, that would be a good reason to reject the hypothesis.

Worldwide, religious believers outnumber atheists, even if we exclude people who nominally belong to a religion but don't practise it. However, across the board, the world's religions find it virtually impossible to agree on the supernatural features of their belief systems. They often seem to agree on fundamentals such as a god – but which god? Each religion, each sect, has a god that – it tells us – demands a different set of rituals, a different form of worship, different prayers. Each is in the minority, so at most one can be correct. But they all appeal to the *same* reasoning: faith. Since their own beliefs disagree, faith clearly doesn't hack it. Thus the apparent majority turns out to be smoke and mirrors.

The writer and comedian Ricky Gervais* made a similar point more pithily in 2010:

The dictionary definition of God is 'a supernatural creator and overseer of the universe'. Included in this definition are all

---

* http://blogs.wsj.com/speakeasy/2010/12/19/a-holiday-message-from-ricky-gervais-why-im-an-atheist

deities, goddesses and supernatural beings. Since the beginning of recorded history, which is defined by the invention of writing by the Sumerians around 6000 years ago, historians have catalogued over 3,700 supernatural beings, of which 2,870 can be considered deities. So next time someone tells me they believe in God, I'll say 'Oh, which one? Zeus? Hades? Jupiter? Mars? Odin? Thor? Krishna? Vishnu? Ra … ?' If they say, 'Just God. I only believe in the one God,' I'll point out that they are nearly as atheistic as me. I don't believe in 2,870 gods, and they don't believe in 2,869.

Ultimately, religious beliefs are based not on objective evidence, but on faith. Religions are belief systems, and many proclaim this as an advantage: faith is a test, set by God. If you don't agree with them, you've failed. Many religionists – and a proportion of post-modernists – have claimed that science is also a belief system; in effect, just an alternative religion. Not so. They have failed to understand the key difference between science and belief: in science, the highest points are given to those who *disprove* the tenets of the alleged faith, especially its central tenets. In science there is no continuing central dogma, such a strong characteristic of religions. Indeed, that is what defines any particular religion: its central creed. Rationality, or indeed science, continually matches ideas against each other – and for science, to the extent that it's possible, against events in the real world – and is prepared to change its stance according to the way they do or do not agree. For religions, in contrast, events in the real world are held up to the dogma. If they match, they are accepted; if they don't, they are either ignored or declared to be evil, needing to be destroyed.

Science can't disprove religious beliefs. *Nothing* can. That's the problem. It's like trying to prove that our universe does not sit on a shelf in Unseen University, a region of the multiverse that is forever inaccessible to us. But the inability of science to disprove religious beliefs in the supernatural does not make it a belief system, even if it may sometimes lead people not to believe in the supernatural. When presented with extraordinary hypotheses, disbelief is not the opposite of belief. It is the default, neutral stance: 'I'm not interested in playing this game, it makes no sense.'

Many religious people try to reject atheism by portraying it as merely another form of belief, with the natural position being what they call agnosticism. They then interpret that stance as the view that the chances of God existing are about 50-50. So by being neutral, you are already halfway towards agreeing with them. This is nonsense. As Christopher Hitchens has said: if we are asked to accept a proposition without evidence, we are also entitled to dismiss it without evidence.

The *default* is to disbelieve. An atheist is not someone who believes that God doesn't exist. It is someone who doesn't believe that God *does* exist. If you think those are the same, ponder this statement by the comedian Penn Jillette: 'Atheism is a religion like not collecting stamps is a hobby.'

L-SPACE

 What Marjorie Daw was not was the kind of person who goes around saying to herself, 'Oh, it must have been a dream.' But by the fourth day she was beginning to question her own sanity with some force.

Her first days home had been a whirlwind as she really got back to grips with her work: seeing to the new books, beefing up the science fiction section, arguing with the council treasurers for more funding – even with the Libraries Committee itself – and demanding that she should be the arbiter of all that came into the library and how it was displayed.

And *that* meant putting the Bible onto the fantasy shelf.

The committee looked into her eyes, and didn't disagree.

One evening, when Marjorie, who was as always the last to leave, was turning out the lights in the library, feeling rather angry because somebody had defaced a book by Richard Dawkins with a lot of squiggles and phrases like 'God is not mocked!' she thought she heard a noise and smelled a mildly pungent smell.

She found, suddenly prominent on her desk, a large ripe banana …

Overhead, a voice said: 'Ook!'

INDEX

ALSO AVAILABLE IN PAPERBACK AND eBOOK

THE SCIENCE OF DISCWORLD® BOOKS
BY TERRY PRATCHETT,
IAN STEWART, AND JACK COHEN

A creative, mind-bending mash-up of fiction and fact.
A wizard's-eye view of our world that will
forever change how you look at the universe.

Terry Pratchett and acclaimed science writers Ian Stewart and Jack Cohen have authored four Science of Discworld books. Each title is an original Discworld story interwoven with an exploration of key ideas in science, philosophy, and religion, and an explanation of important milestones in human history.

THE SCIENCE OF DISCWORLD
The first in the series, in which Roundworld is accidentally created.

THE SCIENCE OF DISCWORLD II: THE GLOBE
In a madcap journey through the development of the human mind and the development of culture, the wizards battle the elves to determine the future of humanity on Roundworld.

THE SCIENCE OF DISCWORLD III: DARWIN'S WATCH
When an obscure English vicar named Charles Darwin publishes his bestselling book *Theology of Species*, derailing Roundworld's scientific evolution, the wizards must set things right.

THE SCIENCE OF DISCWORLD IV: JUDGMENT DAY
The wizards are obliged to defend their godlike creation of Roundworld in court against the noble, religious Omnians.

ANCHOR BOOKS ——— Ⓐ ——— AnchorBooks.com

ALSO AVAILABLE IN PAPERBACK AND eBOOK

THE FOLKLORE OF DISCWORLD
BY TERRY PRATCHETT
AND JACQUELINE SIMPSON

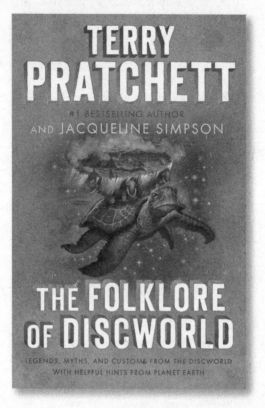

LEGENDS, MYTHS, AND CUSTOMS FROM THE DISCWORLD
WITH HELPFUL HINTS FROM PLANET EARTH

Offering insights into all forty Discworld® novels, such as
- why cheeses roll downhill;
- the hazards of treacle mining;
- what's so uncanny about the humble hare;
- the origins of orcs (which are not the same as goblins!); and
- why witches come in threes.

ANCHOR BOOKS ———— ———— **AnchorBooks.com**

ALSO AVAILABLE IN PAPERBACK AND eBOOK
BY TERRY PRATCHETT

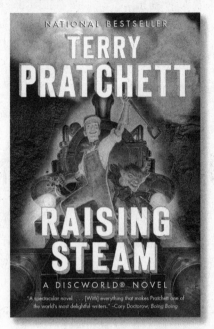

RAISING STEAM
A DISCWORLD® NOVEL

Mister Simnel has produced a great clanging monster of a machine that harnesses the power of all the elements—earth, air, fire, and water—and it's soon drawing astonished crowds. To the consternation of Ankh-Morpork's formidable patrician, Lord Vetinari, no one is in charge of this new invention. Who better to take the lead than the man he has already appointed master of the Post Office, the Mint, and the Royal Bank?

Moist von Lipwig is not a man who enjoys hard work—unless it is dependent on words, which are not very heavy and don't always need greasing. He does enjoy being alive, however, which makes a new job offer from Vetinari hard to refuse. Moist will have to grapple with gallons of grease, goblins, a controller with a history of throwing employees down the stairs, and some very angry dwarfs if he's going to stop it all from going off the rails.

ANCHOR BOOKS —————— —————— AnchorBooks.com

ALSO BY TERRY PRATCHETT

IN PAPERBACK AND eBOOK	IN HARDCOVER AND eBOOK

A SLIP OF THE KEYBOARD
Collected Nonfiction
Foreword by Neil Gaiman

A BLINK OF THE SCREEN
Collected Shorter Fiction
Foreword by A. S. Byatt

IN HARDCOVER

THE COMPLEAT ANKH-MORPORK
Aided and Abetted by
the Discworld Emporium

MISS FELICITY BEEDLE'S
THE WORLD OF POO

Available everywhere books are sold.

ANCHOR BOOKS

Doubleday